Baby, it's You

JOANNE TRACEY

First published in Australia in 2019

by Joanne Tracey

https://joannetracey.com

Copyright © Joanne Tracey 2019

Print ISBN 978-0-6484533-3-8

Kindle ISBN 978-0-9943134-0-9

Epub ISBN 978-0-9943134-1-6

Cover design by Lana Pecherczyk of Author Zoo

A catalogue record for this book is available from the National Library of Australia

For Grant and Sarah...

Always

CHAPTER ONE

'Strap your boobs up, put your trainers on and just do it. One foot after another – how hard could it be? It could be fun.'

Josh Booth took a mouthful of beer, raised his eyebrows, and waited for my reaction.

'Fun? Really? Cavemen only started running because some mean, sabre-toothed animal – a cross between a really angry giant cat and a crocodile – was chasing them. And newsflash, Booth, we don't have any of them in Melbourne.'

He laughed – one of those head back, deep-gutted belly laughs that made anyone near him instantly feel happier, even if they'd had, like I'd had, a really bad week. The men on the bar stools near us grinned.

'I wouldn't be so sure about that. What about that knuckle-dragger who was trying to pick you up last Friday night? He could have been the missing link.'

I giggled. 'True, he was a little Neanderthalic. Anyway, since when did you become such an expert on running?'

'Since I added it to my bucket list.'

'How busy is this place getting?' Suse Turner, the other member of our little gang of three, dropped a light kiss on my head as she squeezed into the space between me and Booth on the corner lounge we'd managed to snaffle. 'We need to find a new Friday night regular.'

Booth shook his head. 'You say that every week. The usual?' At her grin he headed for the bar.

'Hey, Suse.' I shifted across to make room. 'All good?'

'Yeah, shit of a week though. Georgia's teething, Toby's decided his new favourite word is "no" and his new favourite thing is to throw food around the kitchen. Richard's working stupid hours and ignores the chaos on the rare occasion he is home, and that bitch of a general manager of mine is seriously hormonal. If she's having a bad change, she should review her meds and make life easier for the rest of us. Do you know any good doctors?' I shook my head. 'On top of that, I have to retrench half the workforce and tell the other half there won't be any pay rises . . . again.'

Suse was the human resources director for one of the global IT players. She'd make a great CEO one day.

She paused to take a sip of my wine. 'Other than that, things are great. How was your week?'

'You know . . . the usual,' I said with a grimace. 'Same old.'

'You need a new job.' She made the same comment

every Friday night.

My reply was the same every Friday night. 'It's not that bad – Booth keeps it interesting.'

Booth and I worked for the same software development company the three of us met at many years ago. He'd left and come back a couple of times though, and as a result was much more important than me in the pecking order.

'She doesn't need a new job. What she needs is a new challenge.' Booth had returned with the drinks. 'What we all need is a new challenge. Suse, you need something to get you out of the house, and Em needs something to get her out of her comfort zone. And I have just the thing.'

He always had 'just the thing'.

'Did you tell her about my idea?' he asked me.

'Not yet.'

'Why not?'

'Because she only just got here, we've been catching up on the week, and I still don't know what your idea involves.'

He sighed heavily and explained. 'I've decided I want to run a marathon – okay, a half-marathon first. It's on my bucket list. I figured I'd give you two the opportunity to tick it off your bucket lists too.' He looked at us like he expected applause or something.

'A marathon? From the man whose attention span rivals that of a goldfish?'

'Why don't you say what you really think, Em?'

'Oh, ha ha. You can't just keep adding things to your bucket list. You have to decide what's going to be in your bucket and start ticking them off. You just make stuff up as you go along. That isn't how it works. Right, Suse?'

She gave me the sort of smile she probably gave Toby, her three year old. 'I don't know . . . Josh could be on to something here. I need a new challenge – either that or die of boredom – and this would be a great excuse to get out of the house on a regular basis. Richard can look after the kids while I'm training. Running a marathon has always been on my list too, so I might as well start with a half.'

'You have a bucket list too?' I asked.

'Of course I do – doesn't everyone?'

'Em doesn't,' said Booth.

'Says who?'

'Says me.'

Suse thought for a minute. 'That's weird because she has a list for everything else.'

'That's how I know it doesn't exist – Em always writes her lists down.'

Booth had a 'so there' expression on his face. Sometimes he could be so immature.

'You've seen her fridge,' he went on. 'It's plastered with post-it notes for groceries and recipes she's torn out of magazines – and she can't even cook. Empty her bag and you'll find shopping lists on the backs of envelopes, Christmas lists, and those to-do lists for work that she writes on the tram every morning. Do you ever even look at them?'

He reached across the table, grabbed my phone, and entered the four-digit password.

'What are you doing?'

'Showing Suse your lists.'

'How did you know my password?'

He looked at me with pity. 'Oh, derrr. You use my birthday.'

'I can't very well use mine, can I?' I made a mental note to add *change phone password* to my to-do list.

'Here we go. Exhibit one – her notes.'

He held up the phone and scrolled through them.

'That's private,' I said feebly.

'And now we come to her playlists. Who has a list of break-up songs?'

'That would be on high rotation,' muttered Suse.

I gave Suse a dirty look – my record with men mightn't be great, but at least I was prepared for the inevitable.

I snatched my phone back. 'No one understands how I feel better than Celine . . . or Johnny Logan . . . or Abba . . . You certainly never want to listen to me talk about my feelings.'

He laughed. 'Nah, harden the fuck up and move on – that's my motto.'

I wrinkled my nose at him, and Suse giggled.

'If you did have a bucket list, you'd have it written down,' he said. 'That's all I'm saying.'

'If I did have a list – and I'm not admitting that I don't – running any part of a marathon wouldn't be on it!'

'What would be on it then?'

'The usual.'

'Give me one thing,' he urged.

'Okay, but you have to promise not to laugh.'

'I'm not promising anything.'

I took a deep breath. 'I want to wear a bikini on a tropical island.'

They were silent for a minute. Then Booth settled back in his chair and laughed.

Suse said, 'That's it? That's your bucket list? To wear a bikini? You could do that now if you wanted to.'

'Suse is right. Why's it on your list?'

'It's not so much the bikini as the tropical island – somewhere with white sand, palm trees, clear water and pretty fish.'

'You never go on holiday.'

'But I'd wear a bikini if I did.'

Booth shook his head at me. 'Your list, my dear, is lame. You don't even have a valid passport.'

'It expired.'

'Yes, because you haven't been anywhere for years.'

'I went to my dad's wedding in England – that

wasn't so long ago.'

'It was before we even knew you, Em.'

'Really? That long?'

'You haven't been out of Australia in the last ten years, at least. How long have I been telling you to go see your mother?'

My mother lived in Ubud with her partner. They ran tantric empowerment yoga workshops with warrior woman breath work on the side – or something like that. I'd been meaning to visit but the vaccinations got in the way. You could get bitten by anything up there – I was sure the mosquitoes carried exotic-sounding diseases and the monkeys were lethal. Apparently there was a huge problem with rabies. Then there was tetanus and hepatitis. *A Current Affair* had a story about a guy who got HIV or hepatitis – or was it both? – from a tattoo he got in Kuta. Not that I was thinking of getting a tattoo.

'Craig's been talking about us going away together. I think he might be about to surprise me with somewhere special.'

Craig was my boyfriend. He'd lasted four months, which was something of a record for me.

The look on Booth's face was sceptical. 'I wouldn't be getting your hopes up.'

'I really think he's building up to something big. I've lodged a passport renewal. So there.'

'Maybe he's planning a holiday to a tropical island

where you can wear your bucket-list bikini,' suggested Booth.

'I do have other things I want to do, you know.'

'Like what?' asked Suse.

'Grown-up stuff . . . like learning to cook, and fixing up my apartment. And maybe one day leaving my job and buying a one-way ticket somewhere. I might even get a tattoo – just not in Bali.'

'Is that before or after you throw in your job and jet off to the tropical island to wear your bikini?' asked Booth.

'Oh, ha ha.'

'About this half-marathon?' Booth didn't like the spotlight to stray too far away from him. 'I'm signing up for it in September.'

'Count me in,' said Suse. 'I used to run at school. It'll be a good excuse to drag out the trainers again.'

'What about you, Em?' he asked.

'September's only six months away.'

Suse raised her eyebrows at me.

'I don't have anything to wear. Then there's the suspension issue – everything will bounce about.'

'Buy something to wear. And, as I said, strap them up.' Booth always had an answer for my excuses.

'It's not that easy. You don't just wake up one day and decide you're going to run a marathon.'

'Of course it's not easy. If it was, everyone would be doing it. That's the whole point of the challenge.'

When I still didn't look convinced, he tried another angle. 'Go out tomorrow and buy yourself something to run in, and we'll go on a training run on Sunday morning. We'll ease into it from walking. If you really hate it, you don't have to do it again. Deal?'

I reluctantly agreed. 'And if I don't like it, you'll never mention it again?'

'Cross my heart.'

I didn't believe him.

'You know you love an excuse to shop,' Suse said. 'I'll come with you tomorrow – Richard can do some kid-wrangling for a change.' She checked her watch and finished her drink. 'Well, that's my limit. Back to the madhouse. See you in the morning, Em. And see you next week, Josh.'

She kissed us both and was gone. I took the opportunity to make a move too. Booth's attention had already switched to a group of girls in the corner of the bar.

'I think I'll be off too.' I motioned to the girls. 'You have fun.'

'I will,' he said with a grin, kissing my cheek. He was on his feet before I'd even reached the door.

The next morning, Suse dragged me into the first sports shop we came to, where a perky pony-tailed assistant bored me with a description of the cutting-edge technology that every item of clothing seemed to possess. I chose a sky-blue T-shirt made from some space-age fabric that clung to every curve but would, I was assured, 'wick' the moisture away from my body, and some black lycra tights. The price made me gasp.

'They'll allow you to be more comfortable in your stride,' explained Ms Perky, 'and will aid with muscle recovery.'

'Oh, I don't think I'll need that – I'm in reasonable shape.'

Suse looked sceptical. 'When was the last time you went to the gym?'

'I've thought about going to the gym.' Once I'd even contemplated something called a pump class, which turned out to be very different to what I'd thought it would be. 'I run around town every day, in heels – and cover miles and miles when I shop.'

Unconvinced, she handed me the miracle tights to try on.

Change rooms without mirrors had been responsible for almost every bad retail decision I'd ever made. You paraded around in public in something that didn't look any good on you while sales assistants oohed and aaahed, then you put it on when you got home and thought, seriously? And stuffed it straight to the back of the wardrobe.

This was a change room without a mirror, but when I modelled the outfit for Suse, she raised her eyebrows.

'What's wrong?' I asked.

'It's just . . . well, it clings a little – don't you think?'

'Oh.' I smoothed down the top. 'Do you think it's too small?'

'No, the size is fine, I'd just forgotten you were built like that.'

'I look too fat, don't I?'

I held my tummy in and turned side on. I wasn't fat, just a little soft. I thought it suited me. The boob fairy had been kind to me, the hip fairy had been overly generous, and for those times when my waist appeared a little squidgy I could fake it. There were few body issues that couldn't be remedied with some clever underwear choices and accessorising. In my opinion, a little wiggle in your skirt was a good thing – but not, apparently, when it came to running.

'Fat isn't the word that comes to mind.' Suse grinned, 'Josh is going to get a surprise tomorrow morning.'

I screwed my nose up at her.

Ms Perky stepped in and looked me over. 'Hmmm, I think we're going to need some extra containment for your breasts. And judging by the potential bounce there, we'll also need to step up the support in your shoes.'

I paid a ridiculous amount of money for a bra with suspension an off-road vehicle would be proud of, and an even more ridiculous amount on a pair of running shoes that weren't even Italian. I said as much to Miss Perky, who didn't see the irony and again started justifying the science behind them. I held up my hand to stop her.

'Enough already! Unless they can do the running for me, I don't need to understand how they work.'

I used the rest of my limited preparation time wisely.

I'd read somewhere that footballers didn't have sex before a big game because it drained the strength from their legs. Craig was out with his mates so I had an early night. No sex – tick.

Booth was picking me up at ten, so I lay in bed until nine thirty, luxuriating in having the whole space to myself. Ease into match day – tick.

I bolted down a couple of croissants and a coffee before dressing in my new exercise gear. Carbohydrates and fluids – tick.

When Booth arrived, he looked me up and down and grinned wickedly.

'What's wrong?' I asked, pulling at the hem of my top.

'Wow, that shirt certainly, umm, clings. Are you sure you're adequately restrained under there?'

'Oh, ha flipping ha. I'll have you know that this top will wick away my sweat. And NASA engineered this bra – it defies gravity. Trust me, these puppies aren't going anywhere.'

He laughed. 'Did you get a decent night's sleep?'

'Yep.'

'No Craig?'

'Poker game.'

'Have you had some carbs and plenty to drink this morning?'

'Yep.' It was a large coffee.

'Coffee and croissants don't count.'

Sometimes I thought we'd been friends for too long.

'Your shoes look new – have you broken them in?'

'You know I only bought them yesterday.'

He shook his head. 'Blisters, babe.'

'Won't be a problem. These things cost so much they have to include blister-proofing technology.'

Booth proposed a gentle jog along the river, where, apparently, the track was mostly flat. 'It's your first time so we won't push it. We'll alternate walking with running, so just keep to your own pace and you'll be fine.'

I lasted, oh, two whole minutes before slowing (very slightly) to a walk. Who knew two minutes could seem so long?

We continued with the jogging, walking, coughing, whining rhythm for about thirty minutes – until the spewing started . . .

'It's not supposed to be like this. It all sounded so easy at the pub on Friday night.'

'Most things do, my dear. How was it supposed to be?'

'Oh, you know – me gliding gracefully along, my ponytail bouncing in time with the rhythm of my feet, keeping up with you . . . of course. Blue sky, no pain and absolutely no spew.'

I expected him to laugh or tell me to harden up, but instead he gently held my hair back from my face as I vomited a lung onto the side of the track.

'I told you not to eat right before we ran.'

'I can't exercise on an empty stomach,' I replied between heaves.

'You should have got up earlier then.'

'It's Sunday. You don't get lycra *and* an early morning on a Sunday. It's one or the other.'

He said nothing as I brought up the other lung. I bet Ms Perky from the sportswear store wouldn't be doubled over by the side of the Yarra with vomit flecks in her perfect ponytail.

'Just take it at your own pace on the way back.'

'What the fuck do you think this is? This is as fast as it gets!' I glared at him through glazed eyes and turned for home.

'What doesn't kill you makes you stronger,' he offered. 'Like in the song. Just think of the coffee and choc-chip muffin when we're finished.'

I muttered under my breath. I was beginning to feel the blisters – blisters on top of blisters.

'What was that?' he asked.

'I was just saying that the only thing I'm thinking

about right now is your head under the nearest tram.'

'No need to be like that.'

By the time I'd limped back to Booth's car, my expensive new shoes were heavily stained with blood. To top the morning off beautifully, it was raining. Heavily. And my T-shirt's moisture-wicking technology wasn't working. I was on high beam and could have won a wet T-shirt competition for a men's magazine. Not one of those pretend-to-be-tasteful-with-articles-about-building-your-core-strength mags, but a really tacky one that was all about the cleavage on the cover.

'These shoes cost me a fortune,' I wailed. 'This wouldn't have happened if they were Italian. Maybe that's why Italian designers don't do training shoes – because humans aren't meant to run?'

'It doesn't matter how much they cost – new trainers need to be worn in. You should have at least put some plasters on your heels before going out.'

'So now you're going to say you told me so?'

'Shut up for a minute and let me fix your feet. There's a packet of bandaids in the car.'

I passed them down to him. 'Thank you. But that doesn't take away from the fact that this was a disaster, and everything hurts, and it's all your fault.'

He grinned. 'You'll feel better when your shoes are off and you're dry. Speaking of which,' he raised his head and got an eyeful of my chest, 'we might keep you in those wet clothes for just a little longer. The view's great from this angle.'

I crossed my arms in front of my chest to hide my nipples. 'Oh, fuck off.' I pushed at him with my bare foot so he overbalanced.

CHAPTER TWO

Craig was waiting for me at home. He and Booth greeted each other with their normal amount of enthusiasm.

'Craig.'

'Josh.'

Craig raised his eyebrows at my clinging clothes and bandaided bare feet. 'Where have you been? You look soaked . . . No, don't tell me now – get changed first.'

'What? No hello kiss?'

'Not until you're dry and decent.'

Booth watched the exchange with a half smile. 'He's right, no matter how great the view is from here, you'll end up sick if you don't get out of those wet clothes.'

His gaze lingered on my T-shirt, earning him a glare from Craig. Cheeky bugger.

'I'll put the kettle on while you're getting changed,' he added. 'Tea or coffee, Em? Craig, can I get you anything?'

I shook my head at his blatant attempt to irritate Craig by taking over my kitchen.

It had worked. Craig sounded annoyed. 'Don't you have somewhere to be, Josh?'

'Nope,' he replied, scrounging around in my cupboards. 'Hey, Em, where do you keep your biscuits these days? Do you still hide them so you won't be tempted?'

'They're where they always are. Didn't you promise me muffins?'

'That was before the rain came down and the blisters came out. You'll need to make do with chocolate digestives and instant coffee.'

'Whatever. I'm getting changed – the testosterone in here is making me gag.'

Booth's laugh followed me as I left the room.

He stayed just long enough to drink his coffee, demolish the best part of a packet of biscuits – I didn't know where he put it all – and thoroughly piss off Craig.

'I'll be off then,' he finally announced. 'Thanks for the run, Em. It was . . . illuminating, but my job here is done.' He glanced at Craig who scowled at him.

'I know you don't like Craig, but I wish you wouldn't be so obvious,' I said at the door.

'He makes it too easy.'

'Perhaps, but it makes life difficult for me.'

'Like that is it? Oh well, you know what they say: your bed, you made it, you sleep in it.'

'Thanks.'

'You're welcome.' He kissed my forehead, which

was the only part of me that wouldn't be hurting tomorrow.

Back in the sitting room, Craig had turned off the TV. His eyes had turned down in the sulky puppy look that he'd been cultivating of late. It wasn't attractive.

'You've never wanted to exercise with me,' he said.

'You've never asked me.'

Craig always made it clear that his gym nights were his time, and referred to his 'program', and 'delts' and 'quads' and 'lats', as if I should know what he was talking about. I did know where those muscles were, I just didn't need to know in detail how to 'activate' them.

'If I knew that you seriously wanted to do something about your fitness, I would have helped you,' he said.

'It wasn't planned. We were talking at the pub on Friday night about bucket lists and how Booth and Suse want to run a marathon, and one thing led to another.'

I smiled, but he didn't smile back.

'You're not exactly built for running – and I'm glad you're not,' he added when he saw me frown.

'I think I can safely say that I'll never, ever run again. Boy, am I going to feel these muscles tomorrow!'

Craig seemed to relax. 'Remind me to teach you some stretches tonight when we get back.'

'Back from where?'

'Sally and Stu's engagement barbecue – I knew you'd forgotten!'

Craig had presented me to his friends after we'd been together only a couple of weeks. I saw it as a sign of how serious he was about me. The men welcomed me, and then turned back to the football. The women were more reticent. Sally, a top-heavy, reed-thin blonde in super-skinny jeans, a spray-on white top and four-inch heels, had looked me up and down, whispered to a pretty, more evenly balanced redhead named Angela, and turned away.

Craig had handed me a drink and an encouraging smile, and left me to the girls' gossip. That night in bed, we were spooning when he asked me what I thought about his friends. 'They're great, aren't they?'

Given that he'd answered his own question, I just nodded.

'What did you think of Sally?'

I thought she was a bitch, but I was really enjoying the spooning, and judging by the stirring of something against my lower back, so was he.

'She seemed okay.'

I felt his smile as he nuzzled the back of my neck. 'She would have been checking you out – we dated for a while.'

Great. I seemed to have a thing about men who wound up back with the woman they were rebounding from. Suse reckoned it was the dating equivalent of doing your house up in order to sell it to someone else.

'How long is "a while"?' I'd asked.

His hand had reached around to play with my nipple, and he playfully bit at my earlobe. 'I dunno . . . two, three years? It had been over for about six months before you and I met – if that's what's worrying you.'

The hand that had been tweaking my nipple moved down, and strayed across the part of my hip that was ticklish. I jerked away and he murmured, 'You like that spot, don't you?'

I didn't, but we were too new for me to be telling him what I liked and what I didn't. I arched my hip enough to encourage his hand to move.

'It doesn't worry me,' I said, 'but it must have been a whirlwind romance with Stu. Aren't they getting married in the spring?'

'In October, after the football finishes, but before the spring racing starts. Sal would never miss Ladies Day – she plans her outfit a year in advance.'

There was a fondness in his voice that I wasn't keen on, but as his lips moved from my neck to trace the line of my shoulders, and his fingers found their way to a spot that absolutely wasn't ticklish, I wasn't overly concerned.

'Don't you think it's . . . ohhhhh . . . strange how your ex is now with your best mate and you're . . . going to be groomsman?'

'No, not really. As you said, Stu's my best mate. As for you, sweet Emily, let me tell you what I'm about to do to you . . .'

Craig might have found the whole situation perfectly normal, but I didn't. If Suse had taken off with someone I'd been in a relationship with, six months wouldn't have been sufficient time for me to be able to look at her, let alone be her bridesmaid. And yes, I was aware that the likelihood of her running off with any man of mine was pretty low. Number one, she was married with two kids; and number two, my track record with men wasn't that great. But if it did happen, there was no way I'd be as comfortable with the situation as Craig seemed to be.

Later, I found out that Stu had been part of a work syndicate that won some decent money in the lottery – cue drum roll – two weeks before Sally left Craig. Stu had used some of the money to buy Sally a new pair of breasts for her last birthday. She got them on one of those cosmetic surgery holidays to Thailand. Angela had hers done too, but Angela's were, in comparison, quite modest. At Stu's request (well, it was his money) Sally had gone for two cups too many, which looked unbalanced on her small frame. But he loved them, which I supposed was the main thing, and he seemed proud of the attention they got. Sally ensured they were on display a lot of the time, so the other men in the group spent a lot of time admiring them too. I'd even overheard Craig commenting to Angela's husband, Jason, that if Sally'd had those boobs when they were together, he might not have let her go so easily. I didn't think he knew I'd heard — and it had hurt too much for me to volunteer the information.

By the time we arrived at Sally's and Stu's, having detoured to the supermarket for a pre-packaged salad and a tray of meat, the party was in full swing. The men were gathered at one end of the pergola around the barbecue, within arm's reach of the esky. The women were at the opposite end, close to the kitchen. Kids of various ages were running around the lawn under a now blue sky. Melbourne weather was a fickle lady.

Stu was the first to spot us. 'Maaaaate, you made it!' He lightly punched Craig's arm, took the beers and meat from him, and shoved a cold stubby in his hand. 'And the gorgeous Em.' He kissed my cheek. 'Go on, tell me, what's he got that I don't?' He stepped back and opened his arms, a wide grin on his face.

'For starters, he has hold of my bottle of wine. As for the rest,' I winked and leaned closer, 'I'll have to tell you later.'

Sally had looked up when we arrived, smiled at Craig, ignored me, and continued with whatever celebrity gossip was so fascinating that week.

I stepped over a football and held the coleslaw over my head to make room for three hollering boys to run past. Ouch. How did I hurt those muscles? Since when did you use your arms to run?

Angela grabbed the lead boy by his arm. 'Kai, how

many times have I told you? Don't run mud through the house! And watch where you're going – you nearly wore that coleslaw.' He nodded, smiled, and ran off.

'And Brock?' Angela called after one of the others. 'That goes for you too!' She stood and greeted me with an air kiss. 'Sorry about that, Em. Sometimes I think those two will be the death of me . . . but I wouldn't swap them for anything. I try to be stern, but they only need to smile and I melt. They're both as bad as their father.' She looked across at Jason, who raised a beer in her direction.

'Here, give me that slaw, and pop your wine in the ice bucket. There are glasses over there.' She pointed towards the covered trestle tables set up under the kitchen window.

I poured a drink and pulled up a chair, worried that if my muscles continued to stiffen the way they were, I'd have problems getting back out of it. Sally was holding court, so I settled back to listen.

'So I said to him, "How on earth can I be expected to plan a wedding with anything less than five bridesmaids?"' She looked around at the others for approval. A lot of nodding was taking place. To the other women in the group, Sally was like the most popular girl in school. 'Stu was just going to ask Craig to be his best man, and that wouldn't work. We have to make a statement, you know, do it properly. I've asked my dressmaker to copy Mariah Carey's wedding dress.

I'm tall enough to carry it off, and now I've had my boobs done I think I'll look just like her. She needed six attendants to carry her train, it was that long.'

Sally was finally interrupted when a little girl twirled too close to the food table and knocked over a bottle of soft drink. The sticky, orange mess pooled on the vinyl, and a smaller girl in a pink princess costume stuck her hand in it and splashed it in the direction of the mothers.

'Jesus, Makayla!' yelled her father from the barbecue. 'Keep an eye on the kids, will you, Kerry?'

'They're your kids too! Brianna, get your hands out of the soft drink. Don't you dare wipe them on your dress!'

'Maybe we should put the food out?' Angela suggested to Sally.

I managed to pull myself out of the chair, and stood back while the kids descended on the sausages. Craig came up behind me, kissed my neck and squeezed my bum affectionately. I flinched as his fingers dug into my stiffening muscles. He laughed and pulled me back against him.

'Look at the kids,' he said softly. 'Brock and Kai are great boys.'

As he said it, Kai reached across and grabbed Brianna's pigtail and pulled hard.

'Owwwww-a!' she shrieked.

Jason laughed and ruffled Kai's hair.

'Don't you think they're a little wild?' I said.

'Nah.' Craig wrapped his arms around my middle. 'Just high-spirited. I want a few just like them.' He rested his chin on top of my head. 'Three boys would be nice. You'd make a great mum.'

I was saved from answering by Angela calling to us. 'Come on, you lovebirds. Grab a plate.'

Craig was always frisky after a few drinks. I spent the drive home slapping his hand away from my thigh.

'I'm trying to drive, Craig.'

When we did finally make it home, he was quickly satisfied. Afterwards, as I lay in the curve of his arms, my mistreated muscles sinking gratefully into the mattress, he brought up the subject of children again.

'Em?'

'Hmmmm?'

'You want kids, don't you?'

'Sure, one day.'

'Do you want to keep working when you do? Or will you be like Ange and just take something part-time?'

He wanted to talk about this now? I yawned – only partly because I was tired. 'I don't know. I've got a mortgage to pay.'

'I was thinking we could sell your place and use the equity to buy something together. Something more modern – maybe closer to my work and our friends.

Like Sal and Stu's place, or Jase and Ange's.'

'But that would be further for me to travel to work.'

My routine was built around a triple snooze button scenario and a short commute. Did the trams even run that far out?

'You don't want to live in the inner city forever, do you? When we have kids, we'll want something bigger and newer – and we won't get that here. With the money from this place we should be able to afford something really nice. A couple of years of knuckling down, and you can work part-time.'

'Oh.' I leaned across to take a sip from the water glass beside the bed, but had trouble swallowing it.

'I know you don't like change, but things can't always stay the same.' He looked around the room. 'And this place won't suit us forever. It's called settling down. Neither of us is getting any younger.'

But what if I don't want to settle down?

I turned to tell him that, but he'd gone to sleep, so I pushed the thought back into whatever hole in my brain it had crawled out of.

What if Craig isn't the one?

Of course he was the one. He was talking about forever plans. He was offering everything I'd always wanted – a stable, secure relationship, someone to help out with the mortgage, someone who wanted to come home to me – and our kids – every night. Someone who was committed, reliable and safe. What he was offering was everything I hadn't had growing up, and everything I'd sworn I'd give to my children.

But what if there's something more? Something I haven't done yet? Something I don't know yet that I want to do?

Meerkat thoughts. I mentally jumped on each of them as they popped up.

Beside me in the dark, Craig was snoring softly. Knowing his sleep patterns as I did, I could tell he was about to roll onto the side facing me and do that snorting thing he did. Predictable. Predictable was good.

There was something about lying awake when someone else was asleep that made everything seem so much bleaker.

What if there's nothing else I want to do? What if this is all there is?

It couldn't be.

This was another reason to never run again — it messed with the brain chemistry.

CHAPTER THREE

I was wrong. By Monday, even the part of my forehead that Booth had kissed on Sunday hurt. It hurt to stand, it hurt to walk, it hurt to move, it even hurt to think about moving. Doing up my bra required a dexterity that had abandoned me; and to sit on the toilet I had to grip one side of the seat and slowly, painfully lower myself down – and then reverse the movement to get back up. All with accompanying sound effects.

It was something to do with the muscles in my bum, the muscles at the front of my legs, the muscles at the back of my legs, the muscles in between my legs, and the muscles in my back. I would have taken to my bed for the rest of the week, except that it hurt to roll over.

At first Craig thought it was funny.

'Come over here and give me a kiss,' he urged on Monday night, grinning as he watched me lever myself out of the chair.

On Tuesday night he offered to teach me some stretches that he said would help. I almost said yes except that: (a) I couldn't bear to move any more than

I had to; (b) judging by the look on his face, stretching wasn't what he had in mind; and (c) if stretching wasn't what he had in mind, I couldn't bear to move any more than I had to.

By Wednesday he'd switched from any sort of sympathy into 'I don't want to hear about it, it's self-inflicted' mode.

As for Booth, the cause of all my pain? He laughed on Monday morning when I hobbled – in flat shoes – into the weekly risk meeting; and again on Tuesday when I grimaced as I gripped the top of the chair in order to sit down to eat my lunch.

'It's not funny,' I growled.

'From this angle it's pretty hilarious. I'm still having interesting dreams about you in that wet T-shirt.'

I waved his comment away. 'I'm walking like an over-worked porn star. How the hell did running hurt those muscles?'

He looked at me with bemusement, or was it amusement?

'I said that out loud, didn't I?'

He nodded slowly. 'Yes, sweetheart, you did. It's another picture I don't need in my head.'

By Thursday I was beginning to feel vaguely human. I was able to wear heels again, and could manage to sit down without groaning – although anything more physical than that was out of the question.

To celebrate being able to move again I treated

myself to a long lunch of the retail variety. It was Suse's birthday tomorrow night, and as Richard had booked a French restaurant in Prahran that looked like it had just stepped out of 1960s' Paris, I wanted something suitably bombshell in nature. Something that would make me feel like Sophia Loren or Elizabeth Taylor, before she got messy. And when a girl needed a bombshell dress, there was only one thing for it. Fitzroy.

I called Suse.

'You want me to help you indulge that dreadful habit you have for other people's clothes?'

'It's called vintage – and there are some real treasures to be found. Remember that Dinnigan kimono I found last summer? Barely worn, and a fraction of what it cost new.'

We vintage shoppers tended to keep a list of our successes – they sustained us through the lean periods. I'd always remember the Marc Jacobs slingbacks – mine for just twenty dollars – and the Zampatti little black dress that I bought for next to nothing. It would be perfect if I ever needed to go to the opera, or the ballet, or somewhere I needed to look polished and professional. I was still searching for the holy grail – the real thing by Chanel.

In one of the new designer boutiques, Suse found a soft blue leather bag and some tangerine boots.

'I'm not even going to attempt to justify the cost of these to Richard,' she said of the boots. 'This colour is so amazing I'll only be able to wear them a couple of times this winter.'

In my favourite vintage store, I snaffled two long, narrow striped scarfs in the softest of mohair that wound around and around my neck.

'I can't believe that you choose to wear someone else's junk when you have enough of your own at home,' Suse said.

She'd never understood my love of vintage. Nor did Booth. 'Other people's crap,' he always said. 'Clothes that smell like people have died in them.' Inevitably he added, 'Hey, what if someone did die in them?'

'After Sunday's effort I'll be adding the engineered lycra to my spare room closet too,' I told Suse. 'Never to be seen again.' She laughed as I pretended sadness for the sports gear. 'But to answer your question, vintage is about the design and the character. A few accessories, a bit of styling and it's a new outfit. Like seeing a house that isn't perfect but has great potential.'

'Or a man who's a little bruised but can be made whole again?'

'Yeah . . . a bit like that.'

I scanned the racks with the eyes of a practised vintage shopper and spied a classic 1960s-style tight-skirted dress that put the bomb in bombshell. I held it up for Suse – who nodded her approval – and disappeared into the change rooms.

'Is Craig coming tomorrow?' she asked as I

emerged to model the outfit.

'He sure is. Why?'

'The last couple of times he's made a last-minute excuse.'

'Not this time. What do you think?' I twirled.

'Are you sure he's the one?'

'About the dress, I meant.'

'Oh. The dress is great. That green is almost the same colour as your eyes.'

The shop assistant handed me a narrow black belt to cinch my waist even further. Yes, with the right underwear . . .

'I'm not sure if he's the one,' I said, doing a final twirl in the dress. 'You've told me before that no relationship is perfect. This dress, however, is.' I checked the price tag. 'And look – it's better value than that moisture-wicking running shirt.'

As I was waiting to pay, I saw a suede sleeve poking out from an over-stuffed rack of jackets. That colour, a deep ink blue, would work well against my almost black hair. The sleeve belonged to a three-quarter-length suede coat. It was soft, it was gorgeous, it was Italian, and when I tried it on it fitted like a glove.

'I'd forgotten that was there,' said the shop assistant. 'It could have been made for you.'

'I hate to admit it, but she's right,' said Suse.

'And at this price, it's bound to get a whole lot more wear than the dreaded sneakers ever will.'

•

I modelled the coat for Mum that evening – virtually, of course, her being in Bali and all. We Skyped every Thursday evening. Mum laughed at the predictability of it, but I knew that secretly she loved this particular routine.

'I love the coat,' she said.

'Isn't it gorgeous?' I unbuttoned the coat and laid it over a chair.

'Tell me about Sally and Stu's barbecue,' she said. 'Was it as bad as you expected?'

'Worse. First I forgot it was on. Booth and I went running and –'

'Running? Why?'

'I know. Ridiculous, right?'

I poured myself a glass of wine. It was another part of our ritual – Mum drank beer and I drank wine, as if we were having a drink together. Mum said it encouraged easy conversation.

'It's to do with this bucket list that Booth's decided he has to have. Now Suse is on the bandwagon and signing up for a half-marathon too. I promised him I'd give running a go, but,' I paused to take a sip, 'no way. It was dreadful. I couldn't walk for a week.'

'Poor darling. Was Craig suitably sympathetic?'

'You'd think he would be, but no – despite all my moaning. Booth thought it was great fun.'

'I'll bet he did.'

Mum's partner, Steph, popped her head around the screen. 'What's this about you running?'

'Don't worry, it won't be happening again.'

'I'm pleased to hear it.' She blew me a kiss and moved out of sight.

'So you forgot the barbecue was on?' Mum prompted.

'Yeah. I don't know why Craig needed me there anyway. He's in one corner with the men, and I'm in the other listening to celebrity magazine crap – who's shagging who, who's broken up, who's pregnant. Sally was showing off this bag that Stu bought her "just because".' I made rabbit ears for emphasis. 'She's going on like it's a Prada or something, then says in a hushed tone, "It's a Kardashian, you know," as if we were supposed to be impressed. The others seemed to be. And the kids – don't get me started on the kids.' I wrinkled my nose at the memory of Mikayla – or was it Brianna? – and the orange fizzy drink that had splattered all over Kerry's white spray-on pants. 'I can't believe Craig wants all of that.'

'Hang on . . . are you saying that Craig's been talking marriage and kids?'

'Not marriage, but definitely kids. He thinks we should move in together.'

'Don't you think that's a little quick, sweetheart?'

'Well . . . we've been together four months now.

We're not getting any younger. Anyway, you fell for Dad in shorter time than that.'

'Yes – and look how that turned out. You're right though, I did fall hard and fast for your father. I was madly in love with him for a time – we couldn't keep our hands off each other.'

My parents met in London in 1979. Mum was twenty-one, just out of uni and backpacking around Europe. She'd started with one of those 18–25 tours – twenty countries in twenty days. She didn't remember too much of it – she'd slept all day on the bus so she could party all night. 'It was Tuesday, so we must have been in Amsterdam . . .' That sort of thing. By the time she arrived in London, she had enough money for a cheap share flat and not a lot else. She quickly scored a job in a bar, where she met Dad, who was moonlighting as a DJ. I'd seen the pictures from back then. Dad had a head full of dark curls and jeans so tight I was surprised I'd been conceived at all. He looked a bit like the cute guy from that British cop show, *The Professionals*. Mum was small and slim, with long tawny hair that she used to tease and curl. Her jeans were also tight and she wore her T-shirt tucked into them. She had a mass of crucifixes and chains hanging around her neck, and huge hoops dangling from her ears. My mother was Madonna before Madonna was Madonna.

'Don't forget, it was love at first sight for you and Steph too,' I reminded her. 'And that seems to be working.'

'Yes, but was it love at first sight for you?'

'Craig and I make sense, Mum.'

'Perhaps. But sometimes the best things are the ones that don't make sense. I think underneath your sensible lists you could be more like me than you like to admit.'

'What's that supposed to mean?'

'It means there's a lot you haven't done and experienced yet, and I don't want you to wake up when you're forty and regret the sensible choices you've made. Before you make any decisions, why don't you come and visit us? You must be overdue a holiday – and didn't you say you thought Craig was looking to surprise you with one?'

'I'll think about it.'

'Promise?'

'I promise.' I heard Craig's key in the door. 'I must go . . . love you both.'

'Love you too,' and she was gone.

'Was that your mum?' Craig asked, leaning in to kiss me. Thursday was one of his gym nights so it was a sweaty kiss.

'Uh huh. She's asked us up to Bali for a break.'

'That's nice.' He seemed distracted as he opened a beer.

'I picked up our usual takeaway – is that okay?'

He nodded. 'Sure.'

'How about you have a shower while I heat it up?'

He grinned cheekily and wrapped his arms around me from the back. 'Are you saying I'm smelly?' One arm held me firmly, while the other hand grabbed a boob.

'Ouch – that hurt.' I pulled back.

'Okay, after dinner then.' He patted my bum and headed into the bedroom to get changed, leaving his sweaty gym shirt where it fell.

'Do you want to pick that up?' I called.

When I got no answer I sighed heavily and took the offending garment into the laundry, holding it gingerly with my fingertips. Ugh.

While he was showering, I dished out our takeaway: beef and black bean. Craig liked to eat in front of the telly most nights. We chewed in silence for a few minutes.

'Oh, I forgot to mention,' he said. 'Jase managed to snare some tickets in a corporate box for tomorrow night's game. Geelong v the Maggies. Sal's parents are in town to help with the wedding, so it's a good reason for Stu to make himself scarce. We figure it'll be like a bucks' night.'

'You're going too?'

'Yeah, isn't that what I just said?'

'What about Suse's birthday dinner?'

'Sorry, babe. What can I do? My best mate is getting married – I have to be there to support him.'

'The wedding isn't for months yet. Surely they'll organise something else closer to the time?'

He shrugged. 'Will you still go tomorrow night?'

'Sure. Why wouldn't I?'

'I just thought you might want to get together with Sally and Ange – take an interest in the wedding plans.'

Seriously? 'No.'

'So you're happy to go without me?'

'Sorry, babe, what can I do? It's my best friend's birthday – I have to be there.'

He raised his eyebrows at my attempted parody of him.

'I'll ring Booth,' I added. 'He's not seeing anyone at the moment, so we can go together.'

He pursed his lips, but said nothing. There was silence – except for the noise he made when he chewed . . . and the one he made when he swallowed. Why hadn't I noticed that before?

'Craig, do you have a bucket list?'

He screwed his face into a thinking arrangement. 'No. Should I?'

I pushed my food around the plate. 'I don't know. Maybe.'

'What's brought this on?'

'Booth and Suse were talking about it at the pub last Friday. It's why we went running – because they both want to run marathons. And I was wondering whether I should have one too. What would I put on it?'

'No one ever does the things on their list, so what would be the point?'

'If you had a list, what would you put on it?'

He held his fork in the air while he thought about it. There was still a pea speared on one of the prongs.

'I want to buy a house, settle down and have kids.' He looked at me and smiled.

I laughed. 'You're not getting out of it that easily. Really, what do you want to do?'

'That is what I want to do. A nice home in the suburbs, a good woman, a few kids and my friends . . . I'd be happy with that.'

'What about wanting to play for Geelong, or . . . wearing the baggy green? Things that all guys want?'

He shook his head. 'Nah, they're just dreams. They can't be real, so you can't say they're on a bucket list.'

'Oh.' I pushed the rice around some more. Did we really have to eat the same meal every Thursday night? 'What do you reckon I should have on my list?'

'Most people say they want to do things like marathons or skydives. Or they say they want to buy a house, meet the love of their life, travel the world, and lose twenty kilos. You've already bought a house, you don't ever want to run again, and I can't see you jumping out of something.'

'Why not?'

'It's not your deal, is it? You don't like uncertainty, and there's nothing very certain about putting your life in the hands of a giant rubber band, or jumping out of a plane.'

'I guess.'

'And you don't need to lose twenty kilos – five, perhaps ten, would be plenty. You should go to the gym with Sally and Ange.' He smiled encouragingly. 'Those girls will help get you back into skinny jeans.'

I didn't wear skinny jeans; I'd never worn skinny jeans. My brand of curves didn't do skinny jeans.

'Then there's the travel part. You don't like to travel, so there's no point having that on your list either. You're like me – happy to holiday close to home with your friends. In fact,' he paused, 'you know how we were talking about going away together?'

Here it came . . . I knew he'd been planning something in the background.

'Yes, why?'

It was a good thing I'd put my passport application in. Wait till Booth heard about this.

'Well, Stu's suggested that we join him and Sal, and Jase and Ange and the kids, for a week down at Sorrento. It'll be fun . . . don't you think?'

Fun? Coastal Victoria in the winter? The blokes out playing golf, and me in an enclosed space with Sal, Ange and two boys with cabin fever?

I chose my words carefully. 'I was thinking of just you and me, somewhere warmer and more tropical . . . Maybe we could take Mum up on her offer?'

'I don't see the point in spending a fortune on airfares when we've got places right here we can go for a fraction of the price. It'll be a good opportunity for you to really get to know the girls before the wedding. And as for finding the love of your life, well, we've found each other, haven't we?'

He beamed at me. I saw the remnants of a black bean on his tooth.

I smiled, but the image that came into my mind was handcuffs – and not the fun sort. Not that I'd ever done anything with handcuffs, but I'd heard that in the right company, with the right safe word, they could be fun.

'Let's face it, Em, Josh isn't one for settling down, and Suse strikes me as being the type who could be a little bit . . . well, you know.'

'Actually, no, I don't know. What type is Suse?'

'I just think she's the type who's not easily pleased, and would look elsewhere if things aren't perfect. A bucket list just gives her the excuse to feel discontented and run off and do whatever she wants and blame it on her "bucket list".' He used his fingers to make quotation marks. 'You're more sensible than that. More responsible – not as flighty.' He smiled as if it was a good thing. 'You don't need anything like that. We don't need anything like that. It's probably good that when we move, you won't be seeing as much of them. I know they're your friends, but I don't think they're the best influence on you.' He fished a piece of broccoli out of his meal and set it to the side of his plate with all the other vegetables he'd picked out. 'It'll do you good to have some girl time. The other guys are convinced that you're fooling around with Josh.'

'I don't think it's anyone else's business who I choose to spend my time with,' I said firmly. 'So what if the guys have a problem with it?'

'It's not just them. Sal was only saying the other day how if you really cared anything for me, you'd stop seeing him.' He was silent for a few seconds, perhaps wondering whether to push the conversation to the next level, then added, 'She says that men and women can never be friends without sex getting in the way. She says men will always want to sleep with a woman unless she's really unattractive, and even then they probably still would after a few beers. And, given that you're fairly hot, it's obvious that Josh wants to shag you.'

'Sally didn't make that up. She got it from the movie *When Harry Met Sally.*'

'That doesn't make it wrong.'

'Whatever,' I muttered and pushed my half-eaten food away. 'But it's okay to still be mates with the guy who's shagging your ex-girlfriend?'

He was quiet for a minute, and then he absolutely took it there. 'For my sake, would you consider cutting back on your friendship with Josh? I'd like to make our relationship more permanent, but there's no way I'd do it while he's hanging around.'

What. The. Fuck? A blackness came from the back of my head and whirred around my brain, sending me into a cold and nauseous sweat. I made it to the bathroom just in time.

When I came back, he asked, 'Are you okay?'

'Yeah, fine. Probably a dodgy prawn in the rice . . . or maybe I'm coming down with something. I'm feeling a bit tired.'

'It would serve you right for getting soaked on the weekend.'

I busied myself cleaning the plates.

'Actually, no,' I said as I shoved a takeaway container into the bin. 'I'm not okay. I don't want to go to Sorrento with your friends and their out-of-control kids. I want to go to Bali to see my mother. And another thing.' I turned to face him. 'Don't ask me to choose between you and my friends. You won't like the answer.'

He stared at me, then put down his empty beer bottle. 'If that's how you feel, I'd better go.'

He didn't move.

'Yes, maybe you'd better.'

When he slammed the door behind him, I should have felt miserable, but I didn't. I felt relieved.

CHAPTER FOUR

Craig didn't call all Friday. And I didn't phone him either. He'd take any move from me as an apology, and I had nothing to apologise for.

Booth and I were almost the last to arrive at Suse's dinner – my fault. First, I couldn't decide whether to pile my hair up or leave it down. Booth said it looked better down. I thought he only said that because it would be quicker than me re-doing it. Then I couldn't decide what heels to team with the bombshell dress I'd squeezed into. He leaned patiently against the kitchen counter as I appeared first in red, then black stilettos, finally exploding as I was dithering over where I'd put my black patent peep-toe heels.

'For fuck's sake, black is black. Go with the pointy-toe ones and let's get out of here.'

'These pointy toes, or these? Do you think I need a coat? It's a bit chilly out.'

'Just take this one and be done with it.' He grabbed my new suede jacket from its resting position on the back of the chair.

'What about the whole blue and green should never be seen together thing?'

'Really? We're having this discussion now?'

Richard greeted us with open arms and a roar of pleasure. Judging by the flush in his cheeks and the exuberance of his welcome, he'd started partying a few hours earlier.

'No Craig, hey, Em? I knew it was only a matter of time before you and Josh got together properly.' He shook Booth's hand vigorously. Suse caught my eye and smiled in apology. 'After all, Josh, who could resist this sexy package for long?' He pretended to leer as he looked me up and down.

Booth put an arm around my (artificially cinched-in) waist and pulled me close. 'She certainly has more wiggle in that tight skirt tonight,' he agreed, matching Richard's pretend perv.

'I bet you say that to all the girls.' I laughed and thumped him lightly before moving away to hug Suse. 'Happy birthday, love. Are you going to set Richard straight, or will I?'

She sighed. 'He knows, but continues to live in hope.'

Richard had been hoping for a happy ending between Booth and me for as long as I'd known him.

'One day you won't disappoint me,' he said, leading us to the table for introductions and drinks.

Booth leaned in and whispered, 'He's right – you're

looking dangerously hot tonight. Pity Craig isn't here to appreciate it.'

I tapped him on the cheek. 'Sorry to disappoint you, sweetheart, but what you see is mostly the result of expensively engineered underwear. And trust me – it's not at all sexy underneath.'

He laughed. 'How to destroy my dreams, Em!'

'Besides, Craig told me I need to lose weight. Five, maybe ten kilos, he said.'

'Really? From where I'm standing it all looks well distributed to me.'

I dropped my eyes from his. 'As I said, all created by Spanx. I don't know about you, but I need a drink.'

At dinner, we were seated opposite Richard and Suse, and another couple, Liz and Randall, who remembered us from Suse and Richard's wedding.

'I've never been to a wedding before where the bride had a man as the bridesmaid.' Randall laughed at the memory. 'Yet Richard didn't seem to find anything strange about it.'

Richard hadn't batted an eyelid when Suse announced that she wanted Booth and me as her attendants. Richard's ability to accept most things was one of the many things I loved about him. I had a list, naturally. His bear-like exterior hid a soft, trusting and non-judgemental heart; and he adored the ground that Suse walked on. I couldn't have chosen better for my friend if I'd advertised for the position.

We'd joked about that before the wedding. I'd said that her ad would read:

Wanted – big-hearted man looking for independent, slightly manic woman. I'm my own worst enemy, and you'll be my best friend.

She'd laughed and said that mine would read:

Wanted – a renovator's delight.

I hadn't been sure that she was joking.

Booth turned to me. 'How do you reckon Craig would take it if you had Suse and me as your bridesmaids – if you two ever do the deed?'

'Oh, I'm sorry,' said Liz. 'We thought you two were together.'

'No. Josh and I are just friends.' I smiled to let her know she didn't need to feel embarrassed.

Suse jumped in. 'Emily has a boyfriend – Craig, who couldn't be here tonight – and Josh is in between attachments. And thank goodness for that. His track record isn't great. He's been married twice before,' she explained to Liz. 'Neither of them lasted long . . . thankfully.' She turned to Booth. 'I still remember the look on Mandy-sorry-Amanda's face when you told her you wanted Em as your best man.'

'I told her that at least she didn't need to worry about the bucks' night getting out of hand, but, no, she wasn't happy.'

The bucks' night had been fun – what I remembered of it. Booth and Suse remembered even less than I did

– someone had to be responsible. At least there'd been no naked chaining to anything, or shaving cream and razors used anywhere they shouldn't have been used. Booth had walked down the aisle with both eyebrows intact and no limbs encased in plaster. Not that Mandy had been grateful.

'And then afterwards she banned you from having anything to do with us,' Suse went on, 'which was a problem as you and Em were still working together.'

'Yeah, that marriage cost me a job and my friends.'

'Actually, that last part was probably my fault,' Suse admitted. 'I saw her watching you and Em dancing at the wedding, and told her not to worry – that you'd shagged once and gotten it out of your systems. I think she took it the wrong way.'

Booth reached over and patted her hand. 'Don't worry about it, Suse. She was always going to go down that path.'

'So,' Suse said to Liz, 'the last thing we need in our little group is another Mandy or, heaven forbid, Shayla.'

'Aaaah yes,' Booth nodded, 'Shayla . . . not one of my finest moments.'

'Those Bo-Peep outfits she wanted for her bridesmaids were a high point!' Suse remembered with a laugh.

'The dresses were bad enough, but thank goodness I convinced her that flowers would be better than those sheep hook things she wanted her girls to carry!'

'You're not serious?' Liz looked horrified.

'Sadly, he is,' Suse said. 'Shayla wanted her bridesmaids dressed in these powder blue, pouffy numbers. The full toilet-roll-doll extravaganza – puffy sleeves, puffy skirts, puffy hair, and powder blue lace over the top of everything. At first Em and I thought she was joking. But it quickly became obvious that she was deadly serious. She also wanted Em and me in boy shepherd outfits, like those breech things the Gone Troppo kids wear – is that their name? The ones from *The Sound of Music*?'

'I think you'll find it's the Von Trapp family singers,' offered Randall.

'Yes, them. She wanted us to wear those things. Em was trying to keep the peace because of the Mandy-sorry-Amanda thing, but there was no way I was letting Shayla dress us up like some braces-wearing puppets.' She made hand movements as if she was dancing puppets around a stage.

Booth and I looked at each other and sang, '*High on the hill stood a lonely goatherd . . .*'

'*Yodel-ady, yodel-ady, yodelay-ee-ah,*' the others joined in.

When the laughter died down, Liz asked, 'So did you have to wear them?'

'No. Thankfully Josh stepped in and told her he'd already been married once and it was a disaster, and he wasn't going to let her turn this one into a circus. She cried and wailed a bit, and told him that she'd always dreamed of a themed wedding.'

'It was at that point I was sure I was making another mistake,' Booth said, 'but by then it was too late to back out. I don't think she ever forgave me for ruining her wedding, but some dreams should stay in the bucket.'

'Not that it mattered,' I said. 'My peace-keeping came to nothing when Shayla's father came on to Suse at the pre-wedding dinner. Do you remember that, Suse?'

She shuddered.

'Suse slapped him, and Josh defended her, so Shayla accused Josh of having feelings for Suse.'

'I told her that was rubbish. I think I said something like, "God, no, Emily's the one who shagged him — but that's out of their system now." Not surprisingly, it didn't improve the situation.'

The others laughed, but I couldn't. I was remembering how much it had hurt when Shayla banned Booth from having anything to do with us. At least that time it hadn't involved him having to change jobs, but still, he'd been gone.

'Yep,' he said. 'That's twelve months of my life I'll never get back.'

'The marriage only lasted twelve months?' asked Liz.

'Nope, the marriage lasted six — the whole relationship lasted twelve.' He grinned. 'You could say that I rushed into it.'

'What about you, Emily? Have you been married before?'

'Me? No.'

Booth and Suse looked at each other and giggled.

'Em's not great with commitment,' Suse said.

'Maybe she just hasn't met the right man yet.' Liz smiled at me.

I nodded gratefully. 'Maybe.'

'And when she does,' added Richard, leaning over to top everyone's glasses up again, 'she'll be happy to blow you two off if he asks her to.'

I took a sip of my wine and changed the subject. After last night, Richard didn't know how close to the truth he was.

Later, as Suse and Richard saw out the last of their guests, Booth and I relocated to a corner. He slumped into a comfy-looking but low-lying lounge. I eyed it off and dragged a dining chair over instead.

'Can't that dress get down this far?' he asked, grinning.

'I'm not game enough to try,' I admitted. 'If I get down, I'm not sure I'll get back up elegantly.'

'I'll help you. Pass me your drink.'

I did, and he placed it on the side table next to his, and held out his hand. I took it and collapsed heavily beside him. We sat chatting and sipping, until Suse and Richard joined us with the remains of a bottle of wine and my suede coat I'd left on the back of my chair. She tossed it across to me.

'I'm getting too old for this,' she complained, manoeuvring into a chair.

'You poor old girl.' Richard smiled lovingly as he filled her glass. 'Running should be interesting on Sunday morning.'

'Yep, I think I'll still be sweating pure alcohol.' She turned to Booth. 'Did I tell you I've joined the running club that meets at The Tan on Sunday mornings? I went for the first time last week – in the rain. You should join too.'

'If Em's not going to be into it, I will.' Booth held out his glass for Richard.

'I'm definitely not going to sign up,' I said, 'so consider yourself released from any obligation to me.'

'Em told me it was a disaster.' Suse stretched in her chair and rubbed at her eyes.

'We were going well until she started spewing.'

'Oh, Em! You didn't!'

'I did. The whole thing was awful. It rained, and then the blisters came out, and there was all this blood in my new shoes . . . I couldn't walk for days.'

Suse tried not to laugh. 'I'm sorry, I shouldn't.'

Richard made no such attempt and roared so loudly the staff, who were tidying up, stopped and looked over at us.

'It was pretty funny,' agreed Booth. 'And when it

rained, that T-shirt left nothing to the imagination. I wanted a pic to look at in my darker moments, but she wouldn't let me.'

Suse grinned. 'I saw her in the change rooms. I'd forgotten she was built like that.'

'I'll never forget again,' Booth said, and sighed dramatically.

'Oh, shut up about that already,' I growled. 'There is nothing on earth that could compel me to go through that hell again. How did my glass get empty already?'

'I'll fix that,' said Richard.

The conversation meandered through a range of subjects, with mini arguments breaking out, and being resolved or deflected with the next comment. Richard joined in occasionally, but for the most part was content to sit back and listen.

'I can't keep up with you three,' he said. 'I reckon you've covered at least eight different subjects in the last ten minutes.'

Suse leaned over to kiss his cheek.

'If I move, I'll miss nights like this,' I said, then realised I must be drunk. I hadn't meant to say it out loud.

'What?' Suse and Booth spoke together.

'Are you going somewhere?' asked Richard.

'Maybe. I'm thinking about it.' I shrugged, spilling my wine with the movement. Booth brushed it off my skirt. 'Craig wants to sell my place and buy somewhere in the suburbs. Something bigger for when we have kids.'

Booth stiffened beside me, but said nothing.

'I didn't know it had got that serious,' Suse commented.

'I don't know that it has. It's just what he's been saying. It's got me thinking.'

'Is that what you want?' Suse asked quietly.

I think she meant to ask if Craig was what I wanted. The answer was the same.

'I don't know. Things can't stay the same forever – maybe I need to grow up and accept that. It's not that I'd be letting you guys go, just that I'd be further away.'

'You'd have a good chunk of equity in your apartment now,' observed Richard. 'That was a smart buy. All it needs is a spruce-up and you'll really maximise on the investment. I guess the question is whether you want to sell in this market.'

Richard was my go-to man on all matters of real estate. He and Suse had just started dating when I first bought my place. Once I'd decided on an apartment, he helped me through the process.

'If you move out of Richmond, further out of the city, you'll go from an easy commute to something a lot harder. And let's face it, Em, you still haven't made friends with your alarm clock.'

Suse knew I wasn't much of a morning person.

Booth finally spoke. 'What's he bringing to the deal? Has he got a deposit saved, or is this all going to be with your money?'

'We haven't sorted through the details yet.'

'What does this mean for your bucket list, the bikini on a tropical island – or is that going to be your honeymoon?' Booth didn't look at me as he asked the question.

'Maybe I don't need a bucket list. Maybe I should settle down. Who needs Bali – or Hawaii? Sorrento's supposed to be nice at this time of year.' I faked a smile.

Booth pushed himself to his feet, placing his hand on my leg for leverage. 'Need to see a man about a dog,' he announced, heading in the direction of the bathrooms.

Suse watched him go, then said, 'The way you were talking yesterday, I thought you weren't sure about Craig.'

'You're the one who told me that no relationship is perfect and you have to make compromises in every partnership. He's a nice guy and his biceps are magnificent.'

I smiled to lighten the discussion. She didn't smile back.

'Compromises are one thing, letting him walk all over you is another. Before you do anything, just be sure it's what you want – and that *he's* what you want,' she warned. 'Write a list if you have to, but don't say yes just because he's asked.'

'How do you know something like that? If he's *the*

one?'

Richard's gaze lingered on Suse. 'You just do. I knew straight away – it took Suse a little while longer. You'll know when you meet him, but if you have to ask the question, you haven't met him yet.'

Suse returned his smile. For all that she complained about his travel and their joint responsibilities, it was obvious she loved him.

'What did I miss?' Booth was back.

'Nothing. Are you ready to go?'

'Sure am.' He reached for my hand and pulled me to my feet.

In the taxi he didn't say anything until we pulled up outside my apartment block. 'Are you really going to settle for Craig?'

'Don't you mean am I going to settle down with Craig?'

'No. I meant what I said.'

I couldn't see his face in the dark. 'I don't know. Maybe I've been too picky. Maybe he is the one.'

He searched my face in the darkness. 'Okay, but if he isn't, don't wait until it's too late to work that out.' He kissed me hard on the forehead. 'Go peel yourself out of those engineered layers,' he said, earning himself a light thump to the arm, 'and I'll see you Monday.'

Once inside, I checked my phone again. There was still nothing from Craig. I wasn't going to be the first one to call. Not this time.

CHAPTER FIVE

Saturday morning arrived with a hangover, a need for strong coffee and paracetamol, and no message from Craig.

When we'd first started dating, Craig had ticked every box on my checklist. (It wasn't a very long list.) I tended to fall quickly and indiscriminately into love or lust – whatever you wanted to call it. Often I didn't get past the shoulders and arms. I'd always had a thing for men who looked as if they could swing me over their shoulder and take me back to the cave. It wasn't that I wanted to be treated like that, just that I wanted my man to look like he could do it if I wanted him to. Craig's biceps were good. Big tick.

But as we'd got to know each other better, some of those ticks were turning into half-ticks. It wasn't anything I could specifically put my finger on. He was a nice enough guy (tick), and the sex was . . . well, he had this habit of talking me through his moves before he made them. At first it was sexy – listening to him tell me what he was going to do to me was a turn-on. There were, however, only so many variations on the same theme. Sometimes I felt like he was coaching me, or calling a football game or a Melbourne Cup. I decided to be generous and give a half-tick for regularity and effort.

Apart from my weakness for shoulders and biceps, and being a nice enough guy, next on the checklist was a tolerance for my friends. Booth had sworn to Suse and me that after the debacle with Shayla and Mandy-sorry-Amanda, he'd never allow another woman to keep us apart. Sure, it was 3 am and we were all very drunk and he was celebrating the finalisation of his divorce, but I was positive he'd really meant it.

'I love youse two,' he'd slurred. 'No one's ever going to keep us apart again.'

The three of us drank to that.

At first, Craig had seemed accepting of my friendship with Suse and Booth. Big tick. But after we'd been together for a month or so, he started to turn his mouth down in disapproval if I reminded him that I had Friday-night plans.

'I get that they're your friends, but I don't see why it has to be every Friday night,' he'd complained. Half-tick.

The other week, he'd been waiting at my place when Booth and I had got back from an impromptu lunch. I'd been craving *pho* – that Vietnamese rare beef noodle soup that you pronounced as *fur*, or was it *fa* . . . with a short 'u', like you were puffing out air in a distinctly French way. However you pronounced it, I loved it and Craig didn't. As Craig and I didn't have plans, when Booth called suggesting it, I was quick to agree. We'd been arguing over nothing on the walk home, and when I opened the front door I was still laughing at something ridiculous Booth had said to try and win his point. Craig was on the lounge watching the football with a very grumpy look on his face. Booth made a smart-arse comment or two and left us to it. Not that we had an argument as such. Craig spent the rest of the afternoon sulking, and I spent it stubbornly refusing to notice that he was sulking. I couldn't see why he was so upset. After all, he hadn't mentioned he was coming around, and I'd had a craving for *pho*.

I had to face facts – Craig didn't like my friends. He especially didn't like Booth. That was okay – I didn't like his friends. We had nothing in common. For a start I wouldn't know how to recognise a Kardashian in the wild. Tick rubbed out.

I'd really thought that this time I could make it work. I'd convinced myself that this time, this man, would be *the one*. The one I could use italics with, and tell stories to our kids about how I knew he was *the one*. Yet even before Thursday night, I'd been feeling that the thrill had gone. For a start, since I'd given him a key to my apartment, his things were creeping into every corner of my life. I was far from being a domestic goddess – I couldn't cook, I hated cleaning, and I never threw anything out – but there was a difference between having too much stuff and stuff just left lying around. Half-tick.

Suse was right. The only thing for it was a list. Two lists.

I pulled out my notepaper and labelled two sheets: *Reasons to Stay With Craig*, and *Reasons to Dump Craig*. I underlined the headings.

First, reasons to stay . . .

His biceps. I knew it wasn't a real reason, but they were good.

He was hurt when Sally left him for Stu. I don't want to hurt him again.

We never argue.

He's talking about forever-together stuff.

I crossed through the word *never* and replaced it with *hardly ever. We hardly ever argue.* That was better.

I chewed on the end of my pen. There must be other reasons we were together? Perhaps they'd come to me later.

I pulled out the other list . . . reasons to dump. The words flew from my pen.

He doesn't like my friends.

He wants me to sell my apartment.

He wants me to move away to the suburbs.

He's lazy around the house.

The commentary in bed.

He doesn't listen to what I want or consider my opinion.

Take Bali, for instance. Just how many hints does a girl need to give?

I don't like his friends.

I don't like going out with his friends.

He thinks I should lose weight.

He wants to put me in skinny jeans.

If I stay, I'll never get to visit my mother, wear that bikini on a tropical island, renovate my house, or do any of the other things I might decide I want to do.

I contemplated the list and then added another.

We hardly ever argue.

No matter which way I compared the two lists, the Reasons to Dump list was definitely longer. This raised another question: how to actually do the dumping deed? Somehow I didn't think 'you're dropped' would cut it.

I ran through a mental list of gems from my recent-ish break-ups:

It's not you, it's me. (Yes, really.)

There's no one else.

You're lovely, I'm just not ready to commit.

I think I'm in love with you, but I need some space to be sure.

Thanks so much for helping give me back my confidence. I'll never forget you.

She said he was a mistake and she's lost without me.

No, really, there's no one else.

It's just one of those things.

The timing's not right — if only I'd met you first.

She needs me.

Don't you think thirty-five is too young to promise your life to one person?

I owe it to our history together to give it one more chance.

Maybe we can be together in another lifetime.

Truly, there's no one else.

My astrologer told me that you're not a good match for me.

My counsellor advised me not to get too serious just yet.

Harry Davis has changed his relationship status from 'in a relationship' to 'single'.

All of these had been used on me. One guy was responsible for six of them. None seemed right for this situation.

As I was contemplating my lists, my phone rang. My heart raced for a few brief yet betraying seconds until I realised it was Suse's ringtone, not Craig's. Along with to-do lists, playlists and shopping lists, I also had ringtone lists.

'You made me drink that much last night, so you're responsible for me not being able to tolerate the screaming of my children this morning,' she accused.

'Fair call. Heartstarter?'

I named a coffee shop in South Yarra. Aside from being a purveyor of superior caffeine, it was halfway between her house and my apartment.

'Yep. See you there in twenty.'

•

Neither of us spoke until we'd taken that first restorative sip.

'Last night was fun, Suse. Tell Richard thanks for organising it.'

'Yeah, it was a good night. This morning, though, he refused to help with the kids – hangover, he said. What about mine?'

My headache was finally fading so I managed to smile at that- after all, he was at home with them now.

'He thinks I rained on your parade a bit last night,' she went on, 'when you were talking about you and Craig moving in together.'

'Oh.'

'Did I?'

'No. You were just saying what you think. It's my fault – I'd told you I wasn't sure about us. Anyway, I haven't heard from Craig since Thursday night.'

'Because he didn't come last night?'

'No . . . not really.' I concentrated on stirring my coffee. 'We argued, he stormed out. Not a lot more to say.'

'Is it us? Josh and me? It must be tough for anyone coming into a relationship with the three of us. Neither of Josh's wives could handle it. I'm lucky Richard does, but I had to deliberately make room for him. Maybe you need to declutter a little, get rid of what you don't need, clear some space for him in your life.'

'Since when did you go all new age and woo-wooey?' I asked. 'Have you been talking to my mother?'

'It was on an episode of *Sex and the City*,' she explained. 'Miranda worked out that she was never going to have sex in a bedroom with a peach duvet and ruffles.'

'Nor would I! If Craig wants to move in permanently then I guess I'll make space in a cupboard for his things.'

She pulled out that wise married woman look she does every so often. I'm sure it's the same look she uses when she wants Toby to pack his toys away, or she's telling an employee there's no longer a job for them.

'Tell me, what's changed about him since that night you rang and said, "This is the one, Suse, I know it. Oh my God, you should see his biceps – and he's a PE teacher, so that must mean that he's good with kids and will keep himself healthy, right?" What's changed about him since then?'

I shrugged. 'They deliberately don't let you see their issues until you're too far down the road. It's a conspiracy. Anyway,' I added with authority, 'relationships are like treadmills –'

'When was the last time you were on a treadmill?'

'That's beside the point. It's an analogy. You know how Booth says that when he runs, the first kilometre feels good, but the next couple of kilometres are really hard as his body adjusts and gets into the rhythm of what he's doing? He says that's when most people stop. Apparently, though, if you keep going, you start to feel really good again for the next few kilometres – almost like a second wind. Then you hit a wall near the end, but if you work through it you get to the finish line.'

'Josh hasn't got past five kilometres yet, so I'm not sure he knows all that much about it. And I still don't get what a treadmill has to do with a relationship.'

'I'm one of those people who gets off too early. I don't stay on long enough for my body to adjust to the rhythm of the new partnership. I rarely make it through the getting-to-know-you phase before I press the emergency stop button – not that *I* actually get to press the stop button, they do, but you get the idea.' I searched my mind for the words I needed. 'I've realised that it's the middle part I have trouble with. Once the glow's gone, I start to see them for who they are, and find too many things that annoy me. I think if I could have the excitement of the falling-in-lust bit, and somehow avoid the messy middle bit, I'd be able to move straight into so-happy-together, but it doesn't seem likely that's ever going to happen.'

'Sounds like you need to fall in love with someone you've already gone through the get-to-know-you part with,' she suggested.

'No, it's not that. I'm in love with Craig – I'm sure I am – I just have to stay on the treadmill for a bit longer.'

She raised her eyebrows at that. 'Are you sure

you're in love with him, or is this another one you've talked yourself into?'

'That's unfair.'

'Is it? No relationship is perfect,' she said gently. 'You have to work at things.'

'What if staying with him means I'll never do the things I want to do?'

'Like what?' She looked harder at me. 'Are you talking about the bikini and the travelling and the renovations?'

I wrinkled my nose.

'We didn't think you were serious, Em. You've never mentioned it before, and you've certainly never made any moves to do anything about anything until now. You don't even have a bucket list.'

'I know . . . it's just that I'm wondering if I might want to do those things . . . not now, but someday.'

'Dump him then.'

Suse always has simple answers for complex problems. It's one of the reasons I love her.

'I would,' I explained, 'except that he was so hurt when Sally cheated on him. What right do I have to shatter him again? Maybe I need to make more of an effort. His biceps really are magnificent.'

'Dump him, don't dump him. Just make the decision, and do it quickly. It's like ripping a bandaid off – it only hurts while you're doing it.' Suse had always been the dumper, never the dumpee. 'You'd have a list somewhere of what guys have said to you – pick something off it.'

She beckoned a waiter over. 'Could we get more coffees please- and one of those shiny layered chocolatey things in the window – and two spoons?' Order placed, she turned back to me. 'You know you have to, don't you? Do something about it, I mean. When was the last time you dumped someone?'

I pretended to think about it.

'No way! Really? You've never been the dumper? In all these years? What about Seb? I'm sure you were ready to dump him? Wasn't there something about how he kept calling you his ex's name in bed?'

'Yeah, but he got in first.'

'And James? The one whose astrologer told him you weren't a good match.'

'Uh huh. Got in first. I was glad about that – he had a thing about feet.'

'Should I ask?'

I shook my head.

'What about Harry? You couldn't bear the Sunday morning breakfasts with his mother.'

'Relationship status change on Facebook.'

Somehow it had always been me that got dumped. Sure, it'd usually coincided with me deciding there were more crosses than ticks in the pros column, but they'd always got in first.

'Hmmmm.' Suse carefully separated the chocolate

layers in the creation we'd been served. 'You know what Josh would say about Craig, don't you?'

'I have a fair idea.' I skimmed some of the ganache into my mouth. 'This is good.'

'He'd tell you to push Craig off the pity wagon and leave room for some other poor dumped soul to climb aboard.'

'And that, my dear Suse, is why I won't be talking to Booth about it until I decide what to do. Can we talk about something else? This cake needs our full attention.'

When I got home, Craig was there . . . with a bunch of flowers. I felt a little mushy inside and also a little guilty. I'd been spending the morning planning how to dump him, and he'd been out buying me flowers. Perhaps I shouldn't be so quick to wipe away the ticks. I mentally added *buys me flowers* to the Reasons to Stay sheet.

He did his spaniel-eye thing and asked if he was forgiven, and I threw myself into his arms. Maybe not threw, but I was enthusiastic. I couldn't remember the last time someone had bought me flowers. Sure I would have preferred daisies or gerberas than whatever these were – supermarket carnations probably – but it was the thought that counted.

'Wow, if I knew I'd get that response, I'd buy flowers more often,' he said sometime later as he rolled away from me to get dressed.

'Are you leaving?' I pulled the sheet up to cover

my nakedness.

'Wish I could stay, but I'm playing poker with the boys. Do you want me to drop around after? We could have a repeat performance.'

He waggled his eyebrows. It was supposed to look suggestive, but all it did was make me giggle.

'No. I had a late one last night, and I'm pretty tired . . . even more so now.' I might even have blushed.

'You did come home, though, didn't you? That wasn't you just coming in from last night?'

What was he getting at?

'Of course I came home. I just went out for a coffee with Suse.'

His face had closed up. 'Not Josh?'

I draw in a deep breath – *here we go again. Remember the flowers, Em.* 'No, not Booth.'

He seemed satisfied with my response and leaned over to kiss me, reaching under the sheet to tease my nipple. 'Are you sure you don't want me to come around tonight?'

'No, I'm not sure, but I am tired.'

'Tomorrow?' His hand was now tracing a line under my breast. I bit my lower lip and he smiled. 'A few of us are going to watch the Swans get thrashed tomorrow. How about I drop over afterwards and we can continue this . . . conversation?'

'Uh huh,' I managed.

He laughed and kissed me again. 'Until then, babe.'

CHAPTER SIX

The flowers in their vase greeted me on Sunday morning. I tried not to notice how a few were already starting to droop. If Craig could make the move to bring me 'I'm sorry' flowers, I could make some room for him in my cupboards and, by extension, in my life.

Surely he would be satisfied with some space in the spare room – which, on opening the door, I found in a bigger mess than I remembered. The bed was covered with piles of folded clothes, the closet door didn't shut properly, and whatever was under the bed had been breeding. I stood in the doorway and contemplated a plan of attack. Maybe I could write a list.

Work out whatever is stopping the closet door from shutting and find a home for it.

Find a home for the clothes on the bed.

Be brave and look under the bed.

With the list written, I shut the door on the mess and went down the road for a coffee, which I lingered over until it was lunchtime.

Then I phoned Booth. 'What are you doing?'

'Wondering why I went running this morning.'
'Feel like Vietnamese?'
'No Craig?'
'At the game.'
'Give me ten.'

'Are you sure you don't want to order more of those yummy spring rolls? Don't you need to replenish your energy? We haven't tried these duck ones before. They sound nice.'

Booth looked across the table at me, one eyebrow half-raised in that way that says he thinks I have an ulterior motive. 'No, I don't want any more spring rolls. What I want is to know what you're trying to put off while you're sitting here with me.'

I opened my mouth to deny the accusation.

'No, Em. No bullshit. What's that list burning a hole in your pocket.' He held his hand out. 'Come on, pass it over.'

I sighed, and rummaged through my bag for it.

'What is this?'

'A plan of attack to clean my spare room.' When he continued to look confused, I elaborated. 'I'm trying to clear some floor and shelf space so there'll be room for Craig in my life.'

'Have you been talking to your mother?'

'No. Suse suggested it.'

He motioned for the bill. 'Come on then, move

your arse.'

Booth noticed the 'I'm sorry' flowers the minute he walked into my flat.

'Are those for not coming on Friday night?'

'Something like that. Are you helping me with this job or not?'

If the situation wasn't so serious, I would have laughed out loud at the look on Booth's face when he opened my spare-room door.

'Faaaaaaark,' was all he managed.

'Everyone has some clutter that they need to . . . umm . . . organise, don't they?'

'This is why I've never seen inside this room, and have to sleep on the couch?'

Booth occasionally stayed over if we'd had a big night. It saved on the calls for coffee the next day.

'Yep.'

'Okay.' He took off his jacket and laid it on the bed.

'I wouldn't leave it there.' I pointed to the piles of clothes already covering the bed.

'Good point.' He tossed it on the floor in the hallway. 'What do you think is under the bed?'

I screwed my face up as I thought. 'Probably just the gifts Gillian sends me for birthdays and Christmas.'

Gillian was my stepmother; she and Dad lived in England. Most things she sent me ended up under the spare bed – not because I didn't like them, just that I didn't have any use for them. It wasn't her fault – she meant well and I loved her for it. She just had no idea what to buy me, and why should she? We'd only met a few times. I guessed she bought me the same things she bought for her own two daughters. The differences being: they were both married with children, and both domestic divas, or at least knew their way around a kitchen. They lived in Gloucester, just up the road from Dad and Gillian, and their lives were all about husbands, kids, schools, three-piece suites and double-glazing. Mine was about . . . well, something different to that.

'You don't know?' Booth asked.

I shook my head. 'Mostly it's platters and useful stuff – things that women who entertain and cook for families and friends would use.'

'Hmmmm. Let's leave that for another time and start with what's behind the closet door.'

Booth didn't have the attention span required for this type of activity.

I opened the door, and a few bits and pieces fell out – mostly jumpers and scarves. It was no wonder I could never find anything to wear. My foot banged against something hard. I tried to push it back inside the cupboard, but it was obvious it wasn't going to fit, so I pulled it out instead.

'I'd forgotten this was here.'

'A milk crate? You have a milk crate in your

closet? What are these? Old vinyl records!' He started rifling through them. 'These are collectors' items now. "Tragedy"? Seriously?' He looked at me with disdain. 'This one wouldn't be on any collector's list.'

'It's not like it's the Bee Gees version . . . it's the one Steps did. Most of these are my Dad's. Back when he and Mum met, he was working as a DJ. Even after he stopped doing that he still bought a single most paydays. The daggy stuff was for parties, jobs and for me. They used to go off to dinner at someone's house with this crate in the boot of the car. Some of my favourite memories are of him and Mum dancing to these records.'

'I can't believe you have this stuff.' He was still sorting through the sleeves. 'How come your dad doesn't have them?'

'When he decided to stay over in England, he said I could have them. I added a few more to the crate, but CDs were taking over by then.' I sat on the floor beside him and flipped through the vinyl. 'Here it is: William Shakespeare's "Can't Stop Myself From Loving You". He used to play this whenever they had a fight and he knew it was his fault.' I checked the date on the label. 'Wow, this is from before I was born!'

'You moved around a bit when you were a kid, didn't you?'

'Yeah. Mum never really adjusted to English summers, and Dad couldn't deal with Brisbane ones.'

I focused on the contents of the crate. 'London was a shock to Mum. The days were too grey, the nights too long, and the sky too close. She said it made her feel hemmed in and Mum's never liked enclosed spaces. Oh, look at this: Bay City Rollers. I used to love this song.' I peered at the date on the tartan cover. 'This was from before I was born too.' I put the record back into the crate. 'Where was I? We lived with Dad's family in Gloucester for a bit. Dad was happy – he was working in the family business by day and still spinning records on weekends, but Mum felt trapped. Grandma had her ideas about how I should be raised, and they didn't involve tie-dyed nappies.'

'Tie-dyed nappies? You must have looked so cute.'

'I had matching hand-painted singlets too. Mum has heaps of photos of me toddling about in Brisbane, paddling in the blow-up pool and playing under the sprinkler on the lawn.'

'So you were still little then?'

'Three. Mum convinced Dad we'd all be happier in Brisbane, and for a time we were. Dad found a job quickly, and Mum was happy to be warm again. Dad hated the weather. It was too hot, too humid, and the sky was too far away. I can picture Dad melting in front of the TV, pinging his thongs at the cockroaches climbing the walls of our fibro sweatbox. Then Dad lost his job, and Grandpa offered him his old one back and sent the money for us to move back to England.

With the financial pressure off, the arguments stopped . . . for a while. In all, we packed up and moved back and forth twice more before I was sixteen.'

'That must have been tough.'

I could feel his eyes on me, but didn't look up. 'I suppose. The moves were always done in a hurry, usually with Mum in floods of tears. She'd shove things into boxes, and I'd take them back out again and wrap them in newspaper.'

'So your Mum wasn't into lists?'

'Ha! Her idea of packing was to sweep clothes into suitcases, and then collapse into a heap, cursing Dad. Even at that age I was sensible enough to know that before too long we'd be making the reverse trip. I soon realised the whole process would be less painful if I didn't keep as much stuff. So I didn't. Wow, I've sure made up for that over the last few years!'

'You sure have.'

'During the cease-fires, things were great. The problem was, they didn't last long. Mum told me once that it was all about the make-up sex – they couldn't live with each other, and they couldn't live without each other.' I carefully rubbed a record against my shirt to clean it. 'She said other stuff too, but I blocked my ears for most of it. No one wants to hear about the sex lives of their parents.'

'How old were you when they finally split?'

'Umm, sixteen, I guess. Mum decided I needed

some stability for my final years of school. Dad had already gone back to England, and Mum rang and told him not to bother coming back. It's funny, but once they divorced and didn't have to worry about the love part of things, they decided they actually liked each other. Mum came with me to Dad and Gillian's wedding, and Dad and Gillian came over to Byron to celebrate Mum's fiftieth. They've been to Bali too, to stay with Mum and Steph. It's happy families all round!'

'Is that why you don't like travelling? Because it's associated with being in between things?' It was Booth's turn to focus intently on the records as he asked the question.

'Now who's been talking to my mother?' I joked. 'It probably explains why I need so much stuff around me.' I swept my arms wide to encompass the clutter. 'It makes me feel secure.'

He looked up and our eyes met and held.

'Nah,' he said with a straight face, 'that's complete bullshit.'

'It was, wasn't it?'

'Do you have a turntable? We should give these babies a twirl sometime.'

'Actually I do.' I indicated the closet.

'In there?'

'I think so.'

We both burst out laughing – which was how Craig found us.

'We were just cleaning up,' I explained.

'It certainly looks like it.' He didn't smile.

Booth stood and brushed his jeans down. 'That's my cue to leave. Nice seeing you, Craig.' He bent and kissed my cheek. 'See you tomorrow, Em. Don't forget we have the disaster recovery meeting first up, so make sure you're on time.'

I wrinkled my nose. 'Gee, how to give a girl something to look forward to.'

He grinned, and left.

'How long has he been here?' Craig didn't sound happy.

'Did Geelong lose?'

He stared at me, and I remembered that Geelong was his excuse for Friday night. Oops.

'That's right – you were hoping Sydney would get thrashed, right?'

'I thought that after our talk the other night, you'd agreed to back away from Josh. Instead I come home and find you sitting on the floor in the middle of a heap of old records. Didn't our discussion mean anything?'

I sighed. *Here we go.*

'I even bought you flowers to thank you for seeing sense.'

What. The. Fuck?

'You obviously haven't been waiting around for me. I may as well go back to the pub with the boys.'

I really didn't feel in the mood to deal with this.

'You know what, Craig? We were in the middle of cleaning out some things so you'd be able to keep some stuff here. But I think the dust has got up my nose. Either that or I'm coming down with something.' I sniffed for extra effect. 'So maybe you'd have a better night if you did go to the pub.'

'Do you mean that?'

'What part? The cleaning the room or the coming down with something? Yep, I meant it. Go to the pub with the boys. You don't see enough of them.'

'Maybe I will.' He hesitated at the door.

'Good…go.'

In my head, the remaining ticks were being erased one by one. But I'd deal with that later too. In the meantime I had a Sunday night with no sport on the telly and a list of possible break-up lines to go through.

CHAPTER SEVEN

I was on time for Monday's meeting . . . just. I came crashing in with seconds to spare, earning me a glare from my boss, Diane, a grin from Booth, and a disappointed head-shake from our risk manager, Debra (never, ever Deb – except when Booth set out to annoy her) Martinez.

'Sorry, my tram was late.'

Yesterday I'd told Craig that I wasn't feeling great. Today it was true. My throat felt like it was lined with razor blades, and my eyes were being dragged down to meet my chin. Despite this, I battled through the meeting and even managed to give updates on the issues I was responsible for.

Afterwards, over lunch, Booth and I had a few laughs about how we were driving deliverables and parking or unpacking issues.

'I'm sorry, Em, but the only thing you drive or park is a car, and the only things that can be delivered are pizzas and the post. As for unpacking? That's what you do with a suitcase.'

'I'd have suggested we highlight the risk of there being so many acronyms that no one understands what anyone is talking about, except Debra would have taken it literally. Now that would be a disaster that would be difficult to recover from.'

As Monday progressed, I went downhill. By Tuesday morning, the little fib I'd invented on Sunday afternoon had grown into a great, stinking, snotty head cold.

Head colds had always made me question the whole point to modern medicine. For a start, just where did all that mucus live when you were healthy? It had to come from somewhere. Humans could put a man on the Moon, find markers on genes with groundbreaking implications for curing fatal diseases, but still couldn't cure the common cold. Personally, I didn't think they wanted to. As an industry it was worth way too much.

Take my expenditure over the last couple of days:

- Two boxes of those special 'soft on your nose when you blow it' tissues. One box for work, one for home. The ads were full of clouds of cotton wool and labrador pups, so they must be gentle.
- Super-duper triple-charged vitamins.
- Cold and flu medication that was either so strong, or so attractive to potential manufacturers of illegal pharmaceuticals, that I was only allowed to purchase two days' worth, after showing supporting documentation. Did I look like I

knew how to run an illegal drug lab?

- A box of paracetamol.
- A bottle of cough medicine that looked and smelled like something I'd clean my toilet with. I suspected it tasted the same way too.
- A bottle of single-malt scotch.

Why would you mess with an industry like that? And none of it worked. The vitamins did nothing but turn my pee a scary colour; and while the drugs gave me really colourful nightmares, they did nothing to stem the flow from my nose. Only the whisky made me feel a little better, and apparently it wasn't the done thing to drink it at work.

My head felt like someone had taken a sledgehammer to it, and all that mucus I alluded to before had moved into the space between my eyes and the hollows of my cheeks, causing my face to bulge alarmingly. Yet there was still more, flowing freely from a nose that had been rubbed raw from blowing it, despite using the afore-mentioned soft tissues.

I attempted to soldier on, but that amount of fluid on the brain wrecked any power of rational thought. By mid-afternoon on Tuesday Diane ordered me to go home – presumably so I wouldn't infect anyone else. So home I went, to take comfort in my bed, whisky gargles, and the promise of a delivery of chicken noodle soup (with extra chilli) from my favourite Thai takeaway.

I was surprised to see Craig's car parked outside my block. He didn't normally finish work until four-ish, and Tuesday was one of his gym nights. We hadn't spoken since Sunday, and even though I knew I couldn't put off having 'the talk' forever, I'd been hoping to avoid it until I was feeling a little less like death warmed up. I took a deep breath before I walked in.

The handbag on the kitchen counter wasn't mine – although I recognised it as the one Sally had been showing off the other day. Her coat was draped across the lounge, and two empty beer bottles sat on the coffee table.

I already knew what I was going to find before I went into the bedroom, but did it anyway. I used to wonder why the heroine always did this in movies – went into the room even though she knew the zombies were there. Now I knew that it was something you couldn't turn away from. Standing at the bedroom door, I watched them for a minute. From this angle, Sally's breasts appeared to have been a good investment.

'Don't mind me,' I finally said, and went back to the kitchen and poured myself a whisky – for medicinal purposes.

I wasn't feeling anything. In fact, if it hadn't been for a wayward drip telling me that my nose was still active, I might have thought the medication was finally working.

Sally was the first one dressed and out. 'I'm so

sorry, Em,' she simpered. 'This has never happened before.'

'What part? The you-having-sex-with-Craig part, or the part about getting caught?'

She stared at me. 'I wouldn't expect you to understand.'

'Understand what? That you're sleeping with my boyfriend – in my bed, in my apartment?'

She dropped her eyes. 'Stu can't know about this. You can't tell him . . . we're getting married in a couple of months.'

'Maybe you should have considered that before you started fucking his best friend. Oh wait, you've done that before, haven't you?' I collected her bag and coat and handed them to her. 'Off you go.'

'You can't talk to me like this.'

'Actually, yes, I can. This is my place.'

At least I now had an explanation for why my fridge needed restocking so often. I suspected I'd been feeding her as well.

She slammed the door behind her.

Once he heard her leave, Craig sauntered out, doing his best to look cute and misunderstood.

'She was always flaunting those new boobs in my face – what was I to do? She didn't have them when we were together.'

I ignored him and headed back into the bedroom with a garbage bag.

'What are you doing?' He followed me as I went through the apartment collecting his crap. 'It was only sex. You have to know I was always going to marry you.'

'Really? And that makes a difference?'

How many clothes had this man left in my house?

'Sally told me you couldn't care that much about me or you'd have put me first. She would have.'

'So that's why you slept with your best mate's fiancée? Because I refused to give up my friend?'

He looked away.

'Well, that's one less thing you need to worry about then, isn't it?'

'I'd be prepared to forgive you for that,' he offered.

I snorted – which wasn't a good idea in my current state of health.

In the bathroom, I swept his razors and deodorants, and something that was supposed to stop his hair from falling out, into the bag. The smell made me sneeze, so I ripped some toilet paper off the roll to use as a tissue. He probably thought I was crying. That would come later – after he'd gone.

'Sally makes me feel like I come first,' he said.

Knowing him, he probably did.

'And the sex is exciting – we do it everywhere. It's like it was when we were first together, but she's got better boobs now.'

I raised my eyebrows and looked at him. 'Really?

You want to tell me about the sex?'

He shrugged.

I resumed packing his things, using the term 'packing' loosely. 'Please tell me you haven't done it on my lounge . . . or in my kitchen?'

'No, just the bed – it didn't seem right to do it anywhere else.'

It was nice to know he had some standards.

'Out of interest, how long has this thing between you and Sally been going on?'

'I don't know – a few months?'

'Most of the time that we've been together?'

'No, just since she got back from Thailand – you know, with the new boobs. Anyway, if you hadn't come home early, you wouldn't have needed to know about it.'

'And that would have made it alright?'

He shrugged again.

'How long have you been using my bed?' I still couldn't get my head around the cheek of this.

'Not long, just a few times. Mostly we go to hers, but Stu's changed some of his shifts around.'

Stu. Poor bugger. I thought he really did love Sally – manipulative, top-heavy, cheating little bitch that she was.

'You never got over her, did you?'

It was the obvious question, and I already knew the answer. While this break-up might have ended in a different way to the others, the end result was the same.

'I really thought I had. I thought you and I could make things work. But remember that first night when I took you to the club? Sally called me afterwards. She said seeing me with someone else had made her realise what she'd thrown away, and that she'd never been able to forget me. I'm not made of stone, you know.'

Obviously.

'What are you doing home early?' he finally asked.

'I live here. I don't need an explanation.' I thrust the bag into his chest and opened the front door.

'I think you're overreacting,' he said. 'Is this because I asked you to give up Josh? I guess I don't mind if you see him occasionally.'

'No, it's not just about that, but I appreciate the generosity of your offer.'

'Is it about Sorrento then? What if we go to Bali instead? You could visit your mother. Sally doesn't really want to leave Stu – he's paying for the wedding of her dreams – so this could still work out between us –'

I slammed the door on him.

CHAPTER EIGHT

Over the years I'd become quite sophisticated about the break-up process. I had a playlist on my phone ready to go. Celine Dion was the headline act – no one did 'All By Myself' quite like she did. I'd even developed this fantasy where I was on stage singing into a microphone instead of a hairbrush. It was *The Voice*, and as I hit that big note right after the drum solo, all the judges turned around. My ritual started with Celine, and finished when I'd consumed my body weight in chocolate and wine. I'd emerge the next day to eat Chinese takeaway and start all over again.

If I was the dumper, not the dumpee, would the playlist still be appropriate? Would I need different songs – perhaps a little more Whitney and a good dose of self-love? Something like Kelly Clarkson, Pink, or Ricki-Lee, to prove how much I didn't miss him? A little Cher – post-knife, of course, to remind me I could live without him. Songs that reinforced how strong and independent I was. Could I still justify an over-consumption of wine and chocolate? Not that it mattered – Craig had got in first. I was the dumpee again. I wasn't sure what hurt the most – the humiliation, again, at not being someone's first choice, or guilt that I was glad he'd gone.

I'd been dumped for an ex before, but this was the first time my boyfriend had used my bed for the deed. I couldn't get over the cheek of it. The whole business had left me sadder- not so much for the dumping itself – than I'd imagined I would be. I was also a teeny bit disappointed that I hadn't got in first.

Thanks to the head cold and my inability to get out of bed on Wednesday, this was the most luxuriant break-up I'd ever had. Rather than painting on a happy face, this time, thanks to genuine illness, I was able to indulge myself properly in some good old-fashioned miserabilism. And yes, spelling police, that was a word. How did I know? It was in a Pet Shop Boys song.

I managed to drag my snotty, sorry arse back to work on Thursday, and was late for the kick-off meeting for a new project for a Sydney-based customer. The sales guys had sold them something they'd sketched out on the back of a drinks coaster over lunch. Somehow my team needed to decipher the requirements and deliver what the customer was expecting for the lowest possible cost in the quickest possible time. Situation normal.

Booth was running the meeting, but this client was so important that Diane, general manager of our division and my direct boss, was sitting in.

Booth began by introducing Tony, the project

manager seconded from another department at the request of Marcus Sweeney, Asia-Pacific head of something or other, and Booth's boss.

'You should all have the scope of works in front of you?' Booth said, once introductions had been completed.

We all nodded.

'Good. Let's turn our attention to the briefing notes.'

'Ummm, Josh?' Tony looked concerned. 'Who prepared these notes?'

'My team did. Why?'

'It's just,' his concerned look got even more concerned, 'it's a little light on detail.'

'Yes, it's a briefing paper. The whole purpose of a briefing paper is to capture the main points.'

'It's just that . . .' Tony's concerned face screwed up even more as he looked across to Diane while still directing his comments at Booth, 'I'm sure you got the memo?'

'The memo?'

'From Marcus . . . He doesn't like the term "briefing notes", or "overview". Or pink highlighters – not that you've used any, but just saying for next time. The memo contained clear instructions for briefing papers, and this document doesn't follow those standards.'

Booth studied Tony briefly with his best 'what the fuck?' look. Seeing nothing but sincerity, he said,

'Well, thank goodness we've stocked up on orange highlighters!'

Neither Diane's nor Tony's expression changed. I bit my lip to stop a giggle, but it made my eyes water and came out as a snort, which turned into a coughing fit, which had me reaching simultaneously for tissues and water.

'Are you quite alright, Emily?' asked Diane.

'Yes, thanks. I'm sure I'm no longer contagious.'

The look she gave me was one of a woman who suspected a hidden meaning.

'Josh,' she suggested, 'in light of the briefing notes issue, perhaps we should move straight into Tony's PowerPoint. I trust you'll convey to your team Marcus's guidelines in the future? I'm surprised you didn't get the memo.'

'Absolutely, Diane. Consider me as having been brought up to speed.'

'Good. Tony, would you like to commence the presentation?'

Tony nodded and fiddled with his laptop. I surreptitiously popped another couple of paracetamols.

'Diane,' Booth said, 'I've just noticed that the PowerPoint's an awfully long document. I was under the impression that today's meeting was to allow everyone to get a helicopter view, as Marcus would say, of the project.'

'Yes, I'm pleased you picked up on that,' Diane

said. 'But in the absence of an acceptable alternative, we'll need to dive more deeply into the detail – just to ensure that we're all singing from the same prayer book.'

A couple of hours later, still in mourning for my dead relationship, I was sitting opposite Booth over a lunch of satay chicken and honey prawns. Comfort Chinese – the final step in my break-up routine.

'That can't be any good for your sinuses,' Booth said, eyeing off the prawns.

I shrugged. 'It can't make them any worse.'

'Fair enough. Hey, where did they pull Tony from? Is that guy for real? Next thing you know, there'll be a memo banning asterisks. And how many slides were in that PowerPoint presentation? It felt like fifty.'

'Don't forget the pink highlighters. Didn't you read the memo?'

'Obviously not. And Diane,' he shook his head, 'that woman's dress sense gets worse every day. Someone needs to tell her that everything doesn't have to match.'

Today Diane was a vision in black and red stripes – from her red lipstick down to her red and black patent-leather court shoes, by way of a red blouse with fine black stripes and black skirt. Naturally, the court shoes had sensible heels.

I smiled. 'She probably thinks she looks like a cover girl for one of those women-in-business mags. Don't be so mean.'

He sighed heavily and picked a prawn from my bowl. 'Hey, this is good, but so fattening . . . I'm meant to be in training. Since when do you do honey prawns at lunchtime?'

The prawn I was chasing around the plate slid away from my chopsticks. 'I just felt like it.'

He thought it over. 'The last time you combined sticky, sweet Chinese food and creamy satay sauce with real fried rice was when you broke up with what's-his-name.'

He looked closely at me. I concentrated on conveying some vegetables from my satay chicken to my mouth. They were easier to catch than the prawns.

'Oh no, Em, not again. What happened?'

'Who knows? It just didn't work out. Anyway, don't pretend to be disappointed – I know you didn't like him.'

'Yeah, I thought he was a wanker, but I still thought this one might last – mainly because you wanted it to.'

'I'd started to think so too. I really wanted to break through to the next stage this time. You know, get past the first flush to the stage where you want to know more.'

He picked up immediately on what I wasn't saying. 'Don't tell me he's gone back to his ex? The one his best mate bought a new set of tits for?'

'Yep, that one.'

He looked sympathetic. 'That's tough luck. What

about all the talk about holidays, selling your apartment and moving in together?'

'Uh huh. On Tuesday, when I went home to my deathbed, I got the whole "It's been fun, but she says she misses me and I couldn't resist her new boobs. You're not too upset are you?"' Booth didn't need to know the full extent of my humiliation.

'That's rough. Are you okay?'

'Yeah, these things happen, I guess.' I concentrated on my plate.

'To you they seem to. You should just do what I do.'

'What? Have a series of single-nighters? You know I don't do casual sex.'

'They're not single-nighters – sometimes we go out a few times. Yours don't last much longer, it's just that you package it all up into something forever-ish and wind up getting hurt. I learnt my lesson years ago. These days I treat sex for what it is – recreational. My way, there are no expectations and no one gets damaged.'

'So you get off the treadmill after the first kilometre, before you get uncomfortable?'

He grinned. 'I sure do – while it still feels great. My mistake in the past was thinking the initial good bit was going to last forever. I got married during that stage, and divorced at the end of the get-to-know-yous.'

'How are you ever going to finish a half-marathon if you don't train for the middle part?'

He leaned back in his chair and laughed. 'I love your logic, babe.' Then he considered me carefully. 'Craig's an idiot for letting you go. Who needs new boobs? Yours are the real thing. Any other man would be very satisfied with that rack. Any other man would be satisfied with you.'

I was suddenly and weirdly embarrassed. Booth didn't often hand out compliments.

'Are you really going to eat all that?' he asked, looking at my still loaded plate.

'Sure,' I said, finally capturing a slippery little sucker and guiding it into my mouth. 'I'm in mourning.'

'From what Suse hinted, I thought he was starting to annoy you?'

'I thought it could have been love – and then it wasn't. It's so disappointing.' I used a couple of fingers to mime the passage of tears down my cheeks.

'Isn't that always the case with you?'

'I remain optimistic.'

'That's what you say, and you go in all enthusiastic, but as soon as it starts to look promising, you start looking for stuff that's wrong. Just what was wrong with Craig? Aside from the fact that he's a dickhead, of course, and can't recognise a good thing when he has it.'

The weird embarrassed thing was back again. I decided I must still be affected by the virus.

'It was the commentary,' I said.

'Commentary?' He looked puzzled.

I nodded. 'When we were . . . well, when we were in bed, he'd give a blow-by-blow description of what was coming next. You know, announce his next move. I'd have preferred less talk and more . . . I really need a filter with you, don't I?'

'Why start now?' He laughed. 'A running commentary, hey? You've got to admit it – you pick some good ones. Remember James?'

'Of course I remember, but I'm beginning to wish I hadn't told you about him.'

James was three mistakes ago. He was the one who'd said his astrologer had told him that Pisces wasn't a good match for him, and how his perfect woman was a Libra – which just happened to be his ex-girlfriend's sign. I'd told Booth the part about him consulting his horoscope, but not the part about the astrologer being his ex-girlfriend.

'My point is –'

'Oh, so you have a point, do you?' I interrupted.

'I do. My point is, you deliberately fall for these guys so you don't have to commit. I reckon that's why you set yourself up as the rebound girl.'

'Now you're talking shit.'

'Is that why you were off sick? Because you were upset?'

'No! When was the last time I took time off because of a break-up? I've had the head cold from hell all week. I was so sick I was beginning to wonder if it was something exotic I should be reporting to the World Health people. Then I put my symptoms into Google and it came out as man flu.'

'Are you sure there's nothing more to the break-up story?'

Surely Booth couldn't know about the cheating-in-my-bed thing?

'Well, I wasn't going to tell you, but he asked me to stop seeing you guys. He said you made him feel less secure about my commitment to him.'

Booth nodded slowly. 'Aaaah, he was *that* guy. I thought he'd get there eventually.'

'He sure was. And the holiday surprise he'd been building up to – the one I renewed my passport for? Sorrento, and not the one in Italy. He wanted us to go with his mates and his blow-up Barbie ex-girlfriend.' I forced a laugh.

'Have you told Suse yet?'

'No, she's having a week of redundancy hell. I'll tell her tomorrow at the pub.'

He stole another honey prawn. 'Are you sure you're okay?'

'Yep – all good. Nothing that a little Celine, some alcohol and comfort food can't fix.'

He laughed. 'I love how you bounce back.' He followed the prawn with a forkful of my satay chicken. 'Why haven't you mentioned the commentary thing before? This I need to know more about. Most men can't multi-task.'

'Trust me when I say this – Craig can't either.'

He laughed again. 'Too funny. Did he like you to do the same?'

'No, he liked to be the only one in the commentary box,' I said with a straight face.

On my Skype call with Mum that night, I told her everything. About Sorrento. About how Craig asked me to stop seeing Booth. And about Sally in my bed.

'Steph,' she called, 'you have to come and listen to this!'

Steph was as appalled as Mum was.

'Are you going to say I told you so?' I asked. Most mothers would.

'Heavens no – but I'm glad it didn't go any further. You weren't in love with him . . . not properly. You know that.'

'I guess.'

'And now you have nothing to stop you coming to see us. Does she, Steph?'

'Nothing at all. Bring Josh. He can tear around on a bike or something while you learn yoga.'

'Maybe . . . I'll think about it.'

CHAPTER NINE

'Did she tell you she split up with Craig?' Booth asked Suse.

It was Friday night and we were in our usual corner at our usual bar.

'I didn't split up with him. He dumped me to go back to his old girlfriend. And I haven't had time to tell her – we only just got here.'

'He went back to Sally? Seriously? I didn't see that one coming.' Suse seemed genuinely surprised.

'Did she tell you he used to give a running commentary when they were doing it? "Here it comes! Help me guide the big fella in for a home run!" Stuff like that.'

Suse laughed. 'Oh, that's just too good.'

'It wasn't like that,' I protested. 'Anyway, Booth, I told you that in confidence.'

'No, you didn't. At no time did you put the vault around it.' He took a mouthful of his beer. 'I told Em that she's the worst type of commitment phobic – she pretends she's in it for the long term, but once she changes her mind, she engineers it so they do the ending.'

'That's not true.'

'Actually, he has a point. You always do that.'

'No, I don't. It's just that the men who are attracted to me have baggage that they go back for.'

'Only after you've fixed them up and turned them into husband material,' Suse said. 'It's like you have some sort of homing signal for guys that need repairing. Once they've been repaired, it's all too real and you're no longer interested.'

'That's not fair . . . I don't like to see anyone in emotional pain.'

'We should put that on your tombstone: *Here lies Emily Porter, Rebound Girl,*' suggested Booth.

'They could build a whole reality show around you,' Suse added. '*Renovation Girl.*'

'Oh, ha ha. Has it occurred to either of you that I could be really upset about Craig?'

A look passed between them, but neither of them said anything.

I gave in. 'Okay, Suse is right. I had been wondering about whether we were right for each other. Then we had a big argument on Thursday night – I told you about that, Suse.'

'You never really said what it was about, though.'

'It was a few things. We'd been talking about going away – I'd left some travel brochures lying around in case he needed a hint. Bali, Hawaii, Thailand. I'd even renewed my passport. What part of that would make him think I'd be happy with Sorrento? With his artificially inflated ex-girlfriend?'

They looked at me over the top of their drinks and let me offload.

'Then there's the assumption that I'd be happy selling up and moving to fuck knows where just so he doesn't have to be too far from where he's lived all his life. What about my friends, my life? He knows how bad I am in the mornings – how much worse would I be if I had to wake up at sparrow's fart to catch a train into work? Then there's the bit about kids.'

'You want kids, though, don't you?' Booth asked.

'One day, sure . . . I guess. Doesn't everyone?'

'Not necessarily.'

'Don't you?'

'Absolutely. But not yet.'

I smiled at him. 'I know what you mean. I feel like there's still things I want to do.'

Suse spluttered on her drink. 'Seriously? What do you have that you want to do? Wear a bikini on a tropical island? We had this conversation the other night.'

'You might laugh, but not wearing a bikini on a tropical island happened to make my Reasons To Dump Craig list,' I said indignantly.

Booth and Suse struggled to keep a straight face. Suse failed and had to turn away, leaving Booth to ask the question.

'So, if you had a Reasons To Dump Craig list, did you have a Reasons To Stay With Craig list?'

'Yep. It was short.'

'What was on it?'

'His biceps for a start. Craig has magnificent arms.'

'You don't stay with a guy just because you like his arms.'

'I know that, but it's not just his arms — it's his shoulders, his chest and his bum. Physically, the package is pretty complete.'

'I'd have to agree with that,' said Suse.

Booth shook his head. 'Still not a good reason to stay. Next?'

'I didn't want to hurt him.'

'Nope. You can't make yourself responsible for what someone else has done in the past. Give me a real reason.'

'Well . . .' I put my thinking face on. 'We never argued.'

'Not arguing isn't necessarily a good thing, you know. We argue all the time.'

'Which is why not arguing also made it onto the Reasons To Leave list. He just assumed that because I didn't disagree with him I was agreeing with him . . . and they're not the same thing. An absence of disagreement doesn't mean a presence of agreement, it just means a great big passive-aggressive black hole that we both stared into for a while before one of us – usually him – just went ahead and did what the other didn't actually disagree with or agree to. I argue more with you guys about trivial crap than I did with Craig about Sorrento . . . or selling my apartment.'

'What else was on the Reasons To Stay list?' Booth asked, idly flipping a coaster over and back, over and back.

'Nope, that's all I've got. Do you want to know what was on my Reasons To Leave list?'

'Sure, why not.'

I pictured my list in my head. While I'd struggled with finding reasons to stay, the reasons to leave had flown from the end of my pen onto the paper way too quickly.

'Actually, you don't need to know. It was mostly stuff about how he doesn't like my friends and I don't like his. No big surprises.'

Booth stopped his flipping and looked steadily at me. His stare was unsettling. 'Was the L word on either of your lists? Did you love him? After all, if you were seriously considering walking away from your apartment, your friends and your life, you shouldn't need to have anything else on that list. You shouldn't need a list – nothing else matters.'

I let out the breath I'd been holding. 'Yeah. I know. I think I tried to talk myself into being in love with him – like I always do. I mistook that early rush of lust and endorphins as love. Maybe I am addicted to the excitement of phase one . . . I sure as hell can't seem to get past phase two. He was talking about kids and living together, but he never told me he loved me either.'

Suse put an arm around me. 'Oh, Em, I'm sorry.'

That was when I started to cry. Tears the size of raindrops. Who'd have thought that after this week's snot fest I'd still have any fluid left in me? I said that, and Suse laughed and rocked me in her arms. Booth said nothing and disappeared in the direction of the bar. By the time he'd returned with fresh drinks, I'd stopped crying and managed to pull myself together.

As he sat down, he ruffled my hair and said, 'If you think a few tears and a tiny cold are going to get you out of the next shout, you've got another think coming.'

Then he smiled and clinked my glass in a silent toast.

It was one of those increasingly rare Friday nights when all three of us had nowhere else we had to be. Richard had flown back from somewhere earlier this afternoon, so Suse didn't need to be home for the kids; Booth didn't have a date; and I was obviously single again. I relaxed back into my chair and smiled as I listened to Booth and Suse compare training programs. The discussion was about fartleks and pacing runs. Apparently a fartlek wasn't as messy as it sounded. Despite the crap this week had thrown at me, right now, here in this pub with my two closest friends, I felt better.

I noticed their glasses were nearly empty so I made my way to the bar for a fresh round. It was after I'd handed around glasses, and as I was putting my change into my suede coat pocket, that I found the piece of paper. *My Bucket List* it said.

It felt like I'd come across someone's secret diary. I looked around to see if anyone was watching before reading on. As a list, it started well: it was on good paper and had an underlined heading. Just the way I liked a list to look. Even the number of items on the list was right – it felt balanced.

1. Run a half-marathon.

Was I the only person in the world who wouldn't put that on a bucket list?

2. Bungy jump.

Predictable. People seemed to feel the need to either run ridiculous distances or hurl themselves off or out of things. Or both. Perhaps a bucket list wasn't really a bucket list unless it had one of those things on it.

3. Learn how to use a power tool.

Speaking of predictable, I knew what sort of power tool Booth would think of if he read that one – the type that took double-A batteries and lived in a bedside table.

4.

'Em – are you listening to us?' Suse asked.

'What's that you've got?' Booth leaned over and took the paper from my hand. 'My Bucket List. Hey,

Suse, Em's finally written a bucket list. I never knew that you wanted to bungy, or that you have a thing about power tools.'

'I don't.' I snatched it back. 'It's not mine – I found it in the pocket of my coat. It must have belonged to the person who owned it before me.'

'I don't get why you need to buy other people's rubbish when you've got so much of your own to throw out,' Booth said. 'Maybe you should put that on your list.'

'I'll have you know that this coat is a designer original, at a fraction of the price, and it feels like it was meant for me. Vintage is about the design and the character. Sometimes clothes, just like us, need to go through owners who don't appreciate them before they find someone they really belong to.'

Suse reached over to take the note from me. 'Let's see what this girl wanted to do with her life. 1. Run a half-marathon – good choice.'

'Do you think walking a very long way would count?' I asked.

'What – like to the end of Gertrude Street and back?' quipped Booth.

Suse pretended to ignore us. '2. *Bungy jump.* Been there, done that.'

'Really?' I interrupted. 'When?'

'A few years ago, in New Zealand. It was an amazing experience – you should try it sometime.'

I shook my head. 'Nope, not going to happen.'

'Your loss. *3. Learn how to use a power tool.*'

'As if she doesn't already have one in her top drawer?' said Booth. 'Every girl has one. You can tell when the batteries are missing from the TV remote.'

'I think she's talking about a different type of power tool,' Suse said. 'Where was I?'

'I don't have one . . . of those,' I said.

'Really?' asked Suse. 'Why not? I have two – I liked the model, so I bought it in two colours, as you do. At least that way you know it'll go with everything. Richard loves it. He says it brings a whole new dimension to –'

'Lalalalalala too much information.' I stuck my fingers in my ears and pretended not to hear.

'Bullshit,' said Booth. 'I bet there's one in your undies drawer. I'm going to check next time I'm over.'

'You won't find anything.'

It was true. I didn't have a sex toy, and wasn't sure I'd know how to use it if I did. My mother had given me a voucher for my birthday a few years ago for an online shop called ladiestoysdotcom. It was during a particularly dry period, sexually speaking, and Mum had been on and on at me about exploring my femininity and removing my inhibitions – hence the voucher. It was just after she'd discovered both herself (with the aid of a hand mirror and a delivery or two from ladiestoysdotcom) and Steph. The voucher had expired, so Booth could go through my undies drawer as much as he liked. He wouldn't find anything requiring batteries.

'Maybe not, but I'll have fun looking.' He grinned wickedly. 'Next you'll be telling me that you only ever have sex in a bed.'

'I do,' I admitted.

'Really? All the time? Even the first time?'

'Yep, even the first time. I still remember his navy blue sheets – I don't think they'd been washed in a while.'

'You've never been carried away anywhere else and just gone for it?'

'Nope. I like to make sure all precautions have been taken.'

'Man, that's dismal.' He shook his head in incomprehension. 'You know you can be safe and spontaneous at the same time? What about phone sex? Tell me you've done that?'

'Nope. Never had any need to.'

'Wow.' He paused and thought some more. 'What about –'

'Josh!' Suse looked between the pair of us in exasperation. '4. *Declutter my apartment and renovate using at least one power tool.* Your place could do with some work, Em. How long have you been talking about ripping your carpet up and painting the living room?'

'I know,' I said. 'It's just –'

Suse waved away my excuses. '5. *Put together a piece of flat-pack furniture using an allen key.* Hey, Josh – this one's for you.'

'Why would I want to? You can outsource shit like that.'

'Em will need storage solutions when she cleans all her rubbish out – you can put it together for her.'

'Not going to happen,' he said confidently.

'Fair enough. *6. Cook at least one meal for my friends using fresh ingredients, saucepans and matching cutlery.* When was the last time either of you cooked?'

Booth and I grinned at each other. Wasn't that why we lived so close to the city – so we didn't have to cook? We had a duty to support our local restaurateurs.

'*7. Have casual sex without convincing myself I'm in love with the guy.* Oh my God, Em, are you sure this isn't your list? Aside from that long ago whatever it was with Josh, have you ever been able to do that?'

I shrugged. What could I say? She was right.

'*8. Fall in love properly with someone who'll love me back.* Oh, that's just too sad. Maybe you should have that on your list too, Em.'

I couldn't argue with that either.

'*9. Finally resign from my job, buy a one-way ticket somewhere exotic that I've never been, and travel on my own.* Wow. Is anyone else getting the feeling that this girl just had her heart broken? Probably by some guy she got in to renovate her flat, put together her flat-pack furniture, and hooked up with afterwards.'

'Maybe he was a marathon-running, bungy-jumping Kiwi guy, and he left her for someone who can cook Thai food,' I suggested. 'At least we know she has great taste in clothes – I love this coat.'

'She probably ate too much when she got her heart broken and couldn't fit into it any more. Maybe the coat carries the karma of an unrequited love affair.'

'Not helpful, Suse. I bought a handbag on eBay once that came with that sort of karma. It was beautiful – all oriental orange, red and black silk on the outside, and Tiffany blue with cherry blossoms on the inside.'

'I remember that bag. It was gorgeous. What do you mean by karma?'

'It was advertised as "the bag that broke a relationship". The girl who owned it paid too much for it, and when her boyfriend found the receipt, he hit the roof about her credit card debt and they broke up. She never even used it. So I got it – brand new with tags – at a really good price. Sadly, I also got the karma. Harry and I split up soon after.'

'The one who dumped you via a Facebook status update?'

Suse had been disgusted by that. Booth had been too, but he'd pretended not to be. Instead, he'd listened to me cry for a day, then said, 'Okay, enough. Step away from Celine and the chardonnay and let's move on already.'

'Yep. That's the one.'

'Whatever. Back to the coat girl – it was probably

just a casual thing and she read too much into it,' said
Booth. 'Chicks do that. Em does it all the time.'

'If a guy tells me something, I'll believe him,' I
said. 'It's not my fault when it turns out to be lies. I feel
sorry for this girl, whoever she is. Poor thing.'

'If you know the guys don't mean it, why do you
still believe them?' asked Booth.

'Because one day someone is going to come along
who doesn't spin me a line.'

'Are you two quite finished?' Suse said. 'There's
one more thing on the list. *10. Wear a bikini on a tropical
island.*'

We were silent, then Suse said what we were all
thinking. 'This list could have been written for you, Em.'

CHAPTER TEN

It was the weekends that were the hardest when you were newly single. Two days of waking up alone with no plans sounded like an absolute treat when you were in a relationship – or deciding whether you wanted to be in the relationship you were in – but stretched into nothing when you were no longer part of a couple.

I lay in bed for a while, luxuriating in the space, stretching my legs across to the side Craig had slept on. It was a perfect morning for it – the first properly cold one of autumn. Melbourne was like that – it muddled along in and out of summer, then at Easter, no matter if it was early or late, the weather turned. By the time Anzac Day rolled around, the season had well and truly changed.

I ventured out mid-morning for coffee, pastries and magazines, and took them back to bed.

Around midday, I opened the fridge. Although there was nothing to eat, Craig's favourite beer was still in there, as was what used to be leftover pizza. I found some crispbreads and peanut butter and took them back to bed too.

By 3 pm my bum was sore from sitting up in bed reading magazines.

I turned on the radio, but the stations were full of the day's games, which reminded me of Craig. Sure, the sport playing constantly on the TV had annoyed me when he was here, but now that he wasn't I missed the noise.

I thought about cleaning out the spare room, but there no longer seemed to be any point. Instead, I put on a load of washing – which I didn't have to collect from all around the apartment. Craig had a habit of leaving clothes where he shed them – sweaty T-shirts in the lounge room, pullovers on the kitchen bench, towels in the bedroom, undies wherever. All of which used to irritate me, but now I wondered whether I'd overreacted. In a way, his boyish laziness had been endearing. Maybe I'd been too hasty. Perhaps it really had been 'just sex' with Sally and her new breasts. He'd said it was me he wanted to settle down and have kids with – that had to mean something, right?

Before I could go too far down that path, I pulled out the lists I'd written just last weekend. Was it only a week ago? I ripped the Reasons to Stay With Craig list into tiny pieces and threw them in the rubbish. There. Gone.

I unfolded the Reasons To Dump Craig list and reread it. No, nothing had changed, only now I could add another entry – he'd cheated on me.

What I needed was a new list.

What I needed was a bucket list – just like Coat Girl's, but my own.

The weather had deteriorated even further, and my apartment was cold. Where was that poncho I'd bought last year? It was vintage, of course, and looked like something you'd wear to ride a horse across Mongolia. Not that I rode horses, or had any inclination to do so in Mongolia, but it would be perfect for list-making on a cold, wet Saturday at the end of April.

I rummaged through my wardrobe, and the closet in the spare room, before remembering that I'd stashed my winter clothes at the top of the linen cupboard. When you lived in Melbourne, the possibility of a cold snap was a reality until after Christmas.

Adequately attired, I found the perfect list-making paper and my favourite list-writing pen.

Emily's Bucket List.

I underlined the title. Much better.

1. Wear a bikini on a tropical island.

There were valid reasons why I hadn't done that yet. It wasn't that I didn't want to travel. It was more about getting vaccinations, a lack of someone I wanted to spend all that time in a confined space with, and . . . yes, I had to admit it – fear.

2.

There had to be more. Didn't there?

Suse had said that Coat Girl's list could have been written for me – just like the coat felt like it had been tailored for me.

I went to my bag and pulled her list out, flattening the creases with my finger. Suse was right – aside from numbers one and two, Coat Girl could very well have written her list for me. Perhaps she did – she wrote it for the person who would buy her coat. Maybe that was why the coat had been hiding among all those other coats – it was waiting for me to come along.

I crumpled up my list and took my pen to Coat Girl's instead.

Run a marathon.

Not happening. Ever. I could, however, commit to a long walk. I could enter a ten-kilometre race, maybe. Best not to be too specific. I crossed it out and wrote:

Walk a very long way.

There was no way I'd ever bungy, or jump off or out of anything high. But I could still write something about facing my fears. I amended number two to: Do something in another country that scares me.

I only needed to open the spare-room door to know that numbers three, four and five were relevant to me. All my wardrobes were overflowing. Suse was right – I didn't have room in my life, or my home, for a partner.

If I was going to declutter, I'd also need to organise – and that meant storage solutions. These days cupboards and shelves all came in flat-packs and needed to be put together with an allen key. I had no idea what an allen key looked like, but I was guessing not like a regular key.

While I was at it, I should probably do something about the magnolia paint and floral wallpaper border in my bedroom, which I'd been complaining about for years. I'd need a power tool to remove the screws holding up the curtain rods. My kitchen needed reviving and my living room was dated. Those reality shows made it all look pretty easy. As Booth would say: how hard could it be?

If I was going to remove the clutter and spruce up my flat, I'd be able to have friends around more often. I didn't cook – for myself, or my friends – because I didn't need to. But I realised it was a grown-up, responsible thing to do. Feeding yourself and those you cared about was something every adult person should be able to do, regardless of gender.

I left number six on the list unchanged.

Okay, I was going to have to deal with the love issue. I often said I was in love, but I wasn't sure I'd ever *really* been in love – not the bells-and-whistles, forever-and-ever type of love. I'd tried to convince myself otherwise, but there hadn't truly been anyone who'd turned my life upside down and made me want to stay on the treadmill past phase two. Not yet, anyway.

I thought I was a pretty good catch. I was

financially sound, and had no emotional baggage to speak of. My romantic history had been busy, yet at the same time quite non-eventful. I wasn't especially vain, but I knew that despite my dreadful eating habits and lack of regular exercise, I looked good. I was lucky I had good genes – Mum was still in great shape; and even though I hadn't seen Dad in the flesh for way too many years, from what I could tell from our irregular Skype calls he'd aged well too. Still, Suse frequently told me that now I was in my thirties, I couldn't take that for granted for much longer.

The point was, I'd spent my adult life waiting for that all-consuming, all-singing, all-dancing love where I was a guy's first choice, only and always. Not the sort of love where he went back to his ex after a few months. I wanted the sort of love that lasted after the goosebumps were gone; that had a passion that made you want to make love on the kitchen floor, or in the shower, or anywhere other than a bed. Maybe the problem was that word, *falling*. You *fell* in love. It was accidental. It sounded like it was going to hurt, that you'd hit the ground hard when you finally reached bottom. When you did it my way, talking yourself into thinking you were in love, you felt bruised when it was over, but it was more like a grazed knee than a broken heart. It could be soothed by Celine, chardonnay, chocolate and comfort Chinese. Having said that, I wanted real love. All of it. Ideally with someone who'd love me back in the same way.

Part of my problem, I knew, was that I couldn't separate sex from love. When I thought I was in love, I was really just horny. But I needed to wrap it in something bigger to justify having sex. I'd never had casual sex. Not ever. Not without imagining myself in love. I was too much of a goody-two-shoes. Always had been.

At school, I was the girl who did her homework on a Friday night, handed my assignments in on time, and studied regularly, even when exams were months away. After school, when all my friends went backpacking around Europe or took a gap year, I went straight to uni. I went to no mad parties, had no mad affairs, and no unsuitable boyfriends. All my boyfriends had been eminently suitable, which was why their ex-girlfriends always wanted them back.

Even now, I saved a proportion of my salary, paid more than required on my mortgage to build up a buffer in case I was ever out of work or the interest rate returned to 1992 levels, kept my insurances up to date, and did my tax return on time. I'd never locked my keys in the car, lost my wallet, or accidentally set off my house alarm. When I did have to travel for work, I packed well in advance, kept to a list, and layered my business suits with tissue paper.

I'd never smoked anything I shouldn't have, taken any pharmaceutical not provided by a bona fide chemist, or drunk so much that I'd forgotten large chunks of the previous night. Although, admittedly, there had been times when my memory had been a little on the hazy side. Sure, my diet and exercise habits weren't great, but I always took my make-up off before I went to bed, moisturised morning and night, wore sunscreen every day, and always used a condom. I even flossed.

I looked at Coat Girl's list again. Casual sex was way outside my comfort zone, yet bucket lists were about expanding your boundaries and living in the moment. So I added to number seven, and left number eight alone.

7a) Have casual sex with someone I'm not in love with. 7b) *Have sex somewhere other than in a bed. 7c) Have phone sex.*

I looked at Coat Girl's number nine: *Finally resign from my job . . .*

On the subject of comfort zones, I was over my job. I'd been over it for years. It wasn't what I wanted to do with my life – but then, I didn't really know what I wanted to do with my life. Rather than climbing the ranks, I'd floated through my career. When I'd been promoted, it was a case of right place, right time, and no one else spectacular enough to choose for the role. When it came to my work, I'd always done exactly what was expected of me – and no more. My job paid well, it was familiar and secure – and I usually told myself you couldn't put a price on that. The thing was, I'd never resigned from a job or a relationship. I knew this one would be easier said than done, but needed to be left on the list.

10. Wear a bikini on a tropical island.

Booth and Suse had laughed at me, but I'd always had this fantasy of a deserted beach on a tropical island, with me in a bikini wading into the warm, turquoise water and into the arms of the man I loved, who didn't look anything like Craig. The sand would be silky and white, and we'd make love as the waves rolled in around us. To qualify for a position on what was now an impressive bucket list, this fantasy needed to be expanded. I crossed out Coat Girl's number ten and wrote my own:

10. Buy a one-way ticket somewhere overseas, and travel there on my own without a list or a plan. Pack my bikini. Perfect.

I took all the takeaway menus and obsolete shopping lists and recipes off the fridge door, and, using a magnet advertising Mum and Steph's villa, stuck Coat Girl's list in the centre. Like the coat, it belonged to me now.

Booth turned up on Sunday morning. Even though it was almost 11 am, I was still in my jammies and ugg boots.

'Okay, you've had nearly a week of mooching, and that's plenty long enough for that fuckwit,' he said. 'It's time to step away from the . . .' He picked up a CD cover. 'Damian Rice . . . really? This shit is depressing.'

'I love it. "The Blower's Daughter" is an amazing song.'

'If you weren't sad at the start, you sure would be by the time it finished.'

'This was the longest relationship I've had,' I protested. 'Surely that entitles me to feel a little bit sorry for myself.'

'Yes, and you've had that time. One day for every month — that's my rule. And you can subtract the month you spent fart-arseing about deciding whether to stay with him. So, by my reckoning, you're well and truly overdue to get that cute little arse out of your PJs and into something you can train in. We're going to sweat him out of your system.'

'You promised me I'd never have to run again,' I whined, wrapping my robe tighter around my body.

'Who said anything about running? I've already been for a run this morning. We're going for a walk, followed by a late lunch, and then I've volunteered our babysitting services to Suse so she and Richard can go out for dinner.'

'But —'

'No buts. Get dressed,' he ordered.

'I was only going to say that I'm in the middle of going through that closet we started on last week, but a walk sounds like fun.'

He looked at me with suspicion. 'You're okay

about the walk? You'll need to wear your trainers.'

'I said it sounds like fun.' It was number one on my list underway.

'Hmmmm.'

Booth's idea of a walk was the St Kilda to Brighton coast path. Not surprisingly, I'd never done it before. When we started, it was one of those gorgeous autumn days that Melbourne does so very well – blue skies, breeze light but comfortable. By the time we got to Brighton, the wind was strong enough to send spray from Port Phillip Bay into our faces, and whip my ponytail from its elastic. The skies had darkened and a light drizzle started.

'What is it with you, exercise and rain?' I complained, huddling into my hooded jacket.

He laughed. 'At least you're more appropriately attired today.'

'True.'

'And you've got to admit, it feels good to be outside, right?'

'It does,' I acknowledged. 'It would just feel better if it wasn't raining.'

At Brighton we stopped to catch our breath – okay, to catch my breath – and wandered around the brightly painted beach houses.

'How much do you reckon one of these would sell for?' I asked.

'Probably the same amount as your apartment . . .

maybe more. Richard would know.'

'Are you serious? It's just a box with some paint slapped on it.'

'In case you hadn't noticed, it's a box with some paint slapped on it on Brighton Beach in the sand. That blue-ish wet stuff out there is the Bay. These things never go on the market, and when they do, the demand ensures that the price is out of the reach of people like you and me.'

We found a pub to have some lunch and shelter from the rain, which was now bucketing down. Aaaaah, Melbourne, four seasons in one day. I was still in comfort-food mode so we ate dude food – hamburgers, chips, gravy and beer.

'This was top of my Reasons to Dump Craig list, you know,' I told Booth as we clinked our glasses in a toast to whatever.

'What was?'

'He wanted me to give you guys up. I think he actually believed I would.' I took a mouthful of my beer. 'I don't know, perhaps I would have . . .'

'No, you wouldn't. You were already looking for a way out – you just hadn't got around to it.'

'How did you do it?' He raised his eyebrows. 'Choose Mandy-sorry-Amanda and Shayla?' I added.

He shrugged. 'I don't know. I guess it's what you do when you're in love – or think you're in love. You want to keep them happy. But it doesn't work. When you give in on that, there's something else, and then something else. It's just how it works. If you were truly in love with Craig, you wouldn't have had to think about it. If he really loved you, he wouldn't have asked. With Mandy and Shayla it was a power thing. They wanted to control me.'

'I always thought that falling in love would just *happen*. Surely I shouldn't have to try so hard to do something other people manage accidentally? No one plans to fall over, or to fall into something. We don't plan to fall in love. It's just supposed to happen – isn't it?'

'You'll get that lightning bolt when you least expect it.'

'Do you really think that?'

'I know that.'

He raised his eyes to mine and I believed him.

Outside the rain was pelting against the windows.

'Do you think it's ever going to stop?' I said.

'Nah, it'll keep going until it's Monday again.' Booth laughed. 'Isn't that the way? Doesn't matter, we're warm in here, I have nowhere I need to be. Do you?'

I shook my head.

'Good, it's your shout.'

As I put a fresh beer in front of him, he said, 'I know exactly what you need. You need to write a list. Call it a bucket list if you like, but you need one.'

'I have one.'

'Em, we went through this the other week.'

'No, I really do have one. I wrote it yesterday. I'll show you.'

I'd spent some time yesterday afternoon transferring the list to the notes app on my phone. It was looking impressive.

He read through it and handed the phone back. 'This is just the Coat Girl's list.'

'With a few tweaks. Anyway, it was you guys who said her list could have been mine. Now it is. What do you think?'

'About what?'

'My list, of course.'

'Yeah, good job.'

Well, that was disappointing.

'Are you going to show me yours?'

He grinned cheekily. 'Sweetheart! All you had to do was ask.'

'Not that, you idiot – when am I going to see your bucket list?'

'One day. Now drink up,' he looked outside, 'I reckon we've got a small window of clear sky to make a run for the train.'

CHAPTER ELEVEN

My passport arrived in the mail on Monday, so at lunch on Tuesday I picked up some brochures on Bali and Thailand to replace those I'd thrown out after the Sorrento disappointment. Mum and Steph's villa was advertised in the Bali brochure. If it wasn't for needing vaccinations, cash in the appropriate currency and someone to go with, I could have booked the ticket right now.

After a lengthy meeting on Tuesday afternoon about yet another change to the business requirements for the big Sydney client, I went home, poured a large glass of wine, and researched airfares. I had plenty of holiday leave accrued, so could fly out tomorrow if I wanted to – or next week, if I was being responsible. I'd counted to ten so many times in the last two days at work, I was even prepared to take a risk and skip the vaccinations.

Wednesday was completely feral. It was one of those days where I ran from unrelated random issue to unrelated random issue – with a pointless session on the correct use of PowerPoint in between. Marcus had relaxed the bullet-point ruling, but had got Tony working on a revised process that outlined the appropriate number of words per bullet point, the optimum number of bullet points per slide, and just how many slides per minute you should budget for. That was ninety minutes I'd never get back.

I went home, poured a very large glass of wine, and dusted off my CV. Everyone these days had a networking profile, so I set one up and sent friend invites to Booth and Suse – although apparently on networking sites no one had friends, they had 'connections'.

Just for a bit of fun, I browsed a couple of the job sites, and, after the third large glass of wine, I even applied for a couple. Just for fun. Jobs that were so far out of my league in both seniority and salary that I knew I didn't stand a chance.

Thursday morning was the monthly all-hands meeting – one of those sessions that everyone has to clear their diaries and divert their phones for, unless they're out physically selling a solution on a drinks coaster to a customer. The Powers That Be had started referring to the meeting as 'the State of the Nation'. Yes, I was serious. I vaguely recalled seeing a memo about the name change. Some consultant or other probably got paid the equivalent of the pay rises we weren't getting this year to come up with that.

Even though I was on time, the room was full when I arrived, so I rested my bum against a table beside Booth. Diane was already there, laughing (I thought I even saw her flick her hair) with a man whose chin would have entered the room long before he did. It was Marcus Sweeney, our Big Boss of Everything. He'd always reminded me of someone, but I'd never been able to work out who. Now it hit me.

'Oh my God. He's Roger Ramjet!' I said to Booth.

'Who?'

'Marcus – he looks just like Roger Ramjet. I can't believe I hadn't worked it out before.' Booth's face remained blank. 'You know, the cartoon guy with the big jaw – Roger Ramjet and his eagles . . .' I sang the theme song for him. 'It's one of those tunes that once it's in your head it rolls round and round and round.'

'An earworm,' he said. 'It's what boy bands and Kylie Minogue use to sell pop songs.'

'I like Kylie and boy bands.'

'I know you do – the daggier the better.' He grinned. 'They do earworm songs – the sort you can't get out of your head.'

I sang some of the Kylie song of the same name.

'That's the one. The only way to get rid of an earworm is to sing the Banana Splits song instead.'

'What?'

'You know . . . *One banana, two banana, three banana, four . . .*' He sang it for me, complete with the nah-nah-

nahs – until Marcus started talking and we were forced to be quiet.

Now that I'd noticed it, Marcus's likeness to Roger Ramjet was so strong it was disturbing. Even more disturbing was the idea of Diane flirting with him.

'He could get a job on a shaving commercial . . . or a soap opera,' said Booth under the cover of his hand. 'He'd have a name like Brick or Thunder, marry his daughter-in-law five times, and gaze off into the distance at every ad break.'

He mimed the classic chisel-jawed daytime-soap pose. With his cheeky grin and pushed-up-and-about boy-band hair, he looked nothing like a brooding Brick. I swallowed a giggle.

The equivalent of the bonuses we wouldn't be paid next year had gone into creating a pyramid with single-line mantras that sounded like movies Bruce Willis would star in. Marcus ran through them. Maybe Jason Statham would be interested in taking the lead, I thought. I'd possibly have more interest in the strategy if he were starring in it . . . without a shirt . . .

'Stand and Deliver,' Marcus said, announcing mantra three on the list . . . or was it four?

'Wasn't that an Adam Ant song?' I whispered.

He elbowed me. 'Shush.'

Around the room, our colleagues were perched on chairs, the sides of tables, and standing in corners. Some were pretending to check important messages on their cells, but I knew they were really checking their social media. Those at the front of the room, or in full visibility, were pretending to listen intently.

Booth drew a picture of a bee on his notebook. He was a crap drawer, but I knew it was a bee because it had a little balloon coming out of its mouth saying 'buzzz'. Diane, resplendent in coordinated yellow blazer, black shift dress, and black shoes with a yellow ankle strap, looked across at us. Her suspicious expression changed to a smile when I nodded seriously at Booth's notebook. She liked it when people took notes.

I was still trying to hold in the giggles when I felt a prickle in my back. Looking around the room, I saw a man I didn't know leaning against the doorframe. His gaze was concentrated on me. My laughter died and I shivered as if I were cold.

Booth must have felt the movement. 'Are you okay?'

I nodded, but couldn't stop staring at the man in the doorway. It was as if the world had stopped and the only two people breathing were the two of us – and I wasn't entirely sure that I was breathing. In the background, I was vaguely aware of everyone clapping. Marcus must finally be finished.

'What was that about?' asked Booth.

'I don't know.' I turned back to the door, but the man had gone.

'Em,' Booth said.

He was chatting to the man from the doorway. How had he got from there to here so quickly? Maybe the world had stopped spinning, or time had stopped, or something.

'Em, this is Jamie Aldridge, our new project director. Like me, he's reporting direct to Marcus, but will have responsibility for all projects. Jamie, meet Emily Porter. She runs the development team, so if you need a business analyst, developer or tester, she's your girl.'

Jamie held out his hand and I shook it. A strange jolt ran from the top of my head, straight through my spine and out through my heels. If I believed in auras, mine would be glowing.

'Pleased to meet you,' I managed.

'I look forward to getting to know you,' he said, holding both my gaze and my hand.

I pulled my hand away and looked at the floor. 'Ummm, I'd better get back to work. Lots to do. Lovely to meet you, Jamie. See you later, Josh.'

Back at my desk I attempted to absorb myself in the release notes and installation instructions for the software package we were working on. As fascinating as they were, they didn't distract me for long. Oh, he was cute. About Booth's height, six foot-ish or so, with dark hair, pale skin and piercing blue eyes. The men in romance novels all seemed to have piercing blue eyes, but Jamie really did. They were the sort of eyes that could cut right to the heart of a girl. When he looked into mine, it was as though he knew exactly what I was thinking – and was thinking it too. It was like being in the middle of a Kylie song. He even had an English accent. He was a walking cliché. Seriously cute – I'd already said that, hadn't I? I was sure there was a good set of biceps under the civility of that white business shirt.

'What was that bullshit about this morning?' Booth asked at lunch.

I moved the salad around on my plate. 'I don't know what you mean.'

'Come on, you were like poor little Bambi caught in headlights.'

'I so was not.'

'Were too.'

'You are so immature, Booth.' I picked some more at my salad. I wished I'd ordered a curry, but I wasn't sure my tummy could cope with it – it was far too busy doing somersaults and releasing butterflies. 'So,' I hesitated, 'I got the impression you know him?'

'Who?'

'Don't pretend you don't know who I'm talking about...'

He grinned. 'I worked with him at GNA a few years ago. What else do you want to know?'

'What else do you know?'

'Well . . . we've crossed paths a few times at

industry conferences. Had a beer, you know how it is.'

I didn't. If I'd crossed paths with Jamie Aldridge at industry conferences, I wouldn't be that casual about it.

'I'm going to tip this salad over your head shortly,' I warned.

'Speaking of which – why are you eating salad?'

'I just felt like making a few healthy choices to make up for the running I won't be doing.' Then I said it. 'This is him. This is *the guy*. The one I can use italics with. I just know it.'

'Get real – you only met him for five minutes, less than that. You've only just broken up with Craig.'

'I know, but oh, Booth, isn't that how it happens sometimes? Like you said – when I least expect it?'

'Eyes meeting across a crowded State of the Nation wasn't exactly what I had in mind,' he muttered.

I ignored him. 'It was his eyes, his piercing eyes – when they hit mine . . . Surely you felt it too?'

'Nope, I can't say that I did. Strangely enough he does nothing for me. Piercing eyes, did you say?'

I flipped some cucumber at him, and reached over to spear a piece of his chicken. 'I know you're laughing at me and I don't care. I have an excellent sense for these things, and it feels like this is him – the one.'

'Wasn't Craig the one at the start too?'

'No, I didn't get anything like this vibe from Craig. I just thought that with a little perseverance . . .'

'I hate to be the one to rain on your parade, but

you have no sense for these things, no taste when it comes to men, and a completely faulty radar.'

'Fuck off.'

'You know I'm right.'

I waved his rightness away. 'Perhaps. But this time I just know. What else do you know about him? Tell me everything.'

'What you mean to ask is, do I know if he's single?' Booth seemed to be really enjoying himself.

'Okay, yes, that's what I really want to know. Is he?'

'Is he what?'

'Is he single?'

'No.'

'No? Seriously? No way could he give a vibe like that and not be single. His eyes met mine. When he held my hand there was that jolt thing and the cartwheels in my tummy. My heart is flip-flopping. He has to be single.'

'Are you going to throw any more of that salad at me?'

I shook my head.

'Last I knew, he was in a long-term relationship. Carly I think her name is . . . Kelly…Callie…something like that. I've met her – she seems nice. I don't think I've heard anything about him getting married, but he's definitely off the market.'

'But the vibe?'

'I can't explain that, but there's nothing about him

that needs saving or fixing.'

'Oh.'

He pushed his plate towards me. 'Have some curry, and some rice. You need the carbohydrates – your brain chemistry is obviously impaired.'

'I tell you, Suse, he's the complete package. Those eyes, that voice, and his shoulders. When he looked at me I had no idea what had hit me. I really think this is it.'

It was Saturday afternoon and I'd dropped by at Suse's so I could fill her in on the accidental job search – and so I could talk some more about Jamie.

'The lightning bolt, you say?' Suse turned away from me to put something that might have once been pumpkin into the microwave. 'Can you grab Georgia and pop her in the high chair?'

'Sure.' I lifted the squirming little girl into her chair, tickling her until she giggled so much that she forgot to wriggle. 'When did she get so heavy?'

'You should try carrying her for any distance.' Suse emptied the orange mush into an acrylic bowl.

'Booth laughed at me, but when Jamie held my hand and looked into my eyes, I couldn't move. It was just like a Kylie song. The stars came out and everything.'

She grimaced as she aimed a spoonful of food in the direction of Georgia's mouth. 'Seriously, Em? You're quoting Kylie?'

'It's the only music that fits.'

'Everything doesn't have to have a soundtrack, you know.'

'Maybe not, but this does.' I added a sigh so she knew to take me seriously.

'Is he single?'

'According to Booth, no. But what right does he have to go around giving out that sort of vibe to random strangers if he's attached? Isn't it ironic – I meet the man of my dreams, the one I'd clear some room for, and he's off the market.'

'Maybe he's an Alanis Morissette song,' she commented wryly. 'Can you please pass me that cloth? Georgia got more of her lunch on me than she got into her stomach.'

I took the dish from her, and swapped it for the washer on the sink. 'It's his piercing eyes, and the accent. He looks like Hugh Grant, but not *Bridget Jones* Hugh. More *Four Weddings* or *Notting Hill* Hugh. Hugh without the floppy hair and with better arms. Actually,' I considered, 'he doesn't look anything like Hugh Grant, but he sounds like him. Did I tell you he has an accent?'

'Yes, you did. Last night at the pub – at least twice. Where's Richard when I need him?'

'Outside kicking the football around with Toby.'

'It was a hypothetical, Em. He and Tobe are supposed to be raking leaves.'

'Oh.'

As if he'd read her mind, Richard barrelled through the door, a squealing Toby under his arm. Richard put his finger to his lips and said in an exaggerated hushed tone, 'Inside voices, Tobes.' Both attempted a straight face for about a second before laughter burst out of their mouths.

Even Suse couldn't pretend to be impatient for long. 'Come here, you noisy boy.' She took Toby from Richard's arms and hugged him tight.

Richard kissed her head, and lifted Georgia out of the high chair. 'Come on, Tobes, let's go change your sister and let Mum have a chat with Aunty Em.'

When they'd disappeared upstairs, Suse and I took our coffee out to the deck and what was left of the weak afternoon sun.

'I accidentally applied for another job,' I told her.

'Accidentally? How does that happen?'

'I was just looking to see what's out there, and I figured I had nothing to lose. You should see how much some places offer for the same job I'm doing. Anyway, you're always telling me I need a change.'

She sipped thoughtfully at her coffee. 'Yes, you do. Does Josh know about this?'

In the corner of the yard, a magpie was scratching beneath some fallen leaves. I watched as his partner landed beside him to help. They were probably the leaves Richard was supposed to be raking.

'You haven't told him,' she said. It wasn't a

question.

I shook my head. 'No, I'm not seriously looking. I'll tell him if something comes up. Besides, now that Jamie's started there, perhaps I shouldn't be thinking of leaving.'

'Staying for a hot guy who's already attached isn't a good idea. You know the rules. And you need something new.'

'I do.'

We both watched the magpie pair for a bit longer.

'He could have been the one, Suse.'

'Yeah . . . but he isn't.'

CHAPTER TWELVE

Over the next few weeks, Booth and Jamie got quite pally. I knew it was about time Booth got himself some proper man friends. Guys needed other guys, and even though he had Suse and me and we talked about everything – except for me accidentally looking for a new job – it wasn't the same. There was some stuff that we really shouldn't talk about. For example, I didn't need to know how many calories he'd worked off on Saturday night, or with whom and how.

Part of me resented the time Booth was spending with Jamie, but another part of me was used to it. He'd abandoned me before over the years. I didn't see him at all when he was married, and he often disappeared from regular contact for a week or so at a time if he had a new interest. I no longer took his absences personally – he always came back when his concentration waned. A bromance was different to a woman, though. For a start it would probably last longer than his hook-ups usually did, and wouldn't involve a calorie count.

He'd even persuaded Jamie to sign up for the half-marathon. How did I know? I'd been at a loose end one Sunday and called him, but he was off at some post-run lunch thing with Suse and Jamie. I shouldn't have felt excluded – after all, I had said never, ever to running, and I still had the blister scars – but I did. I'd pulled on my trainers and gone for a walk instead.

Since then I'd built up quite a fantasy during my downtime. It involved me in running gear lining up at the start of the half-marathon in September. Suse and Booth stare open-mouthed as I jog lightly and easily on the line. Jamie isn't able to take his eyes off me. When the starter pistol fires, I take off, my ponytail bouncing perkily in time with my stride. Jamie's beside me for the whole twenty-one kilometres. When it's over, he kisses me and says something like, 'You're one amazing woman, Em'. Or maybe even, 'Tell me that you love me as much as I love you'.

Twenty-one kilometres . . . I'd forgotten about that part. Maybe I'd sign up to walk the ten kay instead – how hard could it be? Ten kilometres would qualify as walking a very long way and give me a tick on my bucket list. I'd like to get my money's worth from my purchases, and those trainers had cost a fortune. I wouldn't tell the others until I'd decided for sure.

On Saturday, I checked out some of the local design stores – on foot. I even visited some open homes in the area. Not that I was looking to sell, more for decorating ideas. At one, a two-bedroom flat of a similar vintage to mine, I ran into a girl I'd been to school with up in Brisbane. I'd moved down to Melbourne to study, while she'd gone to Sydney to do law, and we'd lost touch.

'Andi? Andrea Shaw? Wow – it is you!'

She looked intently at me, long enough for me to be concerned that I'd got it wrong, then her face lit up in recognition. 'Emily Porter! How random to see you here. Are you buying this place?'

'No, just checking out ideas – I'm looking at renovating mine. And you?'

'Heavens, no. I've got a place over in Albert Park.' She took my arm and whispered conspiratorially, 'But I do have my eye on the agent. I met him last night and might have mentioned I was in the market.' She looked across at him and dimpled prettily.

'Just not for an apartment?' I guessed.

She grinned, and just like that we were back in the schoolyard giggling over boys.

As we talked, a tall, suited woman entered the apartment and kissed the agent lightly on the mouth. 'All okay here, darling?' When she laid her hand on his arm, we both noticed the wedding ring.

'Damn,' said Andi. 'I should have known he was married – he's exactly my type. Want to come for coffee? We can catch up.'

So we did.

We covered careers – she'd done really well; I'd stagnated.

We covered men – neither of us had had much luck on that front. I told her about my weakness for rebounders; she told me about hers for married men.

'They should have their ring tattooed on. By the time I find out they're attached, it's too late – I've already fallen for them.'

We covered family. Her parents had retired to the Fraser Coast, and both of her sisters had popped out multiple children.

'I think Mum's disappointed in me,' she said. 'What about your parents?'

'Dad's remarried and living back in Gloucester. His wife's lovely and they're happy. We talk regularly.'

'And your mother? Please tell me she's living in a new age commune in Byron or somewhere?'

I laughed. 'Close. She was in Byron for a while. She and her partner, Steph, moved to Ubud in Bali. They have a guest villa and do tantric breath-work or something. I love that she's still alternative.'

'Do you get up there much?'

'No, never. I keep meaning to, but . . .'

'Oh, you must go! I've just come back. My girlfriend Abby went through a nasty break-up, so we had a week or so up there. Well, not in Ubud as such – we were on the coast – but we went there for the day. I did this cooking class . . . Hang on, I have the card in my wallet – you can have it for when you go.'

'Oh, I don't cook.'

'Neither did I, but I figured it was about time I learnt. I had it on my bucket list for this year – learn to cook. And to fall in love with someone who wasn't already in love with someone else. At least that's one tick in the box, I guess!'

'You have a bucket list?'

At school Andi always seemed too much of a dreamer to plan ahead. If there was a cloud nearby to pop her head into, she'd find it. It was one of the reasons we'd got on so well.

'Sure, doesn't everyone?'

Coffee turned into a wine or two, until Andi declared, 'Look at the time! I've got a date tonight.'

I hesitated before asking, 'With the apartment man?'

'No – especially not now I know he's married. No, this isn't really a date as such – just a catch-up with Abby's ex-boyfriend's best friend. I don't even really like him, but we have Abby and Brad in common, so I can make the effort for one night.'

Her girlfriend's ex-boyfriend's best friend. I couldn't even try to work that out. 'Didn't you say they've broken up?'

'Yes, but we're hoping to change that. It's a long story. Anyhoo, I'm off – where's your phone? I'll pop my number in and prank-call myself so we can stay in touch. Okay?'

•

On Monday, I took myself off to Noodleicious for lunch, alone because Booth and Jamie had been out at a clients' office all morning. I knew Jamie was off the market, but that didn't stop the shivers that ran through me each time our eyes met over a conference table. If anything, the effect he had on me was getting stronger. I'd never felt anything quite like it. If this incredible rush was what falling in love was all about, it was no wonder people got addicted to it. I hadn't been able to see anything or anyone else through the haze of Jamie. If he was in the room, I'd be waiting for him to lift his head and catch my eyes with his. When he was talking during a meeting I'd be watching his mouth and his hands and wondering what they'd feel like on my body. The pictures in my mind certainly spiced up our project meetings.

I was just finishing off my noodles when Booth and Jamie walked in.

'You don't mind if we join you, do you?' asked Jamie.

As if I'd mind spending more time with you.

Almost as if I'd said it out loud, Booth raised his eyebrows and shook his head.

I glared at him and said, 'Of course I don't mind.'

He pushed himself into the, ahem, booth beside me, leaving the seat opposite for Jamie. If Booth had been trying to head off temptation, it wasn't a successful tactic. Jamie was able to give me the full force of his piercing eyes; and when he stretched his legs out, one rested against mine, sending little jolts of electricity through my body.

The next time he caught my eyes, I held his gaze and flicked my hair back.

Booth interrupted our eye action. 'So, buddy, how's Carly? Have you made an honest woman of her yet?'

Under the table, I moved my leg away. Above the table, I concentrated on my noodles.

'It's Callie – didn't I tell you? We split up.'

I moved my leg back beside Jamie's. His eyes caught mine again and I flicked my hair some more.

'Really? You never mentioned it,' said Booth.

'No, it wasn't the easiest of break-ups.' He looked at me and shrugged his shoulders in the universal code for 'you know how it is'.

'I'm sorry, that must have been tough, Josh said you guys had been together for years.'

'It was . . . but thanks, Em. We'd been limping along for a while. It finished when she found someone else. But I think I'm ready to move on.'

He smiled at me and my heart did a little somersault. Beside me, Booth was playing on his cell phone.

'That's good to hear,' I said and leaned forward just a little more.

His eyes dropped to the buttons on my blouse and

then back up to my face. I smiled and parted my lips. He smiled and moved his attention to my mouth.

My phone alerted me to a text.

'Shouldn't you be getting that?' asked Booth.

'No, it can wait,' I said, still smiling at Jamie.

'What if it can't?' asked Booth.

I sighed heavily, apologised to Jamie, and checked my message. It was from Booth.

Don't go there . . .

Really? I turned back to Jamie. 'Where were we?'

'Oh, please,' muttered Booth under his breath.

'Do you have something to say?' I asked him.

'Actually, yes. I was just thinking how great it would be if Jamie came along on Saturday night.'

I looked at him with confusion. What was Saturday night? I didn't recall us having any plans.

'Emily and I are cooking dinner for Suse on Saturday night,' Booth told Jamie. 'You remember her from running club?'

Dinner on Saturday night? Me cooking? Him cooking? Us cooking? Since when?

'Yes, she seems nice,' said Jamie. 'You guys have all been friends for a while?'

'Uh huh, years, but just lately things have been getting a little rocky.' I glared at Booth. 'It's the running, you see, it's tearing us apart.'

Jamie laughed. 'So, Emily, not only are you cute and funny, but you cook too?'

Even I had to laugh at that. 'Does that line usually work?'

'Not usually,' he admitted.

'And I don't usually cook, but Josh has kindly offered to help me prepare dinner. Apparently he's good in the kitchen – or so he's told me.' I managed to look innocent.

'I am,' Booth agreed with a straight face, 'great in the kitchen. Inventive, even.'

'Whatever.' I turned my attention back to Jamie. 'You're very welcome to join us if you're free. And we'd love to see you, wouldn't we, Josh?'

I smiled sweetly at Booth. He smiled sweetly back. Two could play that game. A tick to the bucket list, and Saturday night with Jamie – that was multi-tasking at its best.

Jamie seemed confused. 'Am I missing something? Is there something between you and Josh?'

Booth and I looked at each other and giggled.

'Nah, we shagged once,' he said.

'Don't listen to him,' I said. 'It seems that he and I – and yes, we're just good friends – are cooking dinner next Saturday night, and you're invited. It's at my place, in Richmond – I'll email you the address. Are you in?'

'Sure, it sounds good. It'll give me an opportunity to talk you into changing your mind about running group,' said Jamie.

I laughed. 'Nothing could get me back into the

dreaded trainers for anything faster than a walk – at least not until the Italians make running shoes.'

CHAPTER THIRTEEN

In rom-coms, there was often a scene where the heroine was about to cook a meal for the man she'd been in love with since before the start of the movie. The aim was to make him fall in love with her – although usually by this stage the audience knew they'd wind up together. But she hadn't worked that out yet, and nor had he. It was a modern twist on the old saying about the way to a man's heart being through his stomach. Maybe that was where I'd been going wrong all these years?

First, though, the heroine had to empty her oven. This was an important point, as it told us that she didn't normally use it for cooking. Depending on how cruel the writers wanted to be to the heroine, the rest of the scene would go one of two ways:

1. The *Bridget Jones's Diary* scenario.

In this scene, the heroine emptied her oven of bills, dirty laundry or shoes. She'd have found a recipe book somewhere, although there weren't any other books in her flat to support this hypothesis. The cookbook would be open to the page she was working from, probably with a tumbler of wine balanced on it to mark the spot. Every square centimetre of kitchen bench space would be covered with ingredients, and each burner on her stovetop would hold a saucepan that was boiling over. From somewhere she'd have unearthed a blender and a food processor, and these too would have liquid spewing out the top onto what was left of the bench space. In short, it was a disaster from go to whoa. The food was completely inedible, the kitchen looked like a bomb had hit it, and before dessert could be served, the leading man and the leading scumbag got involved in a most undignified tussle out on the street to the rhythm of an eighties' disco beat sung by an ex-Spice Girl. Or something like that.

2. The New York, New York scenario.

In this scene, the heroine lived in a walk-up brownstone somewhere in The Village. In her oven were law books and her invitation to the hero's wedding . . . to someone else. Despite not being accustomed to cooking, Miss New York somehow had this one great recipe in her head. We knew it was in her head because she didn't need a cookbook. It was the sort of recipe that meant she had to go market shopping, which gave the director the excuse to film a location shot with our girl walking the streets hugging to her chest two brown paper shopping bags with huge bread sticks, celery heads and a bunch of flowers sticking out the top – yet nothing she later prepared had celery in it.

Miss New York, despite the law books in her oven, chopped all the ingredients with the proficiency of a trained chef. The table was set with matching plates and the flowers that had taken up most of one of the hugged brown shopping bags. Our hero would buzz to be let in (after all, it was New York), he'd kiss her hello and then grab a spoon to taste the tomato sauce that was sumptuously bubbling away in one of those soup pans that looked like a mini cauldron. (I always wondered why she had one of these pans if she didn't cook, and where it had been stored given that the oven was home to law books and wedding invitations.) Despite never having cooked before, our heroine rustled up a meal worthy of a *Masterchef* finalist, and was rewarded with a shag from our hero in the romantic rooftop garden.

If I was a betting girl – which I wasn't – given the way Booth and I had been arguing over menu choices, I'd put money on our dinner party looking more like the former than the latter. Although I didn't own any blue string, and, as far as I knew, there wasn't a resident scumbag or Mr Darcy on the scene. That said, Jamie and his accent would make a very nice Mr Darcy, but with better biceps. For a minute or so, I allowed myself to picture him emerging from an English country lake in a dripping white linen shirt and riding breeches. Hmmmm.

'Em, a little concentration, please,' urged Suse as we sat in the bar on Friday evening.

'Sorry, I just had this vision of Jamie dressed like Mr Darcy – you know, in the lake scene?'

She laughed. 'Of course you did. You know what? You two are hopeless and I'm going home. Richard flew in this morning, so I suppose I'd better go and treat him like a returning hero.' Before leaving, she looked sternly at us. 'You two need to get your act together if you intend putting a meal on the table tomorrow night.'

I giggled. 'If worst comes to worst, we can always phone out for home delivery.'

She smiled and shook her head. 'Not the point, Em.'

'I know. Don't worry – we'll have a menu and a shopping list. This will be the best meal Booth and I have ever cooked. Maybe the first of many.'

'Let's not get too carried away – it'll be the *only* meal you've ever cooked.'

'True. Are you sure Richard can't come? It won't be the same without him.'

'No, Toby's been running a temperature, and Richard's had a full week so he'll stay with Tobes rather than get a sitter. He sends his apologies.' With that she was off.

'What about Italian?' Booth suggested. 'All we need are tomatoes, herbs and meat. Like the colours on the Italian flag.'

'Where did you get the bit about the flag?'

'Mandy used to cook a lot. She tried to teach me,

but I wasn't interested.'

'I've never really asked you . . . what went wrong with her?'

For a minute I didn't think he was going to answer.

'Oh, I don't know . . . it was all too quick – less than two years from start to finish.' He shrugged and took a mouthful of his beer. 'I was way too young to get married – what was I, twenty-four? But she got pregnant and it seemed the right thing to do.'

The surprise must have shown on my face.

'Yeah, it was early days so she didn't want anyone to know. I was mad about her then, so I got carried away with doing the right thing . . . and then she miscarried. It all happened so quickly, I hadn't even really got used to the idea that it – the baby – was there. It hadn't felt real to me, but it did to her. By then the wedding thing was too far down the track, and she threw herself into staying on the same timetable as if the baby was still coming. I wasn't sure we were doing the right thing, but there was no way I could hurt her – not after the miscarriage. Anyway, as I said, I was mad about her then.' He smiled, but there was no humour in it. 'After the wedding and the excitement was over, we finally started to get to know each other, and neither of us was pleased with what we saw. It just took some time for us both to accept that.'

'And Shayla?'

'Aaaaah, well, Shayla was the reason Mandy and I

finally called it quits.'

I searched his face and decided not to pursue the subject. 'Okay, let's agree on Italian. Do you have any recipes?'

He smiled at my change of subject, and stretched his legs out under the table, bumping the edge and spilling my wine. 'Do I look like a walking cookbook? It's minced beef, tomato and herbs. Seriously, Em, how hard can it be?'

'For a start, we have to use the right herbs. On *Masterchef* they talk about getting depth of flavour and layers, so it must be harder than it looks or everyone would be doing it. Besides, this whole let's-invite-the-world-over-for-dinner thing was your idea.'

'It's your bucket list,' he pointed out.

'Yeah, but you were the one who invited everyone.'

'I thought I was helping you out with Jamie.'

'No, you didn't. You were hoping to embarrass me in front of him. I bet he's one of those men who knows how to cook.'

He looked into his beer glass.

'Oh my God, he is one of those guys. You were trying to turn him off me!'

'That's bullshit, Em.'

'No, it's not, you've been trying to turn me off him since we first met. Maybe you think he really is *the one*. I think you're scared that if we get together I'll be hanging out with him instead of you. Or maybe you're worried that if he and I get together, it'll come between this bromance that you two have going on.'

'That's bullshit.'

'No, it's not. After all, you forget all about me whenever you get married or find someone new. You probably figure I'll do the same. I always know when you have a new woman – you stop returning messages, and you leave early or send excuses for Friday night drinks.'

'I don't do that. Do I?' He seemed genuinely concerned.

I nodded. 'You do, you know.'

'But you've never said.'

'I haven't needed to. You get bored pretty quickly so it's not for long – and besides, it gives me a bit of a break from you. You can be exhausting.' I smiled to let him know I was joking.

'Bitch.'

'Anyway, my point is that I've never done that to you – I've never let a man come between us. Not even Craig. Why would you think I would if Jamie and I got together?'

'The only reason you haven't let anyone come between us is because you haven't let anyone get close enough to. When you really fall in love – properly in love – you'll forget all about me and Suse.'

'Ha! So you are worried about it.'

'Maybe a little,' he conceded. 'Also, I don't want

you to get hurt.'

'Oh.' He'd never said anything like that to me before. 'You think Jamie could hurt me?'

'I just think you should be careful, that's all. If you guys get together and it goes wrong, it'll be awkward with the pair of you working together. And I'm not sure you'll deal with it well if that happens. After all, he is on the rebound.'

The look he gave me over the top of his beer glass was one I hadn't seen from him before, and it made me uncomfortable.

'We need to sort this menu,' I said, returning to the list. 'How about we do a platter of cold meats and veggies to start? I think I've got a big plate somewhere that we can use. That way we can get everything we need from the markets.'

He paused before saying, 'I like the sound of that.'

'Then we'll do a spaghetti bolognese – we can ask the market people what herbs we need, and surely there'll be a recipe online?'

'And dessert?'

'Ummmmm, isn't there, like, an Italian trifle?'

'Tiramisu?'

'Yes, that. I think we just buy the bits and put it together.'

I added the items to my list and Booth nodded.

'We've got this, Em. How hard can it be?'

•

I found recipes online for the tiramisu and the pasta. Both looked easy enough to follow – not too many steps, not too many ingredients, not too many techniques we weren't familiar with. In other words, nothing more complicated than chopping and stirring.

As well as a shopping list, I'd drawn up a run-sheet pinpointing the crucial parts of the timing and the steps in the process where we could run into trouble. I'd given us time to have a late breakfast, do our shopping, grab another coffee, dress the room, compile a playlist of appropriate music (mostly Italian), and then start preparing dinner by no later than 3 pm. I'd even allowed time to change and put a face on – after all, Jamie was coming. We'd got this.

I showed my list to Booth when he arrived to pick me up, but he seemed less impressed than he should have been. As far as lists went, this was a good one. I pointed that out to him as we idled over our coffees at Prahran Market.

'So, according to this run-sheet, we're late already,' he commented.

'Uh huh. We should have started shopping about forty minutes ago.'

'And we have ninety minutes to do the shopping?'

'Yep, we can get everything we need right here. In the movies they always shop at markets.'

'Whatever.' He continued to read through the list. 'What's this "dress the room" crap, and why does it take two hours?'

'It's really just setting the table, but on reality shows they don't only set the table, they also dress the room. It's supposed to distract your dinner guests when the food turns out to be not that great.'

'Fair enough, but two hours? We'll have enough alcohol to take care of the distraction factor.'

'I've allowed extra time for me to find everything. Most of it's stashed in cupboards . . . somewhere.'

He shook his head. 'Em, you really need to clean out some of your crap.'

'It's on my bucket list, but I don't see what that has to do with cooking spag bol?'

'A fair bit, I'd say, given you need two hours to find enough plates and glasses to put on a table so you can feed your friends.'

'I don't know that it's going to take two hours – I've just allowed that long as a contingency. That's what project managers do, build in contingency.'

'I still think you need to do a clean-out.'

'We're running too far behind schedule now for me to argue with you.'

We made it around the market without another argument. Stall owners were consulted and herbs sourced. Hopefully we'd be able to remember what each one was, and what it was used for. The run-sheet got left at the butcher's, or perhaps with the lovely man who sold us the herbs.

Back at my place, plastic bags full of plastic containers containing olives and artichokes and other oil and herb-soaked vegetables were unloaded into the fridge. I sent Booth out for alcohol. When he returned, I was on my knees in the spare room with my bum in the air, looking for a platter Gillian had sent me that I was sure I'd stashed under the bed. On the floor around me was an assortment of boxes, tissue paper, more platters, and a variety of plates and glasses.

'I thought you wanted to have the meat on, and the tiramisu underway by now?' he said.

'Yeah,' I replied distractedly. 'I found some platters.'

'So I see . . . and, by the looks of it, a lot more than that. Who would have thought so much stuff could fit under one bed?'

'What's the time?'

'Nearly five.'

'Fuck!' I scrambled for some free space on the floor as leverage to get up. 'Why didn't you tell me?'

'I take it we're still running behind schedule?'

CHAPTER FOURTEEN

We managed to get a passable bolognese sauce bubbling away in a saucepan I located at the back of one of my kitchen cupboards. I also found a stash of old photos that were living in it. 'Oh my God, Em, check out your fringe!' I put them aside to sort through another time.

As long as no one looked too closely at the layers, I thought we'd get away with the tiramisu. All I had to do was whip some cream and shave some chocolate onto it before we served it. I'd practised the chocolate-shaving bit, and nibbled on a few too many pieces, so had to send Booth out for some more.

The table looked good. I had enough plates and glasses for everyone, and I even had time to change and put a face on.

Suse and Jamie arrived just a few minutes apart. Jamie kissed me on the cheek and kept his hand on my waist for just a moment too long. I flushed and turned away to make an unnecessary introduction.

'Suse, I think you already know Jamie? From running club?'

'Harriers, we call it,' corrected Jamie with a cheeky grin. 'Great to see you again, Suse.'

I left them to it and escaped into the kitchen to gulp down some wine, take a few deep breaths, and get the platter of nibbly bits while Booth dealt with drinks for the others.

The food part turned out well.

'That was seriously good.' Suse patted her tummy in appreciation.

Booth laughed. 'You sound surprised.'

'Well, let's face it, you and Em haven't cooked anything that doesn't go ding in, oh, let me think . . . ever.'

'Just because we don't cook doesn't mean we can't,' I countered.

'And last night when I left the pub, the two of you couldn't even decide on a menu. I said to Richard that I wouldn't be surprised to arrive and find takeaway popped into bowls. I didn't even know that you had a table, Em – usually it has washing on it. Look at it now.'

The books and magazines that were usually spread over the living room floor were stacked into neat piles. I'd plumped a few mismatched cushions, and draped an old wool blanket over the stained arm of the sofa. I'd moved the washing pile into the spare bedroom, found a couple of sari cloths – sent by Mum – to use as tablecloths, and popped some flowers (from next-door's garden) into a large glass water jug I'd found under the bed – another present from Gillian. I'd put tea lights into glasses, and their flickering glow made everything look a little magical. My spare room might have looked like a bomb had gone off in it, but as long as the corners remained dark, the living room looked not too bad at all.

'Loved the fresh herbs,' Jamie commented. 'What were they? Oregano? Parsley? Thyme?'

Booth and I exchanged glances.

'You have no idea, do you?' said Suse. 'I bet you guys went to the markets, and Em flicked her hair about and smiled a bit, and some poor Italian guy felt sorry for her and handed over everything you needed.'

Booth and I glanced at each other again and giggled.

'Something like that,' I conceded.

'There was cleavage involved too,' added Booth.

'Well, if you've got it . . .' Jamie smiled at me.

I looked down at the table and then back into his eyes. His little finger reached out to stroke lightly against my thumb.

Suse watched the movement and took a mouthful of wine. 'However you managed it, you guys have done a great job. I'm just relieved to get out for the night.'

'Why's that?' asked Jamie.

'Don't get her started,' warned Booth. 'It'll be something about how she needs some "me" time, and how it's okay for Richard because he gets to travel while she has to stay at home with his children.'

'Well, it is okay for Richard. He doesn't juggle the kids as well as a full-time job. He has the perfect life. Sometimes I think you guys are the only people who know me as "me" rather than Suse Wife or Suse Mother.'

'Told you.' Booth was smiling, but there was concern behind his eyes.

'Just you wait, Josh. One day that'll be you – oh, wait, no it won't, you're the man. You'll be the one flitting in and out, happy as long as you have an ironed shirt, a cooked dinner and the occasional blow job.'

'That's unfair,' I said. 'Richard's a good man, and he adores you and the kids.'

'Yes, he's a good man who's forgotten why he married me. Mark my words, Em, it'll be you one day – if you can ever get over your habit of rebounding, that is.'

'Rebounding?' asked Jamie.

'Yeah, Em has a habit of falling for men who end up back with whoever they were with before her,' Suse explained.

Yep, there was definitely an edge to her voice. Booth heard it too and shot me a raised eyebrow.

'Don't get me wrong,' Suse explained, 'she never goes after anyone who's already attached, just guys who are still a little hung up on someone. She falls for them, fixes them up, and then when they're all new and shiny again, their ex wants them back.'

No one said anything. Jamie's little finger had

stopped its hypnotic stroking and rested against my thumb.

My eyes felt like they had something in them, so I didn't look up as I said, 'Umm, how about I clear the table? Is everyone happy to wait a bit for dessert?'

Jamie stood to help me, but I stopped him. 'No, it's okay, you stay here and drink some more. There's more beer, more wine – drink.'

I stayed in the kitchen until I was sure that whatever was in my eye had gone. When I returned to the table, Booth was telling a story about Marcus and Diane.

'You know they're fucking,' he said, just like that.

My wine went down the wrong way and I choked. The whole table erupted in laughter.

'That's bullshit,' I said once I'd recovered my composure.

'Are we talking about Marcus Sweeney? He was there when I was there,' Suse said. 'He was sleazing about even then. But who's Diane?'

'Emily's boss,' explained Jamie.

'Why do you think it's bullshit?' Booth asked me.

'Well, firstly they're both married. And secondly . . . eeeeeuw. He wouldn't be on any "would do" list of mine.' I wrinkled my nose in disgust.

Booth roared with laughter. 'Jesus, Em, you can be so innocent at times. Just because they're married doesn't mean they can't stray. These things happen, you know.'

'Well, these things shouldn't happen – it's not right. And besides, if she's going to stray, why choose him? As I said, eeeeuw.'

Marcus was, in my opinion, unattractive. He was in his late forties with a fashion sense rooted in the nineties and a penchant for ties worn way too high. Then, of course, there was his Roger Ramjet chin. Diane had the dark, predatory good looks of a woman in her early forties who was confident in her body and wasn't afraid to use it. *Ripe* was the best word to describe her. I wondered if her lingerie was selected to match her clothes too. That was a thought best kept to myself.

Booth pushed on with his story. 'Anyway, they were caught on CCTV in the basement car park. The security guys all saw it. Diane was draped over the bonnet of his Audi, and Marcus had his pants around his ankles.'

This time my wine sprayed out through my nose. Jamie and Suse laughed, and Booth innocently surveyed the ruckus he'd caused.

I had Marcus pegged as a strictly-in-the-marital-bed-in-the-missionary-position-on-a- Saturday-night type. Appearances could obviously be deceiving.

'You know, she asked me to call her Dee Dee,' said Jamie.

'I hope you keep your bonnet waxed,' Suse commented.

'Have you noticed how they like to be the last ones

left in the building at night?' Booth said. 'Marcus doesn't have that private bathroom in his office for no reason.'

This time we all did the 'eeeeuw' thing.

'I had a meeting with Marcus last week,' Jamie said, 'and he used his ensuite. I was *this* close to asking him whether he had to go, or whether he just wanted me to know that he had his own bathroom.'

'Maybe an executive bathroom is the latest in all things phallic,' said Suse.

'And they were seen leaving together after the Christmas party last year,' chimed in Booth, looking at me. 'I can't believe you didn't know, Em.'

'Nor can I. How did I miss that?'

'Hadn't you just broken up with – what was his name? – around that time?' Suse said. 'Michael? Yes. You thought he was the one – until he went back to his ex-girlfriend.'

'Yes, thank you, Suse, that's enough.' I took a quick glance at Jamie.

He grinned at me. 'I want to know who Emily has on her "to do" list.'

I adopted my most innocent expression. 'I don't have a "to do" list, I have a "would do" list, and the contents of that list are none of your business.'

'Hey, it was worth a shot.'

Under the table his knee moved against mine, and he tilted his head to smile at me. His little finger was stroking my thumb again, and parts of me were definitely stirring. I felt Booth's eyes on me, but for some reason I couldn't look away from Jamie.

'Em, do you think maybe we should think about serving dessert?'

'What?'

'Dessert. You know, the layered cake thing we made.'

'Oh. It's called tiramisu, and it needs cream, and chocolate,' I explained to the others, reluctantly dragging all the parts of me that had been connected in some way to Jamie – leg, finger, eyes – away from him and into the kitchen.

No one seemed to mind that the layers were crooked – and in some parts non-existent. Judging by the empty plates and empty bottles, dinner had been a success. Maybe this cooking lark wasn't as hard as everyone made it out to be. Fresh herbs, plenty of cream, chocolate and alcohol seemed to be the keys to winning in the kitchen. I was taking it as a great big tick off my bucket list.

Sometime around midnight Suse announced that she was going home. 'It's been fun, guys. Who'd have thought that Em and Josh could stop arguing for long enough to get a meal on the table.' She smiled to take the edge off her words. 'I'd love to stay and drink some more, but if I don't get home, there's no way Richard will let me out of the house to go running tomorrow.'

'You're not seriously going tomorrow morning?'

I asked.

'Sure, there's a plan we have to keep to. Besides, I'm enjoying the "me" time. I'm so grateful to Josh for suggesting it. Are you sure you won't change your mind, Em? It would probably do you good – there's a few cute single guys that go. Although I'm not sure any of them need fixing.'

'Quite sure,' I said, ignoring the last part of her comment.

Jamie also stood. 'I probably should be going as well. Thanks, Em, thanks, Josh – it's been great.'

'Oh, do you have to go?'

'Yeah, I'll keep Suse safe while she hails a taxi.'

'Of course.' I couldn't argue with that. Besides, I'd just had a flashback to the state of my bedroom floor.

At the door, he pulled me close and brushed a kiss against my cheek, tantalisingly close to my lips. 'Maybe next time,' he whispered in my ear.

I tingled all over, and had a stupid smile plastered to my face as I kissed Suse goodbye too.

'Lucky he didn't stay,' Booth said as I shut the door and leaned against it with a pathetic little sigh.

'Why?'

'Because we have to clean this kitchen in the morning, and after seeing the state of that spare room, I'm sleeping on your couch tonight.'

I yawned. 'You know where the quilt and pillows are.'

CHAPTER FIFTEEN

When I crawled out of bed on Sunday morning, Booth was already elbow deep in washing-up water. He'd turned the heating on, and had been out for coffee and croissants. I took a sip of the former, decided the pastry could wait until after the dishes were done, and grabbed a tea towel.

'How's the head?' he asked.

'Fine.'

'We did pretty well last night, don't you think?'

He must have been on his second coffee. I grunted a response and reached for the next plate.

'Maybe we should go on that reality cooking show. We could be "work colleagues" or "just friends" and all of Australia would wonder whether we were sleeping together. When the magazines ask, we could say "Nah, we shagged once, now we're just friends". The headlines would be amazing.' He waited for a response. 'Well, what do you think?'

'You mean aside from the fact that we can't cook anything other than spag bol and unevenly layered tiramisu? Then there's the easy-to-overlook issue that both of our apartments are tiny.'

'We could use Suse and Richard's house. They'd let us. You don't have to use your own place. Also, I read somewhere that you don't even really have to be able to cook. Apparently they're after personalities, and if you're not great in the kitchen they send you to classes before filming starts. It's more interesting for the audience if you can't cook and there's the possibility of a train wreck.'

I shrugged and reached for a glass.

'Don't you think we'd be great?'

'I don't do bitchy well.'

The coffee was finally having an effect.

'No, but I do.'

'True.'

'You don't think it's a good idea?'

'Not one of your best.'

We worked companionably until most of the dishes were done. I left them piled on the table.

Booth broke the silence. 'Do you think Suse is okay?'

'I'm not sure. I know she talks like that occasionally, but usually it's just a bit of fun. Last night she sounded almost bitter. Something's definitely going on with her.'

'Maybe it was the wine, but a few times she said things that sounded like they were directed at you. I noticed something similar last week at the pub too.'

'Yeah, so did I. Last night wasn't her usual whingeing. I know Richard's away a lot, but he's always travelled and she hasn't seemed to mind. Work's busy, so perhaps she's just having a few problems dealing with everything.'

'You think that's it? She has a nanny and a cleaner to help out. By the time she gets home, the kids have been fed and bathed. No, Em, I think it's more than that. Richard's a good guy – I'm sure he'd help out if she asked.'

'Perhaps the issue's with Richard? You said it yourself, he's a good guy and he adores her. She always used to say that good guys were boring. Remember the tragedies she dated before him?'

'How can I forget?' He laughed. 'You could be right. She says she's enjoying running, but I think she's seemed even more restless over the last couple of weeks.'

'You see her more than me these days. She's always too busy for lunch or a long phone chat.' I stacked the last of the platters on the table. 'Hey, speaking of which, shouldn't you be running now?'

'Nah, I figured I couldn't leave you with this mess. I'll make it to the after-run brunch.'

He smiled, but tried to hide it under the guise of wiping down the sink and kitchen benches. I'd seen *that* smile before.

'What's her name?'

'Who?'

'The girl at Harriers you have your eye on.'

'How do you know there is one?'

'I know that smile – it's the one you have when you're on the chase. So, what's her name?'

'Corinna.'

'And?'

'And nothing. That's all I know. She's hot, she runs and her name's Corinna.'

'Ha! Clever girl.'

'What's that supposed to mean?' He finished wiping down the sink.

'It means, my dear Booth, that she's already worked out the best way to keep you interested for longer. You've got a pretty low boredom threshold.'

I flicked the tea towel at his bum. He caught it and neatly twisted it into a sharp rat-tail, before turning it back on me and chasing me out of the kitchen.

'Are you saying that I'm boring?' He backed me into a corner, threatening me with the towel.

'No . . . just that your attention span when it comes to women isn't long.'

'It's not my long attention span that they're interested in,' he said with a wink.

After Booth had left, the apartment seemed unusually quiet. I contemplated going for a walk, but it looked miserable outside. I thought about going shopping, maybe scrounging around some of the discount designer stores up on Bridge Road, but there was nothing I needed. Besides, last night's plates and platters needed to be put away . . . somewhere.

I opened a cupboard in the kitchen to look for a place to store the platters. The shelves were jam-packed full of paper – paid bills, magazines, birthday cards, photos, postcards, catalogues and other non-kitchen essentials. The cupboard beside it was full of jumpers.

I wasn't sure how it happened, but one minute I was looking at cupboards full of things that shouldn't be there, and the next I was sitting in the middle of the kitchen floor surrounded by paper, sweaters and chipped plates. Once I'd got that far, I had two choices: jam it all back in, or do something with it. I chose the latter. The alternative was sitting around waiting for Jamie to call and tell me how wonderful last night was and how he couldn't wait for us to be together again.

I recovered all of Gillian's gifts from where they were stashed under the spare-room bed, and set to work. Into a bin bag went:

- Damaged crockery, glasses, platters and jugs, saucepans with loose handles or missing lids, and lids without matching saucepans.
- Most of the contents of my kitchen drawers. How many melon-ballers did one girl need? I didn't recall ever having bought one, and I certainly didn't recall ever having used one. The

same applied to the apple-corers (at least I was hoping that's what they were) and those little bright plastic things that apparently you peeled oranges with. I didn't even eat oranges.

- All warranties, receipts and paid bills more than twelve months old, or not needed for tax purposes. Anything I needed to keep was filed into clearly labelled folders.

I examined the clothing, and popped all items that hadn't been worn in the last season but were still in good condition into another bag for delivery to the charity bin. Everything else got thrown. My rationale was that if it had been living unnoticed in the kitchen, I wasn't likely to wear it again soon.

The photos took a little longer. Any that involved old boyfriends went straight into the bin. I popped one of Booth, Suse and myself at Suse's wedding under a magnet on the fridge. Booth and I had our arms around Suse. She was wearing a deceptively plain, strapless cream dress. As maid of honour, I had the same dress, but in a deep plum. Suse's fine blonde hair was pulled back from her face in a severe bun, making her look even taller and slimmer. She was smiling, and her head was tilted back as if expecting rose petals, or something equally as lovely, to rain down on her face. Booth and I were laughing, and the three of us looked as happy as I'd ever seen us. I found other photos of Booth and me, Suse and me, the three of us together, but in none did we all look so . . . I don't know . . . radiant, as if nothing and no one could ever damage our friendship.

Six hours later I stood back, poured a wine, ate leftover tiramisu, and surveyed my handiwork. My kitchen cupboards and drawers now contained items that belonged in a kitchen, and the surfaces were gleaming. More to the point, I had surfaces. The shelves were tidy and full of neatly stacked plates and glasses. All platters, jugs and saucepans were where they needed to be. My oven was clean and free of law books. Just kidding – there hadn't been any law books in my oven, or wedding invitations. There had, however, been four years worth of tax returns and a pair of ancient training shoes that smelled of ex-boyfriend.

Just before going to bed, I checked my emails. In amongst the offers of penis extensions and lottery wins was an invitation from DotPoint to attend an interview.

Even though I'd applied by accident and knew I had no chance at all of success, I emailed back to say I'd be delighted to accept. The interview practice would do me good.

CHAPTER SIXTEEN

In the two weeks since Booth and I had cooked dinner, the flirtation between Jamie and me had intensified, but still nothing had happened. Even the flirtation wasn't anything anyone else would have noticed – it was way more subtle and exciting than that. Jamie managed to turn the simple act of taking a coffee cup into something more. He'd hold the cup and slowly brush his fingers against the back of mine. The first time he did it, I thought I was imagining things – until I looked up at him and saw his eyes dancing.

Then there were the meetings. He'd wait until I was seated before either deliberately taking a seat beside me or opposite me. If he was beside me, he'd make sure our knees were touching. If he was opposite, it would be the eye thing . . . those piercing eyes. Rather than looking for excuses to send my apologies, I looked forward to meetings – even the ones I used to yawn through.

He'd also taken to dropping into my work station on the flimsiest of excuses – usually to talk about something on my computer screen that he could have seen on his own perfectly well. His hand would rest on my shoulder as he leaned over me, just inches between us. I'd pretend to listen to him, but instead I'd be focusing on the heady scent of his aftershave and the feel of his breath hot on the back of my neck.

Sometimes he'd stop me in the corridor to ask a question he could have asked by email, his hand resting on my arm, his gaze intent. 'Em, is the development on track?' Booth had seen that one and teased me about it later, but I didn't think he'd noticed anything else. Except maybe the screen thing. He saw that once too, but all he said was, 'Doesn't the guy have his own monitor?'

Then there were the instant messages. They always started with something work-related, and very quickly moved into something else.

Hey, Em, can you come along to the 3 pm? We need some clarity around one of the items on the requirement register.

Sure. Send me an invite.

Thanks. I owe you one.

I'll hold you to that.

I didn't tell you what I owed you.

I'll still hold you to that.

As I said, lots of flirting, but no actual action.

On the home front, the decluttering was done and the renovations were being planned. I'd been buying lifestyle magazines – the type with stylists and recipes and gardens. I'd tried some of the easier recipes – cooking wasn't that hard once you got started – and was even contemplating some container-planting on my balcony. My idea of beehives was probably taking it all a step too far.

I suspected Booth was suffering from the same frustration as I was. He'd been short-tempered the last week or so and I guessed that Corinna was still playing hard to get. I'd seen it before – but not as bad as this for a while. Women didn't usually play hard to get with Booth. He told me that was because of his huge . . . charm.

On Tuesday his mood reached boiling point. We were in a meeting to go through yet another change we were making for that important, but indecisive, Sydney-based client.

'Emily, how did we miss this requirement?' he asked.

'We didn't miss it.'

'Well, it's not in the release notes and it's not in the test plan, so again, how did we miss this requirement?'

'If you'd let me finish, Josh, we didn't miss the requirement because it's not on the version of the register we've been working from.'

Tony, the project manager, was pretending to concentrate very hard on something on his laptop.

'Tony, how did we miss this requirement?' Booth asked.

'I'm sure it's in the register – Emily's team obviously didn't pick it up.'

Booth was on top of it. 'We didn't pick it up because even though it was talked about at the original requirements meeting, it didn't make it onto the register.' He flicked through his paperwork. 'Back on March 5, you made the comment that this would be a phase two development requirement. Have you got that document?'

Tony ducked further behind his laptop and said nothing. When Booth was in one of these moods, it was best to stay quiet.

'Em, what version are you looking at?'

I checked through my folder. 'Ummm, May 10 . . . version 2.3.'

'Yep, that's what I have too . . . so why does the directory say that the register was checked out and updated by you, Tony, two weeks ago, *after* the contents of the release was signed off?'

Tony's face turned red.

Booth exploded. 'Tony, this is a critical function that has to be in before Finance will let us invoice – and I want that invoice out before the end of this quarter. How did we let it slip into phase two? Em – is there any way we can fit this into the release?'

'We'll need to clarify the requirements, write the code, complete another round of regression and system testing –'

'Yeah, yeah, yeah – how long?'

'Let me finish,' I warned. 'If, and I'm saying if, the

requirements can be confirmed within the next two days, and if the requirements are what we think they'll be, the code itself isn't too complex. I'd say we can get you the release a week after the current due date. As long as there are no major issues discovered in user testing, you can use the contingency that I'm sure Tony has built into his timetable and still make phase one implementation dates.'

Tony glared at me. Project managers hated it when you called them on the contingencies they told you they hadn't built in.

'Okay.' Booth calmed down a bit. 'Jamie, are you fine with that timing?'

'Yes, we can make it work – there are no dependencies to other changes that can't be juggled without issue. As long as Emily's team can do it, we'll work around that.'

'Good. Em, I need you and Tony in Sydney in front of that client tomorrow.'

Tony came out from behind his laptop. 'Tomorrow? I can't do tomorrow. Emily will need to do it without me.'

Booth stared silently at him. Once he'd given an order, he didn't expect arguments.

'I'm on leave for the rest of the week,' Tony explained.

Booth shook his head slowly and looked at the ceiling. 'Okay, fine. Whatever. We're finished here today. Em – not you. Jamie, do you mind hanging around too?'

He waited until everyone else had left. 'Em, no bullshitting about, can your team make this work?'

'Yes, as long as the requirements are what we think they are.'

'What if they aren't?'

'Then we have an issue around the agreed scope, the agreed cost and how late we'll be in delivering. If it comes to that, this will need to wait until phase two – if you want to deliver at all.'

'How the fuck am I going to tell the customer that?' demanded Booth.

'Seriously, Josh? You want to take this out on me?'

'I'll go to Sydney with Em,' offered Jamie, looking across the table at me.

My heart raced and I concentrated on my notes rather than allowing myself to slide ever so pathetically into his eyes.

'Are you sure you can spare the time?' Booth asked, a thoughtful frown on his face.

'Yes, and I think it's important there's a representative from the project team in case negotiation is required.'

'Maybe I should go,' Booth considered, his eyes on me.

'No, I think it's best I do it. Em, I'll talk to the clients and then email you the details.'

'Fine.'

My head was full of the idea of spending a whole day with Jamie. Surely being jammed together in economy seats would do the trick?

Except we weren't jammed together. Due to a mix-up at check-in, there were about five rows between us. It was as if even the airline had conspired to turn this into the longest flirtation in history.

Sydney was wet. The sort of wet that people who don't know better blame Melbourne for, but which Sydney does more often and much less successfully. A dreary, drenching, bring-all-traffic-to-a-complete-standstill sort of wet.

In the taxi to the city, Jamie sat with his legs apart so his knees didn't bang against the front of the seat, his hand resting in the middle close to mine.

He turned to meet my eyes. 'Let me do most of the talking today. I don't want anything outside the contract sneaking in.'

'Sure.'

His hand inched closer and he didn't let go of my eyes.

'All we need out of today is a set of requirements and a sign-off to the revised scope. Okay?'

'Sure.' What had he just said?

His gaze dropped to my lips, moved down to the shadow of my cleavage, before returning to my eyes.

'And then we can be on our way home. Too easy.'

The taxi lurched to a stop to avoid hitting the car in front. I was thrown against Jamie. He steadied me, then left his hand beside mine, touching but barely touching, for the rest of the journey.

Jamie and I met the clients, agreed the new requirements and the timing, and due to traffic issues – Sydney people forgot how to drive as soon as a little moisture rolled from the sky – only just made our flight. At least we were seated together this time. Jamie purchased a couple of beers and snacks onboard in lieu of the dinner we obviously weren't going to have.

'Do you think Tony will be okay with what we've agreed?' I asked.

'Yes, he has no choice – he stuffed up.'

I nodded, and we lapsed back into silence. The man on the other side of me had gone to sleep, his body melting over my armrest. I leaned closer to Jamie. There were definite advantages to economy class.

'And you're sure your team can meet the agreed timetable?' he asked.

Why were we talking about this now?

'Yes. I'd been running on the assumption that the requirements would be as originally discussed, so had the guys look it over yesterday. There won't be a problem.'

Managers of development teams had their own contingencies.

'Good.' He took a large mouthful of beer. 'You and Josh . . . are you sure there's nothing between you?'

At last. 'Absolutely sure. Why do you ask?'

'I don't want to tread on any toes.'

'You're not. We've been friends for years.'

My heart flipped around a little. If he was worried about treading on toes, he had to be interested.

'He said that you two had been together . . . you know, years ago, but I still wondered. And it's just that Suse said. . .'

I could imagine what Suse had said.

'There's nothing between us.' I smiled and changed the subject. 'You and Callie – you'd been together for a while?'

'Five years. Even though things hadn't been great for a while, I didn't want it to end that way.'

'What happened? You don't need to talk about it if you don't want to . . .'

'No, it's fine.' He opened the chip packet up fully before continuing. 'I made a mistake . . . I made a couple of mistakes.' He shrugged. 'She found out. I have no excuses for what I did. Maybe we'd started to take each other for granted. I thought we might have been able to come back from it . . . I thought she was the love of my life.'

'I've never understood that – how . . . well, you know.'

'How I could be with someone else when I loved

her?'

'Yes.'

He shrugged again. 'I don't know . . . it was just sex. It didn't mean anything to me – and I figured she'd never need to know.' He saw the look of disbelief on my face. 'I know how that sounds. I thought things were coming good, but then she was with someone else.'

'And you couldn't forgive that? Even though you'd done the same?'

'It was different. Cal has never been able to separate sex and love. For her it's the same thing. It doesn't hurt so much now.' He smiled. 'Anyway, why are we talking about this? I'd prefer to talk about you.'

'There's not much to tell.'

'Let me be the judge of that.' He took my hand and pretended to examine it.

'So now you're a palm reader?'

'Uh huh, take this line for instance.' He traced the line that ran from the base of my first finger all the way across my hand, looking into my eyes the whole while. 'This is your love line.'

I swallowed hard. 'What does that mean?'

He followed the line back again, leaving little trails of tingles connecting my palm to other, more sensitive, parts of my body.

'It means that you will love deeply.'

'You have no idea what you're talking about, do you?'

'No, but I like holding your hand – and the line is deep, so it could be right.' He smiled into my eyes and my tummy took another dip.

'Okay.' I took his hand and traced the same line, looking into his eyes the whole time. 'What does yours say about you and love?'

'I'm not sure – can you do that again?'

His head moved towards mine, just as the steward said, 'Ladies and gentlemen, we're commencing our descent into Melbourne. Can you now return your seat backs to the upright position, stow your tray tables, switch off all electronic items and fasten your seat belts.'

He pulled back with a smile.

Melbourne was dark and cold, but even the chill of the night air wasn't enough to cool me down.

'It's late,' I said. 'I'd better join this taxi queue. I'll see you in the office tomorrow.'

'No need for that – I'll drop you home.'

'Are you sure?'

'Yeah – it's late, and anyway, it's not really out of my way.' He smiled and my insides turned to mush again.

'Okay, if you're sure.'

His hand covered mine as I picked up my laptop bag. Our eyes met and held.

'Let me,' he said, taking my bag.

In the car, he turned on the radio, and switched through the stations before landing on an old Robbie Williams song, 'Let Me Entertain You'.

'I love this song,' he remarked, turning up the volume.

As we pulled onto the freeway, he put his foot down and the car sped through the night. The windows were down, the cold air whipped through my hair, and we were both singing at the top of our lungs.

We arrived at my block too soon. Before I could say good night and thank you very much, he was out and had retrieved my laptop bag from the back seat. He placed it on the pavement beside me and then very gently pushed me back against the side of the car. He brushed the hair from my face, carefully placing it behind my ears, and then he kissed me.

I placed a lot of stock in first kisses. It was one of those things that you anticipated, but could never have a second go at. If you got the first kiss wrong, it didn't matter whether the second one was great – the memory of the first would always be there. As far as first kisses went, this one was perfect. It had just the right amount of pressure, just the right amount of tongue, just the right amount of tingle.

When Jamie raised his head, he looked deeply into my eyes, smiled, and asked, 'Is this okay?'

'Ummm, yes . . . lovely, thank you. I mean . . . it was lovely . . . the kiss was lovely,' I babbled.

'You're lovely,' he said.

Normally I'd scoff at something so corny, but just now it seemed right. I pulled his head back to mine. This time when we separated, we were both breathing faster.

'And you're sure there's nothing between you and Josh?' he asked, kissing his way down the side of my neck.

Who? Why did he keep asking about Booth?

'Do you want to come up?' I heard myself ask. As this wasn't technically a date, it wouldn't count as a first-night hook-up.

'No, I'd better be getting home. It's been a good day, hasn't it?'

'Yes, it has.'

'I'd better go,' he said unconvincingly, pressing himself deliciously harder against me and resting his forehead on mine.

'If you're sure . . .' I swallowed hard.

He kissed me once more, then wrenched himself away. 'Good night, Em. I'll see you in the office tomorrow.'

'Night,' I said, and watched until his headlights disappeared.

CHAPTER SEVENTEEN

'When a girl lets a guy kiss her, she has certain expectations, you know?' It was Friday night, two days since The Kiss, and Jamie still hadn't followed through with anything more. 'I don't need this level of uncertainty. Things are going well – I'm making progress on my apartment –'

'Progress? What progress?' asked Suse.

'I'm decluttering. I've done the kitchen and the linen cupboard, and made a start on the wardrobe in the spare room. I've got surfaces and floors again – but, boy, do I need new carpet . . . Actually, I might go for floorboards instead. I'd love new kitchen cupboards, but I can't justify that yet. I wonder how hard it would be to take the doors off and paint them?'

'You'd need a power tool,' Suse pointed out.

'Hold on,' interrupted Booth, 'you're decluttering? You're taking this bucket list thing seriously, aren't you?'

'I had to find room to put all the plates and platters away. You'd laugh if you knew what I found in my oven.'

'Law books?' quipped Suse. She'd seen the same

movies I had.

I laughed. 'No, but there was a pair of smelly trainers – I have no idea whose – and some tax returns.'

'Jesus, Em, what if you turned it on?' asked Booth.

'The oven? Like that was going to happen.' I screwed up my nose.

'True, my mistake.'

'The whole thing started accidentally, but now I'm really into it. And it takes my mind off waiting for him to call. I'm not good at sitting around waiting to decipher mixed messages.'

'Maybe he's just not that into you,' said Booth.

'Josh! Not helpful,' Suse warned.

'Sorry, I've just always wanted to say that.'

'It felt like he was into me – or that he wanted to get into me.' If I closed my eyes I could still feel his body urging against mine. I smiled cheekily. 'Parts of him certainly did. A rather large part of him . . .'

'Puh-leeeese!' Booth pretended to put his fingers in his ears.

'Perhaps you need to let the attraction . . . what's the word? Ferment?' suggested Suse.

'You mean I should play hard to get?'

'Why not? It works – doesn't it, Josh?'

'Corinna seems to think so.'

I turned my attention to him. 'Is that why you're in such a shitty mood at work? Because you still haven't caught up with Corinna? Oh my, she's good.'

'This isn't about me,' he said. 'All we're saying is that maybe you should let it brew a bit.'

'Yeah,' I shook my head, 'that's not going to happen. Fermentation is good for wine and not much else.'

'Maybe he's the one playing hard to get – so you'll want him more. If he is, it's obviously working,' said Suse.

I thought about that for half a second before dismissing it just as quickly. 'Guys don't do that – do you?'

Booth shrugged. 'Play hard to get? I haven't had to yet, but I would if I thought I needed to to increase interest.'

'Okay, but how long would you wait?'

'Oh, sweetheart, you know me – my attention span isn't great.'

Suse laughed. 'That's putting it nicely.'

'Maybe you failed the first-kiss test,' he added.

I'd told Booth about the kiss – in detail – almost as soon as I walked into the office yesterday morning, and then again at lunchtime, and again today. After that, I'd got the impression that he didn't want to talk about it any more.

'You're seriously suggesting that? No, I passed the first-kiss test – I put in a great performance. And he passed too. There was promise there. There was . . . well, a guy can't really hide it when he wants more – you know? And let me say this, he wanted more – a lot more. And what's happened since? Nothing. Not. A. Thing.'

'Be fair, Em. He hasn't been in the office. What did you expect? A declaration of undying love?'

'That would have been nice. He doesn't have to be in the office to make a phone call. Two minutes – that's all it would take. "Hi, Em, the kiss was great and I can't wait to see you again." That's all. This silence doesn't make sense. After the performance I gave the other night, I'd kiss me again. You'd kiss me, right?'

Booth and Suse looked at each other, then back at me.

'Who did she direct that question to?' Booth said.

'Either of you. Anyway, I didn't make the first move – he did, with all his hand stuff and his banter. And now? Nothing.'

Suse asked Booth, 'Hand stuff?'

'Don't ask,' he warned. 'I've had this for two days and can't hear it all again. I'm still wondering about the kissing offer.'

I paused for some wine before continuing. 'I've made preparations over the last couple of weeks. Just in case. I got waxed – you know, *waxed* waxed . . . soft bits waxed.'

'Should I be hearing this?' Booth asked Suse.

'I don't think you have a lot of choice.'

'I've spent a small fortune on new underwear – matching, pretty stuff. It's lingerie, not underwear, and it digs into me in places it shouldn't be digging into. Let me just say this – if you could see under my clothes, you'd know just how smoking hot I'm looking.'

'No, I don't think I need to be hearing this,' Booth said.

'Buddy, if I have to, so do you,' Suse muttered.

'Although I'm always open to a discussion about lingerie.'

I glared at him. 'I'm wearing my highest and most uncomfortable heels, because they make my bum look better in my skirts – and for what? Nothing, I tell you. Nothing except a kiss.'

'Yes, you already said that,' said Suse.

'At least twice.'

I glared at them both this time. 'All I want is for him to do something that justifies the pain I'm inflicting on myself – the waxing and the lingerie and the shoes, you know?'

'You could always phone him,' suggested Suse.

'I don't do the asking,' I reminded her. 'The first move has to come from him.'

'It's your call,' said Booth. 'The way I see it, you can sit at home looking at your clean surfaces and wondering why Jamie isn't shagging you, or you can ask him out for a drink. What have you got to lose? You're already waxed – it would be a shame to let that go to waste.'

'Is that who we're talking about?' Suse said. 'Jamie?'

'Yeah . . . who did you think?'

'I've been out of the loop for a few days, so, knowing Em, it could have been anyone. She moves on pretty quickly.' She was smiling, but it was there again – that edge from the night of the dinner.

'I thought you liked Jamie,' I said.

'Of course I do, he's a great guy, it's just that I'm not sure he's for you. What do you think, Josh?'

'Don't bring me into it.' He held his hands up in mock surrender.

'So he kissed you,' Suse said. 'How was it?'

'Do we have to go back through this?' Booth had pain in his voice.

I ignored it. 'It had serious promise. You know how I can tell from the first kiss what a guy's going to be like in –'

'Enough!' Booth turned to me. 'If you want to get into the X-rated details, it can wait until I'm not here. I've heard so much about this fricken kiss that I may as well have been standing on the sidelines watching. And before you ask,' he warned, just as I was about to jump in with something suitably smart-arse, 'I have no interest in watching you get it on with Jamie or anyone else.'

Suse and I looked at Booth for a few seconds before I returned to my deliberations.

'Well, I'm not doing any calling, so I'll wait for him to call me. In the meantime, I want to know why Booth hasn't managed to seal the deal with Corinna.'

'It's complicated,' he said.

'She's playing hard to get,' said Suse, 'and it's driving him mad. That's why I suggested you try it.'

'Is she cute?'

'Yep, exactly Josh's type – long legs, blonde, fit. Fairly smallish tits though.'

'Really? Booth normally likes a decent rack on a girl.'

'Yeah, but he does like them blonde, and he does like them fit.'

'Why don't you girls just pretend that I'm not here?'

'Isn't it your shout for drinks?' I said.

When he'd left for the bar, Suse asked, 'How's the job-hunting going? You haven't mentioned anything.'

'Would you believe I got a response from DotPoint? The money's great and the role sounds really interesting – they're into web design and social media integration. I was supposed to go for an interview on Wednesday, but had to cancel when the Sydney trip came up. I explained the situation, but they haven't responded with a new date. Not that I think I have a chance of getting it – I'm only going along for the practice.'

'If you'd told Josh, I bet he'd have sent someone else to Sydney.'

'Are you kidding? Miss a day with Jamie for a job I don't even know that I want? That was never going to happen.'

'With your track record, you can't afford to make future-based decisions because of a man – no matter how great the first kiss was.' I opened my mouth to protest, but she held her hand up to stop me. 'You know I'm right, Em. Email them again and set a date. If you like, I can help you with preparing for the interview.'

'Thanks, I will.'

'You still don't want to tell Josh?'

The man in question was making his way back through the crowd with our drinks.

'No, not until I'm sure I want to leave.'

I thought about texting Jamie on Saturday night, but talked myself out of it. I didn't want him to think I was too keen. Instead I spent the night in bed with some design magazines, and imagined how Jamie would look in the photos . . . and in the bed beside me.

On Sunday morning I met Andi for breakfast. We'd chosen my favourite – a rustic-looking place surrounded by raised garden beds. It looked a little like a community garden would look if it had been picked up and put down in the middle of Richmond. It even had a few scarecrows, and one cheeky garden gnome.

'Abby's ex, Brad, designed this place,' she told me. 'He's a landscape architect, but he's done a few of the rooftop bars in town as well.'

While we were eating, a dog of disputed breeding pushed its nose through the wire border and into

Andi's lap.

'Bert! What are you doing here, fella?' She ruffled the dog's ears and fed him a piece of toast from her plate.

'I wish you wouldn't do that, A. Brad's going to kill me if I give his dog back with too many bad habits.'

The voice belonged to one of the best-looking men I'd seen in a long time – with the exception of Jamie, of course. He may have been scolding Andi, but his smile told a different story.

'I'm so rude,' Andi said. 'Emily, this is my friend Todd, and this is his friend, Bert. Todd's looking after him while Brad is overseas.'

Ahhh, Todd – the best friend's ex-boyfriend's best friend . . . or something like that.

'Do you want to join us?' Andi asked him.

'No, thanks. I'll grab my coffee and we'll be off. Bert and I have heaps to do today. It was nice meeting you, Emily.' He turned to leave, and doubled back. 'Just one thing – I don't suppose you've heard from Abby this week?'

'Sure – she was off to Sydney for the weekend. Some family thing. Did you need to talk to her?'

'Aaah yes, I forgot about that. No, it's nothing that can't wait. I'll leave you girls to it.'

Once he'd left, I said, 'It looks very much like you no longer dislike Todd as much as you said you did.'

She smiled into her plate. 'Yeah, he's growing on

me. Not my type though – way too single. How did your interview go?'

I wiped up the last of my hollandaise sauce with toast. 'I had to cancel. A last-minute business trip to Sydney with that guy I was telling you about.'

'Really? This sounds like something I need to know more about.'

'Well, you know how you can tell a lot about a guy from the first kiss . . .'

When I arrived for the State of the Nation on Monday morning, Jamie was already perched on the side of a table. He raised his eyebrows and indicated the space beside him.

'I'm glad we've got this time alone,' he said once I'd settled.

'We're hardly alone.' I looked around the room at our colleagues busily checking their phones.

'True.' He grinned. 'What do you reckon they're doing – Candy Crush, Instagram or Facebook? You can't expect me to believe that everyone's as busy as they're pretending to be.'

'You forgot Words With Friends.'

'Exactly. Hey,' he looked into my eyes, 'I wanted to call you, but I knew I'd be busy this weekend. Also, I didn't know how you felt about it – you know, the whole working together and kissing thing.'

'Oh, I hadn't thought about that. I mean, I'd

thought about the kiss obviously,' I felt my cheeks get hot, 'but it hadn't occurred to me that working together could be a problem.'

'I haven't thought about much else the past few days other than kissing you again. I don't want to make life difficult for you – after all, I'm on the rebound and I don't want to hurt you.' He reached behind me to wind a finger around mine. 'The other night – that kiss – it was great, and I want to do it again. Okay?'

I nodded.

Booth chose that minute to walk in. He saw Jamie and me sitting together, raised a questioning brow at me, and sat on my other side. He didn't smile.

When Diane stood and I noticed she was wearing pink and black – hot pink lips, blazer and shoes – I leaned across to whisper to Booth, but he stopped me with a 'shush'. At the end of the meeting, he left the room immediately, offering Jamie and me a terse 'Better keep moving, see you guys later.'

Jamie whispered in my ear, 'I want to kiss you . . . now.'

Heat rushed through me and I nodded. I smiled at him and left the room. He waited a few seconds and followed me. I looked back once, smiled again, and ducked into the fire exit. I didn't need to wait long.

He pushed me against the concrete wall and kissed me. This time there was no softness in his lips, just hard, fierce passion. When his tongue drove its way into my mouth, I met it with pressure of my own. When his knee forced my legs apart, I willingly moved to allow him space. When his hand grasped my breast through my blouse, I moaned.

The slamming of a fire door a couple of floors below us was a reminder of where we were.

I pushed him away and he slumped with his back to the wall, breathing hard. He smiled at me. I smiled back and, after pulling my skirt down below my bum and tucking my blouse back in, kissed him quickly and left.

I took a detour to the bathroom to splash some cold water on my wrists.

Wow. Just wow.

I was midway through pretending to read a release document when my instant messenger alerted me to a new chat.

Jamie: Wow.

Me: Sure was.

Jamie: I'm still hard.

A shiver passed through me.

Me: Can you say that on IM?

Jamie: I don't know – are they watching?

I looked around the office. My team were all in their partitions beavering away at whatever they were supposed to be beavering away at.

Me: I have no idea.

Jamie: So, what are you going to do about it?

Me: About what?

Jamie: About me still being hard.

I knew what I wanted to do about it. I closed my eyes briefly as a shiver ran through me. God, I could still feel him against me, pushing into me.

Me: What do you want me to do about it?

*Jamie: Now *that's* not for IM;) But I'll tell you later . . .*

Me: What did you have in mind?

Jamie: Drinks . . . to start with . . . 8 pm? Your place?

Was my wax still okay? I didn't have time to get another.

Me: Sounds good.

Jamie: Doesn't it? I don't think I can wait that long.

Jamie Aldridge is offline.

CHAPTER EIGHTEEN

But Jamie and I didn't catch up that night – he texted me later in the afternoon to ask for a rain-check. Something about how he'd forgotten he was catching up with an old friend.

You don't mind, do you? The anticipation will make it all so much better.

The following weekend his parents were in town – from Canberra, apparently. When I asked where he was from originally, he kissed me instead of answering the question.

Although we still hadn't seen each other outside the office, there'd been quite a few more encounters in the fire escape, one in the car park, and a risky interlude in the stationery room.

In meetings we acted normally, although I couldn't help catching his glance every now and again. In his eyes would be a reminder of our last assignation and a promise of our next. I couldn't watch him talk without thinking about his mouth on mine, his hand on my breast or his fingers . . . well, no need to go into the details of what they'd been up to. I never knew when he'd take my hand or give me that look, but as soon as he did, I was ready for him. Every part of me craved the next hit, yet it was never quite enough. I wanted more of him, all of him.

At night, in our respective beds, Jamie and I exchanged increasingly raunchy texts – and the occasional call where neither of us said very much at all, but breathed very heavily. Yes, we were doing phone sex. Another tick on the bucket list.

The first time was a couple of nights after that first hot and heavy exchange in the fire escape. He'd called late and I was already in bed. When I told him so, he went quiet. Then he asked, 'What are you wearing?'

I couldn't tell him the truth – that I had a singlet on under a hoody – so I paused and said, 'The usual?'

'Tell me about it,' he encouraged.

When I remained silent, he helped me out. 'Are you naked?'

'Do you want me to be naked?'

'Yep, but not just yet.'

Okay, I was getting the hang of this. 'No, I'm not naked.'

'Do you have a bra and panties on?'

'Uh huh.'

'Tell me about them.'

'Well,' I stretched my leg out and about, 'it's a little red lacy set. The bra is half-cup and doesn't quite hold me in.'

'Can you reach in and pull your boobs out?'

'Sure.'

That first night I felt uncomfortable, and lay there listening to him, pretending to follow his instructions and feeling that the whole thing was just a little bit silly. Since then I'd got more used to it, although I still felt a bit silly.

Jamie had suggested we keep our relationship to ourselves – for now. 'It could make it uncomfortable with Josh and Suse,' he'd said. 'Besides, it might cause problems in the office if anyone knew.' I wasn't even sure we had a relationship – rather just a lot of incredible snogging in increasingly risky locations and way too much frustration.

It made sense, so I'd agreed. As long as this excitement was running through my veins, as long as he continued to do what he was doing to me, I would have agreed to anything. For the first time in my exceedingly disciplined life I wasn't thinking, I wasn't planning, and I wasn't considering the consequences of the risks we were taking. I was desperate for him.

Friday night at the pub, Booth announced that he was only staying for one drink, pleading someplace else to be. Corinna must have finally given in to his considerable charms.

When I said as much, he smiled and said, 'You can

talk.'

I played dumb. 'I have no idea what you mean.'

'You act like you're in some sort of daze whenever Jamie's around.'

'Do you still fancy Jamie?' Suse said. She'd been unusually quiet up until now, and she looked tired. 'You haven't said much about him since the kiss episode, so I thought it had passed.'

'Fancy him? That's the understatement of the decade,' Booth said. 'That sort of unresolved sexual tension could power the grid. I wish they'd hurry up and get it over with.'

He laughed, but Suse didn't.

'He's the man of my naughtiest dreams,' I said.

'Should I step out while you give Suse the X-rated details?'

'Not necessary.'

Usually I couldn't wait to fill Booth and Suse in on all the horny details, but this time it felt different. Even if Jamie hadn't asked me to keep it quiet, I wasn't ready to share what we'd been up to.

'So it's still unresolved then?' Suse asked.

'Come on, Em, tell us – have you two hooked up yet?'

There was an edge to Booth tonight that I wasn't comfortable with. Maybe now he and Corinna were getting it together, he'd mellow out a bit.

'No, we haven't. There's nothing going on –

outside of my head,' I lied.

I didn't know why I'd lied. As the words came tumbling out of my mouth, I wanted to take them back.

He raised his eyebrows and shook his head slowly. I looked into my wine glass.

'So, Suse,' he said, changing the subject, 'are we going to see you at Harriers this weekend?'

'I hope so. It's getting a little difficult to juggle, so I'm doing my training closer to home. Don't worry though, I'll still be ready for the half.'

'Hmmm, Jamie hasn't made it the last couple of weeks either.' He looked at me. 'Do you know anything about that?'

'No, why would I? Maybe he had other things on.' This time I didn't have to lie.

'He mentioned something about his parents being in town, but I thought . . . It doesn't matter what I thought.' He drained his glass and slammed it on the table. 'Well, my dears, it's been fun as always, but I have somewhere I need to be.'

I got Suse and me fresh drinks and a packet of crisps, and settled back for a chat.

'How's the running going?' I asked her. 'Are you still enjoying it?'

She shrugged. 'It gets me out of the house.'

She picked at a crisp and crumbled it onto the table. I watched her and felt the same concern I'd felt the other week.

'Are you okay, Suse?'

'Yeah, why do you ask?'

'For a start, I've never known you not to inhale crisps.'

'I'm fine.'

'You don't seem it.'

She smiled weakly and swirled the wine around in her glass. 'This thing with you and Jamie – is it serious?'

'I really think he could be "the one".' I made little inverted commas in the air. 'Not that I manage to do any thinking about anything when he's around. There's this thing between us, this vibe. I think he likes me too, but every time we make plans to get together outside the office, it doesn't work – there's always a cancellation. We're supposed to be going out tomorrow night . . .' I shrugged. 'Maybe Booth is right, maybe he's just not into me.'

'Hmmmm.' She concentrated on the pile of crisp crumbs.

'What's wrong? You see him at Harriers – has he said something? Do you know something? Don't tell me he's seeing someone?'

'I don't think he's seeing anyone else – he hasn't said so.'

'So what was the hmmmm for? Don't you like him?'

'No, it doesn't mean anything. I like him, he's a nice guy. If you really like him, maybe you should make it happen. But only if you're serious about him. I get the impression that his ex burned him pretty badly, so he doesn't need you treating him as if he's something that needs to be fixed before he can be released back into the wild.'

There it was again – the judgement.

'Are you okay, Suse? I mean really okay? What you just said was mean, and you're not a mean person.'

'I'm sorry. You're right, that wasn't fair. Don't mind me. I'm just going through one of those stages – kids, marriage, the whole trapped thing. Part of me would like the opportunities and the freedom you have, so maybe I'm envious.'

'Oh.' I wasn't sure what to say. 'I thought you and Richard were happy?'

'Em, you have this idea that if you find "the one" it'll all be smooth sailing afterwards – but it's not. Instead of just having your problems, you have his as well. Your issues double, your bills double, but your opportunities are halved. You can do whatever you want, whenever you want. I don't have that choice.'

She looked distracted, or something else that I couldn't put my finger on.

'Listen to me!' she said. 'Actually, no, don't listen to me. I shouldn't have said that – it doesn't mean anything. I'm tired, it was a tough week.'

'It sounds like next weekend's trip will do you good – where are you guys off to?'

'One of the spa retreats in Daylesford. I'm looking forward to it. We're driving up on Friday afternoon, straight after work.'

'That sounds very romantic for a girls' weekend. Who are you going with?'

'A couple of the girls from work. Tanya's getting married in a few weeks – it's just a small occasion, family and close friends only, in Phuket – but we felt we should celebrate in some way.'

'Doesn't sound like it'll do the training any good.' I was attempting to lighten the conversation.

She laughed. 'Probably not, but it'll work wonders for the stress levels. Maybe that's the real issue – work's been tough, Richard's been away. Maybe I just need a change of scenery and some me time.' She took another sip of her wine. 'Look, don't pay any attention to me – I'm going through some stupid stage. Josh would tell me to harden the fuck up and get on with it.'

'He would.'

'Is that what you think?'

'No, sweetie, it's not.'

CHAPTER NINETEEN

Jamie didn't call on Friday night. He texted to say he had somewhere to be, but was absolutely looking forward to our first real date. Then he asked what I was wearing. I got the phone sex thing – to an extent – but sexting? I didn't get that.

On Saturday I woke to a new text:

Sorry, babe, I need to help my mate move. Hate to do this to you again, but I'm going to have to rain-check. Please say you forgive me? You know I'll make it up to you . . .

Confident there was no way he'd cancel me again, I'd planned the perfect pre-date, pre-sex preparation for today. Instead, I dressed in my oldest clothes and took myself down to the local hardware store. Starting today, things were going to change around here.

When I bought my apartment five years ago I'd had Plans. I'd been house-hunting for so long I was sure the local real estate agents were tempted to turn their sign to *Closed* whenever they saw me approach. At first, the problem was that I simply didn't know where I wanted to live. I'd looked at Collingwood,

Fitzroy, South Yarra and Prahran. I'd even looked at some brand-new apartments over in Docklands. I kept coming back to Richmond.

Once I'd decided on a suburb, I had to consider all the other factors. Could I afford two bedrooms? Did I want a ground-floor or top-floor unit? What about a balcony, and which way should it face? Visitor parking? How many bathrooms? Renovated or renovator's delight? Then I found this place. It had two bedrooms, both with built-in wardrobes. The kitchen was small, and partially separated from the living area by an island bench that I'd popped some stools under. I had room for a smallish table and a sofa, coffee table and TV in the rest of the space.

From a location viewpoint it was perfect. There were great shops and restaurants a short stroll away. I was a quick tram run into the city, or down Chapel Street. I was so close to the MCG that I could walk to the football if I wanted – not that I'd been since I'd lived here, even though there were those few weeks when I was dating a player. It didn't last – he went back to his groupies. I could even walk into the city if I was feeling particularly energetic – not that I'd done that either. Anyway, it ticked all the boxes on my list. Other apartments had also ticked the boxes, yet I'd chosen this one. I didn't know what made it different to the others I'd looked at. Maybe it was the balcony that caught the morning sun. Maybe it was the large black and white tiles in the kitchen. It definitely wasn't the fluorescent-green kitchen cupboards. In retrospect, it was probably more that I was sick of looking, and this was the best fit in the right suburb for the money I was prepared to spend without over-committing myself.

As I was saying, when I moved in, I had Plans. To do some serious walking and find a football team to support. To renovate the kitchen, get rid of the gauze curtains with yellow flowers, and change the green cupboards. To rip up the carpet and put down floorboards and rugs. To paint the walls something other than that salmony/pinky/white someone had hopefully christened 'magnolia', and get rid of the wallpaper borders in every bedroom. So far I'd done none of it. Until now.

Two hours later, after a little smiling, hair-flicking and only a teeny amount of cleavage work, I was back home with:

- Several tins of paint – a soft grey for all the rooms, and a darker heathery, plummy colour for a feature wall in what I'd decided to call the dining space.
- Brushes, rollers, paint trays, and these cool little wheelie tools for something called 'cutting in'.
- Some plastery goo that was apparently for filling gaps.
- Sandpaper for sanding down after I'd filled the gaps.

- Blue tape to protect the skirting boards and windowsills.
- Plastic drop-sheets.
- A fold-up stepladder.
- A set of detailed instructions.

I also had an electric screwdriver – or was it a drill? I wasn't sure the difference was important. It was my first power tool and I was very excited. That was another tick for the bucket list.

I decided to start with my bedroom, mainly because I didn't need anyone else to help me move the bed out from the wall. In the throes of unresolved sexual energy last weekend, I'd cleaned out my wardrobe, ripped off the wallpaper border, and taken down the old curtains. Now my window had just a plain blockout roller blind that would do the job until I could style things up a little. Now I had the hang of that word – *styling* – I figured it was one I'd be using a lot.

Using my new power tool, I removed the old curtain rails, filled the holes with the goopy stuff, and sanded them until they were smooth. Then I stood back and gave myself a high-five in congratulation, turned my music up, and opened my first tin of paint.

By the end of Saturday I had two coats of soft grey on the walls, another coat on me, and some ideas to decorate the bed specifically and the room in general. I was also physically incapable of doing much more than collapsing into a hot bath with a book and a very large glass of red wine.

Before leaving the pub on Friday night, I'd arranged to meet Suse for coffee on Sunday after she'd been for her run. She arrived late, in a bad mood, and with both kids in tow. Georgia had bright pink cheeks and an attitude to match her mother's, and Toby had been promised cake and wasn't going to rest until he got it.

'Mummy, no!' He slammed a half-chewed sandwich onto the table, mashing the white-bread slobbery mess into the timber.

'Come on, Toby, you like Vegemite,' urged Suse as she retrieved Georgia's dummy from the folds of the blankets in her pram.

'No, no, no! That!' Toby pointed to the cupcakes on the front counter.

'I'm not giving in to him,' Suse declared with forced conviction. 'Why Richard had to go into work today . . .' She sighed. 'He knew I was meeting you.'

'It's okay,' I soothed. 'It obviously couldn't be helped.'

'No, Em, it's not okay. He hardly spends any time with the kids, and I hardly spend any time without them.' She covered her mouth in horror. 'I can't believe I just said that! Toby, sweetie, if you want a cupcake you can have one – which colour do you want?'

I kept an eye on Georgia, who had stopped crying and was now gurgling happily in her pram, while Suse arranged a cake for Toby. 'Are you sure you want pink? What about this nice blue one? No? Okay, the pink one it is.'

Once Suse had Toby back in his seat and occupied with his pink cupcake, the two of us settled in for a chat.

She broke off a piece of muffin and nibbled at it. 'Are you sure you don't want any of this?'

'Thanks, no.'

She shrugged. 'Suit yourself. What are the plans for this morning? We're in Gertrude Street, so I'm guessing some vintage shopping? I reckon I've got about two hours max with the kids.'

Toby was making patterns in the icing with his fingers – the sugar rush hadn't yet hit his little brain.

'Actually, I'm interested in checking out the design shop across the road – I'm after some cushions and bed linen for my bed, and maybe a big print to hang on the wall. And there's a furniture store in Smith Street that I might wander through.'

She stopped nibbling. 'You? Design stores? Really?'

'Yeah, now that I can see my bedroom floor, I can see it needs updating. How can I expect a man to be comfortable in there if it's not a place I want to spend any time in?'

'Fair enough. Next you'll be out there buying power tools and paintbrushes.'

I laughed, but didn't tell her the truth. For some

reason, I wanted to keep this little project as my secret for as long as possible. And a project it was. I'd mapped out what needed to be done and had set myself a rough timeline, dividing the tasks into Phase One and Phase Two delivery. In my bag was a list with all the items that need to be purchased or ordered now, and those that could wait. Besides, Suse didn't seem to be really interested in my decorating – she had other things on her mind.

'Are you seeing Jamie tonight?' she asked, concentrating on picking out the pink sugar that had found its way into Toby's hair.

'No. He texted this morning. Apparently he has to help a friend move . . . or something.'

'Maybe it's for the best. After all, if you're looking to change jobs, you're not going to want to start something serious, are you?'

'I don't know that I am going to change jobs yet. I still haven't got a confirmed date for an interview at DotPoint. The CEO is back from somewhere or another next week, so it might be then.'

'Will you take it if they offer?'

I laughed. 'I think it's highly unlikely they'll offer.'

'I'm sure I had wipes in here somewhere.' Suse was rifling through the bag hanging over the back of the pram. 'Em, do you think Richard and I are well suited?'

'I've never thought about it,' I said, avoiding answering the question.

'Of course you have. You and Booth – you had to have talked about it. You were both surprised when we got engaged.'

Wipes located, she set about removing the icing from Toby's face and hair.

'Yes,' I admitted, 'we were surprised. Richard was very different to the other guys you'd been out with. For a start, he kept his dick in his pants and didn't try to come on to me.'

She didn't laugh.

I continued with my list. 'He's good-looking, he's got a great job, he's a good father, he's stable –'

'Don't you mean boring?' she interrupted.

'I didn't say that. After the guys you'd been out with, you needed stability – someone who would support you, understand how important your career is, and still be there when you need him. Richard adores the ground you walk on . . . he's perfect for you.'

'Why do I feel like the magic has gone then?'

'Because that's what happens in relationships – or so I've been told.' I gave a short laugh.

'Is that why you choose the guys you do? Because it's the magic that turns you on, and the real life that scares you?'

'Maybe. Maybe it's just that I've never met anyone who I still want to be with once the fairy dust has blown off. That's who I'm looking for – someone I can love after the goosebumps have settled. Richard is a good man – and he loves you to pieces.'

'I know he does, which makes the way I'm feeling so much harder. I'm so ungrateful. Here I am with a man who adores me, two great kids – well, except for when they're teething, or having tantrums – a beautiful house, a senior job, and a closet full of designer brands, and what am I doing? Bitching about being bored.' She grimaced, 'I'm tired, it was a tough run this morning, and I'm annoyed because I was looking forward to a girls' day out, and instead I have about an hour before the tantrums start. Speaking of which, let's go shopping.

Suse had estimated her available time almost to the minute. By then I'd purchased some new bed linen, a soft grey wool throw, a selection of cushions in shades of turquoise, white, jazz green and bamboo designs, and a large art print to hang over the bed.

We were deciding on some lamps for the bedside tables when a text came through on Suse's phone. She cursed and dropped it in the pram, waking up Georgia, who began grizzling as she tried to decide whether or not she was hungry or just missing her dummy.

'Is everything okay?' I asked.

'Yes, fine. Richard's just messaged to let me know he'll be later than planned.'

'Oh. Did you have somewhere you were going after here?'

Suse found the dummy and popped it in Georgia's

mouth. 'Not really, I'd just promised another friend that I'd drop around later if I could. One of the girls I'm going away with. We want to plan something special for Trace in Daylesford next weekend.'

'Trace?'

'I mean Tanya. God, these kids have scrambled my brain.'

It was at that point that Georgia decided she definitely was hungry, and Toby's sugar rush crashed into a tantrum of stellar proportions. Suse hurriedly kissed me goodbye, cursed Richard and his work again, and bundled the kids out of the shop.

Left to my own devices, I deposited my purchases in the boot of my car, then wandered around the corner and down into Collingwood to the furniture store, before returning home with some lights for the bedside tables. The tables themselves, and a comfy armchair, would be delivered later that afternoon. I also had photos and measurements of furniture that I was pretty sure I'd be ordering for the living room.

I spent the rest of Sunday 'dressing' my room — yes, I was aware that I'd probably watched way too much renovation TV — and was thrilled with the result. I'd found some ready-made curtains in a colour similar to the heathery plummy colour I'd be using for the dining space, and had even managed to hang them. The floor still needed doing, but my bedroom looked like it could be in a magazine.

Before putting the power tool back in its box, I took down the dreaded gauzy curtains in the kitchen, and applied a couple of coats of the soft grey. It was after 10 pm by the time I'd finished and cleaned up – too late to call out for takeaway. Instead I made myself a cheese toastie, poured a glass of wine, and took myself off to my new sheets to do star jumps in the super high thread-count.

I could now add ticks against a few items on my bucket list.

1. *Walk a very long way.* I was walking most nights after work, so I was getting there slowly. Half-tick.

3. *Learn how to use a power tool.* Tick.

4. *Declutter my apartment and renovate using at least one power tool.* Tick to the declutter part and half-tick to the renovation.

6. *Cook at least one meal for my friends using fresh ingredients, saucepans and matching cutlery.* Tick.

7c. *Have phone sex.* Tick.

8. *Fall in love properly with someone who'll love me back.* Was this a tick? I had no idea.

I sent a quick text to Jamie. He didn't reply.

9. *Resign my job.* I'd accidentally applied for a job . . . possibly a quarter-tick?

As I sipped my wine, I looked around at my handiwork again. Not bad. This renovation lark was much easier than it was made out to be. Maybe Booth and I could apply to go on one of those shows instead of a cooking one? I made a mental note to suggest it to him, switched off the light and collapsed into the sleep of the completely exhausted.

CHAPTER TWENTY

On Monday, as I raced around the office from meeting to meeting, I changed my mind – this renovation lark was physically exhausting. In fact, I was using the word *racing* loosely. I felt almost as bad as I had after the run. Actually, I felt worse. Not only was I hobbling, but every single muscle in my back, arms, wrists and fingers – and a heap of muscles that lived below those muscles – were screaming for release, or at least a massage. Where was Jamie when I needed him? The only difference between running and painting, as far as I could tell, was the absence of blisters – on my feet. I was sure I had them on my hands – or would have if it didn't hurt so much to unclench my roller grip.

I grimaced as I lowered myself into a chair at lunch. Booth and Jamie looked at each other and laughed.

'Did you go for another run on the weekend and not tell me?' asked Booth, trying his best to look concerned and failing dismally.

'No, I already said that nothing could ever, ever get me out there again.'

'So what's with the hobbling then?'

'I've just been doing a little work around the house.'

'More than a little, I'd say, looking at you.' Jamie winked and smiled widely at me.

Yes, he was definitely into me – so why had he cancelled again?

'Speaking of running,' Booth turned to Jamie, 'where were you yesterday morning?'

He grinned. 'I overslept. I helped a mate move on Saturday afternoon, and stayed for a few beers and ended up crashing at his place. My body felt like it'd been hit by a truck. I expected it probably would so I didn't make any other plans for the weekend.'

Oh. He was telling me why he hadn't called. A smile spread across my face. Booth kicked me under the table.

'You and Suse missed a tough run,' he told Jamie. 'I was pretty spent at the end of it.'

'Suse?' I was confused. 'But I thought . . .'

I didn't know what I thought. She'd said she'd had a tough run – I'd just assumed it was with the group. Booth looked questioningly at me.

I shook my head. 'Nothing, my mistake. Are you guys in that kick-off meeting this afternoon?'

'Yes.' Booth glanced at his watch. 'Speaking of which, I need to finish some slides that Marcus wants to include in the presentation. I'd better get back to it.

Jamie, are you coming?'

He was speaking to Jamie, but he looked at me.

'No, I'll keep Em company while she finishes her lunch,' Jamie said. 'I'll see you back there.'

'Sure. Em?'

'See you, Booth.' I waited until he'd gone before saying what I needed to say. 'Look, it's okay if you want to call a stop to this . . . whatever this is.'

'What do you mean?'

'This thing . . . us . . . the cancellations . . . it's okay.'

Instead of answering, he leaned over and kissed me softly on the lips. 'Does that feel like I'm not interested?' He sat back in his chair and, still holding my hand, studied my face.

'No, I guess not. Then why haven't we managed to catch up? Even for a drink?'

'Weekends have been tough recently – things have come up at the last minute that I haven't been able to get out of. I wanted to see you, but it just hasn't worked. Okay?'

His thumb idly stroked the back of my hand and my stiff muscles began to soften.

'Okay.' I smiled back at him. 'Maybe this weekend?' It was a three-day weekend.

His eyes didn't leave mine. 'Sorry, babe, I'm away. It's a bucks' weekend for a mate – we're heading out on Friday night. But after that things should be getting back to normal. Then I'll be all yours.'

There was something else I wanted to ask him, but he leaned forward and kissed me again . . . and nope, it was gone.

'We'd better get back,' he said, and let go of my hand.

Jodie Lawrence from DotPoint emailed on Tuesday to set up an interview for next week. I phoned Suse immediately to tell her. She didn't sound as interested as I'd expected.

'They don't seem very organised,' she commented. 'It's taken a while to get to this stage.'

'The CEO's been overseas. Anyway, I was the one who cancelled originally.'

'Hmmmm, maybe.'

'Should I go?'

'Do you want to go?'

'Well, I guess. I don't know what's happening with Jamie and me, so I should go, I suppose. Even if it comes to nothing it'll be good practice . . . right?'

'Maybe.'

I pictured her reading through emails or texts, balancing her phone between her chin and her shoulder – she certainly didn't sound like she was listening to me.

'Suse!'

'Go, don't go . . . just make your mind up.'

'It's just that I'm not sure this is the best time to such a big change.'

'It's an interview for a job that you're unlikely to get. No one's asking you to make a decision yet.'

There wasn't anything I could say to that.

'You're the one who said you didn't stand a chance,' she added.

'Yeah, but you didn't have to tell it like it is.'

I heard her sigh. 'You're right. Sorry, darl . . . I'm in the middle of something – I've got a shitload of work to get through before I head out on Friday. Daylesford, remember?' I'd forgotten. 'Go along to the interview – you've got nothing to lose. Just don't make your decision on the basis of whatever might or might not happen between you and Jamie. I'll call you when I'm back.'

Mum had much the same advice when I told her on Thursday night, although she was more supportive than Suse had been.

'Don't sell yourself short, love,' she said. 'They wouldn't want to talk to you if they didn't think you were capable.'

'But what if they offer it to me?'

'Deal with that when it happens. What does Josh have to say about it?'

I turned away from the computer screen.

'You haven't told him, have you?'

I shook my head. 'I don't want him to rain on my parade before I've decided what I'm going to do next. You know what he's like – he has this idea of how things should be, and there's no arguing with him.'

'I see,' she said, although I didn't think that she did. 'Why don't you go along for the interview. Even if nothing comes of it, the practice will be good. The fact that you applied for the job –'

'It was accidental,' I reminded her.

'The fact that you accidentally applied for the job means you're ready for a change. Why not take a break and come up here? It'll give you space to think about what you want to do next. Ask Josh to come too – we'd love to see him.'

'I'll think about it. I'd need to organise vaccinations and currency though, and travel insurance.'

'Just be spontaneous – how hard can it all be?' Mum waved her hands around as she said it.

'It's just that things are sensitive right now with Jamie. What if he finds someone else while I'm away?'

'If that's the case, he doesn't deserve you.'

Speaking of Booth, he'd been uncharacteristically quiet, which was dangerous. His moods were normally like a Melbourne day – changeable. It was an attention-span thing. His temper was quick, but his really bad moods festered. And when he finally blew, it was an eruption.

We were supposed to have lunch on Wednesday. Just us – his words – so we could talk. But then Jamie suggested we take our lunch to the park – not that we did much eating. I made a mental note to pop that skirt into the dry cleaners. I'd texted Booth and given him some excuse about being too busy.

His mood finally blew on Friday afternoon at the project meeting. We were at the pointy end of the implementation now, so it was all about the detail.

'I don't want to hear what you can't do,' he said. 'I don't want to hear the word no. What I need from you are solutions.'

Patrick, the manager of the support team, spoke up. 'If you'd asked me, I could have told you this wouldn't work. That type of network card is unstable in those servers. We saw a similar incident in Singapore last year. I wouldn't have expected you to know about that, but if you'd asked me what the risks were –'

'If I'd asked you?' Booth's voice was dangerously quiet.

I closed my eyes briefly in expectation of his outburst. Patrick, however, was smiling in what he'd soon find out was misguided triumph.

'Yes,' he said. 'I've had plenty of experience in these issues.'

Booth nodded slowly. Here it came.

'So,' he started, 'if you have so much experience in these issues, why didn't you highlight it as a risk in the project meetings, and why didn't you fix it when you first saw it happening again? No,' he held up a finger, 'why didn't you fix it properly on each of those other times it occurred? Or does it make you feel special and important to be the only one in the room with the information?'

Despite his anger, Booth's voice still hadn't risen, which was way scarier than if he'd flown into a rage. Patrick slunk back into his chair.

'For the rest of you – what's in here,' Booth tapped his head, 'doesn't mean a thing. Don't go thinking that if the axe falls you'll be any safer just because you think you know something someone else doesn't. I don't give a flying fuck how important you think you are, or how much experience you think you've had. Here, in this room, we volunteer information – we don't *wait* to be asked.' He stared straight at Patrick. 'If you can't do that, go play on another team – I don't want you.'

He paused and looked around the room before continuing. 'In future, I want every issue logged, and the root cause and solution updated *before* it's closed off. I want a report on all open issues at this meeting every fortnight. Emily, how's that automated tracking system going?'

'We still need to enter the users and test the workflow. I put it down the priority list in order to get the release out.'

He looked at the ceiling briefly, as if searching for something. Divine intervention? Someone to save him from the curse of incompetent staff?

'Isn't your team capable of doing more than one thing at a time?' he asked me. 'Do you have to spoon-feed them? Or are you going to tell me that you've dropped the ball too?'

I counted to ten before replying. 'Josh, I'd remind you that at our last meeting you stressed that everything else could be delayed in order to get the release completed by the original date – despite the addition of those last-minute requirements. That's being packaged up as we speak, so once it's complete, the team can get the finishing touches done on your tracking system.'

We locked eyes, and he was the first to look away.

'Fine,' he said. 'See that it's done. And that release had better be fucking perfect when it hits the testing platform.'

He left the room and the rest of us let out the breaths we'd been holding in. Monica, one of the specialists on Booth's team, approached me as I bundled up my notes.

'I know you're busy, but do you have any idea what's got Josh in this mood?' she asked.

'Is he in a mood? I hadn't noticed.' Of course I'd noticed.

'He's never this bad-tempered for this long – he's been in a shit of a mood most of the week.'

'Patrick deserved what he got today,' I said. 'It's not the first time he's taken that attitude – I think he's still dirty at being overlooked for the IT director's role.'

'I didn't know he'd applied for it.'

'He didn't. He was waiting for someone to ask him to apply, and then got shitty because no one did.'

Monica laughed.

'Besides, Josh is right,' I added. 'That issue should have been fixed a long time ago – that server outage could have cost us a lot in penalties. Patrick's been allowed to ride in on his white horse and save the day on too many occasions. He loves being held up as the saviour, but if he'd done his job when the issue first raised its ugly, pus-filled head, he wouldn't need to be a hero.'

'I know,' she acknowledged. 'But you get what I'm saying?'

'Yes, I know. I think he's just under the pump from management on a few different fronts. Besides, it's Friday and it's a long weekend. Let's see how he is on Tuesday after a decent break.'

'You're probably right, Em. I'll leave you to it.'

Monica was right to be concerned- Booth wasn't normally able to hold onto a bad mood for this long. On the way back to my work station, I made a detour to the hallowed halls of the management floor, and popped my head around Booth's office door. 'Hey.'

'Hey yourself. What brings you up here?'

'I was just passing and thought I'd drop in.'

'Passing from where?'

'Okay, I don't come up here often,' I conceded. 'Maybe I just wanted to see your smiling face.'

He didn't smile. 'I'd have thought you had better things to be doing – like checking that release again?'

'That's all under control, my friend.' I plonked myself into a chair.

'Pleased to hear it. So, to what do I owe this honour?'

I jumped straight in. 'Are you okay?'

'Yeah, all good, just busy,' he said, concentrating on whatever was on his laptop screen.

'Really? If I didn't know better I'd think you were upset with me.'

I attempted a half-laugh while I waited for him to tell me that I was being ridiculous – of course he wasn't upset with me. He shrugged and continued to work.

I tried again. 'Booth . . . your temper is shocking, your tolerance is non-existent, and you've been ignoring me all week. I haven't spoken to you properly since the pub on Friday night – and you only stayed for one drink.'

He didn't look up. 'I had somewhere I needed to be. Besides, I figured you would have too – somewhere else you needed to be.'

'No, nowhere else.'

'I tried to see you on Wednesday, but you obviously had a better offer.'

He'd got me there. I countered with, 'I called you on Saturday and you didn't pick up.'

'I was busy.'

'With Corinna?'

He smiled. 'Yes, with Corinna.'

'It's about time. Is it going well?'

'So far.'

'You haven't said.' Normally we'd talk about this kind of stuff.

'You've been . . . occupied.'

'What's this about, Josh? This mood?'

He sighed and closed the laptop. 'You're not going to go away, are you?'

I shook my head.

'What's it about? It's about you and Jamie. I don't know what's going on between you two, but it needs to be toned down in the office.'

What the fuck? 'You know about us?' I thought we'd been playing it cool.

'Em – I'm not stupid.'

'We haven't done anything in the office,' I protested.

As long as your definition of office was limited to . . . well, my office, which wasn't really an office, rather a partition. It still made me tingle thinking about this morning in the fire escape – Jamie's hand over my breast, his thumb playing with the nipple through my silk shirt as his tongue duelled with mine, his hardness pressed into me, both of us stopping too soon and panting for release.

Booth watched it all play across my face. 'Really?'

'Sure there was an incident in the fire stairs, and in the photocopy room . . . and in the car park . . . but no one saw us. I'm almost positive.'

'I saw you coming out of the fire exit this morning,' he said. 'It didn't look like there was any legitimate fire drilling going on. As for the car park? I have five words to say to you – Marcus and Diane, security cameras.'

I shrugged.

'All I'm saying is that it's starting to affect your work, and if you stuff up because you're thinking with your . . . well, if you're not thinking clearly, I can't support you. He's more senior than you, so if it doesn't end well, it's not going to end well for you – if you know what I mean.'

'That's unfair, Booth. Nothing has slipped.'

'What about that tracking fuck-up? I wouldn't normally need to remind you about that.'

For the second time today I counted to ten. 'You and I both know that's a bad example.'

He paused for a second. 'Perhaps. But you know what I'm saying.'

I shook my head. 'Actually, no, I don't.'

'Maybe not yet, but can you look me in the eye and tell me that you're not distracted? That's cool if you are – hell, you need to have some fun – but only as long as you stay focused on the job as well. Instead you're fucking around waiting for him to call or message or whatever it is that's going on. That's not like you.'

'I'm a big girl, Booth – all growed up, you know.' I smiled to try and bring some levity to the conversation.

'If that's the case, why did you lie to me the other

night? You've never done that before.'

I looked away. 'I thought you'd guessed.'

'And Wednesday? He called, so you blew me off.'

'It wasn't like that,' I said, attempting to justify the unjustifiable.

'Em, how long have I known you? You've never lied to me before – about anything. Not even those it-doesn't-matter lies that you tell other people when you're trying to be nice.'

'I know . . . it's just that Jamie . . . well, Jamie suggested it was probably best if we didn't talk too much about it until we'd managed to at least get out on a date. He said he was worried about how you and Suse would be because of the running thing.'

He nodded slowly. 'Fair enough. I'm just concerned about you. It's not like you to do what you're doing – the fire exits and stationery room. You don't take those kinds of risks. Please tell me you haven't shagged in the boardroom?'

Did he know about that kiss? A shiver ran through me at that particular memory.

'God, no, Em!'

'Calm down. We haven't shagged anywhere – not yet. Not that it's any of your business.'

He acknowledged the dig with a wry half-smile. 'You know I adore you, but I think you're out of your league with Jamie.'

'I thought he was your friend?'

'He is. He's a great guy, but I don't think I want my best friend to be his girlfriend. He's not looking for anything serious – and this time I think you might be.'

'I really like him. He makes me feel like, wow, I can't describe it. That vibe I felt that first day – it's still there. I can't stop thinking about him, and I can't stay away from him. I know we're taking risks, but I can't help it. It's like he's bewitched me.'

He watched me for a few seconds, then asked, 'Are you in love with him?'

'I don't know. Maybe. I can't think straight when I'm with him, but we really haven't had a chance to get to know each other. We haven't even been on a date yet, and I want him more because of that.' Booth's mouth turned up in a half-smile. 'I know, don't say I told you so. It's all a little too unreal – kissing in corners and sneaking around.'

He nodded slowly. 'Okay. Promise me you'll talk to me if things get out of control.'

My confusion must have shown on my face.

'I don't mean anything by it,' he clarified. 'Just that I care about you and don't want you to get hurt.'

My eyes began to prickle.

He saw it. 'Hey, none of that. See, this is what happens when we start talking soppy shit. Now, get your arse out of my office. It's nearly beer o'clock, and I can't be late at the pub because –'

'I know, you have a date afterwards.'

'I sure do. Hey, speaking of the pub, what's going on with Suse?'

'I think it's the five-year itch . . . or something. She's busy at work, Richard's away a lot and she's feeling neglected. She's off to Daylesford tonight, so will probably come back all refreshed and loving her life again.'

He considered this. 'Maybe. Who did you say she's going with?'

'Some girls from work – we don't know them. As long as it does her some good.'

'Maybe she just needs to buy some sexy underwear and quit whingeing.'

'Don't you think that's a little harsh?'

'No, actually, I don't. I think she's lucky to have found someone who loves her as much as Richard does, and it's about time she grew up and realised that.'

I looked hard at him. 'Wow, Booth.'

He shrugged. 'Just calling it as I see it. Now, get your arse out of here so we can have a drink after work.'

'Before your date.'

'Yep, Corinna is about to get very lucky . . . again.'

'Okay, that's my cue to leave.'

CHAPTER TWENTY-ONE

With Suse in Daylesford, Booth staying for just one drink, and Jamie away on that bucks' weekend, I had a quiet Friday night in. That was okay – I got an early start on my long-weekend to-do list and got the first coat of paint on the spare room and living room.

By midday Sunday I'd finished painting, and had all of my cupboard doors off their hinges. I removed the existing knobs, sanded the surfaces lightly, and primed them all with some one-coat wonder product. When that had dried I'd cover the lime green with something called Wild Plum, which should work in beautifully with the soft greys and heather tones I now had through the sitting area. Thankfully the kitchen benches had been redone in neutral shades before I bought the apartment – after all, what went with lime green?

I couldn't justify the cost of a new kitchen, but Guy, the guy at the hardware store —yes, that was his real name – had given me instructions on how to redo the doors, and had tried talking me into attempting to transform the splashback tiles too. I'd decided to wait and see how the cupboard experiment worked out first. Guy had quickly become one of my favourite people. I'd turn up with a new paint chart and a new request for help, and he'd stop what he was doing and answer my questions. And it wasn't just because I flicked my hair and showed my cleavage – I didn't even need to do that any more.

He'd commented on that yesterday morning. 'The first time you came in, you almost seemed embarrassed to be here. You had make-up on and, although they might have been old, your clothes were clean. Now you come with no make-up and dressed in the remains of last week's paint job. You've caught the bug.'

I'd protested of course, but he was right. It wasn't the hair-flicking or cleavage that had prompted Guy to help me – although I was sure that had helped – it was the fact that I really wanted to learn, and I kept coming back. I did have the bug.

By early afternoon, I was waiting for the first coat of paint to dry on the cupboards when my doorbell rang. I turned my music down, put down the paintbrushes I'd been using as drumsticks, and checked the intercom. It was Booth so I buzzed him up.

He eyed my paint-spattered attire with surprise, and pushed past me to gaze around the living room.

'What the fuck?' He turned to me. 'Did you do this?'

'Yep,' I said proudly.

'Shit, Em, this looks great.' He sounded surprised. 'Is that couch new? And the TV stand?'

'Yep. I still have some work to do in here – there's a huge print that I want for the dining-space wall. I'll go pick it up tomorrow – it's in that design shop in Church Street.'

'This looks like you've been in a room reveal.' He laughed. 'Nothing matches, but it sort of does.'

'That's the point. You should see my bedroom – I've finished styling that.'

He raised his eyebrows at my 'styling' comment. 'Is that an invitation?'

'Oh, ha flipping ha. Just go and have a look.'

He did. 'This is incredible. It looks . . . it looks just like a bought one. And you did it yourself?'

'Yep.'

'Even the curtains?'

'They're ready-made, but yes, I hung them – with the help of a power tool.'

He laughed. 'A different type of power tool than the one I expected you to be using.' He shook his head slowly as he took it all in. 'It's a completely different apartment . . . And look at you, you're getting muscles.'

He squeezed my developing biceps through the threadbare T-shirt I was wearing, then wandered into the spare room and opened the cupboard doors. 'What's happened to all the crap?'

'I had a clean-out. I threw some, I sold some, I

donated some.'

I stopped talking because he wasn't listening.

'Wow, Em . . . just wow.' He turned back to me and said it again. 'Wow.'

'I told you I was doing some renovating.'

'Yeah, but I thought you meant you were decluttering, throwing a few old clothes out, not that you were . . . Wow.'

'So you like it?'

'How did you know how to do it?'

'The guy in the hardware store – Guy is his name – took pity on me and gave me such good instructions that I couldn't go wrong. I bought some magazines, I looked in some design shops, and I've been doing a little bit every weekend.'

'I just assumed you were out with Jamie.'

'No. I told you yesterday that we haven't got that far yet.'

'I feel pretty bad that I haven't been asking about your weekends.'

'It's okay, I know you're in a new thing too. And then there's the running.'

'Still, it's no excuse. I've been a crap friend.' He grabbed me for a hug. 'I'm proud of you. This is incredible . . . and you did it yourself?'

His arms felt warm and comfortable, so I burrowed in for a few seconds before pulling back with an embarrassed laugh. 'There was no point waiting for someone to do it for me. What brings you here anyway?'

'I thought you might want to come out for a coffee or late lunch or something – just the two of us, like we used to do. Things just don't seem the same lately.'

That tension between the three of us that I'd been feeling wasn't just in my imagination.

I smiled at him. 'I can't put another coat on the kitchen cupboards for another couple of hours, so if you want to spend some time together, I know exactly where we can go.'

'Sure, but before we go I need to test out the sofa.'

'What for?'

'To see if it's comfy enough for me to sleep on.'

'There's room for you in the spare room now.'

'Your room looks comfortable.'

He grinned at me. I thumped him.

'Do people really buy these things?' Booth asked. The aisles we were pushing our trolley through contained nothing but cardboard boxes of varying shapes and sizes. 'None of this is put together.'

'That's the point. They keep the price low by keeping it flat-packed – it doesn't cost as much for them to store or transport. Take this table,' I indicated an outdoor setting, 'it would cost double to buy it pre-made.'

'But it would be already made.'

'True, but where's the challenge in that?'

He looked hard at me. 'Isn't that my line?'

I laughed, and checked out the people in the queue in front of us. We were in flat-pack heaven – or hell, depending on your attitude. My trolley was filled with a variety of photo frames, cushions in colours I never would have considered just a few months ago, woollen throws, and two bookcases that I intended wrestling with later this afternoon.

The girls in front of us had two trolleys loaded up with long flat boxes.

Booth studied the contents. 'Are they going to be drawers?'

'It looks like it.'

He raised both brows in a look of silent respect. 'What about that one? Is that going to be a chair?'

'I'd say so.'

'They have two trolleys full of this shit,' he observed, bemusement written all over his face.

'They do.'

He shook his head in disbelief. 'Man, are they going to be in a world of fucked-up mess tonight.'

I couldn't help giggling.

Back at my place, he helped me carry my purchases inside.

'Are you going to put these together now?' he asked.

'I was going to give it a go. Do you want to help?

There'll be dinner in it for you afterwards.' I saw his expression change and clapped my hand to my mouth. 'I'm sorry, I forgot – you probably already have plans. It's okay – I got carried away.'

'No, I don't have any plans, but I thought you would.' He rummaged through my kitchen drawers for a knife to open the boxes. 'You've even cleaned these drawers out.'

'Jamie, you mean? No, he's away – a bucks' weekend.'

He'd phoned last night to tell me he was thinking about me, and texted this morning with the same message. It had made me feel warm all over.

Booth appeared thoughtful. 'Do you know where?'

'He didn't say. Somewhere in the country, I think. I did ask, but he distracted me.' I felt my cheeks go warm.

Booth looked as if he was about to say more, and changed his mind. 'I tell you what, we'll have a go at these together, and then grab some takeaway and have a few drinks. We haven't done that, just us, for ages.'

'No, we haven't. Not since before Craig.'

'That is, unless you're cooking now as well?' He opened my fridge. 'Shit, there's real food in here as well as wine . . . Oh good, and some beer.' He closed the fridge and looked closely at me. 'Next you'll be telling me that you've secretly signed up for the half-marathon and intend surprising us at the start line.' He raised his eyebrows. 'Well?'

I blushed – he wasn't too far from the truth – and ducked my head so my hair hid my face. 'That's a big no to the half-marathon, but I have been walking during the week, and I have mucked around with a few simple things on the stove.'

'Any particular reason?' he asked, his head still buried in my cupboards.

'Hello? Remember my bucket list? The house stuff started because I had to find room for the platters we used for the dinner. Then when everything was where it needed to be, I could see the wall, so I painted it. Then I needed inspiration so I bought some magazines and cooked a few simple things. It might sound strange, but I really enjoyed preparing the meal that night with you.'

He lifted his head and returned my smile. 'Yeah, me too. It was fun.'

'It might have been accidental when I started, but the work has helped me get through the Craig thing, and it's kept me busy instead of waiting endlessly for Jamie to ring. And I love the result.'

I thought I saw a strange look flash across his face at the mention of Jamie, but he quickly recovered. 'You're looking good with it too. Muscles, power tools – you're turning into Wonder Woman. You've got the hair and the shape for it. Pretty tough to resist.' He eyed me up and down and flashed that cheeky grin. 'Are you sure you don't have some sort of golden lasso or handcuffs hidden away?'

'Puh-leese.' I flicked a tea towel at him. 'You'd like that, wouldn't you?'

He leered. 'I've gotta say, it sounds pretty hot.'

'Grab your allen key, sweetheart, you have some building to do. Come and flex those muscles of yours in this direction . . . Oh, that's right, you run instead of lift. I guess I'll need to provide the power this time round.'

Two hours and two beers each later, we had two (relatively stable) bookcases built. In between building, I'd managed a second coat of paint on the cupboard doors. Guy was right – they'd come up a treat. Booth and I sat on the floor of my living room with the remnants of flat-pack packaging around us, and fresh beers beside us.

'Well, that was more painful than it should have been.' Booth collapsed back against the sofa.

'Only because you refused to read the instructions.' I took a mouthful of beer.

'And when you did open the instructions, we had it up the wrong way.'

'You could have helped.'

'I was doing fine without them.'

I leaned back against the sofa next to him and we contemplated our handiwork.

'You know, I read something only the other day about how IKEA is killing sex lives,' Booth commented.

'Really? Because of the arguments over flat-pack

construction?'

'Possibly. Can you imagine the night those poor buggers in the queue in front of us are having?'

I laughed.

'No,' he added, 'it's because of the squeaking. Would you want to shag on a bed made of this crap that makes more noise than you do? And is in danger of falling apart?'

He had a point. 'I guess not. But they're usually put together pretty well.'

'Maybe. What do you reckon these screws are supposed to hold up?' He displayed five leftover screws for my attention.

'I neither know nor care, sweetheart – but I am hungry.'

'Hmmm, me too.' He raised the bottle to his mouth.

'It looks like rain,' I said. 'And it's cold out there.'

'So you're suggesting I go out for food? I can't drive.' He indicated the empties.

'After all that painting, I need a shower –'

'Yeah, you do.' He pretended to sniff the air, earning himself a thump. 'Ouch,' he rubbed at his bicep, 'you want to watch that right hook. You don't know your own strength any more.'

I giggled. 'I'll call up to order, and can you walk around to collect it? I can clean up here while you're gone.'

CHAPTER TWENTY-TWO

I disposed of the flat-pack boxes, the empty bottles and the leftover screws, and cleaned away my painting kit. The doors should be dry enough in the morning to hang, but for now I stepped around them on the kitchen floor. I changed in the laundry, leaving my painting clothes on the floor, and did the nudey run to the bathroom, grabbing a clean set of underwear from my bedroom on the way through.

At some point during my shower, Booth knocked on the door to let me know it was him who had entered the apartment, and not some knife-wielding intruder.

'I'm hungry – get your arse out of there,' he called.

I'd forgotten to bring in fresh clothes, so did the undie run between bathroom and bedroom, surprising Booth, who was rifling through my linen cupboard looking for placemats. We stopped and stared at each other for a few long seconds, him staring at my body and me staring at him staring at my body, but neither of us saying anything.

I recovered first, smiled, shrugged, and made for

the shelter of my bedroom. Honestly, Booth had seen me in swimmers before – this was no different. Except for the fact that the swimmers in question had covered a lot more of me than my lacy bra and pants did. Besides, this was my house – he was lucky I'd even remembered to take a bra and knickers into the bathroom with me.

The way he'd stared at me reminded me of how he'd looked at me after our run. I realised I enjoyed it, and my body had definitely responded positively – some parts more than others. I shook my head to dislodge the thought from my brain. This was Booth, for God's sake. Of course he was going to look at me like that – he was a red-blooded man, and I was half-dressed. That equation was always going to give the same answer. And I'd be insulted if he didn't notice, so there was no need for me to get ridiculous about it. As for my reaction – well, that could be explained by the weeks of waiting for Jamie. That was all. Nothing more to see here.

By the time I was fully dressed, all girlie bits safely hidden under layers of rugby jumper and old trackpants, I'd managed to convince myself that I'd imagined anything in his eyes that might have hinted at anything like *a moment* between us.

Booth had helped himself to another beer and poured me a glass of wine. He'd also set the table – with matching plates – popped the takeaway into bowls for serving purposes, and even found some tea lights and matches.

'Candles? Seriously?'

'Why not? It's been such a long time since we've done this, I figured we'd make it an occasion. We can celebrate your new bookcases and . . .' he looked around for inspiration, 'all your hard work, your new muscles, and the picture you're buying tomorrow for this wall.'

We clinked glasses to that, and the football on the telly provided a comfortable soundtrack to our Thai takeaway and banter. After dinner had been cleared away, we pulled out Dad's milk crate and my turntable (now permanently in the corner of the living room), and played music – laughing, singing and reminiscing. Actually, most of the laughing was from Booth at my bad singing and dancing.

'Oh my God, you really have this?'

'Don't make fun of Wax, my friend. This is a classic.'

'Oh, Em, we have to have this one next – it's from *Ferris Bueller*, and was playing the first time I had sex.' He held up Yello's 'Oh Yeah'. 'And you have the twelve-inch version – I reckon the song will last longer than I did! Just so you know, my game's improved since then.'

'I should hope so.'

We looked at each other and giggled, before singing together, 'Dum dum . . . chicka chicka!'

We bored quickly of Yello.

'Your turn,' he said.

'This one.' I pulled out The Waterboys' 'The

Whole of the Moon'. 'It was playing when I was standing on a balcony one New Year's Eve kissing a muso. I remember he asked me back to his place, and I had no idea that he was asking me back for sex. I was so innocent still.' I smiled as I remembered. 'The next morning I found one of my shoes in a bowl of prawns. I still have no idea how that happened.'

'The story of your life,' he said, grinning. 'What was playing when you first did it?'

'Had sex? Ummmm, let's see, I was twenty . . . so, it would have been . . . You know, I have no idea. I remember the guy, I remember his not-so-clean navy sheets, and I remember wondering what the fuss was about, but I don't remember the music.' I thought a little harder. 'He broke up with me by playing me The Cardigans' "Lovefool".'

'Oh, Em, that's too sad.'

Sometime much later we migrated back to the sofa, curling up on either end, nursing our drinks, the open bottle on the floor beside Booth.

'Em . . .' he started.

'Hmmm?' I replied drowsily.

'You're really serious about that bucket list, aren't you?'

I smiled, but didn't reply.

'You've started exercising –'

'I have no plans to run a marathon,' I interrupted.

'I know that. But you are exercising, and you could

do the ten-kay if you decided to walk it. That qualifies as walking a very long way. Then there's your things – you've got rid of a lot of stuff.'

'So there's room for more,' I said, smiling.

He didn't smile in return. 'No, it's more than that. It's like you're making room for . . . I don't know . . . something . . . or someone?'

I laughed, but it was an uncomfortable laugh. 'How much have you had to drink?'

'Obviously enough to start talking like a new-age therapist.' He smiled ruefully.

'Maybe, in the immortal words of Marcia Hines, I realised there was something missing . . . in my life. I've got that song somewhere here.'

'Ha ha. You've ticked off decluttering, cooking, renovations, power tools and flat-packs. You've only got something scary, casual sex, phone sex, falling in love, and leaving your job to travel the world left to do.'

'If you pull my bucket list off the fridge, you'll see there's a tick beside phone sex.'

'Did I need to know that?'

'Just saying.'

'Any other ticks you haven't told me about?'

'Well, it's unlikely I'll do the casual shagging thing – you know I can't separate sex from love. And as for leaving my job – I can't see that happening any time soon, not after what I've just spent on this place.'

'Come on, Em. You've been squirrelling away spare

cash for a rainy day ever since I've known you. You've put aside money for holidays you've never taken, and renovations that you've kept putting off. You've always been sensible with money – you'd be fine if you needed to be for a few months.'

Booth leaned across and topped up both our glasses. I was going to have one hell of a head tomorrow.

'Regarding the falling in love part,' he said, 'do you think Jamie might be the one?'

There it was again, that tinge of something . . . disapproval?

'You don't like him for me . . . do you?'

He paused and considered his wine before answering. 'No, Em, I don't. Don't ask me why, I just don't. I get that it's all so exciting, and I get that it's doing you good to have a bit of that, and a bit of risk – but I think you're in over your head.'

'That's what makes it so addictive.'

'I know that. Are you sure he's not hiding something from you? Don't get me wrong, I like the guy, but as I said before, I wouldn't want my best friend to be his girlfriend. Besides, I'll have to pick up the pieces after he's finished with you, so really this is all about me.'

'Oh.' I couldn't laugh at him or banter this one away.

'Look, I know you're not going to stop seeing him –'

'I can't stop, not until –'

'I know that. I'm just saying when – sorry, if it doesn't work out, don't feel that just because I've said this, now, tonight, that I won't be there for you.'

I nodded.

'Promise?'

I nodded again.

'Anyway,' he laughed, 'it's not like I'll remember this tomorrow morning in any case!'

I returned his smile and stretched my legs out over his. 'So, mister . . . you and Corinna, what's the story there? Usually at this stage of a relationship you spend every spare moment with whoever it is. I never see you.'

He pulled one of the new woollen throws off the back of the couch and parcelled my feet up into it. 'I'm that predictable, am I?'

'Uh huh. Usually. It's a long weekend, and instead of having sex with her, you're sitting on my couch having deep and meaningfuls with me. I did tell you there was no sex on offer, didn't I?'

'When you put it like that . . .' He pretended to leave.

'No, you don't!' I warned. 'My feet are toasty, and I'm comfortable.'

He smiled, and rubbed my feet through the blanket. 'I was over there last night. I had to chase pretty hard at the start – you were right, she played the game well. Now she's pushing too much too soon.' He screwed his nose up. 'The whole meet my friends and family shit. It's too soon for that. You know what Mum's like.'

'I do.'

Booth's parents lived in Ballarat but came to town semi-regularly, and I was often included in the family dinners when they did. Since Mum moved to Bali I'd spent the last two Christmases with Booth and his large family – he had a brother, two sisters, and what seemed like a lot of nieces and nephews – in Ballarat.

'She still asks when we're going to wake up and realise what we've been missing.'

'Really? You never told me that.'

He shrugged. 'She thinks we're perfect for each other.'

'Possibly.' The alcohol had made me philosophical. 'We might have been once, but I think we missed that window. There was a time, back when we first met, when I could have shagged you.' I contemplated that for a second. 'Wow, I'd almost forgotten that. I was sure you knew – I was almost drooling over you.'

He laughed. 'But not now?'

'Now you're Booth, my buddy. Besides, I've seen how you treat your women. They love you and you leave them. I couldn't lose you. We wouldn't be here now if we'd ever had sex.'

'I guess . . . but you and me – don't you think we'd be different? There's none of that getting-to-know-you shit and ending up disappointed – we've already done that. That's the point where we both run into trouble in our relationships, so if there was a way of skipping it, surely that would be a good thing?'

He stopped rubbing my foot while he topped my glass up again.

'Maybe. The thing is, you can't expect to look at someone you've known forever and suddenly see something different, something you haven't seen before. By then you've gone past the point where you can get goosebumps and butterflies.'

'Goosebumps and butterflies? Really? Anyway, who says you can't get that later?'

'All the songs and books. No one sings about any sort of bolt from the blue with someone you've known forever. Well, Augie March does in "One Crowded Hour", but that's different- and it doesn't have a happy ending. Remember the part about how bolts and glorified screws can't hold you together?'

'That's more about how you mistake lust at first sight for love at first sight. I always took that as being you've got a better chance with someone who hasn't hit you like a bolt from the blue. Or maybe it's that you know someone so well and suddenly it's like you're seeing them for the first time.'

'I just wonder whether the bolts and screws are leftover from something he bought at IKEA and that's why it's falling apart.'

'Oh, Em, for all your romantic talk of goosebumps

and butterflies, you crack me up.'

Our eyes met and he stopped laughing. Instead there was that same intensity I'd seen earlier. And I felt goosebumps on top of goosebumps.

To hide my confusion, I drained my wine. 'I think you'd better tell your mum that our window has passed – but it's sweet that she thinks so.'

'I'll tell her. So there was a window and I missed it?'

'Yep, you did. It was there . . . and then it was gone.' I attempted to make a sweeping, clicking movement with my fingers, but couldn't quite get them to coordinate.

'If it comes around again, be sure to tell me.'

I laughed. 'Why? Are you bored with Corinna already?'

'I wouldn't say that. It's early days yet. We're in the get-to-know-you phase now. Who knows? I might persevere a bit longer. She ticks a lot of the boxes.'

'What? Blonde. Fit. Perky ponytail?'

'Something like that.'

'It sounds like you could be changing your relationship status soon,' I joked.

'I could be,' he said, watching my face. 'How would you feel about that?'

Booth in a relationship? I should be happy for him, but . . . A flash of that look in his eyes this afternoon, and again just now, snuck into the front of my brain.

Every time Booth was in a relationship I lost him as a friend. I got that – what woman wanted another woman hanging around, getting drunk with her man, and then lying on sofas and getting wonderful foot rubs from him? That was what all this was about. It wasn't really a *moment*, it was just me reacting to the possibility of losing him again. Nothing else. I certainly wasn't jealous. I didn't do jealous.

'I'd be happy for you, of course.' I pulled my feet back and unwrapped the throw. 'Anyway, it's late, I think I'm drunk, and you're not going anywhere tonight. Do you want the couch or the spare bed?'

His smile told me he was satisfied with whatever he saw on my face, and his raised eyebrows asked a different question.

I got in first. 'Those are your only options.'

He grinned, and whatever it was that I must have imagined was gone. 'In that case, I'll take the spare bed.'

He rescued our glasses and the now empty wine bottle and took them into the kitchen. Then he leaned over me, ruffled my hair again, and kissed me gently on the forehead.

'Good night, sweetheart, sleep well.'

I smiled, patted his cheek lightly, and took his hand to pull myself up off the couch.

In bed, I checked my phone before I turned off the light. There were three messages from Jamie.

Hey there, missing you.

Hey there, wish you were here.

Hi, don't know what you're up to, but would like to be doing it with you.

I stretched a little in bed, and replied:

Now, that would have been interesting . . . if you're still around, we can discuss it . . .

His reply came back within a couple of minutes:

Sorry, babe, can't do it now, but hold that thought.

I lay there listening to Booth settling next door, and wondering what Jamie was doing that meant he couldn't indulge in a little light sexting. When I did fall asleep, it was to dream of both of them.

CHAPTER TWENTY-THREE

I was still in the leftovers of the dream when I woke –
not the juicy part. This bit was much more for a general
audience. Booth had his arms around my middle, pulling
me back into him. He was wearing running gear and
smelled of sweat. I didn't even know you could smell
in dreams, but you must be able to, because I knew
that he smelled sweaty. I turned my head to look up
at him and he smiled that wonderful Booth smile and
kissed me. I said, 'Your sweat smells of coffee, but that's
okay because it's you and it's sort of sexy.' And he said,
'You're asleep, and when you're asleep you can't smell.'

'Hey.'

I must have still been dreaming, because he was
sitting on the edge of my bed with the smile I'd just
seen in my dream – a tender smile, wide and gentle.
I must have still been dreaming, because I smiled the
same one back at him.

'Wow, what have I done to deserve that?' the real-
life Booth asked.

I groaned and buried my head under the covers.

It had been a rough night. He dragged the covers back off me.

'Excuse me! What if I wasn't decent?'

'Aaaah, I live in hope.' He grinned as I reluctantly struggled into an upright position. 'I brought you in some coffee – I thought you'd be needing it.' He indicated the takeaway cup on my bedside table.

'And pastries too? Oh, you beautiful man.'

He smiled again, and I had to be hungover because something was stirring in my belly that felt suspiciously like butterflies. Maybe it was because of the dream. Or the way he was looking at me. No, definitely a combination of dream and hangover. I'd feel like this about any halfway shaggable guy sitting on the edge of my bed on a Sunday morning offering coffee and pastries.

He watched me for a few seconds, then leaned over and tucked a strand of hair behind my ears. 'Well, my dear, it's been lovely, but I'd better be going. You have doors to hang and pictures to buy.'

I wanted to ask him to stay and help me hang cupboard doors. I wanted to ask him to stay – but I was afraid this weirdness would stay with him, so it was best that he left.

'And I have a lunch date with Corinna,' he continued.

Oh. I hoped I'd caught my face before it fell. At least he couldn't see the butterflies in my tummy dive-bomb. Damn this hangover.

'Okay,' I said. 'Thanks for coming over yesterday, and for the shopping and the bookshelves and everything.' I knew I sounded over the top and forced; he must have heard it too.

'My pleasure. It's been fun.'

'Um okay, then. Well, I guess I'll see you in the office.'

'That you will.' He kissed me, just missing my lips, then flashed me that cheeky, irresistible Boothy grin – the one from my dream.

I drank my coffee, ate my pastries, and wished I knew why I wanted him to stay. I texted Jamie, but he didn't reply.

The cupboard doors went back on without too many hassles, and the new handles looked amazing. I texted Jamie again, finished off last night's leftover Thai, and headed out to buy my picture.

Once in the store, I couldn't decide between two prints – both large, both striking, both similar prices. It was at times like these that I wished Suse were with me. She'd know which one to choose. I took photos of both and sent them through to her. While I was waiting for her to respond, I ducked out to the coffee shop next door.

Her response came as I sat perched at the bar, my hands wrapped around the cup for warmth.

Wow, print shopping? You're taking this styling thing seriously. Next thing you'll be telling me you've bought power tools and paint!

I confessed. *Well, as a matter of fact . . . I've painted the dining room wall this plummy heathery colour.*

In that case, go for the one with the yellow.

Thanks. How's the weekend?

Yeah, great. I feel like a new woman.

Pleased to hear it. Talk during the week.

I finished my coffee and gathered my bag. As I waited in line to pay, I scanned the cafe. Sitting at a table near the only exit were Booth and a very hot-looking blonde – if you liked the tall, leggy, athletic type. The perky, bouncy ponytail type. Suse was right – no tits. They weren't touching, but she was flicking her hair about, touching her lips, tracing the salt and pepper shakers suggestively with her finger, pushing forward her non-existent chest, maintaining eye contact with him. Every girl within the vicinity would know he was taken. He looked like he was lapping it up.

I turned away and paid my bill, wondering how I could get past them without him seeing me. I looked back over to see him smiling at her and leaning in. I looked away again quickly before I had to see him kiss her.

I decided on the march-through-and–pretend-I-can't-see-them tactic. If I fumbled with my wallet and my handbag, it wouldn't look too obvious. I took a deep breath and walked past.

'Em . . . hey!'

I looked around as if I wasn't sure where the voice had come from, before allowing my eyes to settle on him.

'Booth, hi . . . what are you doing here?' Nice acting, Em.

'Late lunch.' He turned to his companion. 'Corinna, this is my friend Emily – I've told you about her. Em, this is Corinna.'

I held out my hand to her and flashed my biggest smile. 'Nice to meet you, Corinna.'

Booth was looking between the two of us and grinning. She shook my hand, smiled briefly and turned her attention back to her herbal tea. I raised my eyebrows at Booth. Really?

He smiled fondly at her, then said to me, 'Have you bought that print?'

'Not yet, I'm trying to decide between two. I sent the photos to Suse.'

'Show me,' he offered. I did. 'I reckon the one with the red – it'd look striking on that heather wall. The one with the yellow would work well on the other wall though, behind the couch.'

'Really?'

'Yeah, you don't want to hold back on the strong colours, not against that palette.'

My eyebrows went up again. Style speak? Booth?

'I was flicking through some of those magazines you buy,' he said.

Oh. So he'd been reading my magazines this morning while he was waiting to wake me up, but didn't want her to know that he'd spent the night. Whatever.

'Have you heard back from Suse?' he asked.

'Yes – she suggested the yellow one, but she hasn't seen the wall.'

'Is she having a good time?'

'Uh huh. She reckons she's coming back a new woman.'

'That's what I was afraid of,' he muttered.

'Sorry?'

'Nothing. I told you what I thought about it the other day.'

I searched his face for whatever it was he wasn't saying to me, and, finding nothing, shrugged. It could wait. Corinna was fiddling with something on her phone.

'I'd better let you two get back to your lunch,' I said. 'It was lovely meeting you, Corinna. I'll see you in the office, Booth.'

She smiled briefly again, and Booth stood to kiss me on the cheek. It was all a little awkward and polite – two things I didn't normally associate with Booth. This was why I got weird about him being in a relationship – he wasn't Booth any more. It had absolutely nothing to do with jealousy; it was about who he became when he was with someone. Less like himself and more like someone pretending to be him. It freaked me out.

I gave it three months before she asked him to choose between her and me. Regular sex versus flat-pack bookcases – of course he'd choose her. How did I know? He'd done it twice before, and each time it had broken my heart. I wasn't sure I could go through it again – that slow decline of phone calls, lunches we didn't do, laughs we didn't have. Then came the uncomfortable talk, the one where he told me that I intimidated Mandy/Shayla/Corinna/whoever, and that for the sake of the relationship he wasn't going to be able to see me any more.

'It's not that she's jealous,' he'd say. 'She's not the possessive type.'

Bullshit, I'd be thinking, *of course she's the possessive type.*

'It's just that our history makes her uncomfortable,' he'd continue.

Of course it does, I'd think. *Every woman wants to know that she's the only woman in her man's life. She doesn't want to think about shared laughs or the possibility of accidental snogs.*

'I think it's for the best,' he'd say. 'Don't you?'

I'd nod and try not to cry. I'd smile and tell him, 'Of course I understand. I only want you to be happy.' Then I'd go home and consume my body weight in chocolate and chardonnay and cry until there were no tears left in me. Just like last time, and the time before.

Then I'd try to imagine a life without him in it, and fail dismally. I wouldn't let anyone know how I felt – not him, and especially not Suse. She'd only wrap it up into other emotions that it absolutely wasn't. I'd wish that I'd never met him, and pretend that he'd just gone away on holiday and wouldn't be back. Then I'd go out and find someone to fall in love with for a while to distract me.

I'd been there before.

Booth sought me out on Tuesday to do a coffee run, and asked the question I'd been dreading. 'What did you think of Corinna? She's great, isn't she?'

'I really didn't get a chance to talk to her,' I said, avoiding answering.

'It was lucky us running into you. I'd been wondering when I could introduce her to you, and there you were.'

'Yes, it was lucky.'

'You don't sound too enthusiastic.'

'She's very pretty, it's just that she didn't say much.'

'You probably intimidate her.'

I raised my eyebrows at that. 'I doubt it, but whatever.'

Jamie was in Sydney with Tony, but we'd resumed our evening phone calls and texts. He was staying up there for his friend's wedding, so wasn't due back in the office until next week. I didn't know how I could wait until then to touch him again, to kiss him again, to feel him against me. God, I sounded desperate – I suppose I was. Absence made the heart grow fonder and all that.

I had the software release in the final stages of testing. So far, so good – a few small issues in the code, but on the whole we were in good shape. One thing about Jamie not being around: I was able to focus on other things – like work.

Marcus announced an offsite for the following week at a conference centre in the Yarra Valley. Something to do with 'planning our way forward' – that whole strategy and future-proofing thing that executives liked to talk about. Invites had been extended to second-tier management, which included me. I didn't get excited about it until I realised that Jamie would be going too. Two nights and three days in the country – surely, surely we could get some time together?

On Thursday I went for the interview at DotPoint.

I still hadn't told Booth about it, so was glad he was with a client all day and didn't see me in my favourite pinstriped Max Mara suit. It was vintage of course, and I usually saved it for client presentations.

Right up until I walked through the doors, I still hadn't decided whether the interview was a good idea or not. Leaving would mean leaving Jamie before we'd even started. On the other hand, leaving would mean not having to leave – or worse, getting left behind – when Corinna finally decided that Booth wasn't allowed to see me any more.

Jodie Lawrence immediately put me at ease with her warm greeting.

'Thanks so much for coming to talk to us, Emily. It must be a huge decision to consider changing companies after so many years. How about we chat about that first, and then I can tell you a bit about what we do here at DotPoint and why it's such a great place to work?'

The hour whirled by. At the end of it, I had no idea how I'd performed, just that if I was successful, she would be lovely to work with.

'We do have a couple of other people that we'd like to talk to,' she told me, 'but the next step would be a meeting with Alex, our CEO. I'll let you know one way or another by the end of next week.'

Back in the office, I called Suse. I'd left messages for her over the last couple of days, but this time she picked up.

'Hiya, what's up?'

'Nothing, I just thought I'd see how your weekend was.'

'Sorry, darl, I got your messages but things have been mad in here. The weekend was great – I'll fill you in tomorrow night. Is everything else okay?'

'It is. I just got back from an interview at DotPoint.'

'Great, I'm glad you went. Anyway, I must run – we'll talk tomorrow, okay?'

She hung up before I could reply.

The phone rang again almost immediately. Andi.

'Hey, sweetie, have you emerged from renovation hell yet?'

I'd told her about my plans last time we met for breakfast. 'I sure have – it's looking great. And, in breaking news, I went for an interview today.'

'DotPoint?'

'Yep.'

'That calls for a celebration. Fancy a drink tonight? That rooftop in Little Lon? You can tell me all about it, and I'll tell you about my latest mistake.'

My one drink with Andi turned into a few too many. We ran into Todd and some of his friends – not entirely by accident, I suspected – and I staggered home somewhere around 1 am after agreeing to meet up with them again on Saturday night.

At the pub on Friday, we were all rather subdued. I was tired. Suse was . . . I didn't really know what Suse was, but she definitely wasn't herself. Booth only stayed for one drink, then left to meet Corinna. It definitely seemed to be getting serious between the two of them – and if that was the case, this time I wasn't going to hang around for the inevitable. I'd find a way to ease myself out of the friendship before he could actually say the words. I'd get in first for a change. Even if the job with DotPoint didn't come off, the time was right to be moving on.

After he'd left, Suse asked, 'Is everything okay between you two?'

'Booth and I? Of course. What could be wrong?'

She shrugged. 'I don't know, there just seems to be something weird. Did you shag again?'

'No.'

'Really? Maybe it's just my imagination.'

'Maybe. I met Corinna. Accidentally. They were having lunch – she was all over him.'

'Aaaah.'

'What's that mean? That "aaaaah".'

'Nothing. It means nothing.'

'It sounded like it means something.'

'Just that I think you could be jealous.'

'Of course I'm not. I don't care who he sleeps with.'

'It's not that you're worried about. It's him falling in love with someone and you losing him again that concerns you.'

'It hasn't crossed my mind,' I lied.

'Come off it, Em. Of course it has. What woman is going to want someone with tits like yours hanging around as the "best friend?"' She made the quotation marks with her fingers. 'You and I both know that he'll have to choose, and given you're both too blind to see the flipping obvious, he'll choose her. He'll end up in another messy split and come running back to you, and we'll start the whole dance again. Or worse – what if this one lasts? What if he never comes back? Have you thought about that? Have you imagined what life without Josh will be like for you?'

Unimaginable. That's what it would be. But I didn't say it. I couldn't even think it.

'In fact, I'm starting to wonder whether the reason that no one has lasted with you is because the one you really want is Josh. And I think he feels the same way about you, but isn't prepared to admit it either.'

'That's ridiculous.' It was – ridiculous.

'Is it?'

'Of course it is. I can't feel like that about Booth – we're way too far down the road. Any window we had is long gone.'

'If you say so.' She didn't look convinced. She'd also got that distant, distracted air about her again.

'You haven't told me about Daylesford yet,' I said.

Her face fell and she fidgeted with a spare drink coaster. 'There's not really a lot to tell. It was a magic weekend and I feel like a new woman.'

'Really? Then why do you look so miserable and as though you haven't slept in weeks?'

She exhaled. 'That's because I haven't.'

'Suse, is everything okay?'

She tapped her coaster on the table. 'No, not really.'

'Do you want to talk about it?'

She took a deep breath and smiled weakly. 'No, but maybe I should. I've made a huge mistake . . . I slept with someone else.'

'Bloody hell, Suse.' I didn't know what else to say.

She sighed. 'I know. I certainly didn't intend it to happen, and I'm sure as hell not proud of it. Things haven't been great between Richard and me since Georgia was born – it's not his fault, he's the same as he always was. It's just that I felt lost and bored . . . and John noticed me. He treated me like I was attractive and sexy and free. I was flattered, I guess. I don't know, I got carried away.'

'Is this John someone at work?'

She paused and sipped her wine. 'Yes.'

'Does Richard know?'

'No – there's no reason for him to. I'm eaten up with guilt. There's no point both of us feeling dreadful.'

I trawled through the bank of trivial information in my brain for something vaguely appropriate to say and came up with nothing.

'You probably hate me now,' she said. 'I risked a perfectly good marriage with a man who worships the ground I walk on for someone who had nothing to lose, and who offered me nothing other than a few hours of,' she smiled, 'absolute bliss.'

'I don't hate you, Suse. I can't understand it, so I have no right to judge you.'

She looked at me, and then back into her glass, but not before I saw the moisture in her eyes. I reached out and touched her hand.

'I wish I could take it back,' she said. 'I wish I could turn the clock back.'

'To when you married Richard?'

'God, no, I love my kids, I love him. I wish I'd never slept with . . . I wish I'd never gone there. It's made a mess of everything.'

'What do you want, Suse?' I considered my next words carefully. 'Does he make you happy?'

She shook her head. 'He makes me miserable, and guilty. I feel like I have "cheater" written over my forehead for everyone to see. I'm so sorry it happened, but I can't imagine it not happening. He makes me desperate – I want him all the time. Even when I'm with Richard, I'm thinking about him. I forget everything when I'm with him. I'm ready for him always – he only has to touch me and I explode. Richard's always so gentle with me, you know? He looks after me and he cares about me, but sometimes I just want him to lose control. Richard and I make love, but sometimes I want him not to care so much – to just, you know, take me, fuck me . . . anywhere.'

She was gazing into space as she talked – as if she'd forgotten I was there.

'John's different. I think he deliberately withholds himself so I don't know when I can have him, when we can be together. We arrange to meet and then he'll cancel. I wait for his call, his texts, anything from him. I've stopped doing things I used to do, just in case I miss his call. I've never experienced anything so exciting – yet I hardly know a thing about him.'

'That sounds like infatuation,' I said bleakly. It also sounded like how I felt about Jamie.

I discounted the idea as soon as it popped into my head. No, it was completely different between Jamie and me. Both of us were free, and the cancellations had been for legitimate reasons.

'Maybe it is.' She shrugged. 'But it's like no crush I've ever experienced before.'

'I think I understand.'

'Is that what it's like with you and Jamie?' she asked after a minute or so.

'It's complicated.'

'But you still fancy him, right?'

'Sure I do. Madly, desperately.' I laughed at myself. 'Listen to me. Next you'll be telling me that it sounds like infatuation, and I'll be saying it's like no crush I've experienced before.'

'Is it?' she asked. 'Infatuation?'

'It's like no other crush I've experienced before.'

CHAPTER TWENTY-FOUR

'I don't want to be *advocatus diaboli*, you understand.' Marcus paused, green highlighter pen poised over the paper on the presentation stand.

'What sort of avocado?' Booth whispered into my ear.

'Devil's advocate,' I whispered back.

He nodded his understanding. 'Fair enough.'

Marcus was still talking. 'But I'm not sure you've thought this all the way through, Paul. We're aiming here for structural rejuvenation, to switch the current paradigm more towards an environment of "can do". This is a great thought bubble, but L to L, I think we need to take a broader, more inclusive perspective.' He used the highlighter to cross through the words.

'So green means "no"?' Booth asked me as Marcus selected an orange highlighter and moved on to the next point on the butcher's paper.

We'd spent the previous session in groups trying to come up with ideas that supported Marcus's vision. The only issue being that Marcus hadn't yet told us what his vision was. I suspected we were meant to come up with that too.

I nodded. 'L to L?'

'Leader to leader,' he replied.

'Right you are.'

'Helen, is this one yours? More stand-ups and fewer meetings?' Marcus stared at the words on the paper while Helen held her breath. Then he nodded and swapped his orange highlighter for pink. 'I like it.'

Booth leaned in again. 'So what does pink mean?'

'That he's relaxed his position on pink highlighters and doesn't mind the idea.'

At the front of the room, Marcus was holding up a flabby basketball. 'Who wants the thought ball next?'

'I'll take it,' volunteered Tony. He caught the ball, held it to his head for a second, then said, 'No, sorry, it's gone.'

Beside me Booth was shaking from the effort of holding in his giggles.

'Come on . . . someone? Anyone?' Tony held the slightly deflated ball above his head.

We all looked at each other, but no one was accepting the thought ball. Maybe someone should have remembered a bike pump.

'I think that's a good time for us to be breaking for a coffee,' Marcus announced when it became clear that the silence was deafening.

Booth and I barely made it outside before

collapsing into belly laughs. Jamie found us doubled over, with Booth parodying Tony. 'No, sorry, it's gone.'

'What sort of avocado?' I asked, sending Booth into fresh fits.

Jamie looked at the pair of us. 'Am I interrupting something?'

I pulled myself together enough to manage to explain. Judging by Jamie's faint smile, it wasn't as funny on the second telling. You must have had to be there.

Booth and I exchanged glances and giggled again.

'When did we stop having meetings and start having stand-ups?' he said. 'Aren't they just meetings without chairs?'

'And without the comedians,' I clarified.

'Okay,' Booth thought it through, 'I think I've got it now. A meeting is something you bring your laptop and pen and paper to. It can go as long as it needs to, but you sit down. A buzz is supposed to be shorter – even though it often goes for longer – and you're just getting talked to. You don't need anything to write on, and you're standing up. A scrum is a buzz that you have first thing in the morning, and a stand-up is a meeting without chairs.'

'Yep, that's about right. You missed the huddle, though.'

'Ah yes, the huddle – commonly confused for the scrum and the buzz, but shorter.'

'And this is all supposed to result in an upward

directional trajectory?' Jamie asked.

'Only if we all keep our eyes on the end game, continue to focus on leveraging positive operational rhythm – collectively speaking – and deliver a step-up approach in our cultural expectations,' I said.

Jamie was nodding seriously. 'I agree. Now isn't the time for gradual change, speaking L to L, that is. Right now, consistently high performance and a complete alignment with back-to-basic principles will form the cornerstone of our success moving forward at a holistic level.'

'Don't forget the low-hanging fruit,' offered Booth. 'We don't want to crawl over the line. We need to keep our eyes on the prize and hit it hard to bring it home.'

We all laughed.

'Christ, this thing's a waste of time,' said Jamie.

'You should have been here yesterday,' Booth said. 'Marcus suggested that we go for a walk through the blame garden, get it all out of our systems, and move through into the light at the end of the tunnel. It was an exercise in expansive visualisation.'

Due to a meeting in Sydney, Jamie had missed yesterday's session and arrived just after breakfast today. We hadn't had a chance to talk yet. In fact, we hadn't been alone for a few weeks. One way or another, he was spending tonight in my bed.

Booth looked between the two of us and made

his excuses. 'I might go back inside – I have a thought bubble I'd like to explore with Diane before the next session. And someone needs to restock the highlighters and pump up the thought ball.'

He flashed me a grin and left us alone.

'So,' I said.

'So,' he said, smiling that smile of his at me. 'Alone at last.'

'Today seems to be the day for that sort of thing – you know, clichés and stuff.'

He laughed. 'Was it like this yesterday?'

'Absolutely.'

'You know, Em, I really need to kiss you.'

He moved closer, close enough to touch. Where did all the air go? I glanced around to check that no one else could see.

'Me too,' I murmured. 'Not here though.'

'Where?'

'I don't know . . . later?'

God, the way he was looking at me . . . maybe just one kiss, in that shadow, behind that tree. One little kiss.

'Later then,' he said softly, reaching out a finger to touch my lips. *Oh.*

Booth popped his head around the corner. 'Hey, you two, here's an interesting thought bubble – get your arses inside. Marcus has stepped up to the plate and is about to grab the ball and run with it, so we better hop on the bus and have our hymn sheets ready to sing along.'

The rest of the day passed in a blur of business babble and acronyms. The basketball remained in the corner. The highlight – or lowlight, no pun intended – was the 53-slide presentation from Tony on a new system of measuring staff performance. In Marcus's words, it 'heralded a bold new step forward into an era of quantitative and qualitative corporate resource measurement'. As well as KPIs (key performance indicators), SLAs (service level agreements), gate-openers (umm, the SLAs and KPIs that had to be met before bonuses – which didn't exist, but apparently might do in the future – could be paid), and BIs (behavioural indicators – how we rated against our key behaviours, such as Stand and Deliver), we now had a system of PPRs (perceived performance ratings – I didn't even ask). Maybe we needed another offsite to come up with more acronyms. We could put them in a pyramid, perhaps.

At the end, Marcus said, 'Well, thanks for that, Tony. You've brought some interesting concepts into sharp focus. I think we've learned a lot this afternoon about the way forward. We're a long way towards my vision of future-proofing the Australian arm of the company. On that note, we'll break for the day. I'm sure you've all got emails and phone calls to catch up on, and then we have a rather special dinner planned in the restaurant. It's a great opportunity for us to bond as a team. Get to know each other better.'

My thoughts exactly.

'I think he and Diane have done enough bonding,' whispered Booth.

'After all,' Marcus continued, 'we're on this journey together.'

Booth made a strained, vomiting noise.

'There you are, Em!' Booth pushed a glass of wine into my hand. 'We wondered what was keeping you.'

'Hello – check the face.'

I'd spent extra time tonight getting ready, choosing a stretch black lace top to wear with slightly flared, flat-fronted black pants. Everything that could be held in was being restrained by a bodysuit so highly structured it could stand up on its own. It exaggerated my curves (all of them) and enhanced my waist. I quite liked the effect, and hoped that Jamie would too. I'd painted my nails red, added inches with black stiletto heels, and scrunched my hair back into curls – it would be a nightmare to straighten tomorrow.

Jamie had been chatting to the barman and came over when he saw me. 'You're looking rather exotic tonight, Em.' His gaze roamed from my red toenails all the way up my body, lingering at my breasts, before finally reaching my eyes.

'That was the idea.'

It felt as though it was his hands rather than his

eyes that had travelled up my body, leaving hot trails of sensation behind. I took a sip of my wine, and then another.

Booth and Tony had started a conversation about the upcoming weekend's football fixtures, and Jamie was soon brought into the discussion. I took the chance to sneak a look at him, remembering the feel of his chest under my hands, the way his biceps flexed when he held me, his . . . oh, I wanted him.

He caught my glance and grinned. 'Alright?' he asked, his hand on my waist.

'Yeah, all good. Why?'

'No reason – you're just quieter than usual.'

'Tired perhaps? Or maybe I'm just thirsty.' I indicated my now empty glass and moved away – just far enough to dislodge his hand. My skin felt warm where it had been.

'I can take a hint. Same again?' I nodded. 'Josh, Tony?'

When the call came to move into the dining room, Jamie steered me across to a spare chair, and slid into the one to my left. Booth took the chair on my other side and immediately assumed control of the conversation.

'Listen to this.' He read from the menu. 'Grass-fed wagyu raised in the Riverina, served with kipfler potatoes from country Victoria and vegetables sourced from the local farmers' market. Now all I need to know is what the cow's name was while it was alive, and who its friends were in the paddock. I don't even know where you guys were raised – well, except for Em, of course – but I know where my dinner's from and what it ate.'

I laughed, but under the table Jamie had moved his leg so his knee was beside mine. On top of the table his arm inched closer to mine until there was only millimetres between us. Every nerve in my body was straining to close the gap. He straightened his little finger and lightly brushed it against mine. A ripple of gooseflesh ran up my spine and, without looking at him, I pushed my knee closer to his under the table and swallowed hard.

Finally dinner was over, and Marcus dropped by to say good night to us all before he retired for the evening. When Diane followed soon after, Booth, Jamie and I looked at each other and giggled.

Marcus's credit card went to bed with him, so someone suggested we relocate to the pub up the road. Jamie put his jacket over my shoulders and threw his arm around me as we walked. Booth was somewhere ahead with Monica, Tony and a few other colleagues. No one could see us back here in the dark, so I leaned into him and he pulled me tighter.

At the bar, we squeezed into a booth with the others. My thigh was against his and my head against his shoulder. He turned to smile into my eyes. Excitement fizzled along every vein and I tossed my hair and smiled back.

Somewhere around midnight Booth suggested moving to another pub.

'Oh, I don't think so,' I said. 'I'm tired and it wouldn't be a good look to fall asleep in tomorrow's session. I could find myself using the wrong colour highlighter.'

'Really?'

'Absolutely. It's bed for me.' I deliberately didn't look at Jamie.

'Okay, I'll walk you back then,' offered Booth.

'I'll go back with Emily. I'm a bit tired from the early start this morning,' said Jamie.

'Are you sure?' Booth directed his question to Jamie, but looked at me.

'Yes, a decent night's sleep might help develop some thought bubbles. I'll see that Em gets back okay.'

'It's okay, Josh.' My eyes were telling him to leave.

'Alright then. Sleep well.'

He finally left with the others, and Jamie and I were alone.

'Let's not go just yet,' he said. 'Finish your drink at least. We haven't really talked all night.'

'Okay.' I sat back down and played with my wine glass.

I could feel him looking at me, willing me to glance up. I'd been burning for him, but now that we were on the brink, I was suddenly not sure.

'You know, you never did tell me who's on your

would-do list.'

I looked at him blankly.

'That night at your place? We were talking about Marcus and Diane and how he wouldn't be on your would-do list?'

I remembered. 'No, I didn't tell you.'

'Have you ever had sex with someone you work with? I mean, other than Josh.'

I swallowed hard and thought carefully about my answer. 'Ummmm, no, have you?'

'Not yet.' His smile sent volts of sensation and flames rippling through my body.

I focused on my glass. 'I think it could be awkward if things go bad.'

'Yeah, I get that – but what if it doesn't go bad?'

I chanced a look at his face and couldn't look away. It was his eyes. They were piercing. He rested his elbow on the table and propped his chin in his hand. He didn't seem to know what to say next, and I certainly had no idea, so we just sat there and gazed at each other for a minute or two – not touching, not speaking, just gazing. My tummy was lodged in my chest and had stopped my breath from coming out.

I bit at my bottom lip. He saw the movement.

'You know what I'm saying, don't you?'

'I think so.'

We'd been leading up to this for weeks. The kisses and banter had all been bringing us to this point.

'So,' he finally asked, 'am I on your would-do list?'

Someone staggered past, bumped our table and spilled my wine over me. I took the interruption as an excuse to visit the bathroom and avoid the question.

When I emerged into the dark corridor, Jamie was waiting for me. He pushed me back into the shadows and kissed me until I had no idea which way was up.

'You didn't answer my question,' he said between kisses.

'No,' I breathed into his mouth.

'Am I on your would-do list?'

He dropped kisses down my throat, each one sending a wave of fresh sensation. I didn't stand a chance.

'Yes,' I said, and his mouth moved back to mine. Even if it wasn't true, I'd say anything just now if it meant he didn't stop kissing me.

Someone stumbled past into the bathroom. 'Get a room, mate.'

'I think we need to go,' I said.

'Yes,' he agreed.

He put his jacket back around my shoulders and I snuggled into the warmth of it. It smelled of him.

We left the pub and walked the short distance back to the hotel. The night seemed so much blacker out here in the country and the road was dark. When I stumbled, he pulled me to him and kissed me again.

'This really means something, Em,' he murmured.

'I don't think I've ever felt like this before.'

I believed him. I hadn't felt like this either – overwhelmed, out of my depth, breathless.

At the hotel, I pulled away from him and we walked separately down the corridor to our respective rooms. I had my room key at the ready, so muttered a good night and let myself in before he had time to respond. Leaning against the closed door, I told myself that nothing had happened that we wouldn't be able to laugh about tomorrow, but I didn't believe it – and I didn't know why I hadn't invited him in.

I'd kicked off my shoes, undressed and popped on a long T-shirt for sleeping, when the knock on the door came. It was Jamie.

He moved me back into the room, kicked the door shut with his foot, and kissed me so hard that my head banged against the wall. His tongue forced its way into my mouth and his body pushed against mine, as mine strained to be closer to his. When he released me I grabbed at him to pull him back, to bring his mouth back to mine, to feel his erection against me, his hand on my breast through the cotton, cupping it, kneading it.

He steadied me and smiled, those eyes piercing mine as he lifted my shirt above my head and pushed my knickers down. I kicked them away and reached for him, but he shook his head slowly and held my hands together above my head in one of his. Using the lightest of touches, he trailed one finger slowly down my body.

Down the line of my throat, between my breasts, around each in a tantalising figure eight, down across my navel, and between my legs. I tried to shut my eyes, but his wouldn't let me. I tried to move my arms, to touch him in the way that he was touching me, but he held me firm. I moaned softly, my legs opening wider as he probed between them. When I cried out and my legs couldn't support me any longer, he held me until they could and said, 'I think it's time, don't you?'

I nodded, and he led me to the bed.

Afterwards, he dressed, kissed me hard on the mouth, looked into my eyes and said, 'Tonight was amazing. Why did we wait so long? I'll call you in the morning – we'll meet for breakfast.'

CHAPTER TWENTY-FIVE

Any second now the phone would ring . . . it would be him. Maybe he'd already rung – perhaps my phone was still on silent? I checked it again. No.

When he did call, I'd let it ring a few times so he didn't think I'd been waiting. I might even try and sound as if I'd just woken up. I'd make my voice sound sexy, as if I was still in bed, not as though I'd been awake for hours – waiting for his call and practising how the conversation would go.

He'd say something like: 'I haven't slept. Last night was great and I'm seriously concerned that I've fallen in love with you.'

Or maybe even: 'I've been counting down the minutes until I can call you. Please tell me that last night meant as much to you as it did to me?'

Possibly this one: 'Was last night a dream? How about I come around now and you can remind me?'

I'd do that breathy little sigh thing people do when they're stretching seductively after being woken from an amazing sleep – or having phone sex – and say something like: 'Oh . . . it's you . . . Sorry, I've just woken up . . .'

Perhaps not.

I took one more disdainful look at the phone – *ring, damn you* – and staggered to the bathroom. The view in the mirror was not pretty. I'd gone to bed last night without taking my make-up off. I always took my make-up off.

Standing under the shower, I reviewed the situation. He'd said that he'd call, and there was no reason for him not to. He'd told me that he'd never felt like this before, that what we had was *special.* The italics were mine, but that's how he'd said it.

Was that the phone? I turned the tap off to be sure. Nope. Nothing.

I replayed his final words to me last night. 'Tonight was *amazing.*' Again the italics were mine.

It was now nearly 8 am and the first session of the day was due to commence at nine. Perhaps I should call him? Maybe the first move needed to come from me?

I checked my phone again – just in case it had rung in the two minutes I was cleaning my teeth.

If he hadn't called by the time I'd put on my make-up, I'd definitely ring him. I'd keep it light and breezy, as if calling him was an afterthought. Maybe I'd say something like: 'Hey, I think I must have been half-asleep last night – did you want to catch up for a chat before the session starts this morning?'

Or maybe: 'This is your friendly wake-up call.'

I grimaced into the mirror. Crap, the bags under my eyes were almost bigger than the bag I still needed to pack this morning. Concealer and white eyeliner would do the trick. Lots of concealer. Possibly best not to wear black this morning, or red – the colours would match my eyes just a little too closely.

As I was finishing my hair, the phone finally rang. My hair-straightener landed on the floor with a bang, and I tripped over the cord in my scramble to answer.

It was Booth.

'Hey, Em, how are you feeling?'

'I'm fine.'

'You don't sound fine.'

'I'm okay, just really tired. You?' I balanced the phone under my chin as I bent to retrieve the straightener.

'Yeah, all good. Hey, are you coming down for breakfast? Do you want me to swing by your room and get you?'

'No . . . thanks though. I'm still trying to get ready, and haven't even started to pack yet.'

'Sure. And you're okay?'

'All cool – just some really bad dark circles that I'm trying to do something about.'

'Okay. I'll let you get on with it then.'

I hung up and continued with the hair.

My cell rang again. It was Jamie. Finally.

'Hi, Em, how are you feeling?'

'Yeah, good.' I tried to inject some sexy-just-woken-up energy into my voice, but failed dismally. 'A little tired, I guess. How are you?'

This was lame.

'Hmmm, much the same. Listen, I'm running behind this morning. I probably won't get to meet you for breakfast. See you in the conference room?'

'Cool. See you then.'

A little pause.

'All okay?' he asked.

'Sure,' I lied.

Booth must have been watching for me. He was talking to Tony and Monica, and inclined his head in an invitation for me to join them. I shook my head in response and busied myself with making a coffee and nibbling at a muffin – triple chocolate, if I wasn't mistaken. Not that it mattered what flavour the muffin was, I couldn't taste it. Entering the room felt a bit like a walk of shame – not that I'd ever done the walk of shame before – I didn't do casual sex, remember. Not that this was casual sex, but . . . At the back of the room was a whiteboard with a schedule of the day's proceedings posted on it. I pretended to take a lot of interest in it. Someone had thoughtfully provided a new stock of highlighters (all colours) and pumped up the basketball.

As soon as the door opened, I knew it was Jamie.

He got a coffee from the table and moved to

stand behind me, so close I could feel his hand resting against mine. His little finger snaked out to twine mine. I felt his breath on the back of my neck and inhaled his aftershave. I closed my eyes briefly, and resisted the urge to lean back into him. God, I must be hungover.

I swallowed hard, and half-turned to face him.

'Later,' he mouthed. He took a step back and said in a louder voice, 'So, Em, any bets as to how much the targets will be moving by this quarter?'

Before I had time to answer, we were joined by Booth. How on earth did he look so fresh when my hangover was printed all over my face? He apologised briefly to Jamie for taking me away, and gently steered me to a chair.

'Are you okay?'

'Absolutely.'

'Are you sure?'

'Absolutely, why wouldn't I be?'

He searched my face and gave my arm a gentle squeeze.

Diane and Marcus walked into the room, so I focused my attention on them – and the whiteboard.

'I hope someone remembered to top up the citrus highlighters,' I said brightly.

'Em –'

'Shush.'

'Feel like bringing that coffee outside?' Jamie asked.

We'd broken for morning tea and I'd poured myself another black coffee.

I nodded, and followed him onto the veranda that wrapped around this wing of the hotel. In my head I'd composed the scene:

We'll have a slightly awkward conversation, following which Jamie will take my hand and lead me around the side of the veranda into the cottage garden. He'll look around to check that no one else has seen us, and then he'll push me against the trunk of one of those wonderful old trees. There, in amongst the lavenders and box hedges, he'll tell me that last night was just the start and how we belong together. Then he'll kiss me.

Instead, we were joined by Booth, who inserted himself between us to discuss an amendment that Tony was proposing to our project.

'I'm pretty sure that Em's team has almost finished the coding. Any further change will impact that,' said Jamie.

I concentrated hard on the indents the heels of my boots were making in the dirt between the brick pavers. I hoped the gardener hadn't spent too long cultivating the mossy stuff that used to be there.

'Well?' Booth directed his question to me.

'What?'

'Is Jamie right? What would be the impact of a change now on the August release?'

'We're too far down the track. Coding is nearly finished and we're about to go into system testing.'

'Yeah, that's what I thought.'

Jamie fussed with his coffee cup.

Booth glanced at my heel patterns.

'Em, how much sleep did you get last night?' he asked.

'Not a lot. Do I really look that bad?'

'No, you've done a good job with the make-up, but you do look tired. Try and stay awake for the next couple of hours, hey?'

I made a face, but said nothing. It was Jamie I wanted to talk to, not Booth. Yet Jamie was making it pretty bloody obvious that he didn't want to be alone with me. So why had he asked me out here?

Booth emptied the remnants of his coffee into the garden bed. 'Let's get this show back on the road so we can finish up early.'

I looked at Jamie. My eyes pleaded with him to make an excuse so we could talk, but he turned away. Beginning to understand, I gathered what was left of my self-respect.

By mid-afternoon we were released to drive back to the city. As I got into Booth's car, Jamie waved goodbye and mouthed, 'I'll call you.'

Booth waited until we'd been on the road for a while before bringing it up. 'I'm guessing that didn't go according to plan?'

I gazed out the passenger window. 'No idea what

you're talking about.'

'You and Jamie. Last night. This morning.'

I shrugged.

'Come on, Em. I had to hear about the kiss and the non-kiss over and fricking over, and now that you've hooked up I get nothing out of you?'

'Maybe I've just decided that there's some information that needs to be kept private.'

He fiddled with the radio station. 'Since when do you apply the filter to your sex life? I'm pretty unshockable, you know.'

I shrugged again, and continued to look out the window.

'You told me about Craig and his commentary position, and Dean and his inadequacies. Then there was Harry and his silence. Do you want me to go on?'

'Yeah, okay, I get your point.'

Harry liked to be quiet while he was having sex. His face just used to screw up into all these weird grimaces. He didn't like me making noise either. If I moaned in appreciation of something clever, he'd stop and frown at me. It fascinated Booth when I told him about it, but at the time it certainly put me off my A-game. As for Dean? The less said about that one the better . . . no pun intended.

'After such a big build-up, I'm thinking there's only two reasons you wouldn't want to talk about it.'

I didn't respond.

'Either it was disappointing, or there was no warm-and-cuddlies afterwards.'

Again, I said nothing.

'Was it disappointing? After the excitement of semi-public places, a hotel room didn't get your motor running? Is that it? Disappointing sex can be worse than no sex, you know. It's the anticipation – you wonder how you read the signs so wrong. Disappointing sex is like falling off a horse, you have to jump back in the saddle and go for another ride.' He looked across at me with his brows raised. 'Well? Had he had too much to drink? Was there a slight case of brewer's droop?'

I sighed heavily.

'Am I on the right track?'

He wasn't going to shut up.

'I'll have you know that technically there were no problems at all. He knows what he's doing.'

Jamie was as good as I'd thought he'd be. He knew it too. As we were lying in bed, catching our breath, he'd sighed and then asked, 'How many times did you come?' I'd cuddled into him and murmured, 'It was great.' He'd seemed to want more from me, so I added, 'You were amazing. Thank you.' He appeared satisfied with that. Sometimes it was polite to lie – the sort of effort he'd put in required some affirmation. But despite the foreplay we'd been engaging in for the last weeks, after that first time against the wall I'd been unable to relax and let go. Perhaps I'd had too much to drink. Maybe I'd built it all up too much and next time would be better. Anyway, it was nice of him to ask – it showed that he cared.

'Oh.' Booth sounded almost disappointed. 'No complaints in that area then?'

I shrugged.

'Okay, if it's not an issue with execution, that leaves the afterwards. Did he at least spend the night?'

'No.'

'How soon after did he leave?'

'Fairly soon.'

He nodded slowly. 'I see. Have you spoken to him today?'

'Not really – you saw the extent of it.'

I felt him looking across at me.

'Keep your eyes on the road,' I said.

'I'm sure there's nothing for you to worry about, Em. Maybe he was concerned about others figuring it out?'

'Perhaps,' I conceded, allowing a little hope to flow back in.

'You don't think so?'

I shrugged again. 'I don't know. It feels different. It's like a light has gone out. He wanted nothing to do with me this morning.'

He was silent for a few seconds. 'I'm sorry, Em.'

'Yeah, I know, and you warned me and all that.'

'I'd never say that I told you so.' He sounded

affronted.

For the first time this trip I turned to look at him. 'I know you wouldn't. That was unfair.'

He reached over and placed his hand on mine. The pressure was brief, but welcome. I bit on the inside of my mouth and swallowed hard.

We travelled the next few kilometres in silence.

'Are you out with Corinna tonight?'

'Yes . . . unless you need me?'

I shook my head and screwed up my nose. 'No, I'm fine. You go out and have fun.'

'Wow, that sounded sincere.'

I tried to lighten the mood. 'You mean you're not bored yet?'

'Bitch.'

We were both quiet for the rest of the drive. I pretended to be asleep, and I was pretty sure he was pretending to listen to the radio.

I kept hoping for a text from Jamie. Something like: *Today was difficult. Can I come over tonight?*

But it didn't come.

What did arrive was an email from DotPoint asking me in for a second interview, or, in Jodie's words, an invitation to a meeting with the CEO, Alexander McInnes.

After what had happened today, the timing couldn't have been better.

•

I didn't hear from Jamie on Saturday morning either.

By mid Saturday afternoon I'd convinced myself that he was waiting for me to make the first move, so I sent him a quick text: *Hi, hope drive back yesterday was fine & hangover gone.*

He replied quickly: *Yeah. All good:)*

I waited but he didn't call.

Sunday was fresh and cold, with that bright blue sky we get in Melbourne on only the freshest and coldest winter days. I decided to stay in, just in case Jamie called or dropped by.

Booth phoned to see if I wanted to go to a football game with him. I thanked him, but told him no, I was baking muffins.

'If you don't want to come with me, you can just say no.'

'I really am baking muffins.'

'More like waiting for Jamie to call.'

'Whatever.'

I rang Suse to talk about Jamie and the accidental one-night stand – that was how I was thinking of it now. Her cell went to voicemail, so I rang her landline instead. When Richard answered he told me she was away for the weekend at an offsite.

'She didn't say,' I said.

'It was a last-minute thing,' he told me. 'Someone

else wasn't able to go, so she needed to.'

By around 5 pm I began to believe there could be something wrong with my doorbell. Perhaps he'd called by and I hadn't heard him. I went outside and buzzed my own number – much to the amusement of the guy in 2B.

'Just testing it,' I said, before slinking back into my apartment.

Around six I began to suspect there was something wrong with my phone that was stopping messages getting to and from me. To be sure, I texted Booth.

Testing 1-2–3

A reply came back quickly.

WTF? I take it he hasn't called so you're pretending that your phone is broken? That's too sad. BTW you missed a good game.

Having established that my phone was working, I decided that the fault must be with Jamie's network, so fired off one last text:

Hi, good weekend? Did you want to talk about what happened before we go back to work tomorrow?

He didn't reply until almost 10 pm.

Yeah, all good here. No need to talk – unless you think we should?

Ummmm . . .

Me: I'm fine if you are. I just thought it might be good to clear the air.

Jamie: Nope, air all clear this end.

CHAPTER TWENTY-SIX

The texts, calls, instant messages and random emails had stopped. At work, Jamie's efforts to avoid being alone with me were, to me, obvious. I saw Booth send me a look the other day that I took as being sympathetic, so now I was trying to avoid him too – just in case my humiliation was contagious . . . or I cried. I wasn't sure which was worse.

Given that there was nothing more I could do around my apartment until I got the floors done, I stepped up my nightly walking sessions just so I wasn't hanging around waiting for calls that weren't coming.

I had my meeting with Alexander McInnes on Wednesday. Because I'd been paying extra attention to my face and my outfit all week – both as a matter of pride and in case Jamie realised what a mistake he'd made – Booth didn't say anything when I came to work in my second-favourite vintage Max Mara suit. I'd gone from not knowing whether I wanted the job to absolutely positively needing it, so was even more nervous about the process than I had been the first time.

Jodie greeted me with a handshake and the same warm tones. 'It's lovely to see you again, Emily. I'll take you through to meet Alex. There's no need to be nervous. This is a casual chat – Alex just wants an idea about who you are. And just to let you know, we're meeting with two other candidates as well.'

I nodded, and must have said something in response.

I was taken to what I assumed was Alexander's office. A collection of different-sized black and white photographs of Melbourne hung together on a red feature wall, and from the window I could see the now leafless plane trees that lined Collins Street far below.

Alexander McInnes was much younger than I'd imagined – probably in his late thirties, I'd guess – and looked nothing at all like the type of executives I was used to dealing with. He looked like he'd be more at home on a beach than in an office. Although he was dressed in business attire, the top button of his shirt was undone, his sleeves were half-rolled, half-pushed up, and his tie was missing. There was an energy about him that was quite compelling.

His smile was wide, and his handshake firm. He directed Jodie and me to a pair of brown leather chairs and, rather than taking his seat behind the desk, leaned against it.

'Tell me, Emily, twelve years is a long time to work in one place – why change now?'

I figured that 'to get away from a man I had an accidental one-night stand with, and to get away from my best friend who's about to tell me that he can no longer work with me' probably wouldn't be the wisest answer. Instead, I settled on a version of the truth.

'I've become too comfortable. The last twelve years have been great, but I'm at a point where I need to deliberately make myself uncomfortable. I need to challenge myself.'

He nodded – whether in approval or understanding, I had no idea. 'Why DotPoint?'

'Because it's about as different to what I'm used to that I could find – while still making the most of my skills. What I've read about DotPoint, I like the sound of. You have a good name for doing some really innovative "think outside the box" development, and everyone I've spoken to has said that your ethos is about possibilities and continuous growth rather than steadfastly sticking to what's been done before.'

'That's certainly what we're aiming for,' he said. 'How do you think you'll fit into that? We've found in the past that some people – especially those coming from more conservatively structured corporations – have had problems with our culture. We don't exist in silos, and we encourage information-sharing. The hardest thing to get used to could be the language.'

'The language?'

'Yes, we're acronym free – we don't deliver or drive

outcomes.'

Really? How did they keep their customers?

Alexander laughed at the confusion playing across my face. 'Pizzas are delivered and cars are driven. We provide solutions to problems that our customers don't even know they have yet – simply by getting to know them and their business. We don't consider ourselves as suppliers, but partners. I don't care how big the company is – if they want to bully us into submission, I'm happy to let the business go.' He looked at Jodie and grinned – it was a cheeky grin, the sort that Booth would grin after he'd pushed a few boundaries away. 'It's a risk, but it's worked in our favour so far.'

Booth would like him. I liked him.

When I left forty minutes later, it was with a promise of a decision the following week. I'd also changed my mind – I no longer saw DotPoint as a way of running away from my problems, but as a company that I really wanted to work with.

I called Suse to tell her, but she didn't pick up.

Speaking of Suse, I still hadn't told her what had happened between Jamie and me.

On Friday, for the first time in I didn't know how long, I avoided the pub. I emailed Booth and Suse in the afternoon saying that I needed to work back. I told them there were issues with the release and I needed to update the test plan and release notes.

Suse seemed to accept my explanation, and replied that she also wouldn't be able to make it, that she needed to spend the evening at home as Richard had just got back from somewhere or other. Booth didn't reply.

He tried phoning me all weekend, but I bounced his calls. I also left the apartment in case he decided to drop by. I went to the football on Saturday, walking all the way to the MCG and then catching a tram home with all the other jubilant supporters. I ate meat pies, drank beer and cheered for Richmond. At least, I thought it was Richmond I was cheering for.

On Sunday I had breakfast with Andi, shopped for floors, and again walked for miles, returning home to collapse into bed to stare at my beautifully painted ceiling some more. There was a spot in the corner I'd missed.

On Monday Booth dragged me to lunch with him – despite me protesting that I wasn't hungry and needed to work through.

Once he had me sitting down with a plate of comfort Chinese in front of me, he said, 'I thought you weren't going to lie to me any more.'

'I'm not,' I protested. 'I haven't.'

Not telling him about the job wasn't technically lying – was it?

'Friday night? What was that about?'

'I worked. I told you that. I left here after eight – I wanted to make sure the release got through the latest round of testing.'

He searched my face for something more.

'Why did you think I'd lied?'

He hesitated before answering. 'Because when you cancelled I asked Jamie for a drink and he told me he had a date. I assumed it was with you.'

I shook my head sadly. 'You were testing me?'

He nodded. 'Yeah, I guess I was.'

'His date wasn't with me. He's obviously moved on already.'

'I'm sorry, Em.'

I shrugged. 'It's okay.'

'No, babe, it's not. He treated you badly and –'

'Booth, leave it. I appreciate that you want to come in all noble, but honestly, I'll be fine. I'm just a little bruised.'

'Is that why you're avoiding me? We usually talk through this stuff and then you bounce back and laugh about it.'

'This time it's different. I don't know how or where to start talking to you about it.'

We ate in silence for a few moments.

'I called around on Saturday, you weren't home.'

'No, I went to the football.'

'On your own? You should have called me.'

'I didn't feel like company.'

'Not even mine?'

I shook my head.

'And Sunday?'

'You dropped in then too?'

'Yeah, I wanted to make sure you were okay, and when you weren't home both days, I guess I thought . . .' He shrugged. 'I guess I thought he'd called.'

'And I'd gone running to him?'

He nodded.

'No. He didn't call. I went shopping for floors.'

Something that could almost be relief crossed his face, but was quickly gone.

'So . . . you went to the footy? On your own?'

'Yep. I ate a pie and drank beer.'

He grinned. 'Did you know who you were cheering for?'

'Everyone to start with, then I worked out which colours Richmond was playing in. The guy beside me told me. He also told me that you shouldn't cheer for Collingwood unless you're born a Collingwood supporter.'

'Did you like it?'

My smile was wide. 'I loved it. The energy was amazing.'

'You'll need to come with me next time I ask — rather than waiting at home making muffins.'

'Wouldn't three be a crowd?'

'Three?'

'Me, you and Corinna? I got the impression she didn't really want to see much more of me than what she did that day we met.'

'She doesn't know you,' he said with a grin. 'But you're part of my life and she's going to have to learn how to deal with that. Anyway, she likes to get at least one long run in on the weekends, and isn't really into the footy.'

I smiled, but wasn't comforted. I knew it was just a matter of time before I lost him too. Against regular sex with a perky blonde I didn't stand a chance.

'Fair enough. I might see if Suse wants to come too.'

'Sounds like a plan. She's still being a bit weird. It's got worse, not better, since she got back from Daylesford. Are she and Richard having problems?'

I hesitated.

'Em, what are you keeping from me?'

'I'm not sure I should be saying anything . . .'

'She's having an affair, isn't she?'

I nodded.

'I was afraid of that. Do you know who with?'

I shook my head. 'Some guy from work apparently. She says it's over.'

'Some guy from work? Is that what she told you?'

'Yeah. She said she couldn't help it. She wasn't in a good place when I spoke to her about it.'

'I thought it was something like that. Stupid girl. Just fucking stupid.' He spat the words out.

'I don't think it's helpful for us to judge. Who's to

know what goes on in a marriage?'

'Seriously, Em? Seriously? Doesn't she know how lucky she is? To have someone love her the way Richard does? I know she's bored, but that doesn't give her the right to run off and shag someone else. She's got a responsibility to him and the kids to try and work it out. She signed up for the long haul. I can't believe she's doing this.'

'She said it's over.'

'Did she? Do you believe her? Where was she on Friday night?'

'She said she was staying in – Richard had just got back from somewhere. Why wouldn't I believe her?'

'If she's lying to her husband, she's not going to stop at us. When was the last time she stayed in on a Friday night because Richard was coming home? Usually she'd stay for one or two wines and then head off. And Daylesford – are you sure that was with "the girls"?' He waggled his fingers to do the quotation marks. 'Seriously, Em, it's no wonder you –' He stopped short.

'What? What were you going to say? It's no wonder I get played for an idiot by every man I fall for? Is that what you were going to say?'

'I was just going to say that you trust too easily. It doesn't occur to you that other things can be going on.'

'And why should it? Why shouldn't I think the best of people?'

He looked away.

'Hang on, do you know something? About Jamie?'

'No. Not for sure. I have suspicions.'

I waited for him to elaborate.

'They're just suspicions. It's like I said before – I like the guy, I just wouldn't trust him if I were his girlfriend. That's all.' He watched my face cloud over. 'Fuck, I'm sorry, sweetheart. I know you're hurting.'

I tried to smile, but it didn't come out right. 'I just wish I knew what I did that was so wrong. I don't know how it changed so quickly.'

'You need to talk to him.'

'I know.'

'You're not going to be able to move on until you know one way or another why he chased you like that and then stopped once he had you.'

And then I was angry. 'I don't know, Booth. I've seen you do it heaps of times. Chase someone until they're convinced that they're the most sparkling thing in your universe and then, once you sleep with them, that's it. It's over. Why do *you* do it?'

'I'm not the enemy.' He stared at me until I looked away. 'I've never been cruel – and I always made sure that they knew the score.'

'Oh yes, the score. Just how does that work? What do you do? Tell them at the start that you're just in it for the drive-by? Do you sort that bit out before or after you get naked?'

'Em –'

'You should be high-fiving him. After all, he's done to me exactly what you've done to others. Now I know how they felt.'

My eyes filled with tears.

'I'm not the enemy,' he said again, more softly this time.

I rummaged in my bag for a tissue. 'I know you're not. I'm sorry. This is why I don't do one-night stands. I don't know the score, I don't know how it's supposed to work.'

'You fell for him – he made sure of that. You read the messages he was sending out, there's no need to be embarrassed.'

I sniffed.

'Talk to him, Em. Hear what he has to say and then move on.'

'I will,' I promised.

On Wednesday afternoon, Jamie and I were alone in a meeting room having just finished a teleconference. It was the first time we'd been alone since it happened.

'So, Em, that thing from the other week?'

Here it came. I'd played this moment through repeatedly and hoped it would go something like: 'I've been thinking about you constantly – we have unfinished business.'

Or: 'I can't get you off my mind. What are we going to do about that?'

Or: 'I still want you. Can we try again?'

I hadn't quite decided on the final version yet, but it certainly wasn't anything like what he now said: 'You're cool about it, right? I mean, let's not complicate it any further.'

My heart was pounding as I saw that he just wanted to pretend we'd never happened.

'You're right – it's probably best forgotten about,' I managed. 'We'd both drunk too much . . . no harm done.'

If that's the case why do I feel so bad? As if I want to double over and hold myself in?

He seemed relieved.

Tears welled in my eyes and my throat closed over. I looked away, biting at the inside of my mouth in an effort to stop the tears from making a run for it.

He stepped closer. 'All okay?'

My head was screaming at him, *No, it's not okay!* But of course I didn't say it.

At that point, Tony and some other colleagues came in. 'Sorry, guys, we have this room booked. Jamie, you're on this call too, aren't you? Are you and Em finished?'

'Yeah, we're done,' Jamie answered.

I guessed we were. Done.

I controlled the tears for as long as it took me to cover the distance between the meeting room and the bathroom. Once safely inside the stall, I let them flow freely, my fist in my mouth so my sobs wouldn't be heard. Booth called, so I switched my phone to silent, and sat there until I knew the tears were spent.

I worked back so there was no chance of running into Jamie again. Rather than going home to a miserable microwave classic, I decided to satisfy a craving for carbohydrates and walked up Bourke St hill to my favourite pasta bar. I sat at the bar with a glass of red and a bowl of fettucine, and allowed my spirits to be lifted. Italian waiters and quality carbs always worked when Celine wasn't available.

Dinner over, I retrieved my coat and scarf and stepped out into the dark to head home. The after-work rush had quietened, and a slow drizzle of rain started. I wrapped my coat more tightly around me and peered at the pavement to avoid slippery patches.

Outside the bookshop two doors down, a couple were embracing. And by embracing, I meant full-on, winter-in-Paris, romantic-black-and-white-photo-style pashing. Her back was to me, and he was holding his overcoat around her slight figure as they kissed. Then he raised his head and I saw that it was Jamie. A sharp pain ran though me, holding me to the spot, even though the drizzle had now turned into rain.

He spoke a few words to her, and, leaving her under the shelter of the awning, walked towards me.

'You're getting wet.' He drew me out of the rain.

'Yes, it's raining,' I said unnecessarily.

He smiled, but it was an embarrassed smile. 'I'm sorry you had to see that.'

'Who is she?' I looked at the figure in the dark. I could feel her watching us.

'She's Callie.'

'Your ex-girlfriend?'

'Yes, we're back together.'

I closed my eyes briefly and groaned inwardly. Of course they were. *Here we go again.*

'Since when?'

He looked sheepish. 'About a month. It's early days, we're just working through things now.'

I raised my eyebrows. 'Seeing if it'll work while you're sleeping with me? Yes, that's a great plan – or is that what I was? Your plan B in case it didn't work?'

'No, Em, it wasn't like that. I fell for you. It was different with you. And the other night – I just couldn't help myself. You were there and looking so hot, and . . . well, I wanted to finish what we'd started. It was just afterwards I felt so guilty – I owe it to Callie to give it another shot, to give us another shot. But you . . .' he opened his palms out, 'I couldn't help it. It's just bad timing. If we'd met at any other time, it might have been different.'

'But you said –'

'I know. I shouldn't have said the things I did to you. I meant them at the time.'

'So, those nights you cancelled on me, those

weekends, the dates we didn't have – that was Callie?'

'Yes, I'm sorry.'

'Me too.'

As I turned to walk away, he grabbed my arm. From the doorway of the bookstore, Callie was still watching.

'This doesn't need to be weird at work, does it?'

'I don't know, Jamie. You tell me.'

'I'm in Sydney for the next couple of days, and then Cal and I are away for a week. That should give you time to get over it. After all, we were just having fun, weren't we?' He laughed. 'It's not like either of us was in it for more than the kicks?'

A week and three days to get over it? I shook my head and walked away. I passed Callie huddling in the bookstore doorway and didn't look at her. I didn't need to see her face.

CHAPTER TWENTY-SEVEN

I walked down the hill, into Swanston Street, and then left towards Flinders Street and the trams to Richmond. I stayed on past my stop, and got out at Booth's. The rain had started again, so by the time I arrived at his block I was soaked through and looked like a swamp monster – or what I thought a swamp monster would look like if it'd been out in the rain and crying. It was only as I pressed the buzzer for Booth's apartment that it occurred to me that he could have Corinna inside. I decided to risk it anyway – I couldn't possibly feel any worse than I did right now.

His voice came through the intercom. 'Hello?'

'Booth . . . it's me. Can you let me up? Please?'

'Fuck, Em! You're soaked,' he said as he opened the door.

'I know. I'm sorry, I've dripped on your doormat.'

'It's okay. Leave your coat here, and come in and get warm.' He put his arm around me and guided me into the apartment. 'Wait here,' he ordered, disappearing in the direction of the bathroom, returning with a towel and bathrobe. 'Take these and go have a hot shower. I'll make us a drink.'

I smiled a watery smile and did as he said.

When I reappeared in a robe that completely dwarfed me, still towelling my hair dry, he took my wet clothes from me and passed me a glass. 'Here, drink this quickly. It's tequila – you need it. I'll pop these into the dryer, and then you can tell me what that bastard's done to you now.'

'How do you know it's Jamie?'

'I know you. Now drink.'

I grimaced as the alcohol ran through me, but it completed the job the shower had started and warmed me. Booth brought the bottle and the glasses back to his coffee table, and patted the seat on the sofa beside him.

'Okay, talk,' he ordered, pouring us both fresh shots.

So I did. I told him everything. About the texts and messages and calls. About the risks we'd taken and the cancelled dates. I told him about our one-night and how Jamie had said how special it was. I told him about Callie, and how Jamie'd laughed when he said we were both in it for the kicks. I didn't tell him about the pain in my middle, or how I feared that Jamie had broken me, and I didn't tell him about the job.

At the end of the telling Booth's face was expressionless and the bottle was a lot emptier.

'You're disappointed in me, aren't you?' I said.

'You warned me about him – you suspected he was seeing someone, and you were right.'

'Yes, I was right, but I'm still surprised. I'd thought . . . it doesn't matter what I thought. I'm far from being disappointed in you. I just hate that he hurt you and there was nothing I could do to stop it.'

He put his arm around me and pulled me close. I cuddled into his familiar warmth.

'You told me that I trust too easily. That means this is always going to happen to me, isn't it?'

'Oh, sweetheart,' he murmured into my hair, 'I love that you trust people, don't ever change that. It's just that some people don't deserve it. He didn't deserve it.'

'But it's always going to happen – I'm always going to be second choice. They always choose someone else. I know it sounds pathetic, but I just want someone to choose me – and only me. I'm so tired of my goodbyes consisting of "It's been nice, but she's better".'

Tears were running down my face now. It was a combination of the tequila allowing me to say things out loud that hadn't been said before, and Booth's arms, and his warmth – and something else, but I couldn't say it. I didn't intend to kiss him – it was supposed to be a hug and then it changed direction. I didn't know if I reached up to him or he reached down to me, but his lips were on mine and mine on his.

I held on more tightly than I'd ever held on before, and he held me more tightly than I'd ever been held –

as if he couldn't bear to let me go. I literally fell into his kiss . . . and the whole thing was a million times more intensely exciting than having sex with Jamie had been.

It was that intensity that made me break away from him. As a first kiss, this one was extraordinary.

'Oh God, I'm sorry.' My voice was shaking.

Inside I was telling myself over and over again, *it was only a kiss, just a kiss*. But my lips had never felt on fire like this before. The flame that had shot through me was more effective than any amount of tequila I could have drunk. I wanted to throw myself back into his arms and keep kissing him forever. Instead, I sat there beside him with my head down, and pulled the robe back together.

'Em,' he said softly, 'look at me . . .'

So I did, and he was smiling, and it was the most beautiful smile I'd ever seen.

I moved back into his arms as if it was the most natural thing in the world to do, as if kissing him was the only thing I was meant to be doing, as if I'd always meant to be kissing him.

I honestly hadn't seen it coming. Me and Booth. In bed. I hadn't seen it coming, and I didn't think he had either. But now that it had, I couldn't stop thinking about it.

Up until last night, I would have said that Booth and I were living proof that men and women really could be friends without the sex thing getting in the way.

But what about how we shagged once?

To set the record straight, despite what Suse said, Booth and I had never had sex. We'd simply got in the habit of telling everyone that we had – it seemed easier than explaining that we hadn't, or why we didn't want to. We'd been saying it for so long that I thought Booth actually believed we had slept together. I didn't even know how it started. It was probably a Friday night when we'd had a little too much to drink and were bickering a little too loudly. Someone probably said something like, 'Why don't you two just get a room and get it over with?' Booth probably said something like, 'Nah, been there, done that.' He would have laughed, and I would have agreed with something like, 'And not going there again.' Or something like that. Now that everyone thought we had slept together, no one hassled us about when we were going to. It wasn't anything that we'd deliberately decided or spoken about, but it made a strange sort of sense.

It wasn't because we'd never been single together. Trust me, there'd been plenty of opportunities. No, the real reason that Booth and I had never had sex was much more straightforward – neither of us had ever wanted to. Aside from a very brief period at the start, there'd never been a 'moment' between us, not even the tiniest spark of attraction. No occasion when our eyes had met for a little too long, or when the touch of his hand sent a shiver through parts of me. Until recently, there'd been nothing like that.

We'd never talked about it – the no-spark thing. After all, how did you tell your best friend that you weren't attracted to him? Especially a man like Booth who had a, shall we say, healthy level of self-confidence. It certainly wasn't because he wasn't shaggable – he was. Plenty of women thought so. Two of them had even married him. Despite being a little on the thin side, and having rather ordinary biceps, Booth had a sexual confidence that followed him around.

Back when we first met, I was conscious of his looks and his presence. I even wondered what he'd be like in bed. Suse and I discussed it one time.

'He must be good.'

'Why do you say that?'

'Because he never has problems getting women, and when he's finished with them, they're heartbroken. Yep, he must be good.'

'But his attention to detail sucks.'

Her reply wasn't suitable for this forum.

Since then, he'd been Booth, my best mate. He was safe. There was no way I could have slept with him and then 1-2-3 forgotten about it. You didn't just forget about sleeping with your best friend – that wasn't how it worked, not for me. I wasn't good with casual sex.

If I had been okay with it, I would have dusted myself off this morning, kissed him on the forehead and said something like, 'Thanks for the ride and the tequila, babe – it was fun,' before heading out the door with a spring in my step. Or I might have woken him for the repeat performance I so desperately wanted.

If it had been one of those situations where I'd really wanted him and he'd really wanted me and we'd just taken forever to hook up, it would have been easier to deal with. The sun would have crept in through the curtains we'd forgotten to shut and gently woken us. I'd stretch languorously, and he'd turn to me, trace my lips with his finger and say 'Why did we take so long to do this?' Then we'd make love again, phone in sick, and go back to bed for the rest of the day, finally emerging with a glow about us that could light up the MCG. Everyone would look at us, smile knowingly and say something like, 'I knew you two belonged together.' We'd move easily from Booth and Em, best mates, to Josh and Emily, boyfriend and girlfriend.

Of course, that wasn't what happened.

Instead, I woke sometime before dawn with no idea of where I was. I looked across at Booth who was snoring softly, the lines on his forehead relaxed, rough stubble on his jaw. The sheet had slipped down his body, but I resolutely looked away and concentrated instead on being impressed that he knew a thing or two about thread counts and clean linen.

Somehow I managed to find most of last night's clothes, and slunk out of his apartment without waking him. The last thing I wanted was for him to wake up, see me, and try to hide the look of horror when he realised what we'd done. I could deal with most things, but not that – not from Booth.

I didn't indulge in any real what-the-fuck-have-I-done thinking until I was in the taxi and well on my way home in the rain. Yes, it was still raining – which seemed right. There was no spring in my step, no skipping along the streets with a song in my heart, and no noticing how fresh and new and completely beautiful everything was. There were just the rain-soaked streets, the sound of the taxi wipers invading my hangover, and the knowledge that somehow, in the middle of the best night of my life, I'd managed to ruin the best thing in my life.

And it had been the best night of my life – amazing, incredible, overwhelming and a whole lot of other adjectives. Everything was perfect – from the moment he'd opened my robe and gazed at me, before following his eyes with his fingers and then his lips, to the moment I cried out his name, and the moment he moaned as he entered me, his eyes never leaving mine as I came. It was as if he needed to know that I knew who I was with. There was never any doubt of that.

I made a mental note to add a tick beside 7b on my bucket list: *Have sex somewhere other than a bed.*

After that first time, we moved from the couch to the bedroom, drifting in and out of sleep, in and out of each other, in and out of bliss. I wasn't going to give a blow-by-blow, so to speak, account of whose bits went where and who said what, but what Booth and I had last night was cliché sex. The earth moved and waterfalls bubbled over and waves crashed down, and he took me (repeatedly) to a place higher than I'd been before. As I said, it was amazing, he was amazing – we were amazing together. And it could never happen again.

CHAPTER TWENTY-EIGHT

His text came when I was on the tram into work.

Booth: Hi.

Me: Hi.

Booth: All okay?

Me: Sure. You?

A little break. Then:

Booth: All good. Running late – will go straight to client's offices, so won't be able to make lunch today. Sorry.

Me: Okay.

Booth: Are you sure you're okay?

Me: Yep. Just a little slow this morning – you know how it is.

Booth: Okay, talk later?

Me: Sure.

If I'd been into tweeting I would have posted: *#Lame convo after #hookup with #bestie #awkward.*

The similarities to the morning after with Jamie were alarming.

It probably would have been easier if the sex had been disappointing – but as I'd already said, it was far from that. Not only was *he* good, but *we* were – good together. Great, in fact. So great that now, sitting at my desk looking at a requirements register I had absolutely no interest in, I closed my eyes and felt again the tingle of remembered sensation.

If the sex had been disappointing, there would have been an uncomfortable silence for a bit, followed by a been-there-done-that-not-going-back-again shrug. Like we'd been pretending for the last however many years. Now, because it had been so good, I figured we had three options open to us.

1. Friends with benefits.

I'd never really known how this worked. I assumed it was a little like repeated casual sex with a mate. This option had the advantage that not only would I get to keep Booth, but with the added extra of amazing sex when I felt like it and he felt like it. There'd be no commitments and no messiness if things didn't work out. On the downside, I wasn't sure how I'd feel about seeing him with other women. Best not to think about that . . . except, of course, I had to think about that, because Booth was in a relationship, which made my next option something that was already not possible.

2. Relationship.

The whole boyfriend and girlfriend extravaganza. I'd watched Booth in relationships before – his attention span was short. This meant that even if we did end up together, if he did choose me instead of Corinna, once we'd got the initial amazing sex out of our system, he'd start looking around for someone else to hold his interest. After all, he knew me better than anyone else in the world knew me. There were no secrets between us, no mystery for him to unlock, no reason for him to stay around. I'd spend from now until we finished wondering whether he'd chosen me out of loyalty to our friendship. Ultimately I'd lose him to someone else and I'd be broken-hearted – without Booth to help me through it. Basically I'd be buggered.

3. Do nothing.

Pretend nothing had happened. Don't go there again. Plead drunkenness and rebound shagging under the influence. Tequila rarely ended well – Mum had told me that.

Yes, doing nothing was the best option.

We didn't talk until late that afternoon. Booth bounded into the project meeting five minutes before the end and, for a change, didn't cause his usual amount of havoc.

'Where are we on the software delivery date?'

'We're on target for delivery into system testing,' I checked my project plan, 'by next Wednesday, as per the schedule. We've allowed ourselves two weeks to get rid of any major bugs and it should be with the testing team by the end of the month.'

'Okay. Is everything else still on track? Good. Get

your arses back to work. Emily? Can you stay back for a few moments?'

He waited until everyone else had left and then perched himself on the table beside me. A slow, sweet smile spread across his face. 'So . . . last night . . .?' He was watching my face closely. I concentrated on my paperwork so I didn't have to meet his eyes. 'You left this morning without waking me. What was that about?'

'I figured I'd better get home.'

He was silent for a moment. I made some notes in the margin of the meeting minutes.

'I thought we had fun.'

'We did,' I agreed. 'It's just . . . well, it was a mistake. It shouldn't have happened. Don't you think?'

'Do you think it was a mistake?'

'It doesn't matter whether I think it was a mistake.'

'Actually, Em, it does matter. It matters to me. I had a good time, I thought you did too, and then when I woke up you were gone.'

I wished he wouldn't smile at me like that.

'I thought it would be best.'

I drew a flower. With a sun and a rainbow.

'Em . . . are you okay about this?' he asked softly.

I chanced a look at his face. There was an expression there that I didn't want to think about now. If I did, I'd slip into a delicious replay of last night, and given that he was one hundred per cent taken by somebody else, it was a fantasy I couldn't allow myself to indulge in.

'Yeah, Booth. I'm fine, thanks. Everything's fine. I'm tired – and still a little hungover.' I forced a laugh. 'Just how much did we drink last night? I'm so sorry if I said anything stupid, but I'm really having problems remembering everything.'

He tried to hold my gaze, but I looked away first.

'Are we playing the pretend-it-didn't-happen game?' he said. 'The shagging-under-the-influence excuse won't work – neither of us had that much to drink.'

I shrugged.

'If it's okay with you,' he went on, 'I intend remembering everything – especially the part –'

Did he have to make this so hard? 'Please don't.'

'We weren't a one-night stand, Em. It might have just happened the once, but it doesn't mean I hadn't thought about it before that.'

Oh.

'Had you?'

'No,' I lied.

'Not even the other night, when I stayed over? Or the next morning?'

'No.' My lie took longer to come out this time.

'Liar,' he accused, his eyes not leaving mine.

There they were again – the butterflies. A whole chaos of them.

'Maybe there was a moment,' I conceded.

'So why did you leave?'

'Because I didn't want to see your face when you woke up and realised what we'd done.'

'Why?'

I coloured in the petals on my flower. 'It was too much.'

Why wasn't he saying anything?

'Josh?'

'I was too much? We were too much? Just what was too much, Em?'

'No, you were lovely.' I goosepimpled up at just how lovely he was. 'It was lovely. God, it was more than lovely. It's just –'

'Just that I'm not Jamie?'

What the fuck?

'Were you thinking about Jamie?'

'God, no! Is that what you think? That I left because I realised you weren't Jamie?' I watched his face. His expression didn't change, but there was a firmness to his jaw that I wanted to kiss away. 'You couldn't be more wrong. I left because I didn't want you to wake up and be disappointed.'

That came out all wrong.

'What the fuck?' He said it out loud.

'You know . . . disappointed that I'm not Corinna.'

'Em, I was under no illusions about that.'

Now, what's that supposed to mean?

'See, that makes it worse – it makes it more of a mistake. I don't sleep with men who I know are in relationships. You're with Corinna – we shouldn't have done what we did.'

'About that . . . what if I wasn't with Corinna?'

I waved his comment away. 'Then there's the issue of us – you and me. You're my best friend – I've seen you in relationships, and you've seen me. I attach easily, and you bore quickly. You'll break my heart, and it'll be so much worse than anything else – because I'll have lost you and this time you wouldn't be coming back.'

'It doesn't have to be like that. Are you still hung up on Jamie. Is that the real issue here?'

'Of course I'm not.'

'Well, what is it then?'

'I told you – I can't be the other woman. I can't be anyone's Plan B – especially not yours.'

'Is that really what you think? That you're my back-up plan?'

I paused, and forced a confident smile – like I thought a girl who was used to having casual sex with her best friend might smile. 'You know what? It's okay, really. I was upset . . . it was just one of those things. I guess it was bound to happen sooner or later.'

'We mightn't have planned it, but I'm glad it happened. It was pretty wonderful.'

'I'm not.' I hadn't meant for that to come out loud. 'It was a mistake.'

This time when I looked at him, I saw his jaw tighten with tension, and something that could be pain, or maybe self-reproach, in his eyes.

He stood and walked to the door. 'Yeah, I guess you're right – it was just one of those things. There's no need to make it bigger than that. And, as you've reminded me, you're on the rebound from Jamie.'

I felt something dip in my tummy, an emptiness that I couldn't explain. I wanted him to say something different. I wanted him to insist that we talk about it. For a brief moment I wanted him to say that he was going to break up with Corinna and we should give it a go –give us, Josh and Em, a go. I wanted to see blue skies and trees, and hear trilling music to skip to. I wanted Michael Bublé on my playlist, with trumpets, feeling good. Instead all I felt was grey.

I'd read somewhere that the Inuit had fifty words to describe snow. I was pretty sure they were the people who did that weird-sounding throat-singing. Not that it was weird to them, but to a girl brought up on a diet of pop music, it definitely sounded weird. Why did anyone need fifty words to describe snow. Surely it was either snowing or not snowing?

It made more sense to me that the British would have fifty words to describe rain. Apparently they saw a lot of it. Not that I'd seen much – of Britain or the rain there. The year Mum and I went across for Dad's wedding, we only stayed a week and it was an unseasonably warm summer. Everyone said so.

Where was I? Yes, fifty words for rain. Probably more than that if you included the different shades of overcast. My favourite of the overcast words had to be *dreich*. I think it meant that space between manky weather – pissing down with rain and bitterly cold – and overcast. It was something more than grey, but not as vibrant as steel-grey storm clouds. That was how I felt: *dreichy*. In a *dreich* mood. Like all the colour in the world had gone.

I was an idiot to think things could go back to being the same as they had been with Booth. It didn't just feel different, it *was* different.

He spent Friday morning offsite, and most of Friday afternoon in his office. A few times he caught my eye and grinned, but it wasn't the usual Booth grin – it felt forced.

When Diane breezed through in neck-to-toe blue and green stripes, I tried to break the ice with an instant message: *You know what they say about blue and green never being seen together? Now I know why.*

He didn't respond, and almost immediately his status changed. *Joshua Booth is offline.*

He didn't come to the pub that night, but, for a change, Suse did.

'Where's Booth?' she asked.

'At work. He texted me before I left. Some issue with next week's audit, he said.'

'Oh.' She seemed distracted.

'Are you okay?'

'Yes, Georgia's unsettled so I'm not sleeping well. How many teeth can these kids get? And Richard's been away again this week. He gets a comfortable hotel bed and the life of a single man, while I'm stuck at home with his kids. Then when he does come home, he expects me to bring out the dancing girls and the hallelujah chorus. I'd like to see him juggle it all for a change – for longer than a weekend. You know, I got back from the offsite the other week and the house looked like a bomb had hit it. I don't know what he did all weekend.'

'Where was the offsite?'

It seemed easier to ignore the rest of her rant. I happened to know that Richard did more than his fair share around the house, but figured she was in no mood to hear that. Nor did I think she was in the mood for me to point out that having cheated on him, she was in no position to complain when work took him away.

'Oh, the Yarra Valley – one of those places that does conferences and things.'

'I didn't know you had one of those scheduled?'

'I didn't – I was a last-minute invitee. One of the management team dropped out, so I got the call on Friday.'

'Lucky you. Since when do IT firms have the money to throw around on all-expenses-paid weekends in the wine village? Was it the same place we stayed at?'

She looked a little uncomfortable and took a large mouthful of her wine. 'I know, it makes a nice change.

Anyway, what about you? What's been happening?'

'I have no idea where to start,' I said miserably.

'Come on, it can't be that bad – can it?'

'On the stupid scale of one to ten, I've done something that rates an eleven – I slept with Booth on Wednesday night.'

'So? You've been there before. I always assumed you guys had the occasional random hook-up on those nights he stayed over at yours.'

'See, that's the thing, I haven't been there before.'

'But you both always said . . .'

I shrugged. 'Somehow it seemed easier. Everyone was always assuming, so we said we had. Well, Booth said we had, and it sort of stuck.'

'I see.'

I didn't think she did. We sipped in silence for a few minutes.

'Are you in love with him?' she finally asked.

'No, of course not – it's Booth.'

'So what's the problem then?'

'It's changed everything. He's not here tonight.'

'I think you're imagining things, Em.'

I shook my head. 'I'm not. I've thought it all through – I know what Booth is like. He's sworn off relationships, he knows how quickly I attach, and I know how quickly he gets bored. I'd be setting myself up for heartbreak if I fell for him.'

'Is that likely? Falling for him?'

I lifted a shoulder. 'That's not something I even want to think about. After all, this is Booth we're talking about.'

She searched my face. 'Are you sure?'

'Absolutely.' I swirled my wine around the glass. 'I told him it was just one of those things – a shagging-under-the-influence event. We'd been drinking tequila and everyone knows that never ends well. It was a stupid mistake, and I wanted to tell him that in case he felt some sort of obligation to me. I couldn't bear that, so I figured it was up to me to tell him first – that it was a mistake. I thought he'd be relieved, but now he's avoiding me.'

'I'm sure that's not the case. He probably really is busy.'

'Maybe. Anyway, I think it was just a mercy fuck.'

'Why?'

'Because I was so upset about Jamie. He started pouring tequila, and then he comforted me, and one thing led to another.'

'Jamie? What does he have to do with it?'

'See, that's the other thing I haven't told you.' I took a deep breath. 'Jamie and I finally hooked up. I really thought he was the one, you know? And then . . . well, he wasn't. Just like every other man in my life, he chose his ex.'

Susie was staring at me. 'What did you say?'

'Which bit? The part about me and Jamie hooking up – finally – or the part about him dumping me? Not that he dumped me as such. You can't be dumped if it was just a one-night stand.'

'Well, both, I guess. Why didn't you tell me?'

'I don't know . . . Josh knew, of course – he was there when it happened. He watched me humiliate myself. I rang to tell you, but you were away.'

'When did you and Jamie get together?'

'Last week, when we were at that offsite. We had dinner, and he kissed me, and then he came to my room and – well, it finally happened.' I paused for a sip of wine. 'When he left my room, I really thought everything would be fine, but he wouldn't even look at me the next day. When we were leaving he said he'd call me, and I waited around all last weekend, but he didn't call. I even tried texting him, but it was like once he'd had me, he was moving on. So,' I laughed ruefully, 'I accidentally had my first one-night stand. Then, just a few days later, I had my second. All these years of being a goody-two-shoes and I let all my standards slip so completely.'

'Have you spoken to him at all? Jamie, that is.'

'Yeah, Wednesday night. I saw him and Callie kissing out the front of the bookshop at the top end of Bourke Street. It looked like a scene from a movie – all black and white and misty. He told me they'd recently got back together and he felt an obligation to her to see if it would work. If he has such an obligation to her, why did he sleep with me? I felt like such a fool for trusting him. Thank God no one at work, except Booth, knows.

I couldn't bear that.' I sighed deeply. 'So that's why I slept with Booth. And now there's no way of undoing it.'

Suse opened her mouth to say something and closed it again.

'What were you about to say?' I asked.

'We need more drinks,' she said, and went to the bar to rectify the situation.

'Here's to bastards,' she toasted as we clinked glasses.

'Booth's not a bastard,' I said. 'He's the nicest man I know. He doesn't deserve to be lumped in the same category as Jamie.'

She considered that. 'I guess.'

We drank our wine in silence for a few moments.

'How was it?' Suse asked. 'Was he as good as we thought he'd be?'

'Jamie?'

'No, idiot – Josh.'

'Oh, yes. It was good. We were good. We were so good together, it's the sex I'll remember on my deathbed – I'm sure of it. To be honest, Suse, it scared the crap out of me. I'm not sure I can ever look at him in the same way again. It was too real.'

'I guess there's one good thing to come out of this,' she said.

'Tell me quickly – I sure as hell can't think of one.'

'It's another tick off the bucket list. Congratulations, Em, you've just had casual sex.'

CHAPTER TWENTY-NINE

I didn't see Booth at all over the weekend. I didn't phone him and he didn't phone me.

I had my new floors laid on Saturday, so all that was left to buy were a few rugs to soften the oak I'd gone for and every item on my renovation list was ticked off.

Andi called on Saturday and invited me out with Todd and some other friends. Even though I wanted to sit at home and feel sorry for myself, I dressed up, went out and, against all odds, had a fabulous time. Despite what Andi said, there was definitely something brewing between her and Todd.

'He's not my type,' she protested, 'and I'm not his. We're just having some fun while we work out how to get Abby and Brad back together.'

'How's that going?'

She pulled a face. 'Brad's home from Denmark soon, and Abby's back in Bali for a couple of weeks. Hopefully we can make it happen – although they're both digging their heels in. Brad's a Taurus, you see –

stubborn. And Abby's just plain wilful.'

With that, she twirled off to drag Todd onto the dance floor.

Jodie Lawrence phoned on Thursday to let me know that I'd missed out on the job at DotPoint. I was more upset than I'd thought I'd be. Sure, I was using it as a reason to escape Jamie and Booth, but more than that, I really wanted to work there.

'Just so you know, Alex was very impressed with your interview, and we'll be keeping you in mind if anything else comes up. The person we've chosen has more experience with web development and social media platforms, but it was a close call.' Her voice lowered as she added, 'On a personal note, I want to wish you luck for whatever comes next. The way you were talking about pushing your comfort zones – well, that's scary, but also inspiring. I really hope it all works out for you.'

At work, Booth tried to pretend that everything was as it always had been between us, but nothing was the same. I was sure everyone could see it. He'd been working through lunch most days, so we really hadn't spoken at all.

On Friday night, both he and Suse begged off drinks. Richard was away so Suse said she had to stay home with the kids, and Booth said he had somewhere else that he needed to be. I assumed he was with Corinna, and the knowledge of that felt like a great weight in the middle of my chest where my heart used to be. Sure that sounded dramatic, but it was how I felt. As disappointed as I was about the DotPoint job falling through, with the way everything else was falling apart around me, perhaps it was a good thing that I wasn't changing roles as well.

I called Booth on Saturday afternoon to see if he wanted to check out my new floor – yes, I knew how lame that sounded – but he didn't pick up and I didn't leave a message.

On Sunday morning I tried again, this time asking him if he'd like to go to the football with me. Again he didn't pick up, so I went by myself – anything to get out of the apartment and stop me wondering about where he was and what he was doing with Corinna. I couldn't bear the thought of his lips on hers, his mouth on those tiny breasts, his hands on her skin. When I closed my eyes I saw it all – him kissing his way down her neck, behind her perky ponytail, her with her head thrown back and her eyes closed, her long legs wrapped around his body as he thrust into her. In my dreams she turned and looked at me – a triumphant 'he chose me' smile on her face. Even in my sleep it hurt.

On Monday, Jamie was back in the office. He seemed to have forgotten our encounter of the other week and was right back into full flirt mode. On Wednesday he followed me into the filing room and attempted to steal a kiss. I pushed him away, but he just laughed.

'I know you're still angry, babe, but there's no reason why anything has to change,' he said, putting his piercing eyes to good use.

Now I knew there was nothing of substance behind them, they left me cold.

'Don't call me babe. I'm not your babe.' I shook my head and walked away.

His laugh followed me. 'Your loss.'

In the meantime, Booth's temper was deteriorating. Everyone was beginning to notice. In our usual Friday meeting he completely lost it with Tony. Sure, Tony was being his usual overly bureaucratic self, but Booth's reaction was over the top. He followed that with an attack on Patrick.

'I thought I made it clear that all support calls are to be logged and are to remain open until resolved and the solution documented?' He didn't wait for a response. 'So why hasn't the network card issue been entered?'

'Because it happened before the system went live. If Emily's team had got it in on time –'

'So you're blaming someone else for your incompetence? That seems to be your style. Just so you're crystal clear,' he almost spat the words out, 'I want the network card issue – and anything else you're holding up your sleeve because you think it makes you a protected species – entered into the system.'

Patrick stormed out, and the others slunk out,

leaving me alone with Booth.

'That wasn't fair, Josh.'

'It's none of your business, Em.'

'Actually, I think it is.'

He stared at me for a few seconds. 'Perhaps,' he finally conceded. He took a breath and then said slowly, 'Em, this isn't going to work.'

'What isn't?'

'This. I get that you don't want to be with me, but I can't sit back and watch you with Jamie. Not again.'

'But I'm not with Jamie.'

'Don't lie to me, Em. I've been watching the two of you all week. I saw you together on Wednesday. I saw him kiss you.'

'You saw him try to kiss me. If you'd hung around, you would have seen me push him away.'

He didn't seem to be listening.

'He told me that it was all sorted out between you. That it was all just a misunderstanding. He asked me to stay out of it. He said you were too embarrassed to tell me that you'd taken him back.'

'But –'

He held his hand up. 'Don't say it, Em. I don't need to know.' He laughed, but it had no humour in it. 'You've made your choice.'

'I've made my choice? I wasn't aware that I had a choice to make.'

'Of course you did.'

'Are you saying that you don't want us to work together any more?'

He shrugged.

'So which of us should go? You or me?'

He didn't answer.

I rarely lost my temper – I preferred the passive-aggressive method of conflict resolution – but now I exploded.

'Booth, this . . . this conversation is why I left that morning. I knew this would happen. I get that you feel some sort of misguided responsibility for me, but if you really can't work with me any more, just tell me now. Do you want me to resign? It may as well be me this time.'

Booth rarely backed away from a situation, but now he was silent, probably trying to work out how to salvage the argument, or deciding whether it could be salvaged.

'That's not what I'm saying,' he said eventually. 'I'm just saying that I want you to be happy. And if that involves being with Jamie, I can't stay around and watch as he breaks your heart again. Because he will – you know he will.'

And that was when the lightning bolt hit me. Out of the blue. For real. It wasn't Jamie I wanted. I wondered now whether it had ever been about Jamie, or Craig, or any of the others. It was about Booth. It was as if I was seeing him for the very first time. It was like when it'd been raining for weeks and the sun suddenly came out, and everything seemed clearer and brighter and greener. Perhaps it had always been Booth. Didn't he know that I couldn't be happy with anyone but him? Didn't he know that he was the one breaking my heart right now?

I couldn't look at him in case he saw the truth in my eyes, so I left. He didn't stop me.

I took my anger out on the walls in the privacy of the fire stairs, following them down into the car park – all thirty-four levels in these fucking heels.

I was hoping he'd follow me, and hold me and kiss me until I couldn't think about anything else. I wanted him to tell me that he didn't want Corinna, that he only wanted me . . . that he chose me. I wanted to tell him that Jamie meant nothing and he meant everything. I wanted him to tell me that he'd been hit with the same bolt from the blue that I'd been. That he loved me too.

On the way down, I gave myself a stern talking-to.

No, no, no, no, Emily. You can't be in love with Booth. This is just some hormonal reaction, that's all. Nothing else. It's understandable that you're confused – the sex was fantastic. God, yes. Utterly fantastic, and that's part of the problem. It's hormonal. You want to shag him. That's okay, but don't wrap it up in brown paper and tie a pretty bow around it and call it love. Not this time.

I leaned against the concrete wall in the car park and swallowed back the tears that were threatening to stream down my face. A few snuck out and I scrubbed them away with the sleeve of my blouse, remembering too late that (a) it was white, and (b) it was silk, and neither of those things mixed well with mascara and make-up streaks.

Using someone's side mirror, I fixed up my face roughly with my finger before venturing back upstairs – this time via the lift. My feet were killing me.

Back at my desk an email had come through from Booth:

Hey Em,

I don't know what this thing is with you and Jamie, and maybe I should have given you a chance to explain, but he's wrong for you. I can't tell you how I know – not yet – but trust me when I say that I know.

Seeing him kiss you the other day made me realise that I can't sit back and watch this happen. Maybe it means I have to change jobs again. I don't know. Maybe we can get past this. I hope so.

It's best that we don't see each other for a few days, so I won't be at the pub tonight, but we have things to say. I have things I have to tell you, but I think we both need to cool down first. I know I have no right to ask you this, but please don't meet him until we talk? We'll have dinner on Monday night and say what we need to say.

What's happened to the three of us – you, me and Suse? It's different now and I don't know where it went wrong.

Josh x

I was deciding how to respond, when he walked

past my office. He raised his eyebrows and I managed to nod.

When Suse rang later that afternoon to make her apologies for drinks, I told her that I really needed to talk to her.

'I'm sorry, love, but Richard can't be home for the kids, so I need to be. Next week, I promise.'

'What about brunch tomorrow?' I suggested. 'I'll pick you up at ten. We'll go to that place in Abbotsford.'

'I'll have to check with Richard . . .'

'You know you love it there,' I coaxed. 'Please?'

'Okay, fine. I'll see you tomorrow.'

Richard greeted me with a kiss, a smile and an apology. 'Suse is running a little behind this morning. She's still in the shower.'

'That's fine – I'm early. Besides, it's a good chance for us to chat. I feel like I haven't seen you in ages.'

'Why is that?' He pulled a chair out from the kitchen counter for me.

'I have no idea. But Suse has been busy – what with girls' weekends and offsites.'

'Yes, she has. The poor girl has been working late a lot lately.'

'That must be hard with your hours and travel schedule.'

'Normally yes, but thankfully my load hasn't been too bad of late. I've enjoyed being able to be home with the kids. I don't get to spend a lot of time with them during the week, so it's been nice to put the passport away for the last few weeks.'

'So you haven't been travelling?' Hadn't Suse been complaining about him being away?

'No, not for the last six weeks – which is lucky as Suse has been the one who's needed to be away, or out with you guys. Although I can't say she came back relaxed from Daylesford – I thought those places were supposed to send you home glowing and blissed out? She came back more strung out than she went away. And I don't think the offsite the other week went as well as she'd have liked – she's been pretty subdued ever since.'

So it wasn't just my imagination- Richard had noticed that too.

'Maybe she missed the kids?' I suggested. 'Speaking of which – where are they?'

He gestured towards the room off the kitchen, where Toby was lying on his tummy watching a cartoon pig prancing across the TV screen.

'Georgia?' I asked.

'Asleep . . . for now.' He smiled. 'I've been relaxing with the Saturday papers.' He indicated the pile of supplements on the kitchen bench.

'Anything I should know about in those?'

'I don't think so – the usual political malarkey, something about property values again, and there's a recipe involving lamb shanks, barley and a lot of slow cooking that sounds like it could be good.'

'Em! Em!' called Toby, launching his little body into my arms for a wriggling cuddle, before just as quickly turning his attention back to the TV.

'Aaah, the fickle nature of children,' commented Richard. 'Can I do you a coffee while you wait?'

'Please. From that?'

The red and chrome contraption took up half of the kitchen bench, and had so many handles it looked as though it could successfully launch a B-52 – or at the very least, grace the swankiest of Italian cafes.

'Yes – I only just bought it, so you're a guinea pig for me. I finished my training on Wednesday night.' He pulled a bag of coffee beans from the fridge. 'I get these from one of those specialty shops up in Brunswick Street, and I went to a course to learn how to drive this thing, but even so, I think it's going to take me a while before I get it right.'

'You needed to do a course? Do they issue you with a licence or something?'

'Absolutely.' He pointed towards a certificate hanging on the fridge – beside a couple of birthday invitations, Toby's latest finger-painting and a whiteboard shopping list.

The machine made a professional-sounding gurgle, and Richard presented my coffee with a bad Italian accent. It was strong and good, with the perfect amount of crema on top – or so Richard told me. He told me quite a bit about crema and beans and balance of flavours. It was another of the things I loved about him – his enthusiasm for the mundane and everyday. He was the type of guy whose default position was contentment in the now. It made him a very easy man to be around and the perfect foil for Suse.

'Before I did this course, I had no idea just how complex a cup of coffee was,' he said.

'Nor did I.' I grinned.

'Tell me, Em, are you into this running thing with Suse and Josh? You're looking great.'

'Thanks for the compliment, but no, I'm not signed up for the half – I'll let those guys do it on their own. Although, between you and me, I have been doing some training so I might walk the ten-kay event. I haven't told the others though, in case I chicken out.'

He smiled and folded the newspaper supplements away. 'Good on you. Your secret's safe with me. You know, when Suse first joined the running club, I truly didn't expect she'd last, but here we are, a couple of months down the track, and off she goes every Sunday morning – even now it's the middle of winter. I'm very proud of her.'

'But I thought –'

I stopped when I saw Suse standing in the kitchen doorway. I'd always thought that the expression 'my blood ran cold' was exactly that – an expression. Yet that was what happened as the implication of everything Richard had said sank into my brain and jigsaw pieces arranged themselves in my head. An icy chill spread throughout my body.

'There you are, darling,' he went on. 'I was just remarking on how Emily looks like she's been training too.' He turned back to me. 'If you haven't been running, what have you been doing that's made you look so fit?'

'I've been renovating – can you believe that? Me with a power tool, painting and decorating? I've done my whole apartment and it looks great. Losing a few kilos has been a very happy side effect. I'll have to get you both around for dinner now that I'm finished.'

'Renovating, hey? Suse never said. And cooking too? We'll look forward to that. Suse mentioned that you attempted something for the three of you the other month. Where was my invite, hey?'

He grinned to let me know he was teasing, but hadn't Suse said . . .

'It's okay, Em,' he said when he noticed how my face had fallen. 'I know you weren't ready to let anyone else taste it in case it all went wrong.'

'Are you ready to go?' Suse asked me.

'Sure.' I put my coffee cup into the dishwasher. 'Thanks for the coffee, Richard.'

'You're welcome. What are you girls up to this morning?'

'Just brunch – maybe a little shopping. I won't be late.' Suse leaned over and kissed Richard goodbye. 'Love you.'

She said nothing to me until we were in the car.

'Please don't say anything yet, Em. Let's wait until we're there – and then I promise I'll tell you everything.'

There was something that looked like panic in her eyes, and that was when I knew for sure.

CHAPTER THIRTY

'The man you were with – it wasn't some random dude from work, was it?'

Suse carefully took the chocolate off the top of her cappuccino with her teaspoon. 'No.'

'His name wasn't John, was it?'

'No.'

'It wasn't just the once either?'

'No.'

I took a deep breath before asking the question that I was sure I already knew the answer to. 'It was Jamie, wasn't it?'

She paused a second and then nodded. 'Yes.'

I let the breath out. It felt as if I'd been pierced somewhere in my middle and the air had been squeezed from me.

'I probably owe you an explanation, don't I?'

'Yes.'

'It started at Harriers – you probably already figured that part out?'

'I had.'

She paused as our food arrived. 'It began as light banter – that sort of flirting that makes you feel attractive. He kissed me for the first time a couple of weeks before we had dinner at your place. I knew that it shouldn't go any further, but I didn't care. It was all so exciting, you know?'

I know – I've been there, remember? I kept my face expressionless.

'He made me feel sexy again – stolen moments here and there. I never knew when he'd call me, when we could be together. It made it all feel even more clandestine.'

Yes, I've been there too.

'That night at your place I saw him flirting with you too, and I knew I had to make my move before you did. So when we left together, I took him into the lane behind your place and we did it against a wall. Then we spent the next morning together. He took me to his place and we made love. That became every Sunday morning. Richard already knew I was out of the house, so I had no need to tell him anything else. I just had to tell Josh that Richard was making it difficult for me to leave the house and that it was easier to do my training solo, closer to home.'

'And Daylesford? There were no girls from work, were there?'

She picked at her eggs. 'No. It was Jamie and I.'

'I see. And the offsite the other weekend? And the

Friday nights?'

She nodded. 'Yes, Jamie again. I know what you're thinking.'

'I don't think you do.'

She couldn't know – because I wasn't thinking anything. All I was feeling was the physical pain of betrayal. It was worse than what Jamie did to me. Suse is – was – one of my best friends.

'Perhaps not,' she acknowledged. 'I let myself down – I know that. I let my family down. But I also let you down – and you don't deserve that.'

Her eyes were watery and she smiled weakly at me. I couldn't smile back.

'No, I don't. You knew how I felt about him. At any time along that road you could have stopped me with a few words. Instead you let me get all the way to the end – you let him hurt me.'

'I wanted to warn you, but I couldn't see any way of doing it without confessing what I was doing. I felt so helpless, and I knew I was betraying you – I wanted to make what I was feeling go away, but I couldn't. Every time I thought I could, he'd call and it would start again.'

I saw a few tears escape, but I was in no mood to give her any sort of comfort.

'The thing is, Suse, you knew how much I liked him – hell, I made you listen to it over and over. All my agonies about why he wasn't kissing me. And then, when we did sleep together, I told you that too. What did the two of you do? Have a few laughs at my expense? Did he tell you about every time he dragged me into a corner, or the boardroom, or a bathroom? Did the two of you laugh about it? About how we were making out in public, at work? And when he slept with me, did you know about that? Did he tell you how he kissed me, what he said to me, how he touched me? What I said to him? How I touched him? Did it turn you on? Did you talk about it when you were in bed? When he was inside you, was he telling you about what he'd done to me?'

'Don't, Em,' she said quietly.

'The funny thing is, I didn't want to say much to you once it had started. Sure, Jamie asked me not to, but the real reason I didn't tell you was because I knew you weren't happy. I knew how dissatisfied and bored you were, and all of a sudden I was in something that was so incredibly exciting it was like a shot of pure gold. You knew that I was in over my head, and rather than help me put the brakes on, you laughed about it with him!'

'It wasn't like that.'

'All those times he blew me off with stories about family visits, or old friends in town for the night – that was you, wasn't it? He told me it was Callie, but it was you?'

She nodded miserably. 'I think so.'

'Do you want to know what hurts the most? Not that he chose his ex over me – Christ, I'm used to that. What hurts the most is that he chose my best friend over me – and she didn't even warn me. Booth tried to, but I didn't listen.'

'It wasn't like that,' she said softly. 'It wasn't like you said. He knew that I knew how you felt about him. I think he used that to get me in deeper. For a while I was competing with you – and I'm ashamed of that. He told me the day before you guys went on that offsite that it was over between us. He didn't give me a reason, just that it had been fun, and now it was over. I was devastated. I thought my world had ended. And then on the Friday morning he called me again and told me that he'd changed his mind, he couldn't be without me. When you told me that you two had hooked up, I figured that he'd gone straight from you to me. I saw him last night to finish it.'

'So the offsite too?'

She leaned back in her chair and looked at me properly for the first time in this dreadful conversation. 'Yes.'

'In the same conference centre? Seriously?'

'Uh huh. Too tacky, right? I didn't know he was back with Callie – not until you told me.'

'Did he tell you that he tried it on again with me on Wednesday? Did he tell you that he told Booth he and I were back together?'

'Yes.'

A thought occurred to me. 'Did you tell him about Booth and me?'

She delayed answering while the waiter cleared away our half-eaten food. 'Yes. I wanted him to know that you'd moved on.'

'So he could concentrate on you?'

She nodded, but didn't look at me. 'He said he thought there'd been something between you two from the start. Apparently Josh confronted him the other day and told him to leave you alone, so he told Josh that the two of you were back on. He said that he waited until Josh would see before he tried to kiss you – apparently Josh looked like he wanted to hit him. What is happening with you two?'

'Nothing . . . now.' I didn't elaborate.

'So, at the end of the day, I risked my marriage for someone who was just having some fun. And I did, Em, I nearly ruined everything.'

'I can't speak for your marriage. Richard doesn't suspect a thing, and I assume you've learned your lesson.'

'Oh, I have. He's such a good man, and I abused his trust for someone like Jamie. I love Richard – you were right before when you said that he's perfect for me. He is, and for a short while I forgot that. What about us? You and me?'

I shook my head. 'No, Suse, you don't get to ask that yet.'

She poured another glass of water, concentrating on the task.

The words in Booth's email came to mind. 'Booth knew, didn't he?'

She nodded. 'Yes.'

She had tears in her eyes. I tried to ignore them. I didn't fucking believe this.

'Everyone knew,' I said. It wasn't a question. 'Except me. How fucking stupid am I?'

'He guessed, Em.'

'When?'

'It doesn't matter.'

'When?'

'Em, don't do this.'

'When did he know? How did he know?'

'He called me the other day. He put everything together. I think he'd seen something between us in the early days. You know Josh – he tends to just know things.'

'Before me, obviously.'

'Don't take this out on him.'

'I don't know what you're talking about,' I lied. I would be taking this out on him.

She watched me silently for a few seconds. 'I worried so much about losing my marriage, but it never occurred to me that I'd lose you two as well.'

I didn't reply.

'You're not saying anything.'

'I can't, Suse. Not yet.'

'And Jamie? How do you feel about him? I know

he hurt you, but . . .'

'I'm not in love with Jamie. I don't think I ever was – I was just a little blinded there for a time. He really didn't give me any chance to get to know him, not properly. It was a crush, and like all crushes it hit me hard and quickly. The thing is . . . the thing is . . . I'm in love with Booth.' And then I burst into tears.

I loved Booth. I thought somehow I always had done. I remembered the first day I'd met him. He had the same cheeky good looks he has now, perhaps a little more hair, perhaps a little thinner, but I knew then – the minute I met him – that he'd be important. I'd talked myself out of falling for him back then. I'd convinced myself so thoroughly that I was happy to have him as my best friend, that the very idea we could be anything else was ridiculous. Aside from when he was off being married, he'd always been there. Through all of my failed relationships, there was Booth. Always Booth.

Until we made love.

Then I lost him.

Suse let me cry and put her hand over mine.

'I think I've always loved him,' I said. 'I mean, of course I've loved him as my best mate, but it's different now . . . maybe it always has been. It's like I've been waiting to know.'

'Have you told him?' she asked gently.

'How can I? He's with Corinna. I don't want him to be with me because he thinks he has to be. I want him to be with me because he wants to be. I want him to choose me.'

'Maybe he's waiting for you to choose him. Maybe it's time you stopped waiting to be chosen and actually went after the man you want?'

'God, I don't know . . . Maybe that's why I've tried so hard to make it work with the others. The thing is, every time one of them asked me to choose him over Booth, it was the beginning of the end – yet he was able to do it twice. How did he choose Mandy-sorry-Amanda or Shayla over our friendship?'

'He had to, Em. The only way any relationship had a chance was if you weren't part of it.'

'He's going to do it again with Corinna. I'm sure of it. He said we have to talk next week and I just know that's what it's about. I can't bear that. I can't smile and pretend this time.'

Her phone rang and Jamie's name flashed onto the screen. She rejected the call, but I pulled my hand back and scrubbed madly at the tears. For a few minutes there I'd forgotten that she'd forfeited the right to my confidences.

'I can't talk about this with you. Not yet.' I used the napkin to wipe my eyes. 'Let's get the bill.'

We didn't talk on the way back to her house, and when I dropped her off she forced a sad smile.

'I'm really sorry, Em – you have no idea how sorry I am. I know you won't want to talk to me for a while, but please think about what I said. You and Josh have been in love with each other for years – it's just taken you both this long to work it out. Take a chance on it. How hard could it be?'

CHAPTER THIRTY-ONE

I opened the first bottle of Kiwi white just after 3 pm. Personally I thought that showed great strength of character. It wasn't every day that you discovered your best friend had been cheating on her husband with the man you thought you were in love with, and that your other best friend, the one you've just discovered you really are in love with, knew about it. It's not every day you lose your two best friends. Just. Like. That.

I eased into my grief, sipping slowly with a little Backstreet Boys. By the second glass – and Westlife – I was sure I could detect passionfruit in the glass.

Celine came out in time for glass number three, and so did the takeaway menus – home delivery, of course. I was responsible enough to know that I was incapable of driving.

The big guns of tortured love songs – Michael Bolton, Leona Lewis and Whitney Houston – made it onto the playlist as I shovelled in tear-diluted Thai green curry. With the wisdom inspired by Eurovision (thanks, Johnny Logan) I constructed an elaborate fantasy where Booth told me that it was me he loved, but Corinna needed him (for some reason I hadn't worked out yet), and we made love one last amazing time before crying, vowing to love each other forever, and going our separate ways.

By glass five, I began to think about what had gone wrong – not just between Booth and me, or Jamie and me, or even Suse and me, but what had gone wrong between the three of us. It would be easy to blame Jamie, but it wasn't just about him. Adele helped me see the sense of it all. With the clarity that only alcohol can bring, it became blindingly obvious that the root cause of all of this was Booth's bucket list. There was a reason I'd never jumped onto the whole bucket-list bandwagon – because things like this happened. Things like your best friend cheating on her husband. Things like falling in love with your other best friend. Things like everything changing.

If it wasn't for the ridiculous running thing:

- Suse would never have come across Jamie.
- Booth would never have noticed me in *that* way.
- I wouldn't have gone into that vintage shop that day and bought that coat.
- I wouldn't have found Coat Girl's bucket list, and Booth wouldn't have had that great idea for me to cook dinner, thereby giving Jamie and Suse the opportunity to have sex for the first time.
- I wouldn't be sitting here now, drowning my

sorrows and grieving for broken friendships.
- Booth wouldn't have met Corinna.
- Booth and I would be as we always were; Richard and Suse would be as they always were; and my comfort zone would still be . . . well, comfortable.

I still would have met Jamie, and fallen for him. Nothing would have changed that. The difference was, I would have been the only one impacted by the Jamie disaster. And it would have ended in the way these things always ended – with him going back to Callie, and me eating chocolate and comfort Chinese, drinking chardonnay and listening to Celine.

As I drained the last of the first bottle into my glass, I conceded that it hadn't all been bad. If I hadn't found Coat Girl's bucket list, and we hadn't had that dinner party, I would never have started my home improvements. I would still have trainers and tax returns in my oven, and I wouldn't have beginner's biceps.

If Jamie hadn't come along, I would never have been forced to acknowledge just how deeply I loved Booth. (I wasn't sure whether this fell into the pros or cons list.)

Try as I might, I couldn't regret Jamie – and I certainly couldn't regret Booth. I just wished that nothing had changed.

I blamed the colour change – of wine (to a local pinot, in case you were interested) – and playlist change (to Abba) for what happened next.

To: joshuabooth@au.sourcedata.com

From: emporter81@mymail.com

Sunday 28 July 2014, 2.32 am

Subject: Goodbye

Hi Josh,

By the time you read this on Monday, I'll be gone.

That sounds really dramatic, doesn't it? But, as I'm mailing under the influence, a little drama is permitted, and expected.

Last night – or was it earlier this morning? – I accidentally booked a flight to Bali. Apparently I fly out today. I can't remember what I said to Mum – I think I told her that I needed her. Steph's already made up the spare bed, so there's no backing out.

My flight is today, I haven't even packed yet, and I don't have a list so I'll probably forget everything. Mum said not to worry, that I can buy anything I need over there. I haven't done anything about injections or travel insurance or making sure that I've got the right sort of money, but Mum said I'm just trying to make it all harder than it needs to be. By the time you read this, I'll be with Mum and Steph in Ubud. I might even be learning about tantric yoga – or breath-work and feminine empowerment or something.

Because I'm drunk-mailing you, I can say more than I should. You need to know that. It'll take me longer than usual to say it, and some of it might not make sense. You should sit down for it. You don't have to reply – in fact, even if you do, I won't see your answer because I'm not checking my email. I'm not even taking my laptop. That way I won't be tempted to check my email, so I won't be able to worry about whether you've replied or not.

I'm sorry I didn't ring you, but I couldn't face you even on the phone, and I didn't want you to try and talk me out of this. I'm not completely irresponsible though — I emailed Diane and told her that I needed two weeks off to deal with a family emergency. I've got eight weeks' leave up my sleeve (hey, that rhymes), so it will be fine — remember how she was trying to get me to take some holidays? I've dobbed Tony in to cover my meetings, and everything else is fairly well under control.

This means we won't be talking tomorrow night, or tonight if you're reading this on Monday — but I think I know what you're going to say. It will be about how Corinna has asked you to choose her — and I can't hear it. But I need you to hear some of what I need to say — without me being able to see your face when I say it. This is the part you'll need to be sitting down for. Unless you're bored already.

You know those times when you were married? I wasn't okay about it. I know I pretended to be happy for you, but I wasn't. The truth is, my heart broke each time. It was okay while you were just shagging around — I didn't need to see any of them or know about them. But Corinna is different, and this time when you choose her, as I know you will, it will be so much worse than before. I won't blame you — her ponytail is super perky and I'm sure she doesn't vomit when she runs — but I want to plead with you to pick me instead of her. I know that isn't fair, and it isn't an option for you, but that doesn't mean I don't want to say it. I did just say it though, didn't I?

Saying it doesn't mean that I'm not still mad as hell with you for not telling me about Jamie and Suse. I can't believe you let me go into that knowing, or even suspecting, they were together. And before you ask how I found out, it was Richard who dropped her in it – accidentally, of course. The poor bastard doesn't know anything. I don't know that I'll ever be able to forgive Suse for doing what she did, and I miss her already. I'd normally be able to ring her and she'd talk me out of telling you this, but I can't ring her, so here goes.

I'm going to miss you too, because I know that after I tell you this next bit, you'll be looking for a reason to avoid me. I'm running away because I've realised that I love you – and not in the usual fall-into-a-crush way that I do, but a full-on, forever, can't-wait-to-see-you and have-to-be-with-you-and-touch-you way. I tried to drown it out with Celine and chocolates and wine, but it hasn't worked. I've tried – I had my favourite songs on repeat, and drank way more than the usual break-up wine. Not that we've broken up – how could we? We weren't even together. Somehow though it feels like we were together, and now we're not. As an aside, seriously, how did Agnetha sing that song Bjorn wrote? "The Winner Takes It All?" That bit near the end where her voice breaks a little gets me every time. Not that either of us have won.

Where was I? I think it confused me so much because usually I fall in and out so hard, but this time I didn't even notice until I was there. This time I hadn't fallen in love, I'd sort of slipped, or drifted there. Gone to sleep one night and woken up there, in love – like in The Partridge Family song. This time it's different. This time it's as if it's part of me – this love for you. All I know is that I've never felt like this before. It took me until Abba to realise – I've been waiting for you.

I know Jamie told you that he and I were back together. He lied. Suse said he only told you that to annoy you or something blokey like that. He doesn't want me, but he doesn't want you to have me either. And I'm only going to tell you this next bit because I'm drunk-typing, but when Jamie and I had sex, I faked it. Technically he'd made such an effort that he deserved some sort of accolade. But you're not allowed to say anything, okay? That's for the vault. And before you ask, I didn't need to with you — with you everything is so real. That's what I meant when I said it was too much. With you I felt too much, like I had no control, or had lost all control — and that's never happened to me before. It scared me. No one has ever made me feel the way you did, but I couldn't tell you that — because you're with Corinna.

Even though I've told you all of this — and you've probably given up reading to go and do something else, like work — don't think I expect anything from you. If we were together I'd just be waiting for you to get bored, and if we weren't together I'd be wishing we were, so there's no right answer. I'd apologise for embarrassing you, but it's a little late for that.

There. I've said it. All of it. Don't reply — there's nothing you can say — but if you wouldn't mind picking up my mail every so often, please? You've still got the key, I think. If you can't find it, you told me that if you ever couldn't find it, I had to remind you that it was at the back of your undies drawer.

With too much love and a million regrets for what can never be,

Em xxx

CHAPTER THIRTY-TWO

Walking across the tarmac from the plane, the heat hit the remains of my hangover like a brick wall. I'd expected it to be hot – everyone said Bali was hot – I just hadn't expected it to be this hot.

When I was packing this morning I'd figured it would be something like one of the hotter Melbourne February days, the ones that send everyone down to St Kilda and South Melbourne beaches after work to try to cool off. In the middle of winter, though, trying to rekindle how that felt and pack accordingly wasn't that successful – especially when in the grips of a massive hangover.

I'd started to write a list, but got as far as:

- Thongs
- Bathers
- Sunscreen
- Passport

before the pain in my head blocked further thought. Opening my bag was going to be a surprise.

For the flight I'd gone for a turquoise maxi dress

and some wedge-heeled flip-flops. With an oversized pair of sunglasses, I figured that I'd sail down the air-bridge, whizz through customs, and emerge into the sunlight with my dignity and make-up still firmly in place. But this wasn't like any Melbourne February day I'd lived through. This was so much worse. It was like walking into a sauna and finding there was no way out. Sadly, my dress was constructed from some man-made fibre that felt like it was melting onto my skin – even for the short walk from the plane to the arrivals gate. Which brought me to the next miscalculation – no air-bridge. The plane parked in the middle of nowhere, and we had to walk down the stairs, across the steaming tarmac, and through the arrivals door. It mightn't have been far, but it felt like we were walking through the gates of hell. Once inside, the only discernible difference in temperature was caused by the absence of sun. As a result, my make-up and I had parted company on the tarmac somewhere – it slid right off my face.

Come to think of it, I didn't recall packing make-up. Something else to add to tomorrow's list of must-be-dones.

Following the other passengers into the narrow customs hall, I saw my name on a sign. Really? I hadn't even had my passport stamped yet, or done that thing with the visa that I vaguely recalled Mum saying something about last night.

I introduced myself to the holder of the sign, who

in turn introduced himself as Murti – I thought.

'Have you got your passport and visa money?' he asked.

'Sure.' I dug into my bag and found both, as well as the entry form that I'd diligently completed as soon as the cabin crew handed them out.

The man whose name I thought was Murti mumbled something or other about waiting somewhere or other, took my passport and the money I'd set aside for my visa, and disappeared with both. I hadn't even officially entered the country yet and I'd already broken the golden rule of overseas travel – never lose sight of your passport.

It wasn't until I saw the woman beside me do the same thing that I started to relax. After all, he was carrying a sign with my name on it. Mum must have sent him . . . or Steph. Mum had never been the most organised person.

'It's okay,' the woman said, 'it's the VIP visa-on-arrival service – it helps you get through the queues.' She indicated the lines at the other counters. 'You just need to wait at the luggage carousel – your man will find you.'

'Thanks,' I managed, already overwhelmed by the heat, my head and a residual queasy feeling in my tummy.

I turned my phone on. Six missed calls, two voicemails and two text messages.

The first of the texts was from Mum:

There'll be a man waiting for you at Customs. Steph organised him. His name is Murti and it's quite alright for you to leave your passport with him – he'll bring it back after it's been stamped. You'll need to give him the money for the visa, but don't worry about paying him for the service, I've already taken care of that. I'll be waiting for you outside – he'll make sure you find me. Also, don't be tempted to get any local cash at the airport – we'll deal with that in town tomorrow.

I smiled, and bit back the tears that threatened to overflow. I mightn't have lived with Mum in over a decade, but she still knew all my little hang-ups. Well, she used to call them hang-ups; I simply thought I was taking on responsibility for the things she hadn't. I loved my mother dearly, but her attention to detail had always been very different to mine. I remembered earnestly reminding her about sunscreen during the hot Brisbane summers, lecturing her about her untidiness around the house ('I don't know how you can find anything in this mess, Mum') and letting her know that it was a good idea if we included vegetables on our plate every now and again. Whenever we travelled – usually if we were either leaving or going back to England, and vice versa – it would be me running through the checklist. Tickets, money, passport? Mum would laugh it off, but invariably my questions would result in a quick U-turn to the house for something or another. I quickly learned that if we had a 10 am departure to tell Mum that it was really 9.30 am. I thought Steph did the same thing these days. Organisation had never been one of Denise Porter's virtues.

The second text was from Booth, as were the missed calls and voicemails.

I made a deal with myself that if my bag hadn't come out before a plastic-wrapped red bag completed its circuit on the carousel, I'd read it. If not, I'd wait until later.

Bugger. There goes the plastic-wrapped red bag.

I listened to the voicemails first.

'Hey, Em, it's me. Give me a call when you get this?

'Hey, Em. Helloooooooo, are you there? Listen, babe, I saw Suse this morning and she told me . . . well, she told me that you know. I guess you're pretty mad with me, yeah? (Half-laugh) Anyways, give me a bell? Just wanting to know that you're okay. That's all.'

Then I opened the text: *Em, where are you? I'm worried. Are you okay?*

As I was deciding whether or not to respond, my phone rang. I answered it automatically. It was Booth.

'So you're alive, then? Where the fuck have you been?' he said in response to my silence.

'Hi. I'm here.'

'Are you at home? I'm about to order some Thai takeaway and thought you might like to share it with me.'

Thank God – he obviously hadn't read the email I'd sent him. I was buggered if I could remember exactly what I'd said in it. That was probably a good thing, although it was something else I'd never done before – forgotten under the influence. Forgetting under the influence was the antidote to confessing under the influence, dialling under the influence, booking under the influence, mailing under the influence, arriving in a new country without currency or inoculations, and letting someone I'd never seen before disappear with my passport.

'No. I'm at –'

The man who I hoped was Murti had returned with my passport. 'No bag yet?' he asked.

'Excuse me?'

'No bag yet?'

'Er no, it hasn't come out yet.'

'Em, where the fuck are you?'

'The airport.' I saw my suitcase peeking out through the rubbery curtains, and pointed it out to Murti. 'That's it – there.'

'The black one with the purple scarf?'

'Who's that?' Booth asked.

'Yes, that one,' I said to Murti. 'It's Murti – I think,' I said to Booth. 'Steph sent him.'

My hangover hadn't altered my ability to multi-task.

'Which airport?'

'Sorry?'

'Which airport are you at?'

'Denpasar, and this call is costing me a fortune. Roaming costs, you know. I should have thought to buy an international sim card. Can you get international sim cards? I'll add that to my list – as well as money, and make-up. Oh, here's my bag . . . bye, Booth,' and I hung up.

When the phone immediately started to ring again, I turned it onto silent and ignored it. I'd have turned it off, but that would have been irresponsible in case Mum needed to catch me.

Speaking of which, Mum looked fantastic. She'd dressed in a simple violet sundress with floral rubber thongs and long dangly turquoise and silver earrings. Her skin had tanned to a deep nut-brown, and her long grey hair fell in loose waves around her shoulders. She was as slim as she'd always been, and if it wasn't for the grey hair could have easily passed for a woman many years younger, especially from a distance.

She made her way through the sea of people, and gathered me in for the type of hug only a mother could give.

'I'm so pleased that you're here at last,' she said into my hair. 'Now you wait here and I'll go and get the car.'

I wiped a bead of sweat from my brow.

'Don't worry,' she said, 'the car is air conditioned.'

'Is it always like this?' I asked a few minutes later, climbing into the car and feeling the wet patch under my boobs start to spread.

'Pretty well – it just rains more later in the year. This is the most comfortable time to visit. Where we are, in the mountains, it's a little cooler. You do get used to it though,' she assured me.

I couldn't even begin to think what tropical diseases must flourish in this climate. My head was pounding, so I reached into my bag for some more paracetamol and a bottle of water. My phone was ringing again, so I pressed the ignore button.

Mum glanced at me. 'Big night?'

'Uh huh.'

'And a booking under the influence? Not usually your style, my darling.'

'Long story, Mum.'

'Anything to do with why that phone has rung twice since you got in the car?'

'Uh huh.'

I concentrated on the madness of the narrow roads around the airport – and gasped as a motorbike passed us carrying two adults, two children, a dog and an electric fan. Mum saw me wince as we narrowly avoided a collision with a ladder slung over the shoulder of another motorbike rider.

'How about you put whoever that is out of his misery,' she said. 'It might take your mind off the traffic. I don't want to drive all the way to Ubud with you making noises and applying fake brakes every time a dog or a chook ventures onto the road.'

Chooks on the road?

'It's just the bikes,' I said, attempting to justify my fear. 'How many people are they legally allowed to carry?'

'I have no idea,' she replied with a smile. 'As many as will fit, I imagine.'

This time when the phone rang, I answered it. As I'd expected, it was Booth. He didn't give me time for a greeting.

'What the fuck are you doing in Bali?'

'Visiting Mum and Steph.'

'And when was this decided?'

'It was spontaneous.'

'You don't do spontaneous.'

I didn't used to do decluttering or renovations or one-night stands either. But I didn't point this out. Mum didn't need to know the whole story just yet – it would get her too excited, and as far as I could tell, the roads and traffic offered enough of that- even for Mum.

'Well, maybe it's time that I did. Anyway, you'd made it clear that you didn't want to talk until tomorrow. What day is it? It's still Sunday – isn't it?' I looked across at Mum for confirmation. She nodded. 'What time is it there?'

'Half past six,' Booth said. 'There's two hours between here and Bali. Just how spontaneous was this decision?'

'Very,' I admitted. 'Anyway, as I said before, I'm paying a fortune in roaming charges for this call . . .'

'Don't hang up,' he ordered. 'I just need to know that you're okay.'

'Seriously hot. My face fell off on the tarmac and my dress has melted into my skin.'

'You know what I'm asking.'

'Yeah, I do. Booth, now's not the time to talk about it. I sent you an email that I shouldn't have sent, so now you know where I am you don't need to read it, so please just delete it, okay?'

He avoided my question. 'When are you back?'

'Two weeks. We'll talk then – or not. Anyways, I'm turning this phone off – I'll buy a local sim or something.'

'Text me the number when you do?'

'Sure,' I lied.

'Em . . . look after yourself,' he said softly.

I hung up, settled back in the seat and closed my eyes.

'So, you and Josh?' Mum said. 'It's about time. I like him – he's good for you.'

They'd met several times over the past few years, whenever Mum had come to see me. They'd gotten along brilliantly, ganging up on me and trying to convince me to . . . well, to do what I was doing now.

'You should have asked him to come with you,' she added.

'It's a long story,' I said, my eyes still closed.

She reached over and patted my leg lightly. 'That's okay – we've got plenty of time.'

We did. And the best part was, there was nothing here that could remind me of Booth.

CHAPTER THIRTY-THREE

Except Mum and Steph's villa.

Could there be anything more clichéd? Located beside a river, with rice fields all around, the main villa was a square-shaped teak construction with a wrap-around verandah to catch the cool air coming up from the water. In the complex was an open-air pavilion – presumably where they did the tantric yogic astrology, or whatever – a large swimming pool set into lush green gardens, and a couple of other smaller villas. Mum said these were where people stayed while on retreats. The whole place looked like it had sprung from the pages of *Eat, Pray, Love*.

Booth and I had watched the movie a couple of years ago. I was going through a sexual dry spell (yep, when Mum sent me *that* gift voucher) and Booth had come over to watch chick flicks and eat chocolate with me. To be fair, that wasn't what he thought he was coming over for, but given I'd already started watching, and it was rainy and miserable outside, he conceded defeat relatively quickly and settled in on the couch. He didn't even complain until after the closing credits had begun.

'Wow, she was one selfish bitch.'

'Really?' I was surprised. 'I didn't see it that way – I just saw her looking to find herself.'

'Maybe it's a chick thing.'

A couple of weeks later we'd been lunching somewhere or other and Booth was hassling me about when I was going to jump back on the horse – as he so charmingly put it.

'How long has it been since you had a date, Em?'

'I don't know, a while, I guess.'

'This is the longest you've been single in ages.'

'Whatever.' I shrugged.

'Has there been anyone since Harry?'

I shook my head. 'Not really.'

'So,' he persisted, 'why aren't you dating? You need to get back on the horse after you've fallen off or you become afraid – and your bits can grow over.'

'Thanks for that advice, Dr Booth. Anyway, no one's asked me out.'

'Well, if you sit around waiting for that, you'll be waiting a while. You need to put yourself back out there. I know you don't do one-nighters, but that's exactly what you need – a transitional shag. Quick, clean, satisfying and with no strings attached.'

'A what?'

'A transitional shag. In fact, you're probably overdue

for it. It's the shag you have post break-up – with absolutely no ties, complications or commitment. When you need to scratch the itch and give you the confidence to get back out there. It'll also help with your joints.'

He had that look on his face that he got when he reckoned he knew it all. In contrast, all that was on my face was confusion.

'It was in that movie you made me watch,' he clarified. 'That one about the woman who ran away to Italy and ate a lot, and then ended up in Bali after a lot of boring stuff with elephants in India,'

'*Eat, Pray, Love*?' I guessed.

'That's the one. Man, that was two hours of my life I'll never get back.'

I acknowledged the latter part of his statement with an eye roll. 'I still don't see what that movie has to do with me having a transitional shag?'

He looked exasperated. 'The bit where she sees the healer woman after she gets knocked off the bike by that guy you reckoned was hot, and the healer tells her she needs to have sex to keep her joints supple.'

'Aaaah, yes. I remember now. Is that really all you got from that movie?'

'That, and the fact that she justified her selfishness by running away to find herself.'

'Your opinion. I loved it.'

'Whatever, you're changing the subject. You need a shag.'

'That's easier said than done.'

'Well, if you need assistance getting back on the horse, I'm your best friend and I'm here to help. I don't mind providing the occasional benefits.'

'Wow, that's the most unselfish offer I've had in a long while.'

'I'm just trying be useful, babe. And let's face it – I have a wealth of experience. You could do a lot worse.'

I'd laughed at the time, and the conversation had moved on to speculation about whether Mum and Steph lived anywhere near where the movie was made.

'You should go there one day,' he'd said.

'I will. It's just that –'

'I know, injections, planning and all of that. Be spontaneous, Em – just fucking do it. Hell, I'll come with you . . . Now, there's an idea – you and I would have a great time. We'll hire motorbikes to get around on.'

'Motorbikes? Don't you need a special licence for that? Don't tourists get in trouble on bikes? You know, injuries and police trouble? I'm sure I heard someone say how the police target Western tourists – it's the bribes.'

He'd raised his eyebrows at me, and said, 'Yeah, but how much fun would it be? You and me?'

He was right – it would have been fun. My arms around his waist and the warmth of his body holding me safe. So much for nothing up here reminding me of him.

•

My inconvenient memories were interrupted by Steph bowling through the front door and grabbing me for a tight hug. She did that – bowled along – much like an overgrown puppy who hadn't yet grown into her feet.

Where my mother was petite, Steph was long and lanky – all limbs and capability. She wore her (mostly) brown hair in a long ponytail, and today, as usual, was dressed in three-quarter cotton pants, a white cotton vest, a sky-blue linen overshirt, and leather sandals. I wasn't sure that I'd ever seen her in anything but. Even when she came to visit in Melbourne, she just swapped the three-quarter pants for full-length cotton pants, and the sandals for flat suede ankle boots.

Steph and Mum were made for each other; from what Mum had said of their first meeting, it had always been so. Each had been married to men in the past, yet fell in love with one another at first sight. Over the years their love had mellowed and grown into something lasting and strong. I was actually envious of what they had.

I'd also loved Steph since the day we met – although obviously in a very different way. I think it was how Mum was with her – as if she'd come home to find the house warm, a meal cooked, and her fluffy slippers ready for her – metaphorically speaking, of course. When they'd announced that they were buying this villa and moving to Bali, I couldn't have been happier for them. My only regret was that it'd taken me so long to visit.

Steph took my bag and expressed surprise at the weight. 'Wow, Emily, where's your other bag? This one feels as though it's only got your make-up in it.'

'Oh, ha ha. I have no idea what's in it,' I confessed, 'but I doubt there's make-up. I'll need to add that to my list for tomorrow.'

'You won't need it here,' declared Steph. 'It slides straight off your face in this humidity.'

'So I discovered.' I laughed, and then stopped suddenly as Mum opened a door off the wide verandah into what must be my bedroom. 'Oh,' I gasped, 'this is gorgeous. It looks like it's straight out of a travel brochure.'

It did. The polished floorboards were partially covered by a blue and white batik-inspired rug, while the bed itself was pure filmy cotton romance.

'You won't need air conditioning in here,' advised Mum. 'The house is designed to capture the cool air coming up from the river, and the fan,' she indicated the controls beside the light switch, 'will create enough movement for you. These louvres will keep the insects out, but you can let down the mosquito net too.'

I wandered around the room with my mouth open, trying to take in the details. In one corner was a decorative pile of wood in a standing vase, and on the walls were abstract art in shades of red.

Mum saw me looking and explained, 'The wood is cinnamon – smell it.'

'Wow, it smells like chai tea!'

She smiled. 'And the art throughout has been done by local artists. You should have a look at some of the galleries before you leave – and maybe take some home.'

I wandered into the bathroom, and wandered out again quickly.

'What's wrong?' Steph asked.

I pointed out the obvious. 'There are no doors, and no roof.'

Mum and Steph exchanged glances and grinned.

'Okay – you win,' Steph conceded.

'Have you two been taking bets on how I'll react?'

'We sure have,' admitted Mum. 'Just try it – it's very liberating.'

'And it's really very private,' coaxed Steph. 'Trust me – try it, you'll love it. The feel of the air on your bare skin is really quite seductive.'

I raised my eyebrows at them both and reluctantly agreed.

'Besides,' said Mum, 'if you're really uncomfortable, you can use one of the inside toilets. Just make sure you take a torch at night – toilet frogs, you see.'

'What?' I thought this place was supposed to be civilised – people came here on holidays!

'They're harmless, but can give you a shock. You never quite forget the feel of a clammy frog hand on your nether regions.'

'Great.' I managed a weak smile.

'Now, just freshen up and settle in, then come find us. You'll be wanting a cold beer and something to tide you through until dinner. We'll take you to our favourite place in town for a meal later.'

My tummy contracted at the thought of food, and my head was still busy reminding me of the damage I'd inflicted on myself last night.

Steph saw it all flash across my face and laughed. 'Trust us,' she said, 'it's hair of the dog with a difference – you'll be feeling better in no time. Then you'll be able to tell us exactly what happened for you to grace us with your very welcome presence.'

'Let me get this straight,' began Steph. 'You fell madly in lust with Jamie?'

Bellies full, we were lingering in Mum and Steph's favourite restaurant. The food was amazingly good, and not as spicy hot as I'd been expecting. It was also a lot healthier than I'd thought it would be – plenty of local vegetables, and complex-tasting sambals. The faint tinkle of water and rhythmic chimes of the gamelan made for a relaxing soundtrack. I'd just finished giving them the full story of my love-life dramas, and fresh beers had been delivered.

'Madly,' I said. 'I couldn't think straight for wanting him.'

'Aaah, the very best sort of lust to fall into,' commented Mum. 'It was like that with your father.'

'Oh, he was clever too,' I said. 'He kept cancelling dates, but always had a good excuse, and called just often enough to assure me that he felt the same way that I did. We took risks like I've never taken before – at work, in public, places where we could get caught. In hindsight, I was completely lost in him for a few weeks.'

'It's good to be lost for a little while,' Mum mused. 'As long as you find your way back out relatively quickly. Every woman should have at least one of those before she settles for the real thing. Sadly, I married mine.'

'Too true,' Steph agreed. 'Remember me telling you about that guy –'

'Excuse me.' I interrupted their trip down memory lane. 'Isn't this about me?'

'Fair point.' Mum smiled at me indulgently. 'You got as far as saying that Suse admitted that she was sleeping with someone from her work . . .'

'That's right.'

'And it ended up being Jamie?'

'That's right.'

'At the same time as Jamie was with you?'

'Yep.'

'And you had no idea?'

'None at all.'

'And he was also reconciling with his ex-partner?'

'Yep.'

'Busy bastard,' Steph observed. 'And here was I thinking that most men had issues with multi-tasking.'

I shrugged. 'I still don't know why he did what he did. Maybe it was because he didn't know what, or who, he wanted. Maybe it was just because he could. Whatever it was, I fell for it.'

'It sounds like classic narcissistic behaviour,' commented Steph.

Before she and Mum bought the villa and went into new age whatever, she used to be a psychologist back in Melbourne.

'But Suse knew about you and Jamie?' Mum asked.

'Yep.'

Steph shook her head. 'That violates all the codes of friendship.'

'So where does Josh come into it?' Mum asked.

'He was just my mate – well, I thought he was. Then he started to get serious about this running thing, and that's when everything fell apart. If it wasn't for that stupid half marathon idea, Suse would never have met Jamie, and Booth wouldn't have met Corinna, and if Booth hadn't met Corinna –'

'You would have still fallen for Jamie,' Mum pointed out. 'And he still would have hurt you.'

'I know, but –'

'And you wouldn't have worked out how you feel

about Josh,' Mum suggested softly. 'Would you really have missed that?'

'I don't know. Maybe. Maybe not. I'll never forget that, and I can't regret it, but I can't imagine not having him there – at the other end of the phone, or at my door, or watching chick flicks on a Sunday afternoon. I just wish that nothing had changed, that the three of us could have been how we always were. Now it's all different, and I don't know how I'm supposed to be without him.'

Steph said, 'Look at what else has come from it all. You finally decluttered, you started exercising, your flat has been renovated, and, however it happened, you're here now. Those are great outcomes.'

'I guess. But I don't have Suse or Booth.'

'I thought that you two would get together some day,' Mum said. 'I always said that, didn't I, Steph? How good they'd be for each other?'

'You sure did, darl,' Steph agreed. 'You always said that Em was just doing her version of commitment avoidance until she realised who she really wanted.'

'But not without Suse,' I said. 'Why did I have to lose her in the process?'

'She made her own bed, love. I know that you were comfortable, but you were too comfortable – you needed to be jolted out of your comfort zone and to let go of a few things. I've been telling you that for years.'

'Yeah, okay . . . so you knew best.'

'Of course I did. I'm your mother – even though your father and I probably haven't been great role models.'

'Oh, Mum, don't be like that. I've always understood. Besides, the pair of you have got your acts together finally now.'

'I'll ask the tough question,' Steph butted in. 'Have you told Josh how you feel about him?'

'Sort of.'

Mum put her face in her hands. 'Please don't tell me you drunk-dialled him as well as us. No, hang on – it's worse, isn't it? That was the email you were referring to in the car – you drunk-emailed him?'

I nodded. 'I sent it to work so he wouldn't open it before I left, and then I deleted it from my sent box.'

'Why? So that it would magically disappear and you could deny all knowledge?'

'Oh, I don't know. I wasn't thinking straight. Hell, I can't even remember exactly what I wrote, but I'm pretty sure it was a full confession. Maybe that's why I deleted it, so I wouldn't have to face what I wrote. Some part of me probably thought I was being responsible in deleting it afterwards. That's why I'm going to keep my phone turned off. I don't want to be upset if he doesn't ring or message me after he's read it. If my phone is off, I don't have to know. It can be as if I never wrote it.' I caught Steph and Mum looking at each other with concern. 'Anyway, now I've told you, and that's the last

I want to hear about it. Okay?'

'Of course, darling,' Mum said with very little sincerity. 'What did you have planned while you're here?'

'Obviously I didn't have a lot of time to map out an itinerary, but I do have a list for tomorrow.' I reached into my bag for my notebook.

1. Get money. (Note to self – make sure you count it properly. Side note – check out money-counting scams on TripAdvisor.)

2. Buy local SIM card. DON'T send the number to Booth.

3. Buy make-up:

　　3.1 Foundation

　　3.2 Blusher

　　3.3 Mascara

　　3.4 Eye shadow

　　3.5 Two lipsticks

4. Review contents of suitcase and buy clothes.

5. Purchase travel insurance.

6. Investigate immunisations.

'Show me that.' Mum grabbed the notebook from my hands, ripped the page out, and tore it into little pieces. 'You won't be needing this.'

'But –'

'No buts. We'll organise some cash, and I know that you'll feel better with insurance, but you won't need any make-up, and you won't need much more than a few loose dresses and comfy sandals or thongs.

You can get those from the markets. This is a holiday, and the only thing you need to do for the next two weeks is relax by the pool, explore, and walk.'

'It's just that –'

'No, darling, there is no "it's just that". It's perfectly safe to walk the streets – just don't get in the way of the motorbikes. It's even safer through the rice paddies, and the monkeys won't bite you unless you provoke them. Understood?'

I opened my mouth to say something and quickly closed it again.

'Good girl. Now, we have a group arriving tomorrow – astrologers this time –we'll be busy transferring them from the airport and checking them in, so you'll need to make yourself at home. Do some yoga, have a massage, maybe take a cooking class – they do a good one in this restaurant, but there are others in town. Hire a driver and explore a little, or head down the hill into the beach at Kuta or Legian, there's plenty to do. By the time your two weeks is up, I'll be putting good money on you never wanting to go home.'

'It sounds lovely, Mum, but I can assure you that I have to go home. After all, I have a job –'

'That you've outgrown.'

'– and bills to pay.'

'That you've probably got cover for, if I know you.' She turned to Steph. 'Emily always saved a quarter of her pocket money, even when she was a little girl. I don't know where she got that from. It must have been from Keith.'

'I just like to make sure that everything is taken care of,' I said defensively.

'Yes, well, now that everything is taken care of, I think it's time you relaxed into life a bit more and took a few risks – have some fun. You don't need to go mad, just push your boundaries some more. Why not try a free dancing or breath-work class? We had someone in the other day who said it had changed her life. A gorgeous girl – Californian-type, long-stemmed with teeth. She woke the next day and realised she was a woman.'

I raised my eyebrows. 'Seriously?'

'And the tits hadn't given it away before that?' Steph giggled.

'That kind of work is not to be trifled with, Emily – it can bring up some powerful issues.'

'All the more reason for me not to do it then.'

Later, lying in my beautiful bed in my beautiful room, after showering in my open-air bathroom under the watchful eye of a largeish lizard (Mum and Steph were right – it was a liberating and sensual experience), I gave in to the temptation to turn my phone on, just in case.

Booth had left one voicemail message and one text.

I listened to the voicemail first.

'Hey, I know you said you'd turn your phone off, but I

thought I'd try you anyway. (Silence) I can't say what I need to say to a voicemail. (More silence) If you get this, please call me. Ummmm . . . that's all.'

So . . . he'd read it.

I opened the text.

I get that you need time, so I won't pressure you, but we need to talk. Go sit under a lotus flower or something for a few days, gaze at your navel, and then call me. Please?

I turned the phone off. Was there such a thing as a lotus flower? I must remember to ask Mum.

CHAPTER THIRTY-FOUR

I slept late, luxuriated again in my open-air shower, and dressed in the only suitable sundress in my suitcase. What had I been thinking when I packed?

Stepping out onto the verandah I inhaled the green, and noticed some folded clothes, a tourist guide, and a note on the chair outside my room.

Good morning!

There's yoghurt and fruit in the fridge, and I'm assuming you don't have any yoga gear so I've left some here for you. Here's a map of the town. Have a wander, change some cash (I've marked the best places on the map), and remember to bargain if you're buying from the markets. Start at half the quoted price and move up from there.

There's plenty of beer in the fridge and we'll see you for drinks before dinner.

It's so lovely to have you here, darling.

Mum xxx

I spent the day exploring the villa and wandering the streets around the main part of town. I changed some Aussie dollars for rupiah, and was surprised to find myself an instant millionaire. I tentatively (at first) bargained with stall holders at the markets for an armful of light sundresses, sarongs and singlet tops, a few with the ubiquitous Bintang beer label plastered across the front.

In the Monkey Forest, I was terrified when a bunch of official Monkey Forest bananas were torn out of my hands and gobbled up. I stood there and shut my eyes. I didn't think that I screamed, but another couple of tourists laughed and pointed as they walked past me, so I might have done. One monkey treated me like he would a tree, jumping onto my shoulder and scrambling across my head, before feeling for anything loose that he could take off with.

Thankfully Steph had given me the standard tourist warning last night. 'Before you go in, make sure you zip up your handbag – with your sunglasses inside. If they can find something to take, they will, and they'll hold on to it until you give them something to eat. It's like monkey ransom.'

'They sound horrible,' I'd said.

She'd looked across at Mum. 'Denise isn't too keen on them, are you?' Mum shuddered in response. 'But really they're quite cute.'

'Awful, fornicating creatures – constantly wanking,' Mum said, with a completely straight face.

'Seriously? I can't believe you just said that! Steph, can you believe she just said that?'

Steph giggled. 'I absolutely can believe it. They do do a lot of that, but hey, I would if I could too!'

Around midday I followed a queue of people to a *warung*, or local restaurant, down a lane opposite the palace to obtain a plate of *babi guling*, roast suckling pig. I figured that the crowd meant the food wouldn't give me the case of Bali belly that I so feared, but I still took the first bite tentatively – and then closed my eyes briefly to fully appreciate the taste. The meat tasted as though it had been infused in a million different spices before being basted in even more. It tasted of the island.

After lunch I did my first yoga class – and made a mental note not to eat immediately before yoga in the future. Full tummies and downward dogs simply didn't mix. The unfamiliar spices in the *babi guling* and the gases in the beer hit me at possibly the worst time they could hit me. Let's just say I made it to the bathroom in the nick of time.

Although the stretches (they were called poses or *asanas* in yoga) seemed deceptively simple, my body certainly felt as though it had worked. I was even a little bit proud of how my beginner's biceps had stood up to the challenge.

Back at the villa, I changed into my bathers and lathered up with the sunscreen I'd actually remembered to pack, and spent the rest of the afternoon lounging by the pool.

That first day set the pattern for the next ten.

I rose with the birds and greeted the sun with my own salute in a yoga class. I'd bought some yoga gear from one of the local designers in town, and was determined to keep it up when I got home. Even after such a short time, my body was feeling more supple and my mind more zen-like.

I'd follow that with fresh fruit, yoghurt and blissfully strong coffee from Mum and Steph's whizz-bang espresso machine. It took me a few days to get the hang of all the levers and switches, but now it was part of the morning ritual. Then I'd go for a long walk, usually through the rice fields and lanes by the river, sometimes through the town, sometimes a combination of both. I'd wave to the farmers – and their ducks – smile at the kids, and sidestep the offerings in their tiny palm baskets that were left all over the place.

Most days I'd spend the warmest part of the day inside. Sometimes I settled on one of the chaises longues scattered around the verandah with a book and the faint sounds of the river, the gamelan and birds floating in to surround me.

Other days I spent working on Mum and Steph's website. It was stuck in the early noughties and wasn't doing their business any favours. I'd managed to upload a new theme and bring it peacefully up to date. I wanted it to have the same impact that my room had on me that first time I opened the door. Now the site's colours and content felt like that.

They didn't have a social media strategy, so I'd built them one – setting up all the pages that needed to be set up, linking those that needed to be linked, and uploading photos I'd taken around the villas and on my daily walks. I'd even developed a professional-looking newsletter to send to all their previous clients. It had the same theme as the website and the social media pages, and contained titbits of news, happenings and images. I was thinking the next step should be to include a monthly recipe, or a profile of something exquisitely Bali, maybe a local designer. I needed to remember to suggest it to Steph.

They were both very impressed with what I'd done, but really it wasn't that hard once I'd started. Fortunately their original provider had built the site so that even I could find my way around it to restyle. Now all I had to do was get Mum to focus for long enough to learn how to update all the social media accounts I'd set up for them.

Lunch was usually something from one of the *warungs*. Sometimes I'd go back for *babi guling*, other days it would be fried chicken or duck, a bean salad or *nasi campur* – a plate of mixed vegies, usually a curry, an egg and a satay stick. It was all tasty, affordable, and – touch wood – so far I'd avoided any serious non-yoga-related tummy problems.

The afternoons were usually spent reading by the pool, and I tried to get another stroll in before it was time for cocktail hour with Mum and Steph, and dinner out somewhere. Sometimes we'd sit outside with our drinks and listen to the noise from the village drift around, the breeze rustle through the rice stalks, and watch fireflies as they flitted in and around. Then it was back to my beautiful bed in my beautiful room – where I'd toss and turn, and give in to the temptation to dream about Booth.

'You're not with the conference?'

The woman lying under a huge hat in the deckchair beside me interrupted my reading. About my age, she had the sort of red hair that went with skin that needed a hat that size.

'No, just visiting family,' I replied. 'My mother lives here.'

'It's a lovely place for some soul searching,' she commented.

Was that what I'd been doing? Soul searching?

'It's just that I noticed you haven't turned a page in the last ten minutes, so either you're a very slow reader or you're soul searching.'

I smiled. 'You've got me there.' I leaned over and held out my hand. 'Hi, Emily Porter . . . pleased to meet you.'

'Alice Delaney – I'm here with the astrologers. It's the first time I've done a group thing like this, but it's so gorgeous here.'

'It is. I've been here a week or so and already I feel like a new person.'

Saying it out loud to someone else, I knew it to be true.

'It gets you like that,' she agreed. 'Do you mind if I ask what you're working through in your head?'

My eyebrows raised under my sunglasses.

'I know,' she said, 'it's awfully forward of me, but I've seen you walking around the last few days, and you look like a woman with things on her mind. Oh, I just realised how clichéd that sounds.' She laughed at herself.

'No, it's just that you put me on the spot.'

'The usual? Man? Career? Children? All of the above?'

'Just what sort of astrologer are you?' I asked.

'The sort that's interested in people,' she replied with a smile. It was a good answer. 'Don't worry, I'm not touting for business. It's just that sometimes talking to someone not involved helps you get your head around things.'

'I guess.' It wouldn't hurt to run the ridiculous idea that was in my head past someone else, would it? 'Don't go anywhere – this conversation needs a beer. Would you like one?'

'Sure, why not?'

I grabbed a couple of Bintangs from Mum's fridge, popped them into stubby holders, and returned to the pool. We were still the only ones there. We clinked bottles in a silent toast.

'Where's the rest of your group?'

She took a sip of her beer before answering. 'Oh, this is good. Everyone's at a lecture – a visiting "expert" from the US.' She made the bunny ears. 'The older women adore him, but he's a little too glass-half-empty for me. That's the thing with these conferences – sometimes it all gets too earnest for me and I need a break . . . and I felt like a swim. So . . . you . . . man trouble?'

'A week ago I would have said yes. I've just discovered that I'm in love with someone I've known for years. It was like seeing the person I've known forever, but suddenly he was someone different. I came here to get away from that. You see, he's my best buddy – well, he was. I'm not sure what he thinks of me now – I accidentally drunk-emailed him and told him how I feel about him.'

'Wow. What does he think?'

'No idea. I made a booking under the influence and flew straight out here – and then turned my phone off.'

'Good plan.' She drank more of her beer. 'It sounds like something I'd do.'

'Anyway, now I've worked out that I'm not going to get over him – it is what it is. I love him, I've told him that I love him, and there's nothing more I can do really.'

'Well, that's a little more mature than your first plan.'

I grinned. 'Absolutely. No, the thing is, I think I've outgrown my life. Although that makes me sound like a spoiled brat – and I assure you that I'm not.' Her silence encouraged me to continue. 'I've been scared of things, and hung on to things, and now that I've started letting go, I'm realising that I've hung on for too long. Does that make sense?'

'It sure does. Cancer, Taurus or . . . Scorpio?' she guessed. 'Hang on, issues with reality . . . Pisces?'

'Pisces, actually.'

'I reckon the other three signs would be in there somewhere,' she said.

'Possibly. I don't know. Mum had my chart done once, but I didn't pay a lot of attention to what she told me. I've been complaining about my job for years, and I've never done anything about it. God, when I think about it, I've never done anything about anything. I've just drifted. Now, even though I know I need to face Josh – that's his name, but I call him Booth – I don't think I want that job any more. There was another one that I really wanted, but I missed out on it.'

'How long have you been there?'

'It would be more than twelve years, I suppose.'

'Have you been promoted in that time?'

'Yeah, sure, every couple of years or so. When they think I'm ready.'

'Not when you think you're ready?'

That question made me think. 'Actually . . . no.'

'Okay, what do you like about it?'

'Well, the money, the security, the familiarity, I guess. The usual things.'

'Everyone has different things that they stay for, so it's not necessarily the usual things. What would happen if the job wasn't there? Would you be okay? Financially?'

I considered the question. 'Yes, for a while. I don't owe a lot on my mortgage, and I have some savings . . . and long-service leave . . . and I have another six weeks of leave even after this fortnight.'

'How long has it been since you had a holiday? Before now?'

'Years . . . I don't know, I can't remember. I always meant to go somewhere, it was just that . . . I don't know, there was either no one to go with, or it was too hard, or I needed injections, or something.'

Alice smiled at that. 'What do you want to do next?'

'This is going to sound really weird, and I know when I tell my mother, she'll take my temperature first and then do cartwheels, but even though I really wanted the role at DotPoint, I want to travel first. South East Asia, just for a few months, and then do something completely different. I've enjoyed designing the website and social media campaigns here, so maybe something like that? I have no idea. The money and the title just don't seem to matter any more, or whether the release will get in on time, and what deals have been made by management, and whether or not someone has the fucking thought ball. I don't want to make excuses any more.'

'Okay, I don't really understand the thought ball comment, but . . . what's stopping you?'

'It's just that . . . Actually, nothing's stopping me.'

It was true — there wasn't anything stopping me. Not any more.

'Not to play devil's advocate, but are you sure wanting to leave and travel isn't just running away from the man?'

Advocatus diaboli. I giggled. 'What sort of avocado? No. Sorry, I'm not laughing at you, it's just . . . don't worry, it's a location joke — you had to be there.'

People were starting to dribble out around the grounds so Alice reluctantly finished her beer and gathered her things.

'Well, Emily, it's been a delight, but now I need to get back to the tribe. Good luck with it all.'

Impulsively I hugged her. 'Thanks so much.'

'I didn't do anything,' she protested. 'You already knew what you wanted to do, you just had to say it out loud. I'll leave a card with your mother — look me up when you finish travelling.'

'I will,' I said, and, unusually for me, I meant it.

I poked my head into the kitchen, where Steph was putting together a tray of cut fruit. 'Sorry to interrupt, but will you be needing the computer in the next while?'

'Absolutely not, go for it.'

I set up a roaming email account – there was no way I was signing into mine – and drafted my resignation. I addressed it to Diane, requested an immediate release, and offered the company four weeks of my accrued leave in lieu of my normal notice period.

Then I pressed send and immediately logged off.

CHAPTER THIRTY-FIVE

'I have something to say,' I announced over dinner. A dinner that, incidentally, I'd shopped for, prepared and cooked – all from recipes I'd learnt yesterday at the cooking school.

'You're going to stay on as our permanent cook?' suggested Steph, reaching for another chicken satay.

'Close.'

'You're going to stay on as our social media consultant?' suggested Mum.

'Not exactly.'

'Well, tell us then,' she urged.

'You know how I'm meant to be going home on Saturday night? Do you mind if I stay another week? Don't worry, I won't be with you the whole time – I'm going to duck down to the beach for a few days.'

'Of course we don't mind – and I'm glad you're heading down the mountain. What about work? Have you applied for more leave?' Mum leaned across for more of the fragrant water-spinach salad I'd prepared to go with the chicken.

'Not exactly – I resigned.'

Mum dropped the spoon with a clang, spraying flecks of tomato sambal over the table. Steph paused mid-bite and raised her eyebrows.

'Darling, while I think you've made the right move, are you sure that you're doing it for the right reasons? This isn't just a more permanent under-the-influence event?'

'I'm absolutely sure. I've thought a lot about it. Just to clarify, though, I'm not staying up here – but I will be back. I'll go home for a week or so and get everything in order, and then I'm taking the next four to six months to travel. I was thinking of starting in Bangkok and playing it by ear from there. I'd like to head up north to the triple border, and then maybe do some island hopping – Phuket, Koh Samui . . . maybe Vietnam . . . I'll work it out as I go.'

'No plan?'

'No plan.'

'No list?'

'No list.'

'And you're sure this isn't so that you don't have to face Josh?'

I took a deep breath. 'I'm sure, Mum. He's part of what I have to sort out when I get home. I've told him how I feel about him, and I can't take that back now, but at the end of the day, he's my best buddy, and he's done nothing wrong. I'm the one who had to go and mess with what we had, so I owe it to him to say goodbye properly and wish him happiness. Besides, I have ten kays to walk.'

'Oh, darling, I'm so proud.'

I met Steph's raised eyebrows with two of my own. 'Why? Because I'm throwing away my whole life?'

'No, because you're living it.'

Despite what I'd said to Mum and Steph, Diane hadn't accepted my resignation without argument. Instead, I received a brief email with a request for me to phone her. I'd done so earlier that afternoon.

When I turned on my phone to call her, I saw a heap of missed calls and a few texts, all from Booth. I gritted my teeth, ignored them and phoned Diane instead.

She offered me the option of taking my long-service leave and accrued holidays at half-pay, leaving me the ability to come back to work when I'd got this whatever it was out of my system. Her words, not mine.

'Things will look different after you've had a proper break,' she told me.

Perhaps she was right. A little time, a little distance.

'Is this because you're having difficulties working with someone?' she asked.

I guessed she was referring to Jamie. I supposed that gossip had to get out at some point – we'd taken too many risks for someone not to have seen us, or to have thought they'd seen us. I told her no, and meant it.

We left it with me promising to take some more time to think about her offer.

Although I'd resolved to delete Booth's messages without reading or listening to them, after dinner, alone in my beautiful room, the temptation to hear his voice, even if it was on a recorded message, was too much.

'I'm going to leave a message every day until you call me back.'

'Hey, haven't heard from you – hope some monkey hasn't carried you off.'

'How's the surf? Are you near the surf. You've obviously still not turned your phone on.'

'You promised to text me your new number.'

'Thinking of you – have a Bintang for me?'

'Phone still off? Just so you know, I miss you.'

'What I said yesterday, about missing you? I meant it.'

'I meant it, but I'll deny it.'

'What's going on? Diane said you've resigned. You have to come back.'

'Please call me . . .'

With tears rolling down my face, I replayed them all one more time, and then again, as if hearing his voice or reading his words would mean that he was here with me. Somehow.

That was when the phone rang.

'Am I talking to a machine?' he asked.

Oh God, he sounded so near.

'No,' I said softly, swallowing back my tears in case he could see them through the phone.

'It's really you then?'

'Yeah.'

'Did you get my messages?'

'I was just checking them now.'

'Now that I'm talking to you, I don't know what to say.'

'I've never known you to be lost for words before, Booth.'

'I've never found out before that my best friend is leaving without saying goodbye.' He sounded hurt. I guessed he had a right to be. 'Why didn't you tell me what you were thinking? We could have talked about it.'

'No, we couldn't have. Not this time. Anyway, I didn't want you to talk me out of it – and I didn't know I was going to do it until I did it. If I'd talked to you I could have lost my resolve.'

Silence.

'Is it because of me? Or Jamie?'

'A little, but not really. It's just – well, it feels like it's something I need to do before I decide what to do next. Anyway, you and Suse have been telling me for years that I need to get out of my comfort zone.'

I laughed, but he didn't.

'I get that, but I never thought you'd do it without me.'

Neither did I.

'What happened to the three of us, Em?'

'I don't know. Jamie, I guess.'

'Perhaps. Surely it's not just that?'

I shrugged.

'Em?'

'I'm shrugging.'

Silence.

'Are you coming back at all?'

'Yes. I'm definitely back Sunday after next.'

'Okay.'

More silence.

'Em,' he finally said, 'nothing's the same with you gone.'

I couldn't answer him, I was crying too hard. Nothing was the same without him either.

'Are you crying?'

'No,' I lied. 'It must be the connection.'

'About your email . . . we need to talk about it.'

'Do we?' I managed. There was now a combination of tears and snot all over the phone.

'You know we do.'

I nodded.

'Em?'

'I'm nodding. I just can't talk about it like this – on the phone. It's something I feel that I need to see your face for. I promise we will when I'm home.'

'Okay . . . I miss you . . . you know that, right?'

'I know, and I miss you too.'

Silence.

'I finished it with Corinna.'

'There are fireflies in the rice,' I said at the same time.

'Did you hear me? Corinna and I broke up – it was one of the things I wanted to talk to you about.'

Oh. The tingle started in my chest and spread down my arms.

'I heard you. There are fireflies in the rice,' I said again.

He and Corinna . . . really? When? Because of us?

I heard his smile across the miles. 'How'd they get in the packet?'

'No . . . in the rice, the growing rice. It looks like long grass.'

'I've never seen a firefly before. What are they like?'

'Like someone's waving a laser around in the dark. It's all a little magical.'

'Make a wish on one for me.'

'What do you want me to wish for?'

'For both of our dreams to come true.'

I squeezed my eyes tightly shut.

'Em?'

'I'm wishing.'

'Night, sweetheart.'

I switched the phone off before I said what I really wanted to say to him: 'I love you, Booth.'

CHAPTER THIRTY-SIX

On Saturday morning Steph suggested we have another attempt at seeing the volcano. The three of us had driven up there last weekend, braving the crowds of tourists and the hawkers, only for the clouds to come down and obscure what I was sure must have been a good view.

'No,' I said, 'I don't really feel like it. What I would like to do is head over to the markets, and spend the afternoon pottering in the kitchen – maybe try that chicken curry I learnt last week. It can be sort of like a special meal before I head down to the beach tomorrow.'

'It sounds good to me. Denise?'

'Absolutely.' Mum seemed distracted by something on her phone. 'Sorry, Em, it sounds lovely. I have to head into Kuta early this afternoon – I've got a few errands to run before next week's group comes in, so if you need anything, just let me know.'

If Booth could only see me now, I thought, as I wandered through the stalls in my Bintang singlet, long-wrap sarong and flip-flops, picking out herbs and spices from an array of ingredients that only a couple of weeks ago I'd never heard of, let alone seen or prepared a meal with.

My list today was very different to the running sheet I did for the Italian experiment with Booth only a few months ago. We'd all been so happy then, the three of us. Suse with Richard, Booth with his one-nighters, and me busy avoiding commitment with the wrong men and telling myself it was love. Our lives were a predictable pattern of work, Friday night drinks, shopping and not a lot else. And then it all changed. Booth blamed Jamie, I blamed the running. Maybe the mood for change was settled on that Friday evening I found Coat Girl's bucket list. I wondered if she, Coat Girl, had ever achieved anything on it; or if, like for me, the list had started off a chain of disasters.

This time my list was merely a set of ingredients, and even then I'd strayed from it. I'd decided to prepare some satays to have with our beers before dinner. The Balinese did them slightly differently, mixing the meat and spice together to form something that looked like a meaty, spicy paste, and then winding the gloopy mix around the skewer. It wasn't as easy as it looked. To follow would be a chicken and potato curry. I'd serve rice on the side, and maybe even a green bean and coconut salad – if I had time. It was a lot of food, but the curry would freeze well.

Back at the villa, Mum had already left for Kuta,

and Steph was sunning herself by the pool. I ducked my head out to let her know that I was back, waved away her half-hearted offer of assistance, and retreated to the kitchen with my ingredients and my music. I even had a cooking playlist now. Every song on it reminded me of Booth – songs we'd listened to, songs he'd laughed at me for, songs that made me feel how he made me feel, songs that made me feel how I did when he wasn't here.

First on my non-list was the spice paste. I'd use this in everything I was preparing for tonight, so decided to get it out of the way first. Besides, there was lots of bashing and pounding to be done to beat these spices into submission. Ipod in docking station, volume up loud, mortar (or was it pestle – I never could tell) in hand, I began bashing and pounding.

Michael Bublé's 'Feeling Good' shuffled on. My shoulders started to lift in time with the music. I placed the mortar (or pestle) back in the pestle (or was it mortar?) and grabbed some wooden spoons as drumsticks. Hips joined in, and a little boob and shoulder shimmy in time to trumpets. I followed that with my version of a belly-dancing hip wobble, a back arch and leg kick as the trumpets got louder. Wow, these yoga classes were already doing wonders for my flexibility. Major twirl, with One Direction elbow dance across the kitchen, finishing with another shoulder shimmy and dip.

That was when I saw him. Standing in the kitchen doorway, watching me and smiling that slow, sweet, oh so sexy Boothy smile. I stood there for half a heartbeat and did the only thing I could do – I launched myself at him.

'Jesus, Em,' he said as he caught me, 'a little warning would have been nice.'

And then he kissed me, much like an Aussie tourist would attack his first Bintang.

When he lifted his head, it was to hold me even tighter. I finally opened my eyes and saw Mum and Steph grinning in the kitchen door.

'Okay?' Mum mouthed. I nodded in response.

'God, I've missed you,' he muttered.

'Me too.'

He pulled back just enough to tip my chin up and look deeply into my eyes.

'How did you get here?' I asked.

'A Garuda flight and your mother,' he joked.

'But how . . .?'

'How did I get in touch with her? After we spoke the other night, I decided you'd had enough time to sort your shit out. Any longer and you'd start to invent reasons not to come back at all. So I called her, asked her not to say anything to you – just in case you got drunk again and booked a ticket to Bangkok or somewhere – anything to avoid talking about it. Then I told Diane I needed an opportunity to talk you out of resigning, so she convinced Marcus to approve my leave.'

I pulled back. 'So you're only here to try and change my mind?'

'Don't be an idiot. I'm here because I want to be with you. Come back to work, don't come back to work, I don't care. The only thing I care about is losing you.'

He lowered his head to kiss me again. I stopped him.

'I still don't understand how you knew how to contact Mum.'

'I remembered seeing her business card on your fridge. Don't look at me like that – you asked me in your email to check the mail.'

Aaah, yes, my email. I tried to pull away again.

'No,' he held me, 'you're not going anywhere.'

'But –'

'No.' He placed a finger gently against my lips. I nipped on it, then drew it in to suck lightly on it. He closed his eyes for a second, retrieved his finger and said, 'Your email.'

'I should never have sent it. I'm sorry. You know what I'm like – I've never drunk-dialled or drunk-mailed in my life. I can't even remember exactly what I said. Anyway, I deleted it so I can't remember.'

'Yeah, that would work. Did you mean it, what you said? When you said you loved me?'

I nodded, but couldn't look at him.

'I'm glad you sent it, Em. You had the guts to

say how you felt – I didn't. Instead I sat there stupidly nodding as you tried to convince us both that we were just a fling. I thought if that was what you wanted, I could work on the rest.'

'But Corinna?'

'I broke it off with her the day after we made love. I couldn't be with her and feel the way I do about you. I tried to tell you that day, but you kept going on and on with all the reasons why we couldn't be together, and I really thought I was just a rebound.'

'Oh.' Warmth flowed through me. 'So that means . . .'

'Yes, I feel the same way.'

'But you get bored.'

'How long have we been friends? You're the only person who's never bored me.'

'But –'

'No more buts, Em. The way I figure it, we've already done the get-to-know-you stuff and came out the other side of that years ago.' He lowered his head again.

'Does Diane know about us?'

'Sweetheart, everyone knows about us. Shut up and kiss me.'

With pleasure.

This time when we separated it was because Steph had poked her head around the corner.

'Ummmm, I don't want to interrupt, but we're

wondering whether we should be planning to eat out tonight instead?'

I looked at the ingredients spread across the kitchen bench and the half-bashed and pounded mix in the mortar (or was it pestle?) and grinned. 'Nope, I'll still cook. Booth can help me chop stuff.'

He looked around at the mess. 'Babe, I don't even know what half of this shit is.'

'That's okay, I do. I've been learning to cook.'

'So it would seem.'

'Amongst other things,' said Steph.

'Really?'

'Yes, I'll tell you as we chop.'

Sometime later, he came up behind me and wrapped his arms around me, pulling me back into him. 'How long is this going to take us?'

'Not long . . . it's just a matter of putting it all together now. Why?'

'I was thinking a shower would be good.'

Oh my. Something told me that a shower wasn't all that was on his mind.

'Do you need help finding it . . . the shower, that is?'

'Uh huh.' He nuzzled along my neck and nibbled at my ear. 'I have a really bad sense of direction.'

'Besides,' I closed my eyes as his hand found its way under my singlet, 'we've been chopping chillies so should make sure our hands are clean.'

'We should,' he groaned as I wriggled back closer into him, 'and quickly.'

'You know,' I said, my fingers idly playing across his chest, 'I was so concerned about using that shower when I first got here, but now I can't imagine why every house doesn't have one.'

'Possibly because suburban Melbourne isn't surrounded by rainforest and rice paddies.'

'Perhaps.'

'It would give the neighbours something to talk about, though.'

'I've got used to squirrels and lizards and birds watching me.'

'We gave them quite a show in there this afternoon.' He smirked and I blushed. 'I've always wanted to make love in an outdoor shower.'

'Well, that's a tick off your bucket list then.'

Why had I never noticed before how lovely Booth smelled?

'Em . . .'

'Hmmmm.'

'Can I confess something?'

'Should I be worried?'

'Not at all.'

'Well?'

My fingers stepped their way down his body. His hand stopped them before they found their target.

'You know that night I stayed at yours, and the next day you ran into Corinna and me?'

'Uh huh.' My tongue replaced my fingers.

'Mmmmm. Well, that wasn't an accident.'

I stopped what I was doing and looked up at him. 'Sorry?'

'You'd said where you were going to buy those prints, so I arranged to meet Corinna there and then pretended it was a coincidence.'

'Why?'

He shrugged. 'I'd noticed your face when we were talking about her that night, and thought that if you were jealous it could mean that you were starting to think of me as something other than a buddy.'

'Oh.'

His hand stroked my hip as he talked. 'You see, I was already there. There'd been a couple of moments that got me thinking. There was that day we went running.'

'Aaah, yes, the vision of me throwing up would have been irresistible.'

He laughed. 'Absolutely. It was more the memory of you in that wet T-shirt that had me waking up at night.'

'Oh, that.'

'Yes, that. Mostly, though, there was Jamie. I've seen you with guys before and they've all been dickheads, so it hasn't really worried me. I knew they wouldn't last. But Jamie was different. First, he was a mate, and secondly, when I saw you two together . . . well, it was tough – so I tried to block it out with Corinna. I knew for sure, though, that night I stayed over. I lay awake for ages wanting to come into your bed, and knowing that you were probably lying there thinking of him.'

'I dreamed of you that night,' I said.

'Was that smile the next morning for me?'

'Uh huh.' I reached up to kiss him. 'I suppose you want to know when I knew?'

'Yep.'

'That day we had the fight at work. Before I came here. Remember I stormed out? I wanted you to follow me and you didn't, and that's when I knew. It felt like a Partridge Family moment – the whole I think I love you thing. But I think I'd always known . . . you know?'

'Yeah, I know.' His hand moved to cup my breast. 'Em . . . I haven't said it yet, but you know I love you – don't you?'

'I love you too.'

He smiled and slid down the bed, licking and nibbling at anything interesting along the way. Oh, he was distracting. There was still something else I had to tell him. I dragged my brain reluctantly back up to my head.

'About what you said before about a ticket to Bangkok . . .'

'Yes?'

'Well, I've booked one . . . a ticket to Bangkok.'

He looked up at me. 'Were you coming back to Melbourne first?'

'Yes . . . I had to talk to you – and I've got ten kays to walk.'

'So that just leaves the something scary and the bikini to go?'

'I intend doing the bikini next week, but the something scary – not happening, my friend.' I gently pushed his head back to my breast.

'Em . . . did you really fake it with Jamie?'

'Uh huh,' I groaned as his tongue circled my nipple. One day I'd better read that email so I knew exactly what I'd told him . . . or maybe not. Then I remembered something else I needed to ask before rational thought left me.

'Booth . . . what else was on your bucket list – the one you wouldn't let me see?'

'This,' he said into my navel.

'I'm serious.'

He dragged himself back up to face me. 'So am I. It's a short list. Hold that thought.' He padded across the room to get his wallet. 'Here it is.'

He pulled out a piece of paper that had been tucked into the back. It was paper-clipped to a small photo of the two of us at Suse's wedding. On it was scrawled:

1. Run a marathon.

2. Have sex in an outdoor shower.

3. Have sex on a beach somewhere warm.

4. Have sex on a sheepskin rug in front of a fire somewhere cold.

'You've got a one-track mind,' I said.

He grinned. 'And you're taking too long to read that.'

5. Fall in love forever.

The last item had been written in a different ink:

6. Do all of the above with Em.

'I added that last one that night at your house.'

'Do you want me to tick it off for you?'

'Later. Now shut up and let me concentrate – you know I can't multi-task.'

CHAPTER THIRTY-SEVEN

I'd been concerned that once we moved from best mates to lovers, the words and the laughs would dry up, but everything seemed just the same . . . with an added layer of wonderful. We'd slotted together as if we were always meant to. Maybe we were always meant to.

We had a very romantic week at a resort on Seminyak Beach. It was the sort of place that dreams were made of – lazy days and nights full of sun, sand and lovemaking, with our own personal (and thankfully, private) plunge pool.

One day we hired a driver to take us across to the east coast to a restaurant Andi had told me about one day over coffee.

'I haven't been myself,' she'd said, 'but Abby went the last time she was there and said it was amazing. Real food prepared the traditional way from fresh ingredients. Nothing like the tourist traps around Kuta and Legian.'

We stopped along the way at a water palace. I'd seen pictures of it in the travel brochures I'd devoured while Craig was planning our trip to Sorrento. It had koi, lotus flowers, bridges, and an eleven-tiered fountain. Booth and I took turns at taking photos of each other in ridiculous poses in front of the stone gargoyles, and I very nearly came to giggling grief as I jumped across the stepping stones in the man-made lake.

We'd been driving through mile after mile of countryside when our driver stopped outside a family compound.

'This is my village,' he said. 'I need to get something.'

We watched him disappear down the narrow lane.

'He's gone for directions,' I said. I'd been watching him peering at signs for the last twenty minutes or so. 'I think we're lost.'

Booth grinned. 'So do I, but what a place to be lost in.'

We got out of the car and walked to the edge of the road. Below us was a vista of green. Fields of water and rice, coconut palms and small houses. I took a step closer and the grass exploded into a wave of dragonflies – more than I could count, so many more than I could wish on.

Booth put his arm around me and kissed the top of my head. Then he said what I'd been thinking. 'We don't need that many wishes any more.'

Booth wasn't beside me when I woke the next morning.

On the pillow was a note: *Gone for a walk xxx*

He was back by breakfast, full of plans for the day. 'Pop your shorts and bikini on, and we'll pack towels and sunscreen in that backpack we bought the other day. We're off to the beach.'

'Not the one just there, I take it?' I indicated the shimmering blue water visible from our breakfast table.

'Nope, this one's a surprise. Meet me out the front in ten minutes. Trust me – you'll love it.'

He was wrong – I didn't love it. Out the front of the resort stood Booth with two motorcycle helmets and a rented motorbike. He was singing Redgum's 'I've Been To Bali Too'.

'I'm not getting on that thing,' I warned. 'They terrify me – and I don't think my insurance would cover an accident. Do you even know how to ride it?'

'Growing up in Ballarat? Sure I know how to ride one . . . although it's been a while.'

'That's not making me feel any better.'

'Come on,' he urged. 'The wind in your hair, a beach in the middle of nowhere, you and me . . . the last big item on your bucket list. How hard could it be?'

When he kissed me like that . . .

'Nowhere on my bucket list does it say anything about riding a motorbike in Bali.' My protests were getting weaker.

'No, but it does say "Do something in another country that scares you".' He handed me a helmet, smiled and said, 'What could possibly go wrong? Trust me.'

So I did.

It was terrifying and exhilarating at the same time. It also made me more than a little turned on – I think it was the fear, or being so close to him, or the throbbing engine between my legs. Back at the hotel, we parked the bike and sprinted to our room, only just making it inside before our clothes were off.

'Wow,' he said, as I collapsed off him a little later, 'I might buy a bike!'

We flew home together on Saturday night as scheduled. Mum and Steph came down to spend the last afternoon with us.

At the airport Mum held me tight. 'Be happy, darling . . . he's a keeper, you know.'

'I know, Mum.'

'Don't leave it so long next time?'

'I'll be back before you know it.'

Then she hugged Booth. 'Don't break her heart,' she said.

'I won't,' he replied. 'I love her.'

'She said you get bored quickly.'

'Not this time. Besides, she has trouble with commitment.'

'Not this time.'

Booth and I went into the office on Monday

morning so I could talk to Diane. Thankfully we didn't see Jamie, but we did get a few other knowing glances and sniggers from colleagues. I blushed, and Booth grinned.

Resplendent in head-to-toe black and white, Diane was remarkably – and unexpectedly – understanding. 'It's been a long time since you took a holiday, Emily. It's no wonder you need a break.'

'It's not just that,' I told her. 'I really feel like I need a change.'

'Perhaps you'll feel differently after being away.'

'I don't think so.'

'I don't think you know how much we appreciate what you do here. You're a vital member of the team.'

I raised my eyebrows.

'You probably don't believe me.' She tried another approach. 'Look, I know how difficult it can be working with someone you're in a relationship with – perhaps things would be different if you were working in a different department. There's an opening to lead the support team in Business Partnerships that we haven't advertised yet – would you be interested in that? Take a few days to think about it.'

On the way home in the tram, I received a call from Jodie at DotPoint.

'I emailed you last week,' she said, 'but as I hadn't received a response, I thought I'd call.'

'I've been in Bali,' I told her. 'I only got back

yesterday.'

She laughed. 'Lucky girl. If you haven't accepted anything else, and still want to work with us, you might like to consider it. I'm sure you have other plans, but we have someone going on maternity leave in February. It's just a twelve-month contract to start, but if you're really after a change, and want to take a chance with us . . . Tell me you'll at least think about it?'

Booth and I talked about both offers when he got home. I'd cooked us something simple for dinner, and we chatted about our day – just like a real couple.

'It's up to you, babe. You could do the support job on your ear, and we've proven that we can work well together. What's this other job about?'

'It's at DotPoint – web development, social media. I went for a couple of interviews there a while back, in the middle of when everything was happening with Jamie. I didn't tell you because . . . well, I didn't know how to tell you, and I didn't want you to talk me out of it until I knew if I had a choice to make. Anyway, I missed out, so there was nothing to tell.'

He was looking at me with his brows raised.

'Are you upset with me?'

'I should be,' he said, 'I thought that we shared everything. But it was all getting a bit crazy then. What do you want to do?'

'Is that an invitation?' I'd missed him today, and had spent the tram ride home thinking about what I wanted to do with him.

'Concentrate for just a few more minutes,' he said. 'What do you want to do for work?'

'I want to work at DotPoint. The timing is right, and the company is inspiring. It's completely different to anything I've done before, and I know the contract is a risk, but I really want the challenge.'

He nodded slowly. 'I think you're right. Besides, working together, we could have problems getting leave together, and I've got a whole new bucket list of places and things we can explore. Speaking of which . . .'

Later that night in bed, I broached the one subject that neither of us had spoken about – my ticket to Bangkok.

'I think I should still go,' I said. 'Even though I'll miss you like crazy.'

He held me tight. 'Yeah, I think you should too. It feels like it's what you need to do to complete the change circle, although I have no idea how I'll manage without you – especially now. Just promise me you won't turn your phone off again.'

'I promise.' I burrowed closer into him.

'Do you have a plan?'

'Not really. I was thinking Thailand first, then Vietnam, perhaps back to Bali. Maybe you can get some time off and meet me somewhere for Christmas?'

'Koh Samui, or one of the other islands. You can wear that hot bikini, we'll go snorkelling, and we'll find a deserted beach somewhere and make love as the waves come in.'

'You can be on top – I don't want sand burn on my knees.'

'But I don't want sand burn elsewhere.'

'We'll just have to take it in turns then.'

'Or change positions a lot,' he mused. 'Do you think we should practise that?'

'Sounds like a good idea to me.' Booth was full of good ideas. I'd always known that. 'What about the distance?' I added. 'Do you think we'll be okay?'

'We'll be fine, sweetheart. Who knows – Skype sex could be exciting. I already have some ideas about that one.'

'Can we practise those too?'

'I think we should.'

Neither Jamie nor Suse had been back to running club. Nor did they turn up to do the half-marathon on Sunday. We saw Corinna at the starting line, but she turned her back and her perky ponytail on us. Booth had told me that Jamie had approached him at work and said, 'No hard feelings, mate?' Booth had shaken his hand.

Watching Booth run over the line at the end of the race was a moment I wouldn't forget in a while. He was so proud of himself, as was I for him. He grabbed me and kissed me thoroughly as the sweat dripped down his body. He said that next year he'll do the marathon.

I walked the ten-kilometre race – I even ran parts of it, just because I felt like it. I had no inclination to do any more than that. I added another tick to my bucket list when I got home.

And Suse? Booth and I missed her. Most days I still went to pick up the phone and tell her about something I knew she'd laugh at. I missed our Friday nights, and I missed Richard and the kids. When I told Booth the other night, he said that he felt the same. Neither of us had the concentration required to maintain a decent grudge.

Mum said it was because between us we didn't have enough fixed energy, and that's what we needed Suse in our lives for. So when Suse sent me a text to see how things were going, I responded.

Me: All good. I went to Bali to see Mum & now I've resigned and am taking 4 months off to travel – SE Asia.

Suse: I'm pleased. And Josh?

Me: We're together & it's good.

Suse: I always knew you two would work it out some day. Is he going with you?

Me: No.

Suse: Travelling alone? Wow. That's big for you.

Me: How's Richard & the kids?

Suse: Good. We're doing well.

Me: I'm pleased.

Suse: I miss you both. I hope we can be friends again one day?

Me: Me too.

I'd call her when I got back. I didn't think that things would ever be as they were – we'd all grown too much for that – but maybe someday we'd settle into a new sort of normal.

Neither of us slept much the night before I flew out. It was as if we didn't want to waste one single minute of the hours we had left. We made love, talking and dreaming and future-planning in between. I dozed off briefly at one point, and woke to see him propped up on one elbow watching me.

'Should I be doing this?' I whispered in the dark.

'Yes,' he whispered back, 'you should. I wish you weren't, but you have to.'

'I love you.'

'You'd better.'

Booth came to the airport to see me off. He even carried my backpack – yes, I was travelling light and without a list. I figured I'd buy anything else that I needed as I needed it.

At the airport we clung to each other.

'I miss you already,' I said in between watery kisses.

'I miss you more than that,' he said, holding me tight. 'Four months is so long.'

'But I'll see you before that – Christmas on an island somewhere, remember? I'll be the one in the bikini.'

I kissed him one last time.

'We'll get through this,' I said. 'How hard could it be?'

Would we live happily ever after? Who knew . . . forever was a very long time. But Booth told me he had enough faith in us for both of us. And I'd started to believe him.

ACKNOWLEDGEMENTS

There I was scrambling for words that would adequately convey my thanks to everyone who had helped me bring Emily's and Josh's story to the page.

'I don't see why it's so hard,' said my long-suffering hubby. 'Just thank Sarah and me for putting up with your mood swings, rejection tears, and for feeding you; and Kali for snoring under your desk.'

So thanks to my family – Grant, Sarah and Kali the Wonder Spaniel – for everything.

But wait, there's more … I would have given up on this dream years ago if it weren't for my first readers: Daniel and Shelley. I know this book has grown into a very different one to the one you won the right to read as the consequence of a fat bet all those years ago, but I'd still be writing, rewriting and scared to show anyone if it wasn't for you two. I owe you a drink or three.

On the subject of early readers, I'm grateful to Heather and Bec for your comments and feedback. Especially Bec, who rarely reads anything that isn't about a life-altering struggle from adversity to success.

Endless gratitude goes to my editor, Nicola O'Shea, for gently squeezing this manuscript into shape. Thanks also for giving me so much invaluable advice about the self-publishing game.

Who else? To everyone else who has listened to me bang on about this over the last couple of years, and offered support and encouragement. You know who you are.

Last, but definitely not least: thanks to the city of Melbourne for her endless inspiration.

•

If you enjoyed *Baby It's You* I'd love it if you left a review in the usual places. If you'd like to stay up to date with my next happy ending, you can sign up for my newsletter at my website: https://joannetracey.com

You can also drop by and see me — virtually speaking, of course — at any of these places:

My blog: https://andanyways.com
Facebook: https://facebook.com/joannetraceywriter
Instagram: https://instagram/jotracey
Twitter: @jotracey_

ABOUT THE AUTHOR

Joanne Tracey would like to say that she's a thirty-something, perky-pony-tailed marathon runner. Sadly, it wouldn't be true. What is true is that she's sometimes a corporate warrior, sometimes a domestic diva, and absolutely always a believer in happy endings. Jo's novels are inspired by her travels and when she isn't writing words, she's procrastibaking, planning her next adventure or taking way too many photos of sunrises for Instagram.

Also by Joanne Tracey

Big Girls Don't Cry

Wish You Were Here

Happy Ever After